ACCLAIM FOR *WINDS OF FREEDOM*

"Rebecca Carey Lyles once again brings us Kate Neilson, but this time, the reader is thrown into a stunning array of contrasts—the power of loving relationships and the destruction of painful affiliations. Can a tender and freshly minted marriage stand the horrors of the streets? *Winds of Freedom* is a page-turner that will take you from the depths of human depravity to the heights of friendship, loyalty and passion to do right at all costs. This book is a triumph."

—Peter Leavell, award-winning author and historian, author of *Gideon's Call*

"Rebecca Lyles is an author unafraid to shine the light of God's truth in the dark places of this world. At times heart-wrenching, *Winds of Freedom* is a story about the truth that sets us all free."

—Lisa Phillips, Author of *The Ultimate Betrayal*, Love Inspired Suspense, summer 2014

"Hooray! Another chance to join Kate Nielson as she uses the gritty street smarts of her difficult past and the assurance of her unfolding faith to find her way and protect the ones she loves. In *Winds of Freedom*, Rebecca Carey Lyles has once again created authentic characters who confront real-life intrigue and adventure in today's Wild West. From the mountains of Wyoming to the sordid underside of Dallas, Kate and her friends make their way with humor, passion, gentle love and tough determination—and like their Savior, they never leave a friend behind. *Winds of Freedom* is an exciting and moving sequel of loss and redemption,

and like *Winds of Wyoming*, this book will leave readers wanting more of Kate Nielson and more of Rebecca Carey Lyles's fiction."
—Lisa Michelle Hess, editor, author and blogger at
http://worth-of-a-word.blogspot.com

"*Winds of Freedom* by Rebecca Lyles is not only an entertaining read, it is another courageous assault on the hideous crime of human trafficking. I applaud the author's willingness to tackle this topic and to help educate us in the depth of its evil. Awareness is the first step in setting the captives free—and then the challenge to each of us to get involved. Together we can make a difference! Do not miss this excellent book!"
—Kathi Macias (www.boldfiction.com) is an award-winning author of 40 books, including The Freedom Series (*Deliver Me From Evil; Special Delivery; The Deliverer*), novels written around the topic of human trafficking

"Rebecca Carey Lyles weaves a gripping tale filled with eye-opening twists and turns. A few familiar characters from *Winds of Wyoming* hold your hand on this fast-paced rollercoaster suspense ride."
—Heather Humrichouse, freelance writer

"The characters and subject matter in *Winds of Freedom* are well developed and provoke strong emotion. I wanted to swoop in and rescue the victims in the story but knew, as did Kate and Mike, that only God could orchestrate such a rescue."
—Val Gray, 2013 ACFW Genesis semifinalist

"*Winds of Freedom* captures the reality of human trafficking with a vivid look at the fear, manipulation and battle involved. Amy may be a fictional character, but the vulnerability she faces as she overcomes trials, the exploitation she is coerced into and the danger for her and others as she tries to escape is very real and occurs to many young women in our own country. I was inspired by Lyles's story as Amy finds hope and freedom, but I appreciate even more the awareness brought to the issue of human trafficking. As we all work to become aware, we can prevent trafficking victims and help the survivors as Kate did, never giving in and never giving up on her friend."

—Kim Peake, President, Idaho Coalition for Justice, http://www.icjustice.org

"*Winds of Freedom* is consistent with Lyles's first novel's unpretentious look at the paths that bring people to God. This exciting tale takes Kate Neilson from bison pastures in Wyoming to a brothel in Dallas and is a testament to the power of friendship as well as the need we all have for someone who believes in us."

—Hilarey Johnson, 2013 CWG Operation First Novel semifinalist

WINDS
OF
FREEDOM

Rebecca Carey Lyles

PERPEDIT ✓ PUBLISHING, INK

WINDS OF FREEDOM
Copyright ©2013 by Rebecca Carey Lyles

Perpedit Publishing, Ink 2013
Boise, Idaho 83709
http://www.perpedit.com

First eBook Edition: 2013
First Paperback Edition: 2013
ISBN: 978-0-9894624-0-2 (eBook)
ISBN: 978-0-9894624-1-9 (Paperback)

This is a work of fiction. All of the characters, organizations and events portrayed in this novel are either products of the author's imagination or are used fictitiously. Any similarity to a real person, living or dead, organization or event is coincidental and not intended by the author.

Published in the United States of America
Perpedit Publishing, Ink

For my husband, Steve, who encourages every step of my writing journey.

Listen to my cry,
for I am in desperate need;
rescue me from my persecutors,
for they are too strong for me.
Set me free from my prison,
so I can thank you.

Psalm 142:6-7a (NLT/NIV)

CHAPTER ONE

Kate Neilson Duncan knocked a second time on her great-aunt's front door. She waited a moment and then turned to her husband, Mike, who stood beside her on the wide veranda. "When I called last night, Aunt Mary said she'd be home all day."

"Give her some time. She never moves fast." Mike aimed his chin at a little boy riding by on a tricycle. "Cute kid."

Like Kate, the boy wore shorts and a t-shirt on the warm October day. He steered the trike with one hand and pulled a clattering wagon with the other, carefully negotiating the bumpy sidewalk that bordered the old house. But then he lost his grip on the wagon and stopped beneath the wide branches of an autumn-laced maple tree to retrieve the handle. As he bent down, a wind gust swirled a kaleidoscope of leaves over his head and onto the porch.

The breeze lifted Kate's hair, set a rocking chair in motion and scattered the leaves across the neighbor's lawn. She brushed a wayward strand from her cheek and was about to knock again, when the lock clicked and the deadbolt began to retract, metal rasping against metal. Finally, the door opened. Kate could see the chain that stretched the narrow gap between the door and the doorframe, but she couldn't see her aunt.

Mike pointed toward the bottom of the door, where a wiggling, sniffing black nose poked through at ankle height. Aunt Mary's dog had always been more of a sniffer than a barker.

"If you're selling Florida grapefruit," a woman's voice quavered, "I'll tell you what I say every year. My husband's stomach cannot tolerate citrus, so please don't come back. God bless you like he blessed Queen Esther. Goodbye."

Before her aunt could shut them out, Kate shoved her sandal into the crack. "Aunt Mary. It's me, Kate."

A frizz of white hair appeared in the narrow opening and Kate could see Mary squinting at her. "Katy? My sweet Katy Joy?" Mary unhooked the chain lock, opened the door, and held out her arms.

Kate hugged her bony frame, all the while thanking God her aunt recognized her. After the last phone call, in which she'd asked three times who she was, Kate was prepared for the worst.

The older woman leaned back. "You cut off your beautiful brown hair."

"It was this length at the wedding, shoulder length." Something cold and wet touched the back of Kate's knee. She jumped. "Prissy! You startled me."

Mary shook her finger at the dog. "You leave Katy alone."

The curly haired Cockapoo dropped her tail between her legs and sidled over to Mike, who knelt on one Levi-clad knee to pet the dog.

Kate kissed Mary's soft cheek. "I'm so glad to see you again, Aunt Mary. You're looking great. Not even using your walker." Her aunt had developed multiple sclerosis in her fifties, but she hadn't relied on a walker until recent years.

The older woman's sea-green eyes twinkled. She grasped Kate by the shoulders. "Just don't let go."

Kate rotated them both toward Mike, who patted Prissy's head and stood.

"Aunt Mary," Kate said, "do you remember my husband, Mike?"

Mary squinted at the tall blond man for a long moment. And then she smirked. "How could I forget such a handsome brute?"

Kate grinned. It wasn't often she got to see her husband blush.

Mike took Mary's hand from Kate's shoulder and kissed her fingers. "And I haven't forgotten you, either, pretty lady."

Mary beamed.

"Okay, you two. Enough flattery." Kate led Mary to her chair in the living room and helped her sit. She could tell her aunt didn't recognize Mike. Thank God she let him into her home, despite her confusion.

Kate sat on the couch beside Mike. "Time for us to get down to business."

Mary peered at them over the top of her glasses. "Business?"

"The business of getting you moved from Pittsburgh to the Whispering Pines Ranch in Wyoming. Remember how much you like it there?"

Mary picked up a newspaper and began to noisily fold it.

Prissy climbed into Mike's lap. Mike whispered, "Smells weird in here. I don't think it's the dog."

Kate nodded. She couldn't put her finger on the odor. Maybe it had something to do with her aunt's aging body, or maybe she'd forgotten to bathe. Though she'd had MS for a long time, the forgetfulness was new. "How many boxes have you filled, Aunt Mary?"

"Boxes?"

"We need to pack your things for the move. But before we go, we'll have a garage sale for stuff you don't need. Have you been sorting?"

"Sorting?"

Kate glanced at Mike.

The dimple in his cheek twitched.

This was going to be more difficult than she'd expected. "Don't you worry about a thing, Aunt Mary. We'll take care of the details. And Amy will join our work crew in a couple hours."

"Who's that?"

"She's…" How could her aunt forget the animated redhead? "Amy is my best friend. She visits you every week, and she flew to Wyoming with you when Mike and I got married. She was my maid of honor, remember?"

Mary compressed her lips and began to pick at a fingernail.

"Well, anyway, when Amy gets here, we'll order a pizza and have a moving party." Kate couldn't wait to see her friend again. They'd met in prison and supported each other through a host of challenges.

Lately, she'd sensed desperation in Amy's voice when they talked on the phone. Although she was usually upbeat, she hadn't found a job to replace the one she lost almost six months ago. Kate was afraid her impulsive friend would leap at whatever employment came along, good or bad. She knew from experience that unhealthy employment opportunities were often more abundant than good options for ex-felons.

"Moving?" Eyebrows pinched, eyes darting, Mary scrutinized her living room as if seeing it anew. "From my friends? My neighborhood, my home?" Her voice rose with each question. "From my prayer room? From Prissy?"

Kate's heart lurched. She knew the sting of being ripped from all that was familiar. Though they'd talked often on the phone about selling her aunt's home, the conversations must have gotten lost in her head. "We'll take the desk and phone from your prayer room, and we'll take Prissy with us, too. She'll like living in the country."

Mike grunted.

Kate knew what he was thinking. *If the coyotes don't eat her.*

She rubbed the dog's furry head before standing. "We'll take this one step at a time. How about I make us some tea?" Her aunt loved green tea.

Mary's face brightened. "That sounds wonderful. Let's all have a nice cup of tea."

In the kitchen, Kate filled the teapot with water and placed it on the stove. Sensing warmth from a nearby pan, she picked up the lid to find dry carrots and crinkled peas beginning to brown. So that's what they smelled. She shut off the gas and moved the pan to another burner to cool. "Aunt Mary, have you done any baking lately?"

"Uhm, well, I...I'm not sure."

"Don't get up. I'll check the fridge." The first thing Kate saw when she opened the door was a big pan of brownies with a corner piece missing. The second was a platter of hot dogs stacked layer upon layer pyramid style. She stared at the pile. Had to be at least three dozen wieners in the mound.

Her aunt hobbled into the kitchen, pushing her walker.

Kate laughed. "You don't take orders very well."

Mary peered into the open refrigerator. "I forget why I came in here."

"I asked if you'd baked anything recently, and you did. The brownies smell wonderful." Kate slid the pan from the fridge. "But all these hot dogs surprise me. I didn't know you liked them so much."

Mary's eyebrows lowered. "I don't like them, not one bit. Your Uncle Dean is the wiener lover. Buys them by the bushel and eats at least a dozen a day."

"But he's not—"

"Oh, that obstinate man." Mary pursed her lips. "He's been sneaking off to Jimmy's Long Dog Stand in front of the library again. Pays that bandit's outlandish prices, when we have plenty here." She wrinkled her nose. "Throw them out before they turn green."

"Uncle Dean died years ago. Surely these aren't his..."

Mary glared at her. "Don't talk about your uncle that way, Katy Joy, and don't argue with me. I am not in the mood." She reversed her walker and started for the living room.

Kate frowned. What was that about? It wasn't like her aunt to be snippy. Or to talk as if Uncle Dean was alive.

Mary paused at the doorway between the two rooms. "Well, hello, young man." Her voice was cheery again. "Did Katy let you in?"

Oh-oh. Aunt Mary had already forgotten Mike.

"Uh, yes, she did." Kate could hear surprise in his voice. "We're good friends."

Kate snickered. *I certainly hope so.*

"That's nice." Mary rolled her walker into the living room. "I read the book of Esther this morning."

"Esther in the Bible?"

"The very one. It's quite an interesting story about a young Jewish woman who became queen of Persia way back when. Do you know how that happened? The king wanted a new..."

Kate set the brownies on the counter and took out the hot dogs, glad she'd been given permission to toss them in the garbage. Only God knew how old they were. She dumped the pile into the garbage can under the sink and closed the refrigerator door.

She'd been concerned about uprooting her aunt from her vintage Pittsburgh neighborhood and taking her to their mountainside guest ranch. Now it was obvious she needed someone to keep an eye on her. Kate broke off a piece of brownie. Thank God for Mike and her sweet mother-in-law, Laura, who would help her watch over Aunt Mary. Caring for a confused person with MS could be a challenge.

She bit into the brownie and choked. Ugh. Salt. Lots of salt. She turned on the faucet and spit the bite into the garbage disposal.

The teapot began to whistle, the tone starting low and then rising.

In the living room, Mary stopped her story. "Oh-oh. Fire truck coming this way. Better check the police scanner in my prayer room."

Kate set her mug on the porch and rested her elbows against the gray-painted step behind her. Basking in the breeze that came up just then, she watched leaves on the big maple tree surrender to random blusters. The red and orange clusters twirled and danced to the ground to carpet the lawn like a colorful quilt.

Amy Iverson leaned back against the same step. "Sure feels good to sit."

Kate smiled. "You can say that again."

"Sure feels good to sit."

Kate chuckled. "I asked for that."

Amy threw back her head and laughed. Sunlight glistened off her auburn hair.

Prissy crept over to inspect Kate's cup. Amy flicked her fingers at the dog. "Get your snout out of Kate's cider."

The little dog dropped to her stomach, placed her head between her paws, and ogled Amy with woebegone eyes half hidden by silky curls.

"Oh, you silly puppy." She pulled the dog onto her lap. "Now your feelings are hurt." Amy looked at Kate. "Much as I hesitate to say it, this might be a good time to tackle the attic."

Kate groaned. "You're going to make me leave this beautiful yard to crawl inside a hot dusty attic?"

"Seems like a good time to work up there, while your aunt is napping." Amy set Prissy on the porch and stood.

"Good point. Seems like she takes stuff out of boxes faster than we put it in."

"Do you think she'll try to climb the ladder to the attic?"

"I hope not, but you never know." Kate massaged her lower back. "What are we going to do with her things? All of a sudden, she's against having a garage sale, even though she's said for years she needs to get rid of stuff. Doesn't make sense, except I was told people with dementia want to hang onto everything familiar."

"I understand."

"You and me, both." Kate picked up her cup. "Prison makes a person cling to what little they have."

"Yeah." Amy held out her hand to help Kate to her feet. "But we moved on, and we have to help your aunt move on. The more I'm around her, the more I'm convinced she needs to be with you."

Inside the house, they tiptoed up the stairs, past Mary's bedroom. At the end of the hallway, Kate pulled the rope to lower the attic ladder, praying the grate of metal against wood wouldn't be too loud. Amy picked up Prissy and started to climb the ladder.

Kate whispered, "Why are you taking the dog?"

Amy leaned toward her. "So she won't disturb Aunt Mary's nap." Kate suspected Amy's love for animals was the real reason. Yet, the longer Aunt Mary slept, the more they'd accomplish. She followed her friend up the ladder and clambered into the musty garret just in time to muffle a sneeze into the crook of her elbow. "Let's open windows to get some air flow."

Amy deposited the dog on the floor. "I'm not sure we can reach the windows. This place is a jungle of junk."

"Put on your pith helmet, get out your machete, and go for it."

As quietly as they could, they shoved their way in opposite directions and managed to prop open two small casements. The next step was to slide items away from the floor opening to make room for the empty boxes Mike was rounding up.

Prissy trotted from one tantalizing smell to another, nose wiggling, tail wagging.

Amy laughed. "Bet she's never been up here." She swept her hand over the attic's eclectic contents. "How do you want to tackle this?"

Kate picked up a mixer. One beater dangled from its cracked case. "Let's make a pile for worthless stuff like this and other stacks of like items we can box together. You know—all the books together, pictures in another group, Uncle Dean's comic books in a pile, and whatever else we find similar, like Aunt Mary's needlework projects."

They worked in silence for a time, digging through old stacks, forming new ones. When they were close enough to talk without raising their voices, Kate said, "Too bad your boss closed the stables. Grooming horses was a perfect job for you. Do you have any other possibilities?"

"Nada. You know how hard it is for ex-felons to find employment." Amy tilted her head. "I've been meaning to ask. How did you get on at Whispering Pines so easy?"

Kate pointed upward. "It was a God thing. The internship application didn't require criminal history and Laura didn't ask for a background check."

"I need to find something like that."

"Wish we could hire you at the ranch, but we don't keep many people on staff during the off season." She lifted a lid from a shoebox. Marbles. Dozens of marbles of every size and color. "Why do you think they kept marbles?"

"Maybe your uncle saved them when he was a kid."

Kate surveyed the toys and puzzles, magazines and tools scattered across the attic floor. "He apparently saved everything from the day he was born until the day he died." A puff of air blew through the room, leaving a dust cloud in its wake. She sneezed again.

Amy patted her arm. "Bless you."

"Thanks." Kate rubbed her nose with the back of her hand. "Any chance you'd be able to make it on unemployment until next spring, when we could hire you for the tourist season?"

"I'd love that, more than anything, especially if you hire another bunch of good-looking single cowboys, like Clint Barrett."

"Last I heard, Clint and Cyrus Moore's daughter, Susan, are still seeing each other."

"Yeah, I figured as much. Just sayin'. Anyway, I promised my sister, Elaina, she can move in with me after I find a job. Besides the fact that she and my aunt—the one who took Elaina and my brother in when our mom left us—don't get along, she wants to attend the University of Pittsburgh."

"I bet you'd love to be with your sister again."

Amy smiled. "I'm excited, but I already have my dogs and cats to feed, so I want to be sure we can make it financially before she joins me."

"Don't forget your parrots."

"I could never forget Orville and Wilbur, or my guinea pig."

"You and your menagerie." Kate chuckled. "You even have them on your legs. Cute idea to tattoo Orville on one leg and Wilbur on the other."

Amy stretched to examine the backs of her calves. "The artist did a good job, didn't he?"

"He did. Good color. Best I've seen."

"They'd look better if my legs were long like yours."

Kate laughed. "No way. They're perfect on you. Are you going to have the artist do your other animals?"

"Not 'til I get a good-paying job. These things cost a fortune."

"Have you applied at the zoo?"

Amy huffed. "The human-resources lady didn't even try to hide the fact she thought I might do something despicable to the animals or to the kids who visit the zoo, just because I spent time behind bars."

"Ouch, that hurts."

"It's just as well. I was afraid they'd make me feed the snakes and clean their cages." She made a face. "I hate snakes."

"I wouldn't like that either." Kate searched through a pile for the mate to a shoe. "I'm sorry you have to go through the job-hunting humiliation again and again."

"Maybe I'll call the number on that ad I told you about."

Kate opened her mouth, but Amy held up her hand. "I know, I know. It sounds too good to be true. Can't hurt to check it out." She shoved a mound of used clothing aside. "Besides, sometimes beggars can't be choosers."

"Be care—"

"Hey, your name is on this box."

"Really?" Kate scrambled over an old bicycle to gawk at the words printed neatly across the top of the carton. *Katherine Joy Neilson.* Aunt Mary hadn't mentioned storing a box of her stuff in the attic. Was it something she'd left at a foster family's house?

Amy picked up a stained shirt and wiped dust off the top. "Don't just stare at it, Kate. Open it."

CHAPTER TWO

Okay, okay. I get it." Mike silenced the navigation system before the condescending voice could tell him one more time to make an *immediate* U-turn. Thank God he didn't have to depend on technology to get where he needed to go in Wyoming.

He steered the rental car into a medical complex parking lot and maneuvered between buildings and pedestrians, looking for a place to turn around. He couldn't wait to get back home where roads made sense and traffic in town was only bumper-to-bumper for a couple minutes after the ballgame.

His cell phone rang. He slipped it out of his pocket as he pulled into a parking space. Probably Kate wondering what in the world happened to him. She didn't have any trouble finding her way around Pittsburgh, but the cobweb of busy streets made no sense to him. He lifted the phone to his ear. "Hello."

"Hi, Mike. This is Marshall Thompson."

Mike pressed the space between his eyebrows with his fingers. Maybe he wasn't in such a hurry to go home. Marshall, the neighbor rancher who'd purchased several of his bison cows and calves, never called just to shoot the breeze. "What's up, Marshall?"

"Sorry to bother you, Mike. I know you're on vacation, but I have a question for you."

"That's okay. I need a break from traffic. What's the question?"

"Have you seen any red deer over at your place?"

Mike rolled up the windows so he could hear better and switched off the car engine. What was so important about red deer? "You mean elk? Sure, we see them around the ranch all the time."

"No, I mean red deer, as in imports from overseas. You know how Europeans call bucks *stags* and the does *hinds*? Well, I swear I saw a red stag and four hinds in my bison pasture shortly after dawn this morning."

"What makes you think they're imports?"

"Their coloring is different from elk, more reddish, and their coats are sleeker. They look like a cross between deer and elk."

"Where do you suppose they came from?"

"Probably Australia or New Zealand. At least that's what I concluded from my research."

"I mean locally, like from a reserve or a park."

"Oh." He cleared his throat. "I'm betting they came from the Hughes ranch. That's the direction they headed when they took off running. But..." He paused. "No matter where they came from, I'm afraid they could be spreading brucellosis."

Mike grimaced. Ownership of certain exotic species was illegal in Wyoming, partly because the animals sometimes carried disease, including brucellosis, which could induce abortion and premature calving in cattle and bison. "I suppose you already let my loaner bull loose in your cow pasture."

"Yep."

"Me, too. I moved the other bulls in with my cows just before we left on this trip. God only knows how many pregnant bison cows we have between the two of us." Mike shook his head. How did impregnated cows morph so quickly from being a good thing to being a bad thing? He moved the phone to his other ear. "Have you called Game and Fish?"

Marshall snorted. "They laughed at me. Said there were no red deer in Wyoming, except on a reserve up north."

"Too bad. I was hoping they'd test the reds to see if they're carriers. Why do you suspect Todd Hughes?"

"Rumor has it he wants to turn his place into an exotic game ranch and stock animals from all over the world for millionaire hunters hoping to bag trophy heads. I also heard he's trying to enlarge his spread by hundreds, if not thousands more acres. Might explain why he's been bugging me and Dad to sell our ranch to him."

Mike watched cars pass on the street in front of him. Seemed like he was always the last rancher to catch Copperville gossip. Maybe it was because he didn't hang out at the bar, or because the Whispering Pines was different. Theirs was a guest ranch as well as a cattle and bison ranch.

"Still there?"

"Yeah, just trying to sort it all out."

"I know you said RB51 isn't necessarily effective with bison, yet I'm wondering if I should immunize my cows, just in case."

"It'd be risky. I vaccinated all our calves, including the ones I sold to you, but not the cows. Remember the abortion storm in that Pinedale cattle herd a while back? I read that it was caused by inoculating pregnant cows."

Marshall released a long sigh. "I'd better go. I'll scout the area to see if I can find the reds. I hear they're skittish, so it may be a lost cause." He paused. "I'll keep you posted."

"We should return in two or three weeks. Depends how long it takes us to get Kate's great-aunt packed up. We're moving her to the ranch."

"I hope the move goes okay. Drive safe and give me a call when you get back."

"Will do." Mike closed the phone. If there was anything they didn't need, it was brucellosis. The disease could cause the state veterinarian to order the destruction of their herds, and if it spread, Wyoming would lose its brucellosis-free status for the second time in recent years. The livestock sales of every producer in the state would be hindered, maybe stopped. At best, constant testing of their herds would be an expensive nuisance, especially with obstinate buffalo.

Mike combed his fingers through his hair. After years of work, his bison herd was finally to the point where he felt it was large enough to sell cows and stud service to people like Marshall plus offer buffalo meat, horns, skulls and hides for sale. He couldn't imagine starting over.

Laura Duncan finished her cereal and carried the bowl into the kitchen of her log home. What a treat to have strawberries on her oatmeal this late in the year. Almost everything else in the Whispering Pine's mountainside garden had succumbed to the cooling temperatures with the first frost, but by covering the strawberry bed at night, she'd been able to keep the plants active a bit longer.

She placed the cereal bowl in the dishwasher and the leftover berries in the refrigerator, thinking that if Dan were still alive, she wouldn't have leftover strawberries to refrigerate. He loved to eat them fresh from the garden. Laura heaved a sigh and picked up her tea mug.

She took a sip of the cinnamon-spiced tea and gazed out the window above the sink. For the umpteenth time, she reminded herself to live in the present, not the past. Every day was a gift, and today was a special gift. For the first time in two years, she could relax at the conclusion of their guest ranch tourist season and appreciate the advent of fall.

Though she'd tried, she couldn't recall the turning of the leaves that bleak autumn two years ago when Dan left her following a brief battle with cancer. During those dark days, her world had dimmed to gray and then to black. Again and again, she found herself staring through the nearest window, seeing nothing beyond his suffering and her sorrow.

Last fall, she'd gotten caught up in the whirlwind of Mike and Kate's wedding. Their happiness gave her joy in the midst of grief. She smiled. The reception had been the talk of the valley for months.

Laura walked to the deer-antler coatrack by the back door, plucked a sweater from one of the points and stepped outside. As usual, Mike's collie dozed on the deck. He raised his gray muzzle, pounded his bushy tail twice and dropped his head back down, his body sagging against the wide redwood boards.

She knelt to pet the dog. "Sorry I'm not Mike, Tramp. I'm all you've got for a while."

Even in his old age, and though his encounter with wolves a while back slowed him down, Tramp wanted to go wherever Mike went. Since his master's departure, he'd slept on the rug by her bed every night, breathing sad whimpers between restless twitches. Yet, she appreciated the dog's company. The house had echoed with a hollow emptiness after Mike moved into Kate's cabin.

But the silence would end when they settled Kate's aunt in the spare bedroom. Laura patted Tramp one more time and stood. She hoped she and Mary would get along okay.

On the far end of the porch, aspen leaves rustled, flickering hints of yellow and flashes of orange. Like gold coins tossed by a benevolent hand, fallen leaves skittered with the breeze along the edge of the deck. Laura looked beyond the ranch buildings to the Sierra Madre Mountains. Snow was already shimmering on the highest peaks.

She was a lucky woman to live in a region that featured sunshine and blue skies almost every day. This time of year, the canopy above her was a rich, almost purple, shade of blue. Laura settled into the chaise lounge and rested her head against the chair back. Breathing in the crisp fall air, she caught hints of wood smoke, dried leaves, warm deck planks, and even the dusty dog.

A pickup truck rumbled by to stop in front of one of the cabins. As predictable as the seasons, fall hunters replaced summer tourists. She slipped the sweater over her shoulders, thinking of how she'd anticipated this moment for weeks—the moment when the last summer visitor had driven away from the ranch and the cleanup was complete, the moment when she could put her feet up. Why wasn't she giddy with excitement?

She folded her arms. Maybe her lack of enthusiasm was because Kate and Mike's departure had left her with the realization she and Dan would never again travel together, would never again do anything together. Two years since his death, the understanding that he could not, would not return to her was only now beginning to sink in.

Or maybe it was the note she found in her nightstand that put her in a funk. Dan's neatly printed words said he couldn't imagine life without her. That he loved her more and more as time went by. How he wanted to grow old with her.

She plucked a blond hair from the sweater. Even something as miniscule and insignificant as a single hair made her think of her husband. He'd loved the color of her hair and said it reminded him of a ripe wheat field. Would she ever be free from constant reminders of Dan? Did she want to be free?

White clouds drifted above the trees. Thank God heaven was more than sitting on a cloud and strumming a harp, or Dan would be bored out of his mind. Although she was glad he was no longer suffering, she missed him. Oh, how she missed him. Two years had dulled the pain but not the loneliness. If anything, she felt more alone now than the day he died.

Kate cleared a space next to Amy on the attic floor and sat in front of the box. The handwriting on the top was vaguely familiar. She ran her fingers along the yellowed tape.

"Open it, Kate." Amy reached into her back pocket and pulled out the utility knife they'd been using as they packed and taped boxes. "I'm dying of curiosity."

Kate ran the blade through the tape and opened the flaps. In contrast to the clutter of the attic, the items in the box were neatly arranged and protected in plastic bags. She wiped her dusty hands on her shorts and picked up a pouch labeled *Katy's Homecoming Outfit (crocheted by her Great-Aunt Mary)*. Inside, she found tiny white booties with pink ribbons at the ankles and a matching hat, pants and sweater. Ever so carefully, she lifted them out.

Amy touched a bootie. "How adorable."

Kate couldn't respond. Up to this moment, the only tangible proof of her family's existence was a handful of pictures from Aunt Mary. And now, here sat an entire box of family stuff.

Amy reached for another plastic-covered item. "This must be your baby book." She removed the album and fingered the picture that was framed by the padded pink cover. "You were a pretty baby, but it looks like you either had a stomachache or you weren't too happy about having your picture taken."

Kate laughed, flipped her hair behind her shoulders, and took the book from Amy. She rubbed the backs of her fingers across the satin cover. Inside, her birthdate and time of birth were listed, along with weight and length, the color of her eyes, the color of her hair, even the meaning of the names her parents chose for her.

She read the words aloud. "Katherine means pure. May our little jewel remain as pure as the day she was born. Joy means happiness, gaiety, bliss, a source of delight. Such delight God has given us in our precious Katherine Joy. Paul is already calling her Katy Joy. I like it. Fits her perfectly."

Kate pressed her lips together to keep from crying. Dymple Forbes, her feisty elderly friend back home, the one who'd helped her get her feet on the ground after prison, once told her God delighted in her. At the time, she didn't know the meaning of her middle name or believed Dymple. And purity? She'd lost that in the first foster home.

Amy touched Kate's arm. "What's wrong?"

"If my parents were alive..." Kate blinked back tears. "They'd be so disappointed in me. I didn't live up to the names they gave me."

"You're different now. God changed you."

Kate placed the baby book in the box and waited while Amy returned the homecoming outfit to its bag.

"Just think," Amy said. "If you and Mike have a baby girl, she can wear this."

Kate sighed. "My doctor says I might not be able to get pregnant. I've been having a lot of female problems."

"Oh, Kate, I'm so sorry. I didn't know."

"That's because I didn't tell you. Mike is the only one who knows. But I keep praying..."

"I'll pray, too."

"Thanks." Kate took the bag from Amy, set it in the box and closed the flaps.

Amy's eyes widened. "Don't you want to see the other things in there? I'd be ecstatic if I found something that suggested my mom actually cared enough to collect memories for me before she disappeared."

Kate squeezed her friend's hand. In some ways, Amy's loss was more painful than her own. Her mother had abandoned the family long ago, and her dad didn't appear to care about Amy or her siblings. "How sad that you have nothing from your mom."

Amy shrugged. "That's life." She touched a flap. "If you don't mind, I'd enjoy going through your memory box with you."

"I'd love to share it with you later." Kate picked up a broken lamp and stood. "Right now, we need to work while Aunt Mary sleeps." She made her way to the other side of the attic to the fix-or-trash pile.

They'd just discovered a treasure trove in a plain cardboard box, a find far more valuable than cash or jewels. Part of her longed to examine everything in the box. The other part wanted to wait to unlock her treasure chest until she could savor the items one by one. Maybe they would trigger long-forgotten memories and give her stories to tell her children, if she and Mike ever managed to conceive.

Her gynecologist had told her conception and carrying a baby to term could be difficult for her body due to the damage caused by abortion as well as by promiscuity and rape. He'd also said she was young and there was a slight chance she might surprise him.

Was the box a sign from God? A sign she'd have babies who'd wear her booties? Maybe her brother's booties were also in the box. Her dream was to have a girl to dress in frilly outfits and an ornery boy with freckles across his nose to remind her of Philip. Of course, he'd also have Mike's blond hair and blue eyes.

From her desk in the office at the far end of the house, Laura heard the door to the lobby open and the sound of boots striding across the wood floor. The bell on the counter rang. She sent the e-mail she'd been writing and stepped to the doorway that led to the lobby. She stopped. "Todd."

"Laura."

The lanky white-haired man stood on the other side of the counter, a box of chocolates in one hand and a bouquet of flowers in the other. She looked from him to the flowers, thinking they probably came from the grocery store down in Copperville. She clasped her hands. What in the world was Todd Hughes up to now? He was a neighbor whose presence on her ranch usually meant trouble.

He smiled.

She drew in a breath, aware they were the only two people in the building. "What brings you to the Whispering Pines?" She tried to sound upbeat, yet her voice came out flat.

He set the chocolates on the counter and placed his hat beside the box. "I owe you an apology."

"For what?" She could smell his aftershave and wondered if he'd dabbed some on just for her. But that was a silly thought. He probably used aftershave every day.

Todd shifted the flowers to the other hand. "For everything that happened last year with Tara. I should have come by sooner. I guess I was too ashamed."

She folded her arms. "Why should you be the one to apologize? Your daughter is a grown woman responsible for her own behavior."

He rubbed his jawbone just below the sideburn. "I'm the one who brought her up. Folks used to tell me I was spoiling her. I should have listened." He shrugged. "I didn't listen, and you got the raw end of the deal."

She studied his face, thinking *raw end of the deal* was an interesting way to phrase Tara's theft of thousands of dollars from the ranch. Yet, if his sincere expression was any indication, the man was apologizing the best he knew how. "Thank you. I appreciate the thought." The polite thing would be to ask how Tara was doing in prison, but she couldn't bring herself to speak the arrogant woman's name.

He held out the chocolates and the flowers. "My peace offerings."

She lifted an eyebrow. "To share with Kate and Mike?"

"Uh, yeah. But I heard they're on an extended trip back east."

So that's why he showed up now. Maybe she should tell him to take his peace offerings and get off her property. However, that would be an ungrateful response, especially considering the hopeful expression on his face. Besides, the man was a longtime neighbor, one whose intentions seemed honorable.

Laura stepped to the counter and accepted the gifts. "Thank you. The flowers are lovely." Not knowing what else to say, she stood there with her hands full, staring at him. Todd Hughes was a better-looking man than she remembered.

She blinked. Where did that come from?

He rested his hands on his hat. "I thought maybe you'd have time to sit and visit for a spell, since it's after Labor Day. That's when all your guests leave, right?"

She hesitated. Mike wouldn't approve. He was convinced Todd masterminded the theft as well as the bison killings—and that Tara and Darryl, their former ranch hand, were his puppets. But Mike didn't have proof, and he wasn't there to hassle Todd, thank God.

She walked around the counter. "Do you like strawberries?"

CHAPTER THREE

Kate settled onto her mother-in-law's sofa. "I'm so glad to be home, Laura. That was a long trip. I'd forgotten how far Pittsburgh is from the ranch."

"I'm happy to have you back." Laura sat in the recliner and twisted the lever for the footrest. "I missed you and Mike."

Prissy hopped onto Kate's lap, and she began to stroke the dog's head. But then she saw Laura's expression. "Is it okay for Aunt Mary's dog to be on the furniture? She doesn't shed."

"I don't mind, as long as Tramp is outside and can't learn any bad habits." Laura lifted her mug. "You sure you don't want to try this new tea I bought? It's caffeine-free."

"Maybe later. I'm full from that delicious dinner." Kate scratched Prissy under the chin.

"I'm glad you enjoyed the lasagna. I used bison meat."

Mike, who'd just put Tramp out the back door, plopped down next to Kate. "Buffalo tastes good no matter how you fix it."

Laura laughed. "Of course."

Kate patted Mike's leg. "Every place we ate at on the trip, if the restaurant didn't have some form of bison on the menu, Mike asked to speak to the chef. The server would go get the poor cook, who'd have to stand there while Mike lectured him or her on all the reasons to offer buffalo to their customers."

"I did not lecture." Mike folded his arms. "I just informed them about the nutritional qualities and versatility they were missing out on, and then I gave them my card so they could order from our meat processor. It's called PR work, sweetheart. You should know that with your marketing background."

Laura set her cup on a coaster. "I hate to interrupt your, uh, discussion, but I'd like to hear about your trip. We've been so busy getting Mary settled that we haven't talked much."

"Our trip was..." Kate lowered her voice, even though her aunt was bathing in the bathroom down the hall. "Quite the adventure. Aunt Mary's dementia is more advanced than we knew. I'm thinking I should have her tested and get some advice from a professional."

"I'm not sure I'd call it an adventure." Mike laid his arm across the back of the couch. "It was more like a rabbit chase. For an elderly person with MS, she can disappear surprisingly fast." He ran his fingers through his hair. "We had to keep an eye on her every place we stopped, whether it was a rest area, a gas station, a restaurant, a store. Didn't matter. She took off every single time."

Prissy wriggled from Kate's lap to Mike's and rolled onto her back.

He stroked her belly. "Good thing Amy volunteered to come with us to help drive. It took all three of us to keep track of her."

"Speaking of Amy..." Laura looked around. "Where did she go?"

"Over to her cabin to unpack," Kate said. "She'll be back later, unless..." She laughed. "Unless she runs into a handsome cowboy to flirt with."

Laura cocked an eyebrow. "Aren't many single cowboys around the ranch this time of year."

Mike chuckled. "Don't tell Amy." He returned to his story. "Aunt Mary was content in the car. However, the moment she stepped out, she headed east, like she had a homing pigeon in her pocket. She even told a convenience store clerk she needed a bus ticket to get back to the Appalachians, where she was born and raised, because..." He made quotes with his fingers. "*Mom and Pop need me.*"

Laura's eyes widened. "Oh, dear."

Mike put the dog on the floor. "The first night on the road, she locked herself and Prissy out of her hotel room while trying to find the bathroom. Amy heard her and found an employee to let her back in. After that, they shared a room."

"Aunt Mary got up several times a night," Kate added. "She bumped into walls and furniture, and sometimes Prissy, with her walker. That woke Mike and me as well as Amy, and probably other guests. We could hear the dog yelp every time she got smacked."

"We can laugh about it now," Mike said. "However, it wasn't so funny when we were trying to sleep. We were all so tired during the day that we switched drivers between the moving truck and the rental car every couple of hours, so one of us could nap."

"What do you think she'll do here?" Laura pointed to the exits that were visible from where they sat. "We have a lot of doors in this place, and a whole lot of outdoors for her to get lost in."

"We were wondering..." Mike looked at Kate and then at Laura. "Would it be okay for us to sleep in my old bedroom for a week or two, until Mary adjusts? Kate being here might stop her from wandering away. If that doesn't work, I can install keypad locks."

Kate shook her head. "This is too much to ask of you, Laura. You have a ranch to run. I should find a memory care facility for Aunt Mary."

"Let's give Mary time. With you nearby, Kate, I think she'll begin to feel at home." Laura tucked a lock of hair behind her ear. "This is a new experience for all of us. We'll learn as we go and do the best we can to keep her safe and comfortable. And, yes, you can use the bedroom as long as you need."

"Thank you." Kate got up to hug her mother-in-law. "I can't tell you how much I appreciate you doing this for Aunt Mary."

Laura returned the hug. "This place has been way too quiet lately. I'm excited to have a lively household again."

"It'll be real lively," Mike said, "when all those guests come for Thanksgiving dinner next week."

Laura grinned. "I can't wait."

Happy chatter circulated around the Duncan dining room. Kate glanced from smiling face to smiling face. Thanksgiving dinner with her favorite people. What could be better? They'd added two leaves to the table to make room for everyone.

She and Mike, Laura, Aunt Mary and Amy sat across from their guests—Dymple, Cyrus Moore, Clint Barrett, and Marita and Jorge Ortega and their three children. Cyrus was a longtime, multi-talented Whispering Pines ranch hand, Clint was their ranch manager, and Marita worked in the dining hall during guest season. Jorge herded sheep in the summer and played in a mariachi band in the winter.

Mike took Kate's hand and bowed his head to pray.

She closed her eyes, reveling in the moment. After years of foster families, homelessness and incarceration, celebrating holidays with family and friends was the frosting on the cupcake of her new life. The food smelled wonderful. Even better, the sweet camaraderie around the table warmed her heart.

The instant Mike said *amen*, Cyrus slapped his palms on the table. "I've been waiting for this moment for weeks. No one cooks up a turkey like Mrs. D."

Laura smiled. "Thank you, Cyrus. That's quite a compliment coming from our ranch cook."

He arched a gray eyebrow, dragging a latticework of skin from his temple to his hairline. "*Former* ranch cook." His voice sounded like swirling gravel.

"True." Laura said. "But you're always welcome back in the kitchen. Right, Marita?"

Marita's dark eyes twinkled. She patted his shoulder. "Anytime, Mr. Cyrus. Anytime."

Laura handed him a serving fork and knife. "Since you're so anxious, you can carve the turkey, please."

While he sliced, the others passed the side dishes. Amy picked up the fruit salad. "Yum."

Kate smirked. "We're lucky there's any fruit salad left. You don't know how many times I had to slap Amy's fingers while I was making it."

Clint winked at Amy. "I'm a fruit salad fan, myself."

Kate saw a tinge of pink slide up her best friend's neck and onto her cheeks. She understood the attraction. Despite the hat crease in his short dark hair, Clint was a good-looking guy. Even better, he was a really nice man.

Last night, they'd all tackled a jigsaw puzzle together. To everyone's surprise, Aunt Mary found three pieces that fit. Apparently that was enough for her because she, like Laura, went to bed at her usual time. Kate and Mike gave up at midnight, leaving the puzzle half completed and Amy and Clint in deep concentration, their heads nearly touching as they bent over the puzzle. This morning, the picture was complete.

Clint elbowed Manuel, who was seated next to him. "How's your first semester at the University of Wyoming going, dude?"

Manuel's face lit. "Great. After the small classes in Copperville, I wasn't sure how I'd do, but I'm getting As and Bs, so far."

Mike gave Manuel a thumbs-up. "Good for you, buddy."

Clint took a bite and spoke out of the side of his mouth. "Any hot chicks in your pasture?" He grinned at Marita. "Sorry. Guy talk."

She blinked and spoke in her lilting Spanish accent. "I never heard of a chicken pasture. Maybe you should ask my son if he has hot heifers."

Everyone laughed. Cyrus slapped his knee. "Good one."

Clint's eyebrows scrunched. "I'm not sure the womenfolk would appreciate being called heifers."

Amy placed her hands on her waist and cocked her head. "So you think we like to be called chicks?"

Clint held up his hands. "Okay, okay. I give." He turned back to Manuel. "Hey, man, are you dating anyone these days?"

Manuel lowered his gaze.

Kate remembered the first day she saw him walk into the ranch dining hall, head down, shame and regret written all over him. But this time the teenager looked up. A broad grin high-lighted his straight white teeth. "No, but I started a club, and a whole bunch of girls joined it."

"*Girls?* You're in a club with *girls?*" His little brother's eyes were almost as wide as his mouth.

Everyone laughed again.

Kate watched the family. Manuel's sister was smiling up at her big brother. Their parents' expressions, on the other hand, were guarded. So Manuel's club was news to them, too. Their son was off probation, yet his mom and dad worried about him.

Manuel's brother asked, "What's the name of your club?"

"Fop."

"Fop?"

"Yeah. F-O-W-P. Friends of Whispering Pines. You have to know someone who's worked at the ranch to get into the club. Bethany and Trisha must have a million friends, 'cause more and more girls come every week to our meetings."

Jorge brushed crumbs from his dark mustache. "What do you do at these meetings, son?"

"Work." Manuel shook his head, as if in disbelief. "It's amaz-ing what people will do to get a chance to visit here. I tell them they have to attend at least ten meetings or find a way to do the work outside of a meeting if they want to come to the WP for spring break."

Laura, who'd just taken a drink of punch, sputtered. "Here? Spring break?"

"To help you guys get the ranch ready for the guest season. We'll bring our own food and clean up after ourselves."

She got up, walked to his chair and hugged him. "What a thoughtful idea, Manuel."

He ducked his head.

"Tell your friends we'll be happy to feed and house them while they're here, and maybe even provide some entertainment." She sat back down. "Right, Mike?"

"Good idea," Mike said. "Cyrus can yodel for them."

Cyrus waived away the cheers. "I can't yodel worth a hoot, but I might pull out my harmonica, if you'll strum that guitar of yours."

Kate asked Manuel if any of the members were male. Much of the work around the ranch required strong backs and arms.

"My roommate, Jason, is in the club, plus Samuel and Jack. They both worked here one summer."

Mike nodded. "I remember them."

"And some guys who started coming with their girlfriends."

Cyrus lifted his chin. "What kinda work is your gang doin' in Larmee?"

Kate smiled. Most people pronounced Laramie as "Lair-a-mee," but not Cyrus. Considering the small university town was named after a French trapper named Jacques LaRamie, they probably all said it wrong.

"We've raked a few yards, cleaned up mountains of dog poop, hauled broken branches after a windstorm, shoveled walks—that sort of stuff. I called City Hall and told them we'd like to help elderly and disabled people who can't take care of their property. Then Parks and Rec asked us to do some cleanup after the storm."

He sat taller. "Last Saturday, we worked at a horse-boarding place. The owner is in Afghanistan with the Guards. His wife said she kept up with the manure until their tractor broke down. So I got everybody out there with shovels and rakes and wheelbarrows. Took us all day. We'll go every couple of weeks until her husband returns."

Tears glistened on his mother's eyelashes, and his father's chin had a proud lift to it.

Kate smoothed her potatoes with her fork, thinking how much she'd like to give Mike a son.

Dymple, who'd been unusually quiet, asked, "Did your friends do any mister slinging?" She smiled and flipped her long white braid behind her shoulder.

"Uhm..." Manuel started to speak but then stopped.

Mary reached across Amy to pat Dymple's wrinkled hand. "I think she means manure slinging."

Dymple sighed. "Yes, that's what I meant to say."

Although Kate was pleased by her aunt's participation in the conversation, she felt sorry for Dymple. Her elderly friend's messed-up words usually resulted in confused expressions or laughter or both. Dymple took the aphasia in stride and pushed through to clarification, but Kate knew her unintentional word substitutions frustrated her.

Manuel grinned. "The guys threw horse pucky at the girls, who screamed and ran away. You know how girls are."

Everyone chuckled.

Mary folded her hands. "My brother invented a mule-powered cow-patty slinger when he was twelve-years old."

Kate saw clarity in her aunt's eyes. This would be interesting. A story she hadn't heard before.

The men and boys gawked at Mary as if she'd told them where to dig for gold.

"It's true." Her green eyes sparkled. "He and my other brother carried on an ongoing manure battle with the neighbor boys, which they were determined to win once and for all."

"Cool." Manuel rested his elbow on the table, his chin on his fist. "How did it work?"

Mary drew a diagram on her napkin and explained how the device worked. She told of men and boys coming from miles around to see the slinger operate. "In fact..." She blushed. "That's how I met my husband." Her brow furrowed and she peered from one end of the table to the other. "Dean...Where is Dean?"

Amy put her arm around Mary's shoulder. "Did you try the fruit salad yet, Aunt Mary? Kate made it."

Mary picked up her spoon. "The salad looks delicious. I'll have a taste."

Manuel's brother tugged on his dad's sleeve. "Can we make a poop slinger?"

Jorge didn't have a chance to answer before Manuel high-fived the younger boy. "When I'm home this summer, we'll visit Dad out at the sheep pasture and make one there."

Jorge's dark eyebrows lowered. "Sheep make pellets not patties."
Manuel pointed at his brother. "One pellet slinger coming up."
Kate smiled at their optimism. Maybe she and Mike would
have a girl and two boys, like the Ortegas.

CHAPTER FOUR

Kate followed Amy into the kitchen, where they found Laura already at the sink rinsing dishes. She put down the turkey platter, grasped her mother-in-law's shoulders, and steered her out of the room. "Go put your feet up and enjoy your guests. You've been cleaning and cooking for days."

"You girls can't—"

Amy brandished a spatula. "If I were you, lady, I'd think twice before I argued with two ex-cons armed with kitchen utensils."

"Okay, okay." Laura held up her hands, grinned and backed out of the kitchen.

Kate began to load the dishwasher. "I'm glad the raisin cream pie was a hit."

"Is this the first time you tried the recipe?"

"Yes. I finally came up with a use for Aunt Mary's raisins."

"You mean that jar of old raisins we found in her cupboard?" Amy wrinkled her nose. "The raisins she picked out of her cereal one-by-one?"

"They smelled okay and weren't moldy. I had enough to make two pies. And we only have half a pie left."

"I have to admit it was delicious." Amy opened a cupboard and took out plastic containers. "Maybe I'll have another piece later, when I no longer feel like a beached whale."

Kate groaned. "I know the feeling."

"How's it going with Aunt Mary? Is she staying put at night?"

"Not yet. She knocks around with her walker searching for the bathroom every couple of hours." Kate rubbed her temples. "If we don't wake up right away, both dogs start to whine, like they're telling us something's wrong. That's good, but it's hard to feel alert in the daytime when our sleep is interrupted so often."

"I hope she adjusts soon, so you can get some rest."

"I have a feeling we'll be staying in Laura's house longer than we planned." Kate longed to return to the cozy little cabin she and Mike shared, to have their own space again and escape the awkwardness of trying to make babies in a room situated between her aunt's and her mother-in-law's bedrooms.

Amy peeked into the living room before she turned back to Kate. "I don't see Clint. Did he go home?"

"He and Manuel and the kids are in the office playing computer games."

"So what's with him and Susan?" Amy lowered her voice. "They were inseparable at your wedding. I thought she'd be here today."

"So did I." Kate rinsed a bowl. "She's come here for other holidays."

Amy scooped food into a container. "In case you haven't noticed..." She snapped on the lid. "I developed a crush on Clint the day I met him. Every time I'm with him, it seems like things click between us."

"You two were certainly cozy last night. What time did you finish?"

"Around two-thirty. We had such a good time that I hated to leave, but it was nice of him to walk me to my cabin." A dreamy smile crossed her face. "The full moon was bright enough to see the path, yet he held my arm all the way."

"I heard him teasing you about your bird tattoos."

"Clint likes Orville and Wilbur."

Kate grinned. "So that's why you wore a skirt today."

"You caught me." Amy's cheeks colored. "I wanted to show off the new tatts on my legs."

"I like them, too." Kate hugged her friend.

"If Clint and Susan break up, let me know. Okay?"

Kate tapped her lips with her finger. "If he and Susan break up, and if you don't have a job by summer, maybe you could work here until your sister moves to Pittsburgh. That would give you a chance to get to know him better."

"I like that idea." Amy hesitated. "There's one stipulation. You have to promise I won't run into any snakes."

Kate snickered. "Like that won't happen on a ranch." Then she saw Amy's expression. "Sorry, I didn't realize you were serious."

Her friend had a faraway look in her eyes. "I was like nine or ten years old when I saw this huge snake crawling across our backyard. I ran inside the house to tell my dad and then followed him at what I thought was a safe distance when he went outside. He bent down, picked up the snake, and threw it at me. It landed on my shoulder, against my neck." She shuddered. "It was awful. I screamed and screamed."

Kate frowned. "That was mean, really mean. What happened after that?"

"I threw the snake on the ground and ran inside the house." She rubbed her hands on her skirt. "I still remember how the scales felt and my dad laughing at me. He said I was a scaredy-cat, just like my mom."

"Your father is a sick man." Kate sighed and shook her head. "You'll be glad to know snakes rarely come near the ranch buildings. If you went anywhere else on the property, you'd be on a horse or in a pickup."

"I've been wearing my snow boots when I walk back and forth from the cabin, just in case."

Kate suppressed a snicker. "It's too cold for snakes right now. However, if you join us next summer, you'll need to stay alert and wear cowboy boots for protection." She didn't tell Amy what Mike had told her. Rattlesnake fangs were long enough and powerful enough to pierce boot leather. Yet, boots were better than tennis shoes.

"I love cowboy boots." Amy high-fived Kate. "I can't wait to go shopping." She stopped. "But..."

"But, what?"

"I sent my resume to that agency I told you about. If they hire me, I won't be able to work here."

Kate frowned. "I have a funny feeling about that place."

"I haven't come up with any other possibilities."

"God has a perfect job in mind for you. You need to be patient."

Amy crossed her arms. "You have Mike and this ranch to take care of you, Kate. I don't have that luxury, and my unemployment checks won't last forever."

When they'd said goodbye to the last guest, Laura settled in the recliner with a magazine. Too tired to read, she skimmed the pages and relived the good time they'd shared with friends. Thank God she didn't burn the turkey or over-salt the gravy.

She flipped a page, saw an ad for a Las Vegas casino, and thought of Todd. They'd talked twice on the phone since his visit to the ranch. Both times, he'd asked her to travel with him, first to Florida and then to Vegas. She'd laughed off his offers.

Had he eaten a turkey dinner at a casino today? The mental picture of him eating alone surrounded by strangers and noisy slot machines made her sad. Surely he would have preferred a home-cooked meal with friends.

Pine sap crackled and popped in the fire.

Should she have invited the lonely widower to eat with them? What if she'd asked Todd to carve the turkey, instead of Cyrus? Laura heaved a long sigh. About then, Mike would have tossed Todd *and* the turkey into the nearest snowbank.

Mike reached the outskirts of Copperville and slowed his truck to park in the lot next to Grandma's Café. He hurried into the restaurant and was surprised by the bright interior. Maybe he could convince Kate to trying Grandma's again. She'd had a bad experience there when she first came to town, but he'd heard the food and the service improved after the new owners took over.

He spotted Marshall Thompson in a booth and headed that direction. A young waitress followed him. As he slid across the vinyl seat, she asked if she could bring him something to drink. Marshall was already drinking coffee.

"Coffee, please."

"Are those cinnamon rolls I smell?" Marshall asked.

She grinned. "Fresh out of the oven."

He pointed to Mike. "Want one? I'm buying."

"Sounds good."

"Two cinnamon rolls, coming up." The girl turned toward the kitchen, her brown ponytail swinging.

Marshall picked up a sugar packet. "How was your trip?"

"Great. The fall trees in New England were something to see. Kate grew up on the east coast, so she was in seventh heaven."

"Did you sell her aunt's house?"

"Not yet. An agent will list it after some repairs and upgrades are completed."

"Her stuff still in it?"

"I wish." Mike grunted. "Took two big storage units to hold what we left behind, and we filled a stall in the barn with the boxes we brought to the ranch."

"Whoa."

The waitress appeared again, this time with a coffee carafe and two giant cinnamon rolls.

Marshall's eyes widened. "Those are monsters."

She turned over Mike's cup to fill it. "Can I get you gentleman anything else?"

"A refill later would be good," Mike said. "Are you the new owner?"

"My parents own the café. They're in the kitchen discussing menu options right now. If you have something special you'd like us to serve, I can let them know."

Mike and Marshall spoke in unison. "Bison meat."

"Like in buffalo burgers?"

"And steaks, roast and sausage." Mike raised a different finger for each item.

"I'll tell Mom and Dad. Where do they order it?"

Marshall directed his forefinger at Mike and his thumb toward himself, toggling his hand back and forth. "From either of us. I have a brochure in my truck I can leave with you."

Mike grinned. Marshall hadn't been in the business long, but he was proud of his herd and displayed the enthusiasm of a door-to-door salesman.

"Great. Mom and Dad like to buy local as much as they can."

Mike held out his hand. "I'm Mike Duncan from the Whispering Pines Guest Ranch, and this is Marshall Thompson from the Leaning T Ranch. Welcome to Copperville."

"Thank you." She shook his hand and then Marshall's. "I'm Cindy Raeburn. My parents are Joyce and Martin."

Marshall stirred sugar into his coffee. "Where did your family come from?"

"Pittsburgh, Pennsylvania."

Mike, who was opening a tiny cream container, looked up. "I thought your accent sounded familiar. My wife and her aunt are from there. I'll have to bring them in."

"That would be fun." Cindy glanced at a couple who'd just walked in the door. "I'd better get back to work and let you drink your coffee before it gets cold. Nice to meet you both."

Mike stirred the cream into the dark liquid. The colors swirled and blended, like the coffee and cinnamon aromas wafting around him. "What's the latest with the red deer? Are they still hanging around your place?"

Marshall scratched his nose. "No. I've asked other ranchers if they've come across 'em. They just stare at me like I've been chewing locoweed."

"Any word on what Hughes might be up to?"

"That's why I asked you to meet me here. At the Grange supper a couple weeks ago, Leonard Gruber and Arnie Williams told me

Hughes was pressuring them to sell their ranches to him. I'm not the only one he's trying to buy out. And I don't think it's a coincidence that their property, like yours and mine, borders his ranch."

"Huh." Mike pursed his lips. "He used to hassle my dad about selling, but he hasn't bothered me or Mom since that craziness with his daughter last year."

"I think he's trying to expand."

"Why?" Mike sat back. "He has the biggest ranch in the area."

Marshall spoke around a mouthful of cinnamon roll. "My dad checked with the county assessor last week. Hughes has seventy-three thousand, five-hundred and ninety-two acres."

"Which came from his banker father buying out how many ranchers at rock-bottom prices back in the sixties?"

"That's what fries Dad. He says Rodney Hughes was as crooked as a Chicago politician. A lot of men lost land that'd been in their families for generations. He pretended to help them with a high-interest loan during hard times and instead ripped them off." Marshall picked up his coffee. "When they couldn't pay up, he took everything they owned, including family keepsakes."

"I heard he was as heartless and greedy as they come. Did your dad learn anything else?"

"We all know Hughes doesn't do much ranching. Grows a little hay, sells a few head of cattle now and then, nothing substantial. Yet he offered each of us cash." Marshall pushed his glasses higher up the bridge of his nose. "We got to wondering where it was coming from, so Dad started talking with realtors around the state and checking county records. Old Man Hughes owned property all over the place."

"Interesting."

"Even more interesting, Todd Hughes sold three large properties in Natrona County last spring and two in Sweetwater County last summer. A fairly good-sized ranch is up for sale near Devil's Tower along with another nice-looking place not far from Jackson. Wouldn't mind having the Jackson ranch myself, except I'd never trust a Hughes deal. Plus, it's way overpriced." He snorted. "But you can bet some wealthy movie star will snatch it up without blinking twice."

"So he's land rich and cash poor. What's that got to do with us?"

"Could be he's selling all those other places to get money to buy out his neighbors." Marshall rested his forearms on the table. "You sure he stopped bugging your mom?"

Mike shrugged. "She hasn't mentioned it."

"Maybe you should ask her."

"After that fiasco with his daughter..." Mike clenched his fists. "Hughes steers clear of me and I steer clear of him." He leaned closer. "I'm fairly certain he masterminded the theft as well as the bison shootings."

"I wouldn't be surprised. Any more shootings?"

"Nope."

"Wonder what that was all about."

"Me, too. The more I think about it, the less sense it makes."

"Maybe Hughes was trying to scare you away because you wouldn't sell."

"I have to admit I thought about selling the herd, but we've never considered selling the ranch."

Cindy returned with a carafe. "More coffee?"

"Please." Mike pushed his cup to the edge of the table and angled his chin toward the corner. "I see you kept the jukebox. Does it work?"

"People put quarters in now and then."

"Are you going to keep the same songs?"

"Funny you ask." She filled Mike's cup then Marshall's. "My dad found a place online where we can order 45 rpm records. Mom wants more of the old rock-and-roll stuff, like what's already in there. Dad wants country-western and bluegrass, 'cause he thinks that's what Wyoming people like. My brother wants us to get rid of the jukebox and put in speakers so we can play hip-hop and heavy metal."

Mike grinned. "What about you?"

"I just want something more current than Elvis." She slid their cups back. "I can't believe people listen to his music. He died eons ago."

Marshall chuckled. "Not an Elvis fan, I take it."

She crossed her eyes.

"Maybe you could figure out a way to mix it up." Mike took a sip of coffee. "Something for everyone."

"Dad's afraid older people will be offended and never come back if they hear my brother's music in here."

"He has a point." Marshall folded his arms. "You'll have to let us know who wins the battle."

CHAPTER FIVE

A my kicked off her new boots and curled into her overstuffed recliner. Although she loved visiting Wyoming, she was happy to be back in her Pittsburgh duplex, even if it smelled like the litter box was overdue for a change. A cat climbed onto the chair and settled in her lap. Her dogs plopped at her feet.

She picked up the phone and called Kate. After the initial greetings, she asked, "How was your trip to Grand Island?"

"Good." Kate's voice came in loud and clear. "Much better than that drive from the ranch to Cheyenne. We experienced fairly decent roads after we dropped you off at the airport."

"I'm glad to hear that." Amy snapped her fingers at her golden retriever. The dog was displaying way too much interest in her boots. "What's your impression of Nebraska?"

"Flat. Very flat."

Amy laughed. "Not quite like Wyoming, huh?"

"Parts of Wyoming are on the plains, like Nebraska. After all, they're adjoining states. But this area is definitely not Whispering Pines country. Did you have a good flight to Pittsburgh?"

"Yes, except for the boring layover in Denver." Amy ran her hand over her cat's long black fur and felt a purr vibrate its warm body. "How's the bison sale going?"

"So far, Mike has purchased five cows—yearlings, I think they're called. The sales have been interesting. They're like auctions. But I'll be glad to return to the ranch. Motel living gets old fast and I hate to be away from Aunt Mary for long."

The cat rolled over and batted at the phone cord. Amy swung the cord back and forth, glad she'd kept her grandma's ancient phone. "Good news, Kate. I have a job interview tomorrow."

"How exciting. Who's it with?"

Amy shifted. The cat jumped off her lap, hissed at the dogs, and chased them out of the room. She cleared her throat. Kate wasn't going to like this part. "That online place I told you about. They liked my resume."

"Oh."

Amy heard disapproval in her friend's voice. "I'm just checking it out. They're paying for my flights to and from Dallas and an overnight stay in a fancy hotel with a huge indoor swimming pool and an in-room hot tub. I saw pictures online. I also get three gourmet meals at high-class restaurants."

"Tell me again..." Kate sounded doubtful. "What's the name of the company, and what kind of job is this?"

Amy drummed the chair arm with her fingertips. Her best friend ought to be happy she'd finally landed an interview for something other than flipping burgers. "I'll interview with an employment agency called Executive Pride for a personal-assistant position with them that includes other duties, like hosting PR parties and making videos for clients. That's why the interview includes an acting audition." She took a breath. "I don't know much about it, but it sounds fun. I like the idea of variety in my work."

Wrapping the phone cord around her finger, Amy decided not to tell Kate that the woman she talked with asked for her weight, dress size and measurements. Even insisted she put down the phone to measure herself. She admitted that was strange. Yet, if she was going to act for them, they needed to know what size costumes to provide. She nibbled at the edge of a fingernail. Must be why they'd also asked her to send a full-body picture.

Kate interrupted her thoughts. "I thought Elaina was planning to move in with you and go to school in Pittsburgh."

"That's the cool thing about this job. They're a rapidly growing company with divisions all over the U.S. I can work in any large city I choose."

"What about working at the ranch this summer?"

"Did Clint and Susan break up?"

"Not that I know of." Kate sighed. "Is the pay good?"

"The pay is awesome. Far better than what I was making at the stables."

"Almost sounds too good to be true. When do you leave?"

"I fly to Dallas in the morning, interview in the afternoon, spend the night, and fly home Saturday morning. Short and sweet."

One of her parrots squawked. "Short and sweet, short and sweet."

"I heard that." Kate laughed. "Did you get permission from your parole officer for the out-of-state trip?"

"Uh..." Amy hesitated." I haven't told her. I mean, it's only overnight. She'll never know I'm gone. Besides, she's on my case to find a job, so the interview ought to please her."

"Amy..."

"It's too late now. I committed to the interview. The tickets are purchased, and her office is closed for the day."

For a moment, Kate was silent. "I hope it all works out for you. What time will you get home on Saturday?"

"I'm not sure. They'll give me my plane ticket when I get there."

"That's unusual. Seems they'd send you both tickets upfront."

Amy shrugged. "They're the ones buying the tickets."

"Do me a favor."

"What?"

"Memorize my cell phone number and our number at the ranch."

"Why?" Amy asked. "I have your numbers in my phone."

"It just seems like a smart thing to do, in case you drop your phone in the hot tub or whatever."

"Okay. I can do that, I guess. Seems silly."

"Humor me, and call me the minute you get home. I want to hear all about it, okay?"

"Sure." Amy smiled. Even if she didn't get the job, spending a couple days in Dallas would be an adventure. "I'd better go decide what to wear for the interview. Wish me luck."

"I'll be praying for you."

"Thanks."

Kate chuckled.

"What's so funny?"

"I'm surprised you're willing to leave your animals again so soon, even for one night. You worried about them constantly while you were in Wyoming."

"My next-door neighbor's kid, the one who took care of them while I was gone, he said he'd feed them and walk the dogs. I'll sleep better knowing he's checking on them."

"No doubt you'd toss and turn all night in your fancy hotel room if you thought they were missing a meal." Kate paused. "One more thing."

"What's that?"

"Wear your copper-colored blouse with the dark-green pant-suit. You look like a movie star in that outfit."

Laura answered the office phone on the third ring. "Hello."

"Hey, pretty lady. You have a moment to chat?"

She lowered her voice, even though she was alone. "I'm just doing email correspondence."

"I'd like to take you to dinner tomorrow tonight. Return the favor for those strawberries you fed me."

So Todd was back in town. "You don't have to do that."

"I want to."

"I appreciate the offer. However, Kate's aunt just moved in with me. She has dementia, along with multiple sclerosis, and can't be left alone. Kate and Mike are at a bison sale in Nebraska and won't be back until Saturday or Sunday."

He was quiet, as if digesting the information. "So, I'll bring dinner to you and the aunt, complete with candles. How does that sound?"

"You cook?" She couldn't keep the surprise out of her voice. Todd didn't seem like the type to cook anything more complicated than a hamburger.

"What do you think a widower with a child to feed does? Open cans and boxes?"

"Well…"

"I plan to knock your socks off. Be ready with an appetite."

"Goodness, Todd. You don't have to go to all that work. In fact, you shouldn't do anything at all. They were just strawberries from our garden."

"Fabulous strawberries enjoyed with a fabulous lady. I'll be there at six o'clock sharp. Bye."

Laura put the phone down. The man had it all figured out. That thought raised her hackles a bit. Maybe she should call him back and tell him not to come. She started to reach for the phone but stopped. It was nice to have someone notice her and want to spend time with her. One evening with Todd couldn't amount to much, could it? Mary would be their unofficial chaperone, and with any luck, her failing short-term memory would keep her from telling Mike and Kate about Todd's visit.

Amy reached for her bag on the airline carousel just as a masculine hand with long tapered fingers, well-groomed nails and a diamond ring grasped it. "Allow me."

She turned her head and found herself face to face with an incredibly good-looking, good-smelling, olive-skinned man. His jaw and upper lip were tinged by a hint of dark beard. He smiled, revealing perfectly spaced white teeth, and her mind went blank, except for two words: Greek god.

The man lifted the bag and straightened. "Miss Amy Iverson, I presume." Tall, well-built, and wearing a suit, her escort was dressed far better than the others who surrounded the carousel. The curve of a gold watch glinted just below his jacket sleeve.

"Yes..."

In one fluid motion, he set the suitcase on the floor, extended the handle and held out his other hand. Amy cringed at the sight of a snake tattoo that wound from the back of his hand into his sleeve. Fangs protruded from the open mouth.

"I'm Thomas." He took her hand. "I'll be your escort this weekend."

"How do you know who I am?"

"You provided a picture. Remember?"

"Oh, yeah. I mean, yes." As they shook hands, she tried not to touch the tattoo, which was more realistic than any snake tatt she'd seen. And she'd seen a lot of them, especially in prison. Women who thought they were tough or considered themselves sexy tended to be the ones who flaunted serpents winding around their bodies. Her bird tatts were much nicer.

He offered a sly grin. "If you don't mind me saying so, you're far more attractive in person than in your photo."

"Thank you, I think." Was that a compliment or an insult?

He motioned toward the exit. "This way, please."

The instant they exited the building, a black limousine glided to the curb in front of them and stopped. The driver came around to greet them. Thomas handed him her luggage and helped her inside. Then he sat next to her, a wide smile highlighting his tanned face. "Ready for lunch?"

Though she was rarely without words, the man's stunning features took her breath away, not to mention his delectable aftershave. All she could do was smile and gawk at the leather-and-mirror surroundings. She'd never been inside a limo.

The car slid into traffic and merged with all the other vehicles exiting Dallas/Fort Worth International Airport. Thomas indicated the mini bar in front of them. "Would you like me to fix you a drink?"

"No, thank you."

He seemed disappointed, but he didn't push her. Instead, he asked, "Ever been to Dallas before?"

"This is my first visit. I'm anxious to see the city and meet some Texans."

"Oh, you'll get to know its citizens well." His eyes glittered.

"In a weekend?"

"We'll have you back here often for corporate meetings and training sessions. Dallas will become like a second home to you."

"*If* I'm hired."

He smirked. "My guesses so far as to who makes it and who doesn't have been one-hundred percent accurate."

"Really?" She grinned. Did she finally have a job?

"I predict you'll fly through HR."

"You've only known me a few minutes."

Thomas ran a hand over his hair, revealing more of the tattoo that continued up his forearm.

Amy bit her lip. The lifelike reptile looked ready to crawl off his arm and onto the leather seat.

"Call it masculine intuition." He winked. "Or maybe it's that the ones who impress me impress HR."

Within moments, it seemed, they were standing just inside the entrance of a beautiful restaurant high atop an elegant hotel in downtown Dallas. The palatial yet intimate setting was exquisite. She'd never seen anything like it—or smelled such tempting aromas.

Thomas took off his jacket, his muscles rippling seductively under a form-fitting red silk shirt. He adjusted his tie and insisted she leave her jacket as well as her suitcase and purse with the coat clerk. "The employees at this place are so trustworthy they're bonded. Your belongings are probably safer with them than with yourself." He laughed at his joke as if it was the funniest thing he'd ever heard.

Was he laughing at her? Did he know she'd done time for theft?

She could barely understand the menu let alone recognize the food her escort ordered for her, but it was tasty. Delicate flaky pastries melted in her mouth. A savory sauce topped incredibly tender meat. And the buttery vegetables were steamed to perfection. She couldn't begin to imagine what the dessert options might be.

Although she asked for iced tea, Thomas insisted she try the house specialty, a grand mimosa with raspberries. "You'll love it. That's what I always order for my guests."

"I can't go to the job interview with alcohol on my breath."

"You seem tense. A drink would help you relax."

She didn't feel tense. Scrutinizing his flawless features and staring into his beautiful eyes banished all concern. If she could, she'd sit there all afternoon just ogling his perfect body. She lowered her gaze and speared a broccoli floweret—and hoped she used the right fork.

The waiter set their drinks in front of them.

Thomas stirred his and then reached over to stir hers. The tattoo undulated with the movement.

Amy stared out the window at the wide expanse of city below. Why did such a gorgeous man have to ruin his body with a snakehead?

"This restaurant's mimosas are perfect," Thomas was saying, "except I always think they need a couple more swirls to blend in the liqueur just right."

She nodded her gratitude and slowly chewed a bite of meat, relishing the flavor. Thomas watched her eat, but she wasn't about to hurry. No matter how much money they paid her, she had a feeling it would be a long time before she could afford anything this expensive. She swallowed. "What?"

"What do you mean, *what*?"

"I get the feeling you're waiting for me to choke or something."

"No, not at all. Do you like what I ordered for you?"

"Everything tastes fabulous, wonderful, scrumptious. Even if I can't pronounce the names. Thank you for bringing me here. I've never been to such an exotic restaurant. The view from this place is incredible."

"Don't thank me. It's on the company, even the drinks."

"You really think it's okay for me to drink alcohol before the interview?"

He leaned forward, rested his elbows on the table and tented his long fingers. "If it'll make you feel better, just take a couple sips. You'll love it."

Amy reached for the drink. "You have a much better idea of what is expected of me today than I do."

His eyebrows rose. "You'd better believe it, baby. I'm looking forward to it."

What was that supposed to mean?

She tilted the delicate champagne flute, sipping from the rim. It *was* good. She took another, longer drink and smiled at her host. "Mmm. Very nice."

Gourmet meal number one. Two to go. She could get used to this lifestyle.

He lowered his eyelids and loosened his tie.

She set the drink down. The mimosa was delicious, but she couldn't risk ruining the interview of a lifetime.

CHAPTER SIX

Kate twisted away from the hand that gripped her shoulder. "Don't..."

"Wake up, Kate. You're dreaming."

She opened her eyes. Mike's worried face, illuminated by a bedside lamp, filled her vision. Though he was with her, she felt disoriented. "Where are we?"

"In a motel room in Grand Island, Nebraska."

"Oh, I thought..."

"I know." He smoothed her hair away from her cheeks. "Another nightmare."

She dried her eyes with the sheet. "This one felt so real, like when I was in prison and a correctional officer was kicking me in the stomach. Then I was in a lake trying to swim away from him. I couldn't move my arms or—"

She groaned and twisted into a fetal position.

He grabbed her arm. "What's wrong?"

She hugged her abdomen, trying to stop the pain. Black feelers crawled at the edges of her vision. She felt a thick stickiness between her legs, and a familiar metallic odor wormed its way into her awareness. She gritted her teeth. "I think I'm bleeding."

"Where?"

Before she could answer, she heard him draw a fast breath.

"The blankets are soaked. I'm calling an ambulance."

She would have objected if she hadn't lost consciousness.

Amy awakened but couldn't see anything. The streetlight outside her duplex must have burned out again. She tried to sit up and discovered her arms were asleep. She shifted to turn over. Her arms weren't asleep. They were stuck. So were her legs. She'd gotten tangled in the sheets. A loud noise vibrated in her head, and she realized it was the sound of her teeth chattering. Why was she so cold if she was wrapped in bedding?

She struggled to free her arms and legs and felt her skin scrape against cold cement. She searched for a glimmer of light but saw none. The cement's moldy dirt smell saturated her senses, yet it was overpowered by an even stronger sewer-like odor. She must be in the middle of the worst nightmare she'd ever—

"Sleeping Beauty awakens."

Amy gasped and her heart began to pound. The male voice was familiar. Who was it? Where was she?

"Welcome to Executive Pride, Miss Iverson." The husky baritone boomed, as if from surround-sound speakers, vibrating her ribs against the hard floor.

Thomas. She sucked in a breath as it all came back. The flight to Dallas, the limo ride...lunch. What did Thomas do to her?

"How do you like your fancy accommodations? Does the room suit you?" He apparently no longer felt the need to temper the sneering sarcasm she'd seen hints of earlier.

Before she could respond, he jeered, "Lady, you are one good lay." Then he laughed a long loud chortle.

"What?" Surely she would have known. Wouldn't she?

"Just what I said, baby. Nice, real nice. Now it's Damon's turn, and Marco's and Carl's and Alfonzo's and, well, whoever else is in the mood this afternoon to test drive the new whore."

Whore? What was he talking about?

Thomas's voice throttled down a couple notches. "Damon is going to open the door now. Be sure to behave yourself. He's got a temper. He also has a very sharp knife to cut the duct tape, so you can service him properly." The voice became sing-song. "Just remember, if you don't make Damon happy...well, let's just say he knows how to inflict maximum pain without marring that exquisite body of yours."

After the doctor left the room, Kate lay in her hospital bed, staring out the window. Early morning sunlight glared off the snow piled on a nearby roof. She closed her eyes, wishing she could turn off her brain and shut out the doctor's words.

"I know this may seem sudden and surprising to you, Mrs. Duncan." He'd paused then, as if giving her a moment to ready herself for his next words. "Your uterus was a time bomb. I'm surprised it didn't detonate earlier."

Now the time bomb was gone. And with it, her dream of having a family to call her own. Eventually, her body would recuperate from the hysterectomy and blood loss. And the doctor promised she'd soon be free of the pelvic pain that had plagued her for months. But what about the ache in her soul?

This time when Amy awakened, she was in a bed covered with red satin sheets and a silver-and-black comforter. A stripe of sunlight pierced the gap between heavy drapes and splashed across the foot of the bed. Pushing the bedding aside, she tried to sit up but collapsed against the pillows. Why did she feel so hungover? And where was her nightgown? She didn't remember taking it off.

With effort, she rolled onto her side to search for the gown. A sharp pain stabbed her pelvis. She clutched her abdomen, and the horrible night came back in vivid detail, awakening a tremor in the pit of her stomach that spread to her extremities. She yanked the covers over her bruised body and frantically scanned the dim room for a phone, but the nightstands were bare.

She clutched the sheet to her chest, her breath catching in jagged gulps. The room had three doors. The open one looked like it led into a bathroom. The one next to it could be for a closet. And the other door, that had to be the exit.

Amy sat up. How she'd ended up in this room was a mystery, but at least she was no longer chained to that cold hard floor with all those men... She heard a noise and saw that the third doorknob was turning. The latch clicked.

Mike hurried into Kate's hospital room. "Sorry I'm late." He bent to kiss her. "Has the doc been here?"

She hugged him, trying not to disturb the tubes that dangled from her arms. "He just left."

"I overslept." Mike straightened, shaking his head. "I was planning to shower and change my clothes at the motel and then come back to spend the night with you." He rubbed his hand over his unshaven cheek. "Don't know what happened. I sat down on the bed to take off my boots, and that's the last thing I remember until a few minutes ago, when the sound of people rolling their suitcases past our room woke me."

"You needed the sleep." She took his hand. "The doctor didn't say much except that the surgery went okay and I should be able to go home in two or three days."

Mike perched on the edge of the bed. "I've never been so scared." He gripped her hand with both of his. "Your face was white, your lips were blue. There was blood everywhere. And you were moaning, like you were in terrible pain. I thought the ambulance would never get there."

She wrapped her other hand around his. "I'm sorry I put you through such a fright."

"Oh, sweetheart." He kissed her forehead. "I didn't want to picture life without you." He sat up, sucked in a long breath and let it out. "You look a world better today. How do you feel?"

"Drugged." And empty, like the desolate void she'd felt when her family was killed in the car wreck. "The pain is gone for the moment, thanks to morphine. And the doctor says I'll be good as new in a few weeks."

"Great, but I don't want to leave here until it's safe for you to travel." He motioned toward the window. "I heard on the radio on my way over that Grand Island got nine inches last night, but the snow is already melting."

"Maybe the roads will be dry all the way to the ranch." She readjusted her pillow before raising the head of the bed. "Would you like some of my breakfast? I saved it, so we could share." Besides, she didn't feel like eating.

"You need to eat."

"Not all of it. They gave me a huge pile of scrambled eggs and a big chunk of ham plus peach slices and two pieces of toast."

Mike set the lid aside. "Smells good." Steam rose from the eggs. "Okay, I'll help, but you have to eat, too."

Kate watched him slice the ham into bite-size pieces. "I'm sorry, Mike."

"For what?" He speared a piece of ham and offered it to her.

She chewed the salty bite and swallowed. "I'm sorry we can't have a family."

He scooped up a forkful of eggs. "The two of us, we're a family."

"If I hadn't aborted my child, we'd have three members in our family right now, plus we'd be able to have more children."

He put the fork down, pushed the tray aside and took her hands. "The doc back home said it's hard to know exactly what caused all the damage. Your body has been through a lot, Kate."

"Sin has consequences." She lowered her gaze. "I killed my baby. The hysterectomy could be God's repayment, the consequence for what I did."

Mike caressed her cheek and didn't speak until she made eye contact again. "Have you forgotten that God forgave you and wiped your slate clean."

"I know, but we wanted children." From almost the moment they became engaged, they'd talked about starting a family. He'd lost his brother and father. She'd lost her brother and both parents.

He arched an eyebrow. "I'm not enough?"

"Of course you're enough, more than I ever dreamed of in a husband. But what am I supposed to do now? I pictured myself rocking babies and reading to toddlers, attending school programs, helping with homework, teaching our kids how to ride a horse and plant a garden." She shrugged. "It's hard to imagine a future without children."

"You can still do all those things."

Kate looked down, knowing what he was going to say.

"We could adopt."

"No way." She pulled her hands from his grasp and folded her arms. "Been there, done that."

"You were a foster child, not an adopted child."

"Not much difference, is there?"

"There'd be a big difference at our house."

Kate lowered the bed back down and pulled the covers up. "I'm not hungry."

Amy yanked the bed linens to her chin.

Sporting a wide grin, Thomas wheeled a cart into the room. "Good morning, beautiful."

She gaped at him.

"I brought you breakfast."

With drugs in the orange juice, no doubt. "I'm not hungry." Her voice was hoarse. "I want to go home."

He parked the cart and closed the door. Crossing the room, he opened the drapes before settling into a chair next to her.

She scooted to the opposite edge of the king-size bed.

Thomas leaned forward, hands clasped, elbows on his knees. Muscles bulged beneath a canary-yellow silk shirt, muscles she'd admired earlier but now feared. His aftershave was so strong she could taste it, and her stomach rebelled. He offered a patronizing smile, yet she knew violence simmered behind his unreadable black eyes.

"This is your home now, Natasha." His tone was sweet, almost syrupy.

"Natasha?" She spat the word back at him. "That's not my name, and I don't live here."

His eyes darkened even further. "Your name is Natasha." His voice had turned brittle. "And this is your home from now on."

"Where's my luggage, my clothing, my purse?"

He smirked. "You don't need the old rags we found in that shabby suitcase of yours. I brought you classy clothes."

He pulled the cart to the chair and slid a basket from a side shelf. "Shopped for you myself." Lifting a shiny jade top, her favorite shade of green, he said, "Like it?"

She shrunk into the pillows. No way would she dress in front of him. "I hate it. I want my own clothes, no matter how tacky you think they are."

He narrowed his eyelids. "Next time, you'll show some gratitude."

The ice in his voice made Amy shudder.

He pointed a long index finger at her. "You'll say, 'Thank you, Thomas, darling. You have exquisite taste and you treat me better than any man ever treated me before.' Or you'll suffer the consequences of your ingratitude." He sat in the chair again. "We burned your rags and your suitcase."

She stared at him. He was psycho. The sooner she got away from him, the better. She needed her bank card to buy clothing and a ticket to fly home before her parole officer realized she was gone. "Is my purse in this room?"

He chuckled. "You don't need that old thing anymore. I bought you an Armani today." He held a large leather bag above the bed. "It's a beauty, don't you think?"

She refused to even peek at the handbag, though she'd yearned for an Armani for years. "Did you burn my purse, too?"

"No, no, no, Natasha." He dropped the satchel into the bin and shoved it closed. "Your precious little bag has taken on a new life. Just about now..." He lifted the wrist with the gold Rolex. "Law enforcement personnel in one of our higher-class Dallas suburbs should be arriving at the location where you abandoned the Cadillac Escalade, the one you stole after you murdered the owner last night."

"I did no such thing." Amy glared at him. "There are no fingerprints, no witnesses, no evidence of any sort."

"Just the purse you left in your haste to get away when OnStar locked the engine at the request of the authorities—after your victim was found by the side of the road this morning. If you'll recall, that bag contained your driver's license, credit cards, plane ticket..."

She clutched the covers. "And my contact info for Executive Pride."

"Baby, baby." He shook his head, a sadistic smile twisting his lips. "You're gonna learn I'm a whole lot smarter than that."

The first glimmer of hope she'd felt all morning, or day, or whatever it was, surged through her spirit. The police would find her phone in the purse and talk with people on her contact list.

"And your cell phone? We burned it with your luggage."

"But, it had my phone numbers. That's how I keep in touch with my—"

"Friends and family. Blah-blah. That's ancient history, Natasha. The moment I retrieved your trashy little bag at the airport..." His nose wrinkled with distaste, and he wiped his hand on his pant leg. "From that moment, I became everything you'll ever need. I'm your best friend, your boss, your man, your lover."

Lover? "I have a lot of animals." Her voice cracked. "They need me, and I need them."

He looked her up and down.

Despite the bedding, she felt as though he'd just stripped her naked, again.

He lowered his eyelids, and a purr rumbled in his throat. "Natasha, I'm all the animal you'll ever need."

She swallowed the bile rising in her throat.

"Which means…" He paused. "Those silly tattoos are history."

"They were expensive. I can't—"

Something beeped.

He checked his watch. "Gotta go." He stood, looming larger than she remembered. "Welcome to Executive Pride Escorts, Natasha, the best and the busiest escorts in the West."

"Escorts?" She frowned. "That's not what I was told the job would be."

He sneered. "Your job is to make my clients deliriously happy all night, every night."

"I'm not a prostitute, if that's what you mean."

"Pride women are proud of who they are—state of the art, high-class whores—and they don't pretend to be anything else." He stabbed a finger at her. "You are a whore, a harlot, a hooker. My men and I broke you in."

She sat taller. "I don't care what you did to me or what you call me. I could never do that."

"I read your rap sheet. You're a perfect match for the Pride."

"That was before—"

"Oh, yeah. I read about that, too." He sniggered. "Before you got religion. A con getting religion is as believable as water running uphill." He leaned close. "You have a new god, and it's me."

Amy willed herself to return his glare. "You're not a god, you're a pimp."

Thomas jolted upright. "I am not a pimp. I'm a professional personnel manager." He jutted out his chin. "I help individuals— male and female, young and old—fulfill their fantasies."

"Being gang raped was never one of my fantasies."

In an instant, he was on her side of the bed, ripping the sheets away. He grabbed her by the shoulders and jerked her to her feet. "That's enough lip."

"I can't. I won't—"

He flung her onto the bed, ripped a phone from the case at his waist and hit a button. "Damon, new recruit's room. Pronto."

Recruit? She wasn't a recruit. She'd been kidnapped. *Help me, God.*

"Bring the snakes." He snapped the phone shut.

"No!" She jumped up and gripped his arm with both hands. "I'm afraid of snakes."

He shoved her to the floor. "You think I didn't know that?"

Amy cowered at his feet. "I'll do what you want. Please don't—"

He kicked her aside and strode to the door, where he punched a code into a keypad. As he exited the room, another man carrying a wire cage entered and kicked the door shut.

CHAPTER SEVEN

Like an ever-changing melody, snow swirled first one direction and then another outside the window of Mike's childhood bedroom, yet Kate's soul did not sing along. The cloud that descended on her after the hysterectomy was heavier than anything she'd previously experienced, heavier even than when she was alone and starving on the streets of Pittsburgh.

With difficulty, she rolled to her other side and pulled the covers over her shoulders. She knew she should be grateful to be alive, but it hurt to think she'd never have a dimpled blond replica of her handsome husband. Or a little girl to mother in all the ways she'd missed out on as a child.

She heard a knock and saw her aunt standing in the doorway. "Hi, Aunt Mary."

"Hello, Katy, darling. May I come in?"

"Of course. You can move my robe off that chair and lay it on the bed."

Mary scooted her walker to the chair, transferred the robe, and then side-stepped until she could sit. Prissy, her ever-present companion, snuggled into the chair with her.

Kate could tell her aunt was sucking on one of her Canada mints. Mary had often shared the pink wintergreen candies with Kate and her brother when they visited her house years ago. She still loved the smell.

"How's my girl today?"

"Better, I think." Kate shoved two pillows against the headboard before squirming upright to lean against them. "Not as sore today."

"You seem stuck in the doldrums, and that concerns me."

"I don't mean to upset you, Aunt Mary. It's just that..." She hesitated, not wanting to drag her aunt down in the dumps with her. "I'm having a hard time believing Mike and I will never be able to have children."

"I understand. Dean and I were sorry we couldn't have a family."

"Why didn't you, if you don't mind me asking?"

"War injury. Your uncle was shot in his, you know, privates, and couldn't make those little fishy things."

"You mean sperm?"

Mary's cheeks reddened. "Well, I s'pose that's what some people call them."

"I didn't know that was the reason you were childless."

"We didn't talk about it much. Just enjoyed each other and went on with life." She brightened. "You and Philip were our unofficial grandchildren. We wanted to take you in after your family was killed in that awful wreck, but the state wouldn't let us because of our advanced age, as they termed it, and my multiple sclerosis. I kept track of you the best I could and wrote you and sent you school clothes and presents for birthdays and holidays."

The flurry outside rattled the windowpane. Prissy whimpered. Mary patted her head and whispered, "It's okay."

"I remember every package," Kate said. "Sometimes the gifts you sent were the only ones I received. I loved your letters and phone calls and looked forward to hearing your sweet voice." She clasped her aunt's hand on the walker. "You're the reason I survived my childhood. I always knew you loved me, even if no one else did."

"Can I ask you something, Katy?"

"Anything."

"All those times you ran away, why didn't you come to us?"

"Oh, Aunt Mary." Kate squeezed her hand. "I knew the first place they'd look would be your house. They'd find me there and take me back to the latest creepy foster family I'd escaped from. When I got older and the authorities no longer considered me a runaway, they tried to find me for other reasons, bad reasons. I didn't want to embarrass you, or for some drug dealer to harm you."

"I could never be ashamed of you, dear." Mary smiled. "Thank you for considering my safety. Each time you disappeared, a policeman would show up on our porch asking if we'd seen you. That helped me know how to pray. I'd wait a couple weeks and then call social services to ask if you had a new address."

"When I was young," Kate said, "I cried buckets of tears wishing I could grow up in your house instead of all the places I lived. I guess God had a different idea."

Mary nodded. "He has plans for you, Katy Joy. Good plans."

"I'm trying to believe that." Kate sighed.

"God had a plan for Esther in the Bible, although it wasn't obvious at first."

Kate suppressed a smile. Apparently her aunt read the book of Esther every morning, or maybe random verses. Every day she talked about Queen Esther.

"Like you, she was an orphan girl, yet she became queen of all Persia. Isn't that amazing?"

"Yes, truly amazing."

"God used that little girl to save his people. He can use you in the same way."

Kate tilted her head. "You think so?"

Two fat snakes twisted and coiled below Amy's precarious perch on the bathroom counter, their rattles hissing like water splattered onto hot grease.

She screamed and grabbed the faucet for support. Three more snakes slithered across the tiles, heads shifting from side to side, forked tongues flicking in and out, in and out, tasting her scent, searching for her body heat.

Amy backed into the corner to crouch beside the wide mirror. "Help! Someone please help me!"

When no one responded, she ripped the hair blower from the wall mount, pushed the *on* button, and aimed it at the snakes.

A rattler struck at the appliance and missed.

She shrieked and dropped the blower. It bounced against the cabinet door, noisily spewing hot air. Clinging to the hand-towel ring, Amy sobbed so hard she could barely breathe. "Please! I'll do it." She'd never felt so vulnerable and alone in all her life, not even in prison.

The snake struck again. This time it found its plastic target.

The hair dryer ricocheted off the cabinet.

She jerked, slamming the mirror with her knee and breaking off the corner. Blood spurted down her leg. This couldn't be happening to her. She was losing her mind. Tearing at her hair, she rasped, "I give up, give up, give..."

The door clicked open.

Amy choked back a sob. Inch by inch, the opening widened. She clasped her arms about her bloody shins.

Damon stepped in, long tongs in his hand. He glanced at the hair blower swinging from the outlet. "Stupid broad." Reaching down with the tongs, he hoisted a thrashing, rattling, hissing snake into the air.

Her desperate squeak morphed into a guttural groan.

Damon bellowed, "Shut up, whore!" and shoved the reptile at her face.

Amy shrank away from the fangs. Clawing the wall behind her, she stared into the snake's unblinking eyes until the room grew dark.

When Amy regained consciousness, she was seated on Thomas's lap wrapped in a thick terrycloth robe that smelled of lavender.

"Baby, baby..." He held tight her against his hard chest. "You're gonna be okay, gonna be okay." His voice was so tender, she couldn't help but look up at him.

He smiled down at her. "You're awake, darling. I was afraid I'd lost you, Natasha."

She closed her eyes. This time, she remembered the nightmare he'd put her through. He'd tricked her, drugged her, stripped and bound her, and then encouraged men to pin her against a cold cement floor while others raped her, mocked her and kicked her. After that...the snakes. She couldn't stop the spasm of revulsion that jolted her body.

Thomas rocked her, humming a lullaby in her ear.

Amy blinked. She must be hallucinating. This couldn't be real.

He kissed the top of her head again and again.

She was too spent to resist.

"You did it, Natasha. I'm proud of you."

"Did what?" She nearly choked when she realized she'd answered to his name for her.

"You made it through one of the most difficult aspects of your induction into Executive Pride Escorts. Not everyone survives that important step. The next segment will be easier."

"Please," she begged. "Please, Thomas. No more."

He laid a finger on her lips. "You'll love what comes next. You get to meet the rest of my sweet family and learn how to ensure every customer is a return customer."

She could only gawk at him, horrified at the thought of what he might be insinuating.

He caressed her cheek. "That, my dear Natasha, is how to make me happy and keep me happy." He paused. "It's simple. Stay beautiful and healthy. Exceed your quota. Create return business." Lifting her chin, he looked into her eyes. "Do everything you can to please me, and I'll take you places you never imagined and pay you more money than you ever dreamed possible."

❦

Mike cut a bite of buffalo roast and was about to tell his mom how delicious the meat was when Mary clunked her cup onto the dining room table. "I don't like that man." Tea splashed over the cup rim.

"Oh, Aunt Mary, be careful." Using a napkin, Kate dabbed at the thin skin on the back of her aunt's hands. "Did you burn yourself?"

"That man drinks too much. Dean and I can smell it on him."

Laura jumped up. "I'll get a wet cloth."

Although he was concerned about Mary, Mike was glad to see a little life in his wife. She'd been almost catatonic since the surgery.

"What man?" Kate peered into her aunt's eyes.

"Oh, you know—that sneaky one."

Laura returned with the cloth and handed it to Kate, who placed it on Mary's hand.

"Somebody in Pittsburgh?" Mike asked.

Mary's forehead wrinkled. She frowned. "Somewhere."

"More corn, Aunt Mary?" Kate picked up a serving dish. "This came from the garden we grew last summer over by the barn."

Mary pointed at Laura. "She knows I don't like him."

"Yes, Mary, I know." Laura patted her arm.

Mary flipped the cloth off her hand and reached for her walker. "I'm going to join Dean in the bedroom." She hobbled away, her dog at her heels.

Kate slowly got to her feet. "Bed sounds good to me, too."

Mike stood. "Want me to walk you to our room?"

"No, thanks. I'm okay. Just tired."

He kissed her. "Kick Uncle Dean out if he tries to sleep on my side of the bed."

Kate rolled her eyes. "Funny, Mike. Funny."

Laura smiled. "You're doing better and better, Kate. Up longer each day. More color in your cheeks."

"Thanks. I feel better, even though my body is calling it quits tonight."

After she left, Mike sat back down at the table. He sliced another piece of roast and put it on his plate. "Great flavor, Mom. Nice and tender. Thanks."

"I have a feeling I could undercook or overcook bison, or serve it to you raw, and you'd still think it tasted good."

He chuckled. "You're probably right." He took a drink of water. "Question for you."

"Sure. What is it?"

"I talked with Marshall Thompson the other day." Mike set his glass on the table. "He told me Todd Hughes made cash offers to him, Leonard Gruber and Arnie Williams to buy their ranches."

Laura lowered her fork. "So?"

"So, the one thing they all have in common, besides owning land that's been in their families for generations, is owning property contiguous with the Hughes ranch."

She shrugged. "Maybe he wants to enlarge his ranch."

"His place is nearly seventy-five thousand acres, and he barely works it. Spends most of his time at Bogie's Bar. Why would he need more?"

"Maybe he likes to own property. He has a right to do that, you know."

Mike couldn't believe his mother was defending the man. "Marshall asked if Hughes made us an offer. I told him he bugged Dad for years, but he's only asked you a couple times about selling the ranch, as far as I know."

Laura stacked Mary and Kate's plates on top of her own. "Todd...Todd Hughes has not spoken to me recently about buying our ranch. I made it clear to him the last time he asked that the Whispering Pines will remain in the family." A slight flush to her face, she snatched silverware from the table and hurried to the kitchen.

He cut another bite of meat. Why did his mom act so uncomfortable? And why did she defend Hughes? She knew Dad never trusted the man. And she knew Mike suspected Todd was the one who gunned down their bison and masterminded the robbery.

He sat back, wondering if he should tell his mom and Kate about the potential brucellosis disaster looming on their horizon. They should know what was going on around the ranch. Yet, he hadn't seen any red deer, and his wife didn't need anything to further depress her. His mom's hands were full, what with taking care of Kate and Aunt Mary, plus managing the ranch office.

He got up to take scrap meat to Tramp before he let him in for the night. What was Hughes up to, anyway?

CHAPTER EIGHT

Laura filled the dishwasher, surprised by the quiver in her stomach and the tremble in her hands. Yes, Mary's outburst had unnerved her. But Mike's comments were what set her teeth on edge and convinced her she couldn't let Todd come to the house again.

She closed the dishwasher door, leaned against the counter and folded her arms. They'd had a lovely evening together. As he'd promised, Todd brought candles with him. Plus, he'd cooked a surprisingly delicious meal. Mary went to bed right after dinner, so they'd spent the rest of the evening by themselves.

Seated before the fireplace playing checkers and munching popcorn, the two of them visited like old friends while the fire crackled in the background. At one point, she asked about Tara and learned his daughter might get out of prison in a year, if she behaved herself.

That's when Todd placed his hand over hers and apologized again. "As far as I can figure, she got it in her head to marry your son. When Mike didn't offer an engagement ring, she decided your family's money should buy one for her, so she went and stole that cash from your office."

"I trust prison is helping her see things differently."

"I'd like to think so." He leaned back in his chair and stretched. "Let's talk about someone more interesting. How're you doing since Dan passed away? Running a ranch is a big responsibility for a single woman."

"Don't forget I have Mike and Kate and the rest of the staff. They're all smart, hardworking individuals."

"Yet the full responsibility rests on your shoulders, right?"

"No. The three of us are in this together."

"I assumed Dan left the place to you."

"He did, and then I made Mike and Kate co-owners of the Whispering Pines."

At that, Todd arched an eyebrow but made no response.

Laura squeezed out the dishcloth and wiped crumbs from the counter into the sink. Surely he'd given up on buying their ranch. Now that he knew the WP was owned by all three of them, maybe he'd think twice before making another offer, even if the other families decided to sell to him.

Mike walked in with serving dishes. He spooned leftover peaches into the Mason jar, screwed on the lid, and opened the refrigerator. "What's with the socks, Mom?"

"Socks?" She peeked inside. "I think those belong to Mary."

He waggled an eyebrow. "No wonder supper tasted so good."

She laughed. "I found a wad of tissues crammed between the couch cushions yesterday."

Mike reached into the frig to retrieve the socks. "We discovered all kinds of interesting things in nooks and crannies when we moved her out of her house." He handed the socks to Laura. "Like napkins inside the toaster."

"That could be dangerous."

"Yeah. The neighbors were glad we stepped in when we did." He aimed his chin at the stove. "Be sure to check the oven before you turn it on. Might find Prissy in there."

"Mike..."

"You never know, Mom. Aunt Mary is full of surprises." He closed the fridge. "Speaking of neighbors, if Hughes ever..."

"He won't. And if he does, my answer will be the same."

"Will you let me know if he calls or stops by? I'd like to add my two bits, make sure he gets the message."

Laura nodded but ducked her head. If Todd mentioned buying their ranch, she might tell her son about his offer. No way would she report his other phone calls and visits.

Mike hugged her goodnight and left the room.

She released the breath she'd been holding. Mike wouldn't understand how much she enjoyed Todd's company and attention. Flowers had been delivered to the lobby last week with a card that read, "From a grateful guest." She was sure they were from him and pleased he'd been discreet.

This morning, she'd found a box of chocolate-covered almonds on the front seat of her SUV. No note, just a hint of familiar after-shave. Todd was the only one she'd told, other than Dan, how much she loved chocolate-covered nuts, especially almonds. Such a thoughtful gesture.

She added the serving dishes to the dishwasher, along with detergent, and pushed the start button. Maybe she should tell Mike and Kate about Todd. But then she pictured the steam that would surely spurt from her son's ears when he learned she'd let their neighbor into her life. She shook her head. Not a good idea.

Muffled taps against the kitchen window caught her attention. Laura peered through the glass at the aspen trees illuminated by their yard light. Snowing again. It was going to be a long winter.

She draped the dishcloth over the sink divider. The next time Kate and Mike left the ranch, she'd find someone to stay with Mary so she and Todd could have a couple hours to themselves. It would be nice to escape memories and responsibilities for a few minutes. But who could she ask?

Running through a mental list of possible sitters for Mary, her brain stuttered when she thought of Dymple Forbes. Dymple was a good friend and a dear soul. However, her run-ins with Tara Hughes were well-known throughout the valley. Of all the people who might disapprove of a romantic relationship with

Tara's maverick father, Dymple would be at the top of the list, right after Mike. Besides that, she was out of town.

Mike crawled into bed. Moonlight filtered through the window and across the covers, and he could see that Kate was awake. He kissed her. "It's snowing again."

She groaned. "Does it ever stop?"

"Spring is on the way, I promise." He snuggled close. "You seem deep in thought. Are you feeling okay?"

"Just thinking about Aunt Mary and all the changes she's experienced lately." She stroked his cheek. "How about you?"

He thought for a moment. "I guess you could say I'm sad."

"Sad?" She cradled his jaw. "Why?"

"I'm sad you've been so unhappy since the surgery." He wrapped a strand of her dark hair around his finger. "I think your body is getting better, but I'm not so sure about your heart."

She lowered her eyelids. "I'm sorry. I'll try to be cheerier."

"You shouldn't have to try to be happy."

Kate took his hand. "You and God have been so good to me. I have a lot to be thankful for. It's wrong for me to be upset, and sometimes angry, I admit, that we can't have children."

"That's normal. I'm disappointed, too, but I'll always love you, whether we have kids or not."

"And I'll love you forever." She hugged him. "Maybe I'll get over this depression, or whatever it is, when the weather warms up and I can get out more."

"I hope so. If not, it might be a good idea to see a counselor." Mike could feel her body stiffen.

"A counselor can't change my anatomy."

"Of course not." He rubbed her arm. "However, he or she could help you deal with loss and accept the idea of adoption."

She pulled away. "I'm not ready for adoption, Mike. To be honest, I don't know if I'll ever be ready."

"Okay. I'll drop it." He tugged Kate back into his arms and kissed her neck. She smelled good, like always. "Would it help you to get together with Dymple when she comes home?"

"That would be fun. She called from Colorado and tried to cheer me up over the phone, which was nice. Better than the swift kick she'll give me in person."

"Sounds like Dymple." Mike chuckled. "She tells it like it is."

"When I lived with her before we were married, she told me about some of the hard times she's experienced. I have a lot to learn from her." Kate kissed him and moved to her side of the bed.

He adjusted his pillow. "Have you talked with Amy lately?" Kate's best friend was a lively, upbeat person. Maybe she could encourage his wife.

Kate's eyes widened and her head jerked up. "Oh, no."

"What?"

She pushed back to sit against the headboard. "Amy flew to Dallas for a job interview while we were in Nebraska. She was supposed to call me when she got home, but I was in the hospital." Her brow wrinkled. "That was more than two weeks ago and I had my cell phone. Why haven't I heard from her?"

"Maybe they hired her at the interview, and she's been busy ever since."

"She'd make time to call. Knowing Amy, she'd be so excited she couldn't resist calling."

"Give her a buzz in the morning."

"If it wasn't two hours later in Pittsburgh, I'd call right now."

Kate watched Mary spoon a raisin from her cereal and drop it onto a napkin next to a half-dozen other raisins. As anxious as she was to talk with Amy, she didn't want her aunt to eat breakfast alone. She also didn't want to awaken her friend too early on a Saturday. Amy loved to sleep in on her day off.

"Why do you ask Laura to buy Raisin Bran cereal if you're going to remove all the raisins, Aunt Mary?" Kate asked the same question every morning.

And every morning, her aunt offered a different explanation. Today was no exception. "Too sweet."

"Then you should get bran cereal without the raisins."

"No flavor."

"Oh." Kate didn't know what to say. Or what to do with the raisins, other than make another pie. At least Aunt Mary removed the raisins with a spoon, not her fingers, before she added milk.

After breakfast, Kate placed their bowls in the dishwasher and added the raisins to the others she'd collected. Then she walked laps through the house, office and lobby, Prissy at her side. She'd promised the doctor she would walk at least fifteen minutes three times a day.

As she circled the interior of the log building, she pondered Amy's uncharacteristic lack of communication. Could be she didn't get the job and was too embarrassed and disappointed to tell anyone. Or maybe the company hadn't made a final decision as to who to hire. Or... Kate halted in the middle of the lobby.

Prissy gave her a puzzled look and then trotted to a potted plant in the corner to sniff the soil.

Kate rubbed her forehead. What if Amy had been caught violating parole and sent back to prison? She began walking again. *Please, God, help me find my friend.*

Just as disturbing as the questions about Amy were questions about herself. How could she forget her best friend? She could blame the drugs, yet she'd been weaning herself off the painkillers. In fact, today she planned to only use ibuprofen as needed. Was she so enmeshed in self-pity she couldn't think of anyone other than herself?

When they completed the tenth lap, she bent down to pet the little Cockapoo. "We did it, Prissy. Ten laps." Prissy wagged her stub of a tail, and Kate could have sworn the dog was as pleased as she was with their progress.

She dropped the dog off at Mary's room and pulled a quilt from the linen closet. Settling into an easy chair, she arranged the blanket over her legs and prepared for a long Saturday talk with her best friend. But when she dialed Amy's cell phone, the call went immediately to voice mail.

She dialed her home number. It rang and rang. Finally, Kate hung up. She'd try again later. Amy was probably running errands.

Mike's Bible sat next to her on the end table. She opened it to Matthew, chapter ten, where she'd been reading in her own Bible the day before. Maybe she'd find something from Scripture to encourage Amy. She started at verse eleven, learning more about Jesus' instructions to his disciples than she'd known before. Verse sixteen caught her attention and she reread it.

I am sending you out like sheep among wolves. Therefore, be as shrewd as snakes and as innocent as doves. But be on your guard against men...

The words seemed to shimmer on the page, while the surrounding text blurred like an out-of-focus picture. Kate looked at the snow-covered pine trees outside the living room window and then back at Mike's Bible. Though she blinked and smoothed the thin paper with her palm, the letters continued to flicker and call to her.

But she wasn't going anywhere. She was recuperating from surgery and not yet allowed to drive. Besides, the roads to the ranch were closed, blocked by snowdrifts. As to being on guard against men, after a year of marriage to a sweet, kind, considerate man and working with the great guys on the ranch crew, she'd begun to drop her wariness around males, even crotchety old Cyrus.

Shrewd as snakes, innocent as doves. What could that possibly mean? She'd seen several rattlesnakes in Wyoming. Once, when she and Mike and Cyrus were riding fence on horseback, they'd surprised a rattler sunning on a rock. In an instant, the snake coiled, ready to strike, the rattle on the end of its tail buzzing a warning. The horses didn't like the reptile any more than she did and shied away from it, giving their riders several minutes of excitement. Cyrus swore at the snake and called it a low-down sidewinder.

I don't get it, God. You'll have to show me. She picked up the phone and dialed both of Amy's numbers again. Still no answer. If only she'd contacted her earlier. Kate released a long sigh. No matter who called whom, it was strange her best friend hadn't called to tell her all about the interview, like she promised to do.

This time, Kate left a message on the cell phone. If she didn't get a hold of Amy by Monday, she'd call her dad, even though he was a jerk. Maybe he'd know his daughter's whereabouts. If not, she'd have to call the police. Not that she wanted to talk to a cop, but she'd do what was needed to find her friend.

Propped against the headboard later that afternoon, Kate used the bedroom phone to call Amy's cell phone. No response. She dialed the home number. What if she was sick? Or maybe her plane crashed.

"Hello." The voice was young and masculine. Had she dialed the wrong number? "Hi. Is Amy Iverson there?"

"No…"

"Is this a wrong number?"

"No, yes…I mean, this is her number, but I don't know where she is." His voice cracked, and she pictured a boy in his early teens. He cleared his throat. "Do you know her?"

"I'm her best friend. I've been trying to get ahold of her. Who are you?"

"I'm Kevin. I live next door with my mom and dad. Amy asked me to take care of her animals while she went to Dallas for a job interview. She was only supposed to be gone one night, but it's been, like, two weeks."

Kate's pulse began to thump in her neck.

"My mom called her dad and her sister, 'cause Amy wrote their numbers by the phone. They haven't heard from her either. Her dad said she's probably sitting in the Dallas County jail. I didn't think that was very nice."

Kate clenched her fist. Sounded like something Amy's dad would say. "You and I both know she wouldn't leave her animals this long without a good reason. Have you or your parents called the Dallas police?"

"At first, my dad figured she was training for her new job." Kevin's voice cracked again. "Now he says he's going to report her missing to the Dallas police *and* the Pittsburgh police if she doesn't call or come home this weekend."

"Tell your parents I'll call both departments immediately and let you know what I learn. Amy is a responsible person, especially when it comes to her animals. She would have told you if she needed to stay in Dallas."

The receptionist for Pittsburgh's Missing Persons Unit said she'd pass the word and hung up before Kate could ask about the process. She dropped the phone on the bed. How could the woman be so callous about someone who'd vanished?

With a sigh, she picked up the phone again. She shouldn't be surprised. After all, she'd met many individuals on the streets who chose anonymity. Amy was just one more name on a long list of lost people in Pittsburgh.

The Dallas operator, however, connected her with Detective Barker in their Special Investigations Unit. He was all business from the get-go. "Name, please."

Her mouth went dry. She didn't have a reason to fear the man and he was going to help her find Amy. Even so, years of running from the law had created a dread that hadn't quite yet dissolved. She swallowed. "Kate Duncan."

"Address?"

Her life was an open book now. Gripping the phone with one hand and her pen with the other, Kate fought to steady her voice as she gave him the ranch's address.

"Phone number where you can be reached?"

Again, she reminded herself she had nothing to hide. She provided her cell number and then offered the house and ranch numbers.

"What's your relationship with Ms. Iverson?"

Uh-oh. Here came her past to haunt her again. She answered truthfully, without mentioning that they'd met in prison. "Best friends."

"How's that? You live in Wyoming. She's from Pennsylvania." Kate pictured an unsmiling drill-sergeant type seated behind a bare metal desk, his posture perfectly aligned with his straight-backed chair. "We knew each other in Pittsburgh, where I lived before I married a Wyoming rancher."

"What makes you think she's missing, that she's not on vacation or visiting relatives?"

"Amy had an appointment for a job interview in Dallas over two weeks ago." Kate pushed herself higher on the pillows. "She said she'd call to tell me the results. I haven't heard from her, so I called her cell phone and house phone several times today. This afternoon, the neighbor boy who's caring for her animals answered her home phone. He and his parents are worried. She was only supposed to be gone two days."

"You have a phone number for the neighbors?"

She gave him Kevin's name and number.

"Why did you wait so long to check on your best friend?"

Kate squelched the exasperation welling within her. When would the detective quit with the questions and start looking for Amy? "I underwent emergency surgery the weekend she was interviewing and have been kind of out of it ever since." She wouldn't bore him with the details of her depression. "Last night, I remembered she was supposed to call me as soon as she got home."

"According to the Pittsburgh authorities, Miss Iverson has not yet returned. We have evidence she murdered a man here in Dallas and then disappeared."

Kate gasped. "No, that can't be! She was so excited—"

He cut her off, but she didn't mind. She could barely breathe, let alone talk.

"Your friend violated her parole requirements by flying from Pittsburgh to Dallas two weeks ago," the detective said. "Early the following morning, Saturday, the body of a dead man with multiple stab wounds was discovered lying by the side of the road. At our request, OnStar disabled his Cadillac Escalade. The SUV was then abandoned by the driver. When we inspected the vehicle, Miss Iverson's handbag was found on the passenger seat."

"That can't be right. Even if she violated parole..." Kate's voice rose. "Amy is not a murderer."

"Do you know the name of the company where she supposedly interviewed?"

"Executive Pride. She said they were paying for her flights and her hotel."

"Interesting."

She could hear him flipping pages.

"Here it is." The detective cleared his throat. "A one-way ticket from Pittsburgh to Dallas was purchased with Miss Iverson's credit card, but not a return ticket."

She frowned. The company was supposed to pay for her flights.

"What kind of job was this?"

"Personal assistant. According to their website, they're an employment agency, plus they help set up events and create commercials and promotional films for businesses."

"What's the URL?"

"I'm not at a computer. It's something like Executive Pride Services dot org or maybe Executive Pride Employment."

He paused. "Anything else you can add that might help this investigation?"

"This is a mistake. Amy is not a murderer."

"You want to know how many times I've heard that line?"

Kate didn't respond. Like most of the other women she'd been incarcerated with, she'd tried hard to convince anyone who'd listen of her own innocence. But Amy didn't kill anyone. She was sure of that. So why did she disappear? And where in the world did she go?

CHAPTER NINE

Kate found very little online information about Executive Pride outside of the company's website. Two businesses had provided endorsements for Executive's hostess service, and the company seemed to be in good standing with the Better Business Bureau. By all appearances, the place was legitimate. Yet, she couldn't get past the fact they'd used Amy's bank account to purchase her airline ticket to Dallas without providing a return ticket.

She typed *Dallas private investigators* into the search box. Pages of listings came up. She didn't know where to begin, and she was getting tired. *Lead me, God*, she prayed. *I'm clueless. And it's the weekend. They might not even answer their phones.*

To her surprise, she was able to talk with several PIs. Eventually, she selected Walt Harnish, partly because he indicated he could begin the investigation immediately and partly because he appeared to be on good terms with Detective Barker.

Walt called back the following afternoon. "Somethin' mighty fishy about this case, Miz Duncan."

She chewed at her lip while the Texan apparently gathered his thoughts. When she realized she was picturing a rangy guy with a toothpick hanging out the corner of his mouth, she decided she'd read too many novels set in Texas.

"The Escalade owner's prints, his wife's prints, and those of his two dogs were all over the SUV. Yet your friend's prints were found *only* on the purse. She could have used gloves. However, going to the effort to avoid leaving fingerprints doesn't fit with abandoning a purse with her ID inside and her prints on the outside. She'd have to be a couple sandwiches shy of a picnic to do that."

Kate squeezed her eyes shut, not wanting to believe what she was hearing. "Amy's not stupid. She was there for a job interview. She wouldn't mess up a promising future, unless..."

"Unless what?"

She opened her eyes. "I don't know. Maybe the guy attacked her. Maybe it was self-defense. Do you know his history?"

"Retired banker. Active in his homeowners' association. Volunteer. He not only served the community through several charitable organizations, he gave generous donations to each of them. In addition, he was married to the same woman for fifty-two years. Stranger things have happened. Even so, he appears clean as a whistle."

She stared out the living room window. Sunshine broke through the clouds, flashing sparkles across the snow that coated and softened the landscape. "Have you learned anything else about Amy?"

"You might find this interesting." He burped. "S'cuse me, ma'am. I checked all the cab companies to find out who was working when her plane arrived shortly before noon. Showed each driver that picture you emailed to me. One guy thinks he saw someone who looked like your friend and a tall well-dressed man get into a black limousine. Said they were a striking couple, very attractive people who acted like they'd just met. He thought the woman was wearing green, but he wasn't sure."

Kate's heart somersaulted. "That's perfect."

"It wasn't a positive ID."

"It fits with Amy's schedule and the fact someone was supposed to meet her at the airport." She paused. "Did he know where they went from there?"

"Well, just so happens he picked up a couple passengers and ended up following the limo all the way downtown. He dropped his people off in front of some office building and never saw the limo again. Maybe your friend and her escort ate lunch in the area. No lack of restaurants around there."

She switched the phone to the other ear. "Did you check out Executive Pride?" Maybe Walt found something she'd missed in her Internet search. "When I called them, the receptionist said Amy never showed for her appointment."

"Executive checks out okay. It's an employment agency, like your friend thought it was, but..."

"But what?"

He belched again. "Sorry, Miz Duncan. Breakfast burrito backfiring." After a moment, he added, "The taco stand on the corner sells dang tasty chorizo burritos that come back to haunt a fellow."

"Glad you, uh, enjoy them."

"I went to Executive Pride pretending to check out job options and saw ceiling cameras in every corner. Overkill, if you ask me. And a guy who looked more like a bouncer than an employment counselor walked through every few minutes and asked if we had questions. I got the feeling he was keeping an eye on me and the woman at the next computer. My gut says they're hiding something. Whether it's your friend or not, I can't say."

Kate released a long breath. "We've got to find her."

"Maybe she doesn't want to be found."

"Amy was hoping Executive Pride would hire her to work in Pittsburgh, so her sister could move in with her and go to school there."

Kate watched a clump of snow slide off a tree branch and thought of her tearful conversation with Elaina last night. They'd both cried, and she'd promised to do everything she could to find the girl's big sister.

He tapped the phone with what sounded like a pencil. "How far do you want me to run with this, Miz Duncan? I need to get a feel for how much time and money you want to put into the investigation."

"What would you do if this was your wife or daughter?"

"Good question. I'd check every restaurant in downtown Dallas, from cafés to high-class joints. If that search came up dry, I'd flash your friend's picture around stores and talk to cabbies and sidewalk vendors and anyone else who hangs out on the streets. I'd also do some research to see if there's a possible connection with your friend's disappearance and other women who've gone missing and see what else I can learn about that Executive Pride bunch. I can't quite get a handle on it, but something about that place put a bur under my saddle."

"That's what I want. Do everything you can think of."

"That'll take time, and the meter'll be ticking."

"Walt, find my friend. Whatever it takes, find my friend."

The PI called again the next morning. "I think we have some-thing, Miz Duncan. Not much, but it's a start. Sometimes, if I can't get what I need by going through the front door, I cruise the alleys and the hallways. Try to catch the help out takin' a smoke. They're usually willing to talk, sometimes for a few greenbacks, especially if they're puffin' weed."

He paused. "By the way, this contact cost me—and you, ulti-mately—five-hundred big ones."

"I understand." She pushed the button to lower the phone's volume. Walt's loud twang was making the speaker vibrate.

"The guy was a busboy, young and jumpy as a cat in a roomful of rocking chairs. He insisted we take the stairs, separately, down to the bottom floor and find a spot behind some big bushes to talk. He said his restaurant is a high-class establishment that's hush-hush about its ritzy clientele. However, he was perturbed enough about something that happened to talk to me, for a price, of course."

Kate pressed the phone against her ear.

"This guy said a woman who looked like your friend entered the restaurant with a tall man who had dark hair and medium skin. They left a suitcase and a purse and jackets with the coat clerk before ordering some of the most expensive food on the menu. The man didn't eat much. Just watched the woman, who seemed to appreciate the attention as well as the food."

"That sounds like Amy. Did he say she was wearing a copper-colored blouse?"

"He said he's colorblind and wasn't sure what color her clothes were. Anyway, all of a sudden, she slumps onto the table and almost falls off her chair. My contact, who's bussing the table next to them, steps over to help. Before he can, the other guy picks her up and half carries, half drags her to the elevator. 'I called an ambulance,' he says. 'They're on the way.'

"He pushes the elevator button, the door opens, and two medics are standing there with a gurney, like they're waiting for him. They grab the girl and flip her onto the gurney, he grabs their things from the coatroom, and they all disappear. Just that fast. My contact said it gave him a spooky feeling."

Walt grunted. "Bizarre story, huh?"

"That's awful." Kate felt like throwing up. "Did you tell Detective Barker?"

"Not yet. We don't know if your friend was the person the cabbie saw or the person the busboy told me about."

"But..."

"I can tell you that none of the local hospitals list an Amy Iverson as being admitted to the emergency room on that day and none of the ambulance companies reported a client with that name or a call to that particular restaurant."

"That's weird." Kate gazed at the ceiling. *Oh, Amy, where are you?*

"Yeah. Like I said, bizarre."

"So why not call Detective Barker? He could ask to see the restaurant's records. If the guy used a credit card, they'd have his name."

"Barker is after a murder suspect, slash car thief, slash ex-con. You're trying to find your best friend. Totally different viewpoints and approaches. I've been this route before. He's not interested in your victim theory."

"So what's next?"

"I'm fixin' to find someone who saw three men pushing a stretcher down the street, although I have a feeling this was well planned and they all disappeared as fast as they appeared."

Kate gripped the phone. What if the police found Amy before Walt did? She wouldn't stand a chance against a murder charge with her record and the parole violation. "I'm going to Dallas as soon as my doctor gives me permission to travel."

She needed to shake off her funk and get well fast. Walt might be a bit unrefined, yet he seemed to know his stuff. Between the two of them, and prayer, they'd find Amy and prove her innocence.

Mike sat on the side of the bed. "I like Amy—and I hate to think something bad happened to her." He pulled off a boot. "However, I don't see how after nearly bleeding to death and having major surgery you can go to an unfamiliar city by yourself to help her."

Kate closed the atlas with the map of Texas she'd been studying and dropped it on the nightstand. "First off, the doctor says I'm healing right on schedule. I should be able to travel by the first of the year. Secondly, I don't plan to travel alone."

"Do I dare ask *whom* you expect to accompany you?" He leaned over to nibble at her ear, pleased that the notion of rescuing her best friend reignited the fire in his wife's eyes. Though he didn't want her to go to Dallas, he also didn't want to lose her again to depression.

She wrapped her arms around his neck and kissed him. And then kissed him again.

He groaned. "That's not fair. You know I can't resist your kisses. What good can either of us do?"

"If nothing else, we can be there for her."

"Dallas is a huge city, Kate." He straightened. "Amy won't know we're there."

"We can make it a tax deductible trip."

Mike slipped a sock off his foot. "How's that?"

"We could attend the Fort Worth Stock Show instead of the Denver show this year. Clint could cover Denver, and you and I could take business cards and brochures to Dallas and—"

Mike raised his hand. "You had me at 'Fort Worth Stock Show.' I've always wanted to attend that one."

Kate grinned. "We'd promote the guest ranch as well as the bison and bison products. You could also arrange meetings with potential buyers, maybe even host a bison steak dinner."

He tugged at the other boot. "I should have known our marketing manager would be way ahead of me on this one."

"Haven't you talked with a couple Texas ranchers about starting herds? You could meet them in person."

"How would that help Amy?"

"I was thinking of dropping by Executive Pride's office. I'll pretend to job hunt. Say I'm with my husband, a buffalo rancher from Colorado who's attending the stock show and considering expansion into Texas. I'll tell them I do marketing for the ranch and am interested in enlarging my horizons, whether we move to Texas or not. Try to give the impression we're an upwardly mobile couple."

A wind gust rattled branches against their bedroom window. Mike set his boots in the closet, clicked off the lamp and crawled under the covers. "Why Colorado?"

Kate laid her head on his chest. "To protect us and Amy, in case they've seen Wyoming numbers on her cell phone."

"What if they check on us? With the Internet, it would be easy to discover we're imposters."

"We could pick up a couple prepaid phones with Colorado numbers and rent a post office box in Slater. That's not far away. Besides, doesn't your property run into Colorado?"

"*Our* property crosses the Wyoming-Colorado border here and there."

"There you go. We own the Little Snake River Bison Ranch near Slater, Colorado. I'll make a few fake cards on the computer, create a website that says *closed for updating*, and we'll be ready to roll."

"Whoa, whoa, *whoa*." He pulled her close and buried his face in her hair. "I can tell you've put a lot of thought into this, sweetheart. But I don't like the idea of you endangering yourself trying to find Amy. Who knows what kind of viper pit you could stumble into." He paused. "Even if you somehow find her, you'll have to tell the police, who'll toss her in jail. What's the point?"

"You think she did it, don't you?" Kate pulled from his grasp and moved to her side of the bed. "You think she murdered that man."

"It's hard to imagine her doing something like that. Still, she was in prison for a reason."

"So was I. In fact, I did a lot worse things than Amy ever did." Kate pushed up on her elbows. "Yet you trust me, right?"

"I don't know Amy as well as I know you."

"I know her, and I know her spirit. She wouldn't kill someone except possibly in self-defense. Please believe she's innocent, Mike. Something terrible has happened to her."

For a moment, he was silent. "Okay, I'll work on it. In the meantime, we need to take this slow and easy and pray about it."

"Can I at least make arrangements to pay her rent and utilities while she's missing plus pay Kevin to take care of her animals?"

"Of course. That's the least we can do."

Christmas morning, Mike scanned the labels on the packages beneath the blue spruce he and Clint had cut two weeks earlier. They'd both gotten chilled to the bone as they trudged through knee-deep snow searching for the perfect tree, but the women loved it. Kate especially liked the fresh evergreen scent, which made him happy. Her lonely childhood Christmases had been filled with artificial trees as well as artificial families.

He found a package for Mary and handed it to her. "Your turn, Aunt Mary."

"For me? Goodness sakes, this is fun." Her eyes twinkled beneath her halo of white hair. Though they'd seated her near the fireplace, she wore a sweater over her robe and two pairs of socks inside her slippers.

Mike grinned. Sharing Christmas with Kate's aunt was as much fun as sharing it with a child. He took a sugar cookie from the tray on the coffee table and sat beside Kate on the couch.

She leaned forward. "What do you think it is, Aunt Mary?"

"Maybe it's a calendar." Mary toyed with the curled ribbon. "Dean always gets me a calendar."

Laura smiled. "Could be that's just what it is."

Kate knelt beside her aunt to help her remove the ribbon and the wrapping. Then she held the box upside down so Mary could slide out the contents.

Mary squinted at the gift, a framed photograph.

Kate smiled. "Recognize those two?"

Her eyes softened. "It's Dean, my dear husband." She touched the glass. "He's so handsome."

"And you're so beautiful, Aunt Mary. Like Uncle Dean always said, you were the prettiest lady in Pittsburgh." Kate set the wedding picture on the end table.

"Where is Dean?" Mary scanned the room. "He should be here by now."

"Slick roads probably slowed him down." Mike was amazed at how easily they'd all fallen into fabricating stories. "He'll be here soon." None of them wanted to ruin their Christmas festivities by telling her Dean was dead. They'd made that mistake more than once and upset Mary enough she always headed straight for bed.

Kate rummaged under the tree. "I'll pick the next gift." She selected a book-size package and handed it to Mike.

"Aha. I know what this is." He tore at the wrapping.

Kate smirked. "You sound awfully sure of yourself."

He rolled the paper into a ball and tossed it into the fireplace before checking out the box. Huh. Books didn't usually come in boxes, boxes that said... He glanced at Kate. "Is this what I think it is? A book yet not a book?"

She kissed his cheek. "Not just one book, sweetheart. Thousands of books."

"I read the book of Esther this morning," Mary said.

Mike looked up. "Wow, that's great, Aunt Mary. Esther was a terrific lady."

"She was a girl, a young girl, when she became queen."

Laura nodded her agreement. "She must have been very special girl." She looked at Mike. "What is it?"

He opened the box and lifted out the device. "An eReader."

"Oh, how nice," Laura said. "I've heard they're really handy, especially for traveling."

Mike wrapped an arm around Kate. "Thank you." He kissed her forehead. "I'll get a lot of mileage out of this. Can't wait to try it."

Mary folded her hands. "Queen of all Persia, no less."

He grinned. "No kidding?"

Kate tapped the eReader. "Now you can read every word ever written about bison since Zane Grey, including *The Thundering Herd*. I downloaded it for you, even though you've probably read it a hundred times."

Mike grinned. "It's been a couple years. Time to read it again."

"I know exactly how you feel." Mary brushed a cookie crumb off her sweater. "No matter how many times I read the book of Esther, I always want to read it one more time."

Amy leaned her forehead against the cool windowpane. Matchbox-size cars rolled from intersection to intersection on the streets far below. The only clues that it was the Christmas season were the colored lights on top of the other buildings and the reindeer headbands and red teddy negligees Thomas made them wear to amuse their guests. Oh, and the one piece of peppermint candy she'd been allowed to eat.

The empty office building across the street made her think this was the actual holiday. Despite the miniature lights that flickered in some of the windows and the flag that fluttered atop the building, she didn't see anyone seated in front of computers or walking about. She looked downward. Traffic had never before been this sparse.

She traced a circle on the window with her finger. Were her brother and sister having a good time today? She hoped so. Angel Tree volunteers had provided presents for them while she was imprisoned. This year, she'd been excited to shop for them herself and to deliver the gifts in person. Now, they'd never get them. The landlord probably donated her stuff to the Salvation Army store down the street and dropped her pets off at the animal shelter.

Her stomach growled and she sipped water from a plastic cup on the windowsill. When the Duncans invited her to join them for Christmas, she'd told them she wanted to be with her siblings. Kate jokingly tried to bribe her by promising to make fruit salad again. Amy's mouth watered at the thought. These days, her diet rarely included fruit or more than an ounce or two of meat and *never* bread or dessert.

The flag flapped and fell, flapped and fell against the pole. Were Kate and Mike opening gifts right now with Laura and Aunt Mary? Was Clint with Cyrus and Susan? Or did the couple break up? If so, maybe someday... She shook her head. She needed to forget the kindhearted cowboy.

The negligee strap slipped off her bony shoulder. How long since she'd breathed fresh air or felt a breeze ruffle her hair like it ruffled the flag? She touched the cool glass pane again. An airplane flew across the sky and faded into the horizon. How she ached to be on it, flying to freedom. She'd only been out of prison a few months and was just beginning to adjust to life on the outside, when Thomas...

With effort, she turned from the window. Like he'd told her, she couldn't think about her former life. She was lucky to have a roof over her head and food in her stomach, as much as Thomas allowed, anyway. She slid the strap back onto her shoulder. No more dwelling in the past. No more longing for her old life when she had a good-paying job here. The memories were too painful.

A snake slithered across the reptile cage on the other side of the room. She cringed. Instead of removing the rattlesnakes from her quarters, one of Thomas's men had rolled in the terrarium and dropped the creepy things inside.

When she told Thomas she couldn't sleep with snakes in the room, his upper lip had curled. "I know you miss your pets, darling, so I decided to share mine with you. They'll help you remember the lessons you learned." Then he reached inside to stroke their scales.

Amy shuddered. Thank God Thomas didn't make her feed the snakes. However, he'd ordered her to open the drapes on the two big windows every morning when she returned from work, so his pets could get plenty of sunshine. Apparently, it didn't matter to him that she needed to sleep during the daytime.

She twisted to see the backs of her legs. Her birds were barely visible, thanks to laser and dermabrasion treatments. Like the tattoos, the people and animals she once loved would soon fade into the past.

CHAPTER TEN

When Kate heard Mike stomping snow off his boots on the deck, she opened the door. The wave of frigid air that followed him inside made her shiver. "It's really cold out there."

"Pushing twenty below." He closed the door before kissing her. "Clint and I decided to call it quits when the wind came up. We were spending more time inside the barn warming up than outside fixing the gate."

"The tea kettle is simmering. I'll make us some hot chocolate." She took his coat and hung it on the antlers. "Have a seat on the sofa after you take off your boots. I'll sit with you, and you can fill me in on your day."

Kate intended to let Mike talk first, but when she handed him the steaming mug, she blurted, "We need to talk."

He raised an eyebrow. "What about?"

"About going to Dallas. I talked to Walt this morning. He's hitting brick walls every direction he turns."

"What makes you think we can find Amy when a professional investigator can't?" Mike sipped the chocolate. "We don't know anything about PI work, and we don't know anything about Dallas. What are we going to do? Grab a taxi at the airport and tell the driver God will show him or her where to go?"

Kate laid her hand on Mike's knee. "Like I said earlier, I can visit Executive Pride's office and pretend to look for work. I don't know what I'll learn. Maybe nothing. But whether or not it's a good lead, the employment agency is the only lead we have. I can't shake the feeling that Amy's disappearance is directly related to that place. She's been kidnapped, or..."

She stopped, not wanting to take the thought any further. "If I can get inside Executive, I'll get a feel for whether or not the place is on the up and up. I might even run into Amy while I'm there."

Mike's brow lowered. "If these Executive people did something to Amy, and that's a big *if,* then snooping around their office could be dangerous for you."

"I know that."

He pursed his lips. "How about this? As our marketing director, you could do the wining and dining, and I could go to the employment agency."

"Nice try, sweetheart." She leaned her forehead against his. "I appreciate your desire to protect me. However, I believe God wants me to do this, alone. He'll take care of me."

Three days later, Kate stood in the lobby of a Dallas skyscraper searching for "Executive Pride Services" on the directory. When she found the employment agency, she pushed the elevator button for a ride to the top and then sent Mike a text. *Waiting for elevator. Will keep you posted.*

She smoothed her hair and checked her fingernails. Mike had wanted to come with her, yet she knew she would be more effective by herself. Besides, he had a meeting with a potential Texas distributor for the bison products he and Marshall sold. Straightening her jacket, she recalled her husband's reaction when she modeled the red suit and black heels for him. His loud whistle had startled nearby clerks in the downtown Dallas department store.

"Shh," she'd whispered. "You're not on the ranch."

"And you obviously aren't either. Haven't seen you so dressed up since our anniversary dinner."

"You think this is okay to wear?"

"Nope."

She checked the mirror. "What's wrong with it?"

"You're dangerous in that outfit."

"Dangerous?"

"Men will crash cars and trample over each other just to get a second glimpse of you."

"Oh, Mike. Stop it." She didn't tell him how relieved she was that the abdominal swelling she'd experienced following the surgery had abated enough she could fit into the straight skirt.

She studied her reflection in the window. Was she overdressed for posing as someone who was just stopping by the employment agency. It wasn't like she had an appointment for a job interview.

The elevator dinged.

Kate swiveled.

The doors opened, and a half dozen people streamed out, staring straight ahead.

She stepped inside, pushed the button for the fiftieth floor, and sneezed at the aftershave smell that lingered in the tiny enclosure.

"Gesundheit!" A tall well-dressed man hurried into the elevator. He looked her over and then pushed the button for the fifty-first floor, revealing a snake tattoo on the back of his hand.

Kate shivered and focused on the indicator lights. *Is he the one who picked Amy up from the airport, God? He gives me the creeps.* She reeled in her imagination. Just because she'd seen plenty of his kind and he fit the vague description Walt's contacts gave didn't mean he was the guy. Even so, riding alone with him for fifty floors made her claustrophobic. She could feel his eyes undressing her, floor by floor.

When the elevator finally stopped and the doors parted, she strode into the open reception area without acknowledging the man, though she was certain he scrutinized her backside as she departed. She surveyed her surroundings. The walls were colorless, except for random canvases of abstract art.

Apparently Executive leased or owned the entire floor. Seemed a bit much for an employment agency. But then, their website said they made videos and ads. Movie sets sometimes required a lot of space.

She checked the room. No one else in sight, other than the receptionist. Maybe Amy would walk in later.

A woman who wore so much makeup she looked like a porcelain doll sat behind the curved reception desk. Kate stepped forward, hand extended. "Hi, my name is Katherine Reynolds. My husband and I are in town for the stock show, so I don't live here."

The receptionist ignored her hand. "Can I help you?"

Kate rested her arms on the high counter, thinking the woman's liberal display of cleavage was a bit much for an office setting. "I do the marketing for our guest ranch, and I'm thinking of expanding my services." She smiled brightly. "Which is why I'm here."

The woman's false lashes raised and then lowered. "Do you have an actual marketing degree, or do you just sell a few little ads for your ranch?"

Kate tilted her head to study the woman for a moment. "I have an earned degree."

"Well, then..." The woman picked up a folder of papers. "Have a seat at one of the tables. I'll bring the paperwork to get you started."

"I'd rather not fill out anything until I know what's available in this area." She watched the woman's forehead crinkle and wondered if her makeup would crack. "I'm tight on time right now."

The receptionist hesitated but then pointed to monitors on the other side of the room. "You can use a computer to scan the listings. If you see anything that interests you, you'll need to complete the application and do the testing."

"Testing?"

"Generic questions. The test assures us you know your field before we stick our necks out offering your services for hire." Her tweezed, penciled eyebrows froze mid-forehead, as if daring Kate to question her company's protocol.

Kate nodded. "I understand."

The woman stood, came around the desk, and led Kate to the other side of the room. Her perfume tickled Kate's nose, but she held back the sneeze until the receptionist left. Then she clicked the computer mouse to activate the monitor. Under "marketing jobs," she arrowed down a long list of businesses, noting several possibilities. Maybe she wouldn't just pretend to look for work.

"Excuse me."

She swung around in the swivel chair. A meaty man wearing a dark pinstriped suit stood before her, arms folded. One look at his face, and she sensed evil behind his toothy white smile. *As shrewd as snakes, as innocent as doves. Be on your guard against men...*

So this was what God meant. Somehow, this man whose hard eyes examined her body with way too much interest was connected with Amy's disappearance. Was he the one who kidnapped her best friend? He wasn't tall and slender, like the man Walt's contacts described.

"Our receptionist says you didn't complete the paperwork. We require all our applicants to provide employment history."

"I don't consider myself an applicant, yet." She smiled, hoping it was one of her more charming smiles, like the ones she'd used when she competed for johns on Liberty Avenue in Pittsburgh. "I was on my way to do some shopping while my husband is in a meeting and decided to take a few minutes to check out the possibility of picking up extra work in Dallas."

She folded her hands. "If I'm violating company rules, I can come back when I have more time and when my husband has a better idea of whether or not he's going to expand into Texas." She could feel her sinuses objecting to the man's aftershave and knew a sneeze was on the way. Did everyone in Dallas pour on the perfume and aftershave?

"I'd like to talk with you in my office. We have an opportunity that might interest you."

She checked her watch. "I have a couple minutes. I don't want to miss out on shopping. We don't get to the big city often."

Kate followed the man down the long hallway.

He glanced over his shoulder. "Where's your ranch located?"

She raised an eyebrow. The receptionist must have informed him about the ranch. "Northern Colorado."

"You ever go to Denver?"

"Occasionally." She sneezed. "Excuse me. It's a long drive to Denver, so we have to go when we can stay two or three days."

They entered an office decorated in black and chrome. She sat in one of the chairs, and he took the leather couch across from her. Leaning forward, he tented his fingers. "May I call you Katherine?"

Kate nodded. No secrets here, at least from this guy. Either his receptionist was a busybody or they always shared information.

"Katherine, what are the chances of you moving here?"

"At this point, I have no idea. Depends on what my husband learns while we're at the stock show."

"Does he know you're here?"

"Oh, yes, of course. I sent him a text."

The man looked disappointed. He sat back, a quick smile sliding across his smooth face. "Like I said, if you happen to move here, we have something that might interest you."

"What's that?"

"Besides being a traditional employment agency, we also employ attractive women such as yourself to act as hostesses, tour guides, docents, demonstrators, escorts and such. Sometimes we're asked to provide models. You have the perfect body type. The pay is excellent, and our people get to meet fascinating individuals plus participate in events they might not ordinarily be invited to attend."

"Sounds intriguing." Kate rested an elbow on the chair arm. "But I'm married. Would that be a problem?"

He cocked an eyebrow. "Only if you let it be."

She frowned. "What does that mean?"

"Every marriage is different." He opened his hands. "Some husbands are excited for their women—their wives—to have a career, to make great money. Others are the jealous type."

"Your women aren't expected to, you know, do anything illicit, are they?" Kate realized she'd started to swing her foot and halted the motion mid-swing. She put both feet on the floor and sat taller.

"No, no, no." He shook his head. "Nothing of the sort. Our services are provided to organizations that don't have enough manpower to pull off events or shows by themselves. We help them out, and they pay us good money to do it." He lifted his palms. "I can show you the records, if you'd like. We have many satisfied customers, many return customers."

"That won't be necessary." She stood. "I'd better move along." She held out her hand. "I didn't catch your name."

He clasped her hand. "Damon. Damon Giordano." After holding her hand a moment too long, he cleared his throat. "Do you have a card, so we can keep in touch?"

"Yes." She pulled a Colorado business card from her purse. "And I'd like one of yours, if you have one."

They exchanged cards, and she moved toward the doorway. "Thank you for your time, Mr. Giordano. I'll probably be..." She stopped and stared at his card.

He was instantly at her side. "Something wrong?"

"I just got an idea. So obvious, I can't believe I didn't think of it earlier."

His expression was wary.

"You said *escorts* didn't you?"

"That's right."

"I planned to hook up our foreman with a high-school friend for a formal dinner we're going to this week, until I learned she and her boyfriend are getting serious. Maybe..." She tapped the card against her chin. "How much notice do you need?"

"Five to six hours is usually enough time for us to make arrangements. We could set up the escort right now to ensure satisfaction."

"I don't dare make a date for George without consulting him first."

"Give me a call when you're ready. We'll need to know his preference. Height, ethnicity, hair color, eye color, etcetera."

"You mean he can order a woman who looks just the way he wants, like from a catalog?"

Damon smirked. "We aim to please."

"I'll get back to you." Kate walked to the doorway and turned to wave goodbye. His gaze was on her legs. She shivered. The creep was a lecher. She hadn't strutted her stuff on the streets for years, yet he made her feel cheap all over again.

Mike dialed Clint's number on his cell phone and settled into a hard hotel room chair. He eyed Kate. "He's going to think we've lost our minds."

Clint answered. "Hello."

"Hey." Mike could hear voices and music in the background.

"Hi, boss. Sorry about all the noise. I'm in the exhibit hall. How's it going down south?"

"Great. You enjoying the Denver show?"

"Yeah. Been having a good time hanging with a couple rodeo friends. I've handed out almost all the brochures and bid on a couple bison bulls, like you asked. Got one this morning. Think you'll like him. Big sturdy guy with a nice pedigree. Won the People's Choice award."

"Good work. How soon will they deliver?"

"Next month."

"Perfect. How long you staying?"

"I'm thinking I'll catch tonight's rodeo, hand out the rest of the brochures in the morning, and head home tomorrow afternoon. I'd like to beat the blizzard the weather dudes are predicting. Anything you want me to grab before I leave Denver?"

Mike ran his fingers through his hair. "I, uh...well, Kate and I are wondering if you'd like to join us in Fort Worth. See what the stock show is like here."

"Sure, if you think the ranch can survive without the two of us for a few more days."

"I'll let Mom know. She can ask Cyrus to check the livestock."

"You really want me to drive all the way to Texas? That's a lot of gas."

"We'll buy you a plane ticket for this afternoon or evening, if we can find a flight."

"What about the rest of the brochures?"

"We can use them here."

"I'll head for the airport as soon you let me know what time I leave."

"One more thing, Clint." Mike winked at Kate. "Do you mind if we set you up with a date for a banquet tomorrow night?"

"A date? My boss wants to arrange a date for me? That's, uh, different."

"It was Kate's idea."

"That's even weirder. My boss's wife setting me up."

"It's a long story, and your name will be George for the evening. Mine is James and Kate's is Katherine."

"What's the deal?"

"We'll explain later. You game?"

Clint was silent for a moment. "Things have cooled between me and Susan. Neither one of us is willing to relocate, so we've reached an impasse." He paused. "I don't know what you have up your sleeve, dude... But, hey, what could be more exciting for a guy named George than a blind date in Dallas, Texas, especially in the middle of a cold Wyoming winter?"

CHAPTER ELEVEN

Kate dug her Colorado cell phone from her purse, ready to call Damon as soon as Mike told her Clint's response.

He ended the conversation and gave her the high sign.

She dialed the number on the business card and pushed the speaker button. "Hi, Damon. This is Katherine Reynolds."

"Ah, yes, the lovely Katherine from Colorado. It's fabulous to hear your voice again." He finished with a throaty purr.

Kate rolled her eyes and glanced at Mike, who looked equally disgusted. She plunged ahead. "I'm calling for our foreman. His name is George Elliot, and he'd like to reserve an escort for tonight, if it's not too late."

"Never too late for you, darling."

She tried not to gag.

"Did he say what ethnicity he prefers?"

"George likes women with fair skin and reddish hair. You know, that copper color that's so pretty. Is that possible?"

Mike gave her a thumbs-up.

"Anything is possible in our salon, darling." Damon chuckled. "Only the hairdressers know for sure."

She prayed they'd pick Amy with her auburn hair. When he asked about eye color, she suggested hazel, Amy's color.

"Only her optometrist will know."

"Sounds like Executive Pride has it all figured out. What about height? How do you deal with that?"

"That can be a bit of a problem. However, our girls know how to stand short or tall and wear higher heels when needed. What height is your foreman friend wanting?"

"I doubt height is an issue." She chewed at her lip, wishing she knew Amy's exact height. "George isn't real tall. Maybe someone shorter than him would be good. Let's say somewhere in the neighborhood of five-three to five-six. How does that sound?"

"Perfect. We can easily accommodate those numbers."

"Without trimming off the top of someone's head?"

"Even Executive Pride has its limits."

Kate and Mike met Walt Harnish in the hotel lobby. He wasn't the tall, clean-shaven man she'd expected. Instead, the PI was her height and reminded her of men she'd known when she lived on the streets in Pittsburgh. At least three days of brown-gray stubble peppered his cheeks, and graying twists of longish hair curled around the edges of his stained baseball cap. A dark hooded sweatshirt topped a dirty t-shirt. Beneath his ragged jeans, grimy tennis shoes were splitting at the seams.

Walt shook their hands. "Miz Duncan, Mister Duncan."

"First names work for us," Mike said. "And we'll call you 'Walt,' if that's okay with you."

"Fine by me." Walt rubbed his hand across his chest. "My apologies for lookin' like I crawled out from under the porch. Have to blend with the lowlifes I hang with over yonder." He lowered his voice. "I, uh, sniff out...transactions. Dallas isn't all that far from the Mexican border, if you get my drift."

"Searching for my friend must be a bit tame for you," Kate said.

"Things'll heat up soon enough." Walt surveyed the lobby and the adjacent eating area, where several people were taking advantage of the continental breakfast. "How 'bout we go to your room?"

"Good idea," Mike said. "The elevators are over there."

They'd just entered the elevator when Walt let out a loud belch. "S'cuse me, folks."

Kate smirked. "Bet you ate a chorizo burrito for breakfast."

The doors closed.

Walt gave her a funny look. "How'd you know that?"

"Oh, just a wild guess."

They reached their floor, exited the elevator and walked down the hall. With a slide of his card key, Mike unlocked the door to their room and they stepped inside.

Kate opened the drapes. "Have a seat, Walt. I'll get some coffee started."

Mike pulled the desk chair over to the small table in the corner. Within minutes, they were all seated around the table, steaming Styrofoam cups in their hands.

Walt took a sip. "Last week, I heard a drug honcho crowing about a two-for-one hooker helicopter deal. Said it was the best night of his life."

Mike arched an eyebrow. "You mean, two women on a helicopter?"

Walt chuckled. "He mentioned a brothel, so I assume the deal included, uhm, entertainment and a 'copter ride, maybe to a hidden location."

"I thought brothels were illegal."

"That doesn't mean they're not out there."

Kate frowned. "So why are you telling us this?"

"The guy's secrecy caught my attention. He refused to give the name of the place or its location. All he'd say was the women are out of this world and the rest of us couldn't afford them."

"Are you suggesting that Amy...?"

He swirled the liquid in his cup. "Could be why she slipped under the radar."

"No way." Kate jutted her chin. "That's one thing Amy did not do in her wilder days."

Walt picked up two sugar packets, tore them open and poured the contents into his cup. "I talked with your detective friend."

Kate stopped mid-sip and lowered her cup. "And?"

"Barker was none too happy to learn I'm on the hunt for your friend. I promised to feed any information we come up with to him. He admitted they've found no further trace of Iverson. It's like she flew into town, killed a guy and vanished into thin air."

Kate placed her hands on the table. "Amy did not—"

"Right." Walt nodded. "She didn't kill anyone. Just telling you how Barker views the case. My job is to prove him wrong."

Mike set his cup down. "So we know more about her than the cops know?"

"Maybe, maybe not. They're not always forthright with their information." He winked. "But Barker and I get along pretty good. He's an okay hombre."

"That's encouraging." Kate swirled the tea in her cup. If they worked with the police and the police worked with them to find Amy, maybe the department would be open to the notion that Amy was innocent.

"I have to admit," Walt was saying, "I keep running into dead ends. Haven't found anyone who saw the men with the stretcher. They probably had a van waiting in the alley."

"Maybe we'll learn something tonight," Mike said. "We hired an Executive Pride escort to attend a banquet with us and our foreman. We're hoping that person will be Amy."

Standing next to Clint's escort in front of the restroom mirror, Kate decided the woman's hair tint was at least two shades lighter than Amy's. All evening, she'd tried to hide her disappointment that they'd gotten Janessa Valentine rather than Amy Iverson. Mike must have noticed because he'd pulled her close and whispered that they could mine Clint's date for information, which was what she was about to do.

She dropped her hairbrush and lipstick into her handbag and closed the flap. "How do you like working for Executive Pride, Janessa?"

Janessa, who was applying another layer of mascara, looked at Kate in the mirror. "It's an interesting job. I get to meet lots of different people."

"Damon Giordano in the office suggested I work for them if James decides to relocate to the Dallas-Fort Worth area. I'm wondering if that's a good idea for a married woman."

"Good question. As far as I know, most of us are single." Janessa brushed the lashes on her other eyelid. "I rarely talk with any of the other escorts."

Learning that Janessa might not know Amy made Kate's heart fall even further. "Did you find out about Executive escorts the way I did?"

Janessa held the mascara wand midair. "How's that?" Her tone was cautious.

"I went to your headquarters to check on marketing jobs—that's my field, and Damon invited me into his office to chat. Is that how it worked with you?"

Janessa straightened. "I guess you could say Executive Pride found me." The tiny diamonds on her choker necklace sparkled under the fluorescent lights. "I was working at a dress store downtown, and one day this really good-looking guy came in shopping for his girlfriend. At the time, I didn't realize his connection with Executive Pride, but the next thing I knew, I was part of the crew."

"That fast, huh?"

She slid the brush into the tube. "Yeah, it was so fast it was unreal."

"Did you have to fill out an application and be interviewed?"

"Not the way Thomas..." She smoothed her dress and flipped her long hair behind her shoulder. "I'd better get back to work, or George will think he got gypped." She opened the bathroom door. "And I wouldn't want him to think that, because he's a lot nicer than some of the guys I've escorted."

"He's a funny man, isn't he?"

"Yeah, he's a riot. Too bad you won't be in town long."

"If we ever return, and he's with us, we'll be sure to ask for you." Kate followed her into the hallway. "Have any of the not-so-nice clients ever tried to harm you?"

"Executive lets our customers know in advance what the expectations are." She made a face. "Sometimes things get crazy, but I know how to deal with the 'problem boys,' as we call them."

Clint hadn't mentioned any Executive expectations. "That's good," Kate said. "I like your necklace. It's unique."

Sterling silver chains intertwined in a lacelike pattern supported two rows of miniature flowers with tiny diamonds in their centers. A much larger flower was attached at the front of the inch-wide choker, the individual onyx leaves edged with silver. Though the necklace was beautiful, the chains reminded her of the jewelry she wore when she worked the streets.

"Thank you. It was a gift from..." Janessa paused. "From a very special person."

They rejoined Mike and Clint just as the emcee approached the podium to introduce the speaker. Kate glanced at Janessa. Too bad their new friend was forced to listen to a boring talk about cattle futures. On the other hand, she was being paid good money to act interested.

Hoping to prolong their time with Janessa and learn more about Executive Pride, Kate nudged Mike. "Want to go out for drinks and dessert when this is over? This cheesecake tastes like cardboard."

He leaned close. "And it's just as tough to chew."

Later, Kate and Mike followed Clint and Janessa into the small Italian restaurant the escort selected for their after-party, one where garlic and basil scented the air and classical music played in the background. Kate touched Janessa's shoulder. "This is perfect. I've heard enough loud cowboy music to keep my ears ringing for the rest of the winter."

Janessa smiled. "You seem like people who like to hear each other when you talk, so I thought this would be a good place. They have fabulous tiramisu."

"Oh, yum. I haven't eaten tiramisu in ages."

The men looked at each other. Clint frowned. "Isn't that something women wear on their heads?"

Kate laughed. "It's an Italian dessert."

Janessa winked. "Some people call it 'heaven in your mouth.'"

Clint raised his eyebrows. "Guess I'd better try some. Has to be better than that cheesecake, which was about as dull as the speaker."

Mike seemed doubtful. "I don't know…"

Kate patted his arm. "You can order something else and have a taste of mine."

After they'd been seated in a candlelit booth and placed their order, Janessa said, "I'm envious you-all live on a ranch. I grew up on a farm, and I love the outdoors." She sighed. "I'm not real fond of this concrete jungle."

Clint, who sat next to her, said, "I heard you say you're from Kansas. How'd you end up in Dallas?"

Her face clouded. "My dad died when I was a freshman in high school. During my junior year, my mom remarried and moved us all to her husband's house in town. Then my twin brothers joined the Navy and I was the only kid left at home. My mom and step-dad were so caught up in each other, I felt like I was in the way. So when my girlfriend decided to go to beauty school in Dallas, I moved with her and found work at a downtown dress shop."

"That's where someone from Executive Pride discovered her," Kate said.

Mike asked, "Do you like this line of work better than selling clothes?"

"The pay is better." She put her hand on her throat and leaned toward Kate. "Don't do it."

Kate stared at her. "Do what?"

"This…" Janessa pointed to herself. Teardrops danced on her thick eyelashes, reflecting candlelight. She wrapped both hands around her neck. "You're too nice."

Clint touched her arm. "You're nice, too."

She pulled away and dropped her hands to her lap. "Thank you. I've enjoyed my evening with you." Janessa focused on Kate again. "Do you two have any children?"

Kate felt as though she'd missed something in the conversation. "I had a hysterectomy a few weeks ago." She looked down. "We'll never be able..."

"I'm sorry. You must have really wanted kids."

Mike wrapped an arm around Kate's shoulders.

Janessa folded her hands on the tabletop. "In case you're wondering how adoption compares to having biological kids, my parents adopted my brothers and loved them just as much as they loved me. In fact, I used to think Mom and Dad loved the boys more, 'cause they let them do stuff I wasn't allowed to do. The fact that they were I older than I was didn't matter to me."

Clint laughed.

Mike smiled at Kate. "We'll start checking out our options in a couple months."

Kate searched her husband's eyes. Maybe by then she'd be ready to think about alternatives to birthing their own family. At the moment, she wasn't ready to give up her dream of a little boy with Mike's blond hair and dimples.

CHAPTER TWELVE

Laura and Todd stepped from the warmth of the Laramie movie theater onto a snow-covered sidewalk. The crisp night wind whipped her hair and snowflakes pelted her cheeks.

He took her arm. "Great movie. Lots of action." He raised his voice to speak above the wind. "Want to go over to the Rifleman for a drink and pie?"

Snow was already sticking to the streets and Laura was anxious to get back to the ranch and Mary before the roads got bad. "If we don't stay long."

They hurried to his pickup. Once they were both inside, he started the engine and pushed the defrost button. "How long did you say your son and daughter-in-law are planning to be out of town?"

"They should be home tomorrow, unless this storm grounds them." She peered through the windshield at the dark sky. "On second thought, maybe we'd better go straight home. This could get nasty."

He clenched the steering wheel. "Just one drink. All I need is one drink."

Evidently alcohol was a bigger issue with him than Laura realized. Maybe he really was a regular at Bogie's Bar, like Mike said. She pushed hair from her face and wiped fog from the side window. Dan wasn't a drinker, so this was all new territory for her.

Forty-five minutes later, they were on the highway headed home, strawberry-rhubarb pie in their stomachs and a six-pack of beer behind the truck seat. Snow whooshed toward them like a scene from *Star Wars* and clumped on the wiper blades. *Please, God. Get us home.* She didn't want to be stranded with Todd or have to explain to Kate and Mike why she left Mary. Laura pulled her collar up around her neck and prayed Marita would stay until she arrived home, though she wasn't sure God would acknowledge her prayer. If she hadn't snuck away, she wouldn't be in this mess.

The highway was open, but the going was slow. Neither of them spoke. Todd switched on the radio. Although she wasn't in the mood for music, cowboy love songs interspersed with storm warnings covered the silence.

Laura reached into her handbag for her cell phone. "I'd better call Marita while we're in tower range." By calling her cell phone instead of the ranch number, she might avoid waking Mary. She dialed the number. No answer.

Laura sighed. She might be in range, but Marita wasn't. Cell phones rarely worked at the ranch. She called Marita's home number. Jorge answered and told her his wife had left Whispering Pines a half hour earlier. "It started snowing hard, and the aunt was asleep, so I told her to come home."

"Okay, thanks. That's good to know." She didn't blame him for wanting Marita to drive home while she could.

Todd turned down the radio. "Everything okay?"

"Marita left after Mary fell asleep. I don't like for her to be alone. If she wakes up, and no one is there, she might wander out in the snow searching for us, or Dean, her deceased husband. She talks about him all the time and asks where he is."

He placed his hand over hers on the bench seat. "You worry too much. She'll be fine."

She smiled. "You're probably right." His fingers felt warm and strong—just what she needed at the moment. "How are the roads?"

"I've seen worse." He squeezed her fingers. "Your kids flying or driving home from Dallas?"

"Flying. Clint is with them."

"Whispering Pines must be doing okay to afford three round-trip flights."

She studied his face. The lights of the dashboard cast a green hue on his cheeks and stubbled chin. "What does that mean?"

"It's a long drive from Texas in weather like this."

"I mean the affording flights part. Why did you say that?"

"I just thought if you ever needed any help, I could pitch in."

"Pitch in?"

"These are tough times for ranchers. Sometimes people have to partner together to make a go of it."

The heat inside the cab swirled in rhythm with the snow that danced outside the truck. The swirling and dancing combined with the smell of alcohol made her dizzy. "Does this have anything to do with your offers to buy our ranch?"

"No."

"Really?"

"Really." He patted her hand. "I'd rather merge ranches."

She frowned. "I've told you before…"

"I know, I know. But I like eating at your table with you across from me and driving down the road with you in the passenger seat. It feels like, well, you know, like we could be…"

"Married?"

"Well, yeah. I'd like that."

"For goodness sake, Todd, we barely know each other." She yanked her hand out from under his.

He caressed her cheek with the back of his hand. "We've been neighbors for a long time, Laura."

"Watch the road." She pushed his hand away. "We've only spent a few hours together, and you're already talking marriage." They were just friends, a widow and a widower who enjoyed having someone to talk to now and then.

"You're the one who brought it up."

"No, I didn't."

"Yes, you did."

She exhaled. The man was impossible.

Todd chuckled. "You're an intelligent, beautiful woman. I like being with you. The life of a widower is lonely. I'm ready to move on."

"Well, I'm not. Dan hasn't been gone all that long. I still miss him, a lot."

"I understand." He smiled. "That will pass in time."

"Don't go there, Todd."

He slowed the truck, and his words. "I'm a patient man, a very patient man."

"Well, that was disappointing." Kate kicked off her heels and flopped into a chair in their hotel room. She leaned on the windowsill and watched the endless stream of cars below. Was Amy in one of those vehicles? Or trotting along with her sassy swing window shopping with a friend, like she loved to do?

Clint settled into the other chair. "Thanks for treating me to a night on the town."

Mike took off his boots and stretched out on the bed. "Good of you to say that after we used you to try to get to Amy."

"Glad to help." Clint yawned. "Janessa was nice, but I was hoping for Amy."

Kate sighed. "Anything we can glean from this evening?"

Mike drew line in the air. "Number one. Janessa is touchy about her work."

Kate traced a two on the window. "She's also touchy about her employer. Something is not right with that agency."

Clint tilted his chair back. "Did you learn anything about Amy when you were alone with Janessa?"

"Huh-uh." Kate shook her head. "Unless you count the fact Janessa was apparently recommending I not work for Executive Pride."

Mike propped two pillows behind his shoulders. "Do we have anything we can work with, anything to give Walt and the cops?"

"We have names." Lifting one finger at a time, Kate listed the individuals. "There's the escort, Janessa Valentine, the guy in the office, Damon Giordano, and someone named Thomas. He's the one who recruited Janessa."

Mike circled his finger above his prone body. "Number three."

"Maybe he's the man who picked up Amy from the airport. I'll give Walt the name." Kate squinted at Clint. "Did you meet Damon at the Executive Pride office?"

"Nope. I gave the cash to a woman at the front desk, she introduced me to Janessa, and we left."

"That reminds me. Did they give you a list of dos and don'ts?"

"List?"

"You know. What to do and what not do with your escort. Janessa said their clients are given a list of expectations."

"I didn't even get a receipt."

"Too bad. She thinks men know the rules and she's protected." Kate could feel fatigue and pain setting in and promised herself two ibuprofen and bed the moment Clint left their room. Tomorrow was going to be a long day of flying and driving.

Mike tossed a pillow into the air and caught it. "Our flights are scheduled for tomorrow afternoon. Do we have any reason to stay longer?"

"I was hoping we'd see Amy somewhere, somehow," Kate said. "I hate to leave now that I'm even more convinced something awful happened to her."

"What can we do for her here?"

"Pray."

"We can do that at home."

"Right." She massaged her temples. "I'll call Walt in the morning to tell him what little we learned. We can fly home tomorrow, unless Amy calls."

"Of course." Mike unbuttoned a shirt cuff. "If Walt or the police somehow connect with her later, we'll catch the first flight back to Dallas."

"I'd like to come with you." Clint stood. "I'll do whatever I can to help find Amy."

Laura slogged through the drift that covered the porch stairs. She'd insisted Todd drop her off and keep going. She was exhausted and knew he was, too. The drive from Laramie took twice as long as usual.

She dropped her purse on the couch and went back outside to get more firewood. When she returned with a stack of logs in her arms, she saw Mary standing in the middle of the living room. Prissy sat on one side of her and Tramp on the other. The elderly woman leaned on her walker, appearing lost, as usual.

"Mary, what are you doing out of bed?"

"Where have you been?" The older woman's eyes flashed. "Were you with that man again?"

Laura deposited the wood on the hearth, added a log to the fire, and sniffed her coat sleeve. Maybe Todd's aftershave scent had transferred to her coat. "I was getting more wood."

"Oh." Mary gaped at the fireplace.

Laura gave her a hug. "You smell good, Mary. You must have eaten a mint before bed." She helped her turn the walker around. "Let's get you back under the covers before you're chilled."

"I dreamt about Queen Esther in the Bible."

"That must have been interesting."

"Where's Katy?"

"She and Mike are in Texas. They'll be home tomorrow, unless this storm causes flight delays." Laura guided Mary and the walker toward her bedroom. "It's quiet around here without them, isn't it?"

"Too quiet. I miss my Katy."

"I miss her, too." Laura helped Mary climb into bed and then hung up her coat and turned off the lights. Mike and Kate's absence left a huge gap in her life. So why did she sneak around like a wayward teenager the minute they left town?

She thought about her recent lapse into adolescent behavior while she brushed her teeth. Partly, it was the silence. She was so lonely without Dan, even with Mary in the house. And the boredom. What was a single woman supposed to do in a small community with a dearth of single men? Yes, she enjoyed her women friends and kept in touch with couples who'd been friends forever, yet it wasn't the same.

She washed and moisturized her face, put on a flannel night-gown, and stuffed pillows on Dan's side of the bed, like she did every night.

Tramp, who'd followed her into the bedroom, licked her hand and circled three times before he curled on the rug beside the bed.

Sliding between the cold sheets, Laura tucked her feet into her gown and clutched a pillow. She missed snuggling with her warm husband. She pulled the covers over her head. Was Todd a good snuggler? Or someone who kept to his side of the bed? Somehow, she couldn't picture him as the cuddly type, even though he held her hand every chance he got.

She rearranged the feather pillow under her neck. Todd Hughes was a strong-willed man. If she married him, would he dominate her? Would she be caught between him and Mike? How would Kate and Mary fair with Todd in their lives? She already knew Mary's reaction, but her negative feelings wouldn't be an issue for long. In time, she wouldn't know the difference between Todd and any other man who walked in the door.

Laura rolled to her other side. Todd was right. She worried too much. Why was she so concerned about everyone else? What about her need for companionship and love? Was Todd the one to fill her empty life?

Kate settled into the window seat on the plane bound for Denver and fastened her seatbelt. Then she reached inside her purse to turn on her Wyoming phone. She'd shut the phone off at dinner last night and forgotten to turn it back on. If she was quick, she could check for messages and respond before the cabin crew instructed passengers to turn off electronic devices.

The phone chimed almost immediately.

She peered at the screen. A Dallas area code. Maybe Walt found Amy. She read the text. *Do not respond. Not my phone. I have new friends, new job, new lover, new life. Please find good homes for my animals, if they haven't already been adopted.*

"No." Kate's heart thundered against her rib cage. "Please, God. No."

Mike leaned over. "What's the matter?"

She handed him the phone.

He read the message and then read it again. His forehead wrinkled. "Do you think...?"

"It has to be Amy."

"But—"

"I know. It's weird. Show Clint."

He handed the phone to his foreman, who sat in the aisle seat. Clint read the message, a puzzled expression forming on his face. "Amy?"

Mike nodded.

Clint handed the phone back. "Wonder what it means."

She reread the message. "Amy sent this at two-sixteen a.m. If I'd left my phone on, we would have heard it. I feel terrible I missed her call."

"First off, it wasn't a call, and second, she said, 'do not respond.'"

"We could have called Walt or the police, or done something." The plane's engines roared to life. She looked at Mike.

"I hope you're not thinking of getting off this flight. This doesn't give us any new information."

"The police could track her—or whoever owns the phone—through the cell phone company."

"Right," he said. "The police, not you."

"I'd want to be there. They'll arrest her."

"They're going to arrest her when she surfaces, whether you're there or not."

A flight attendant stopped in the aisle next to Clint. "Please turn off your phone, ma'am."

Kate nodded and quickly forwarded the message to Walt with a brief note. She'd tried to pay Amy's phone bills but couldn't without access to her accounts. Service had probably been suspended for both phones. Now there was another number for her. She'd call as soon as they landed in Denver.

Chapter Thirteen

From her high-rise perch, Amy watched tiny cars scurry between traffic lights. How many days—or weeks—had passed since one room and two windows became her daytime existence and since working in the brothel down the hall became her nighttime occupation? She'd worked a lot of jobs but never expected prostitution would one day be the source of her paycheck, if she ever got one. Thomas hadn't mentioned payday, and she was afraid to ask.

She brushed a speck of dust from the window ledge. Kate wouldn't approve of what she was doing. But, no matter what her friend thought, a single woman needed an income. This was the only job offer after months of searching. Besides, her satisfaction rate made Thomas proud. At age twenty-five, she was one of his *mature* women. He'd told her she didn't bring in as much as the kids. Even so, he was happy with her work. And her reward was time alone with him and his sexy body.

Amy twisted a lock of highlighted hair around her finger and eyed the terrarium. If she continued to please Thomas, maybe he'd remove the snakes from her room. She shivered and tried to think about something else.

In the reflection off the windows of the building across the street, she saw a helicopter approach the roof of her building. She heard and felt the thwap of rotors and caught a glimpse of the tail just above her. Looking back at the reflection, she saw the aircraft settle until only the slowing rotors were visible.

More than one of her customers had mentioned a helicopter ride. "The price was outrageous," one said, popping his knuckles between words. "I expect–*crack*–you'll make it–*crack*–worth the dough–*crack, crack.* She smirked. That particular john was convinced he was the greatest athlete ever, in or out of bed.

Apparently, she was on the top floor of a tall building, one so tall she couldn't see the base of the building across the street. The flag on top barely stirred in the breeze.

She heard footsteps outside her door and glanced at the clock Thomas installed above the door when she became a full-fledged member of his organization. He'd also furnished her room with a dresser and an armoire, plus another chair in her sitting area. He said he'd put them on her bill, along with charges for housing, clothing, jewelry, dermabrasion and laser treatments, hair and nail care, housekeeping, and the scanty meals he provided. Even with all those deductions, maybe in time she'd make enough to return to Pittsburgh and buy a place for herself and Elaina to share.

The latch clicked. She frowned. They'd already delivered lunch, what there was of it, and it was way too early for business. For sure, they wouldn't be bringing a snack. Thomas never allowed food between meals.

"You have a few good years left in that aging body of yours," he'd told her. "That is, if we keep a tight rein on your calories." He even tracked her time on the elliptical machine that sat beside her bed, checking the meter and demanding a minimum of an hour a day. Sometimes she did more time out of sheer boredom.

The door opened. Thomas, Damon and Carl strode into the room, their mouths hard and flat.

Amy's gut seized. She crossed her arms and tried to act natural. "Good afternoon, gentlemen."

Thomas pointed at the bed with the bamboo pole he held in his tattooed hand. "On your belly."

She stared at him.

His eyes flashed. "Now!"

Amy dropped onto the bed. "I'm sorry, Thomas. I won't—"

"Grab her feet."

The men grasped her ankles and shoved her knees downward, grinding them into the mattress.

Amy shrieked. What were they doing to her this time?

"Shut up." Thomas's angry shout reverberated around the room. He slapped the bottoms of her feet with the pole and then did it again, and again.

She twitched.

The men held tight.

The blows stung her feet yet they weren't terribly painful. Was this a punishment or a new sex game they were teaching her? Maybe it was a type of spanking. Some clients liked that.

She moved her head to the side in order to breathe and saw Thomas's red face and veins bulging from his temple. This was no game. She dug her fingernails into the comforter. He was punishing her. Amy frantically racked her brain, trying to recall a rule she'd broken or an unhappy customer.

The snake head on Thomas's wrist flipped up and down and the blows increased in frequency and strength and began to hurt. She crammed a knuckle between her teeth to keep from crying out. Thomas despised crybabies.

"You have any clue what this is about?"

Amy pushed up from the mattress. "I'm sorry, Thomas. Really, I am."

The men shoved her back down, slamming her against the mattress.

She bit her tongue. The taste of blood filled her mouth.

Thomas's rhythm did not falter, nor did the strength of his blows. "You stupid tramp. You sent a text on a client's phone to someone who called the cops. You're a wanted woman, so the fuzz leaned on our client, confiscated his phone."

She gasped. Almost as soon as she'd pressed *send*, she'd forgotten about the message to Kate. "He fell asleep. All I did was ask someone to make sure my pets are okay."

He cursed. "I told you to forget those stupid animals." He whacked harder.

Amy groaned. The bottoms of her feet felt like they were crusted with hot blisters that burst and reformed with each strike and then burst again. "I'll never do it again." She sobbed. "I promise."

"Don't worry. There'll never be another cell phone on a john." He slowed the rhythm.

Waiting for the next blow was excruciating. She moaned. "Please, Thomas. Please stop."

"Shut your mouth." He hit her calves with the stick, hard. "I can still see those stupid tattoos. They should be gone by now."

Pain shot through her legs that were already tender due to the treatments. Amy screamed into the comforter and writhed against Damon and Carl's grasp. They held firm.

Words hissed from Thomas's lips. "This is bas-tin-ado, baby." He returned to rhythmically smacking her soles. "It's a clever form of punishment used in eastern countries, the beauty of which, I'm told, lies not in the strength of the blows, but in their longevity."

He cackled the merciless laugh she'd first heard when she awakened on the cement floor. "Bastinado has been known to cause insanity and death. That's what idiot whores like you deserve."

Amy clawed at the bedding, smelling laundry soap mixed with drool and begging God to help her.

Thomas snickered. "I find this form of punishment appropriate for our business..." Smack! Smack, Smack! "Because it leaves no scars. You won't miss a minute of work."

Kate deposited Prissy in Mary's bedroom, closed the door, and walked into the living room, where Mary, Dymple and Cyrus were seated. The coffee and chai tea aromas smelled good mixed together.

Mary poured coffee for Cyrus and set the carafe down. "What would you like, Katy?"

"Chai, please, with cream and honey." Kate hugged Dymple and sat beside her on the couch. "Good to see you again. I missed you."

"It's good to see you, too, sweetie." Dymple motioned toward the coffee table. "I tried a new scone recipe. Lemon ginger this time."

Kate picked up a napkin and reached for a pastry. "Seems like you were gone forever."

"I had a wonderful time visiting my sisters in Colorado. However, it's good to be home."

"I'd like to meet your sisters someday."

"I'll tell them. It's high time they came to Copperville instead of me traipsing to Colorado every time I want to see them."

Cyrus aimed a finger at Dymple. "Tasty eats." A crooked grin lifted his wrinkled cheeks. "Think I'll have another."

With an equally wrinkled hand, Dymple scooted the platter across the coffee table and handed him the butter knife. "Thank God the sun finally came out and the roads thawed enough to get over to your side of the mountain." She paused. "Where are Mike and Laura this morning? I didn't see either of them in the office when I passed."

"Mike and Clint are checking to see how the herds weathered the storm. And Laura said she needed to run in town, now that the snowplow made it this far."

Dymple regarded Kate a moment before she picked up her teacup and turned to Mary. "How do you like living on the ranch, Mary?"

Kate hoped Dymple's feelings weren't hurt by Laura's absence. They hadn't seen much of each other lately. She took the knife from Cyrus and added more butter to her scone.

Mary put down her teacup. "Is this a ranch?" She peered at her surroundings.

"Yeah." Cyrus brandished his coffee mug. "We lost a lot of branches due to the heavy snow last week. It was a wet one."

"You don't say." Mary smiled. "I always liked to swim."

Kate blinked. Between Cyrus's deafness and her aunt's dementia, where was this conversation headed?

Mary motioned to Dymple. "What is your name, miss? If you don't mind me asking."

Kate saw Dymple's lip twitch before she told Mary her name, like she did every time they met. "Dymple. Dymple Forbes. I live on the other side of the mall."

Oh-oh. Dymple's aphasia strikes again. Kate tucked her lips between her teeth to keep from laughing out loud.

"How about that?" Mary's eyes widened. "Do they have a Sears store?"

"No." Cyrus tapped his chair arm. "But there's a hardware store about a mile from there. Good prices on calf pullers right now. Almost calving season. We're gonna need those pullers."

"Oh, my, isn't that marvelous. Dean was once a Fuller Brush salesman, you know."

"Excuse me." Kate hurried into the bathroom, closed the door and grabbed a stack of towels. She dropped onto the edge of the bathtub, buried her face in the towels and laughed so hard she feared she might loosen sutures.

Too bad Mike and Laura weren't there to share the fun. On the other hand, if either of them even hinted at a grin, she would have lost control. Finally, she wiped her eyes with the corner of a towel and stood. It felt good to laugh again.

When she rejoined the others, Cyrus was rising to his feet, one snapping joint at a time. He plucked his insulated denim jacket and bedraggled hat from the coatrack by the back door. "Better tackle those downed limbs while the sun's a blazin'. I hear another storm is headed our way."

Kate groaned. She needed sunshine.

He arched an eyebrow, pulling a wrinkled eyelid upward. "Been a crazy winter. One squall after another." He tipped his hat toward the group before plopping it on his head. "You ladies'll have to finish your gabfest without me."

They said their goodbyes, and Cyrus and his bowed legs hobbled out the door and onto the deck.

Dymple chuckled. "Deep down he's got a heart of gold."

"I've never seen him so mellow." Kate broke off a piece of scone. "We should invite him to tea more often."

Mary sat up tall. "Just don't let that other man come here."

"What man?" Kate bit into the pastry.

"You know." Using her walker for support, Mary pulled herself to her feet. "I need a nap. I'm going to go lie down with Dean." Once she gained her balance, she shuffled toward her bedroom.

Kate poured herself and Dymple more tea. "I hate to see Aunt Mary sleep so much. Seems like she's only up a few hours a day."

"What can she do around here?"

"Not much." Kate shrugged. "She doesn't like to watch television and doesn't seem to have the attention span to read a book, although she says she reads the book of Esther in her Bible every day. It's also hard for her to help in the kitchen. When she tries, she forgets what she's doing and wanders off or gets confused." Kate shifted her position. "If it wasn't so cold, she'd probably like to sit on the deck."

"Does she have any hammers?"

"Hammers?"

Dymple squeezed her wrinkled eyelids closed. "I meant to say..." She opened her eyes. "Hobbies. That's what I meant, hobbies."

Kate grinned. "Aunt Mary did needlework for years but gave it up a while back. Hurt her hands too much. That's when she really got into prayer. Not only did she pray for friends in her church and neighborhood, word got out and people started calling from all over the world. Plus, she had a scanner that picked up police and fire department activity. Every time she heard of an emergency, she prayed."

"Did you bring her radio with you?"

"It's in the barn. Mike stacked a bunch of her boxes in an empty stall. Between my health issues and the weather, we haven't unpacked everything." Kate heard the sound of a chain saw and through the front window saw Cyrus cutting a tree branch into short lengths for firewood.

"Maybe Mike could find the radio."

"He told Aunt Mary he'd set it up for her and install an antenna. But we got so involved with Amy, we forgot all about it." She broke off the tip of a second scone. "As you know, Dymple, we don't have much excitement in these mountains. She'll probably fall asleep on top of her radio."

"Could be. At least she'd have a purpose again. We all need a reason to live, you know."

CHAPTER FOURTEEN

Kate added more cream to her chai. Did she have a purpose? Obviously, she wasn't meant to be a mom. For now, she'd care for Aunt Mary and do all she could to find Amy. Their trip to Dallas may have been futile, and the text from Amy hadn't led anywhere, but she wouldn't give up.

She turned to Dymple. "We didn't shut off Aunt Mary's phone service. Just put it on vacation mode. Maybe we could forward her Pittsburgh calls to the ranch. We have extra lines."

"Good idea."

"We'll have to find her phone." Kate pointed to the cordless phone on the end table. "Newer ones are too confusing."

"She'd also need a desk or a small table and a chair."

"Both of those are already in her room."

"Perfect. Your aunt is blessed to have you and Mike and Laura to care for her." Dymple set her cup and saucer on the coffee table and folded her hands in her lap. "Sounds like we have Mary set up for business. Now, let's talk about you, Kate. How's your recovery going?"

"I'm doing much better, thank you. But..."

Dymple cocked her head. "But what?"

Kate hesitated. She hated to whine. Yet, she knew if anyone could help her find a way through the depression, it would be Dymple. "You, more than most people, know the world I came from and the host of miracles God has done in my life."

Dymple's eyes brightened. "Yes, indeed."

"My dream to work on a Wyoming ranch came true, and then I married a sweet God-fearing man—both miracles beyond my wildest imaginings. Plus, I have the greatest mother-in-law and the best friends in the world, especially you."

Dymple smiled.

Kate looked away. "Still, I'm not satisfied. I want a baby. Three or four babies." She shrugged. "I'm selfish, Dymple. Despite all God has done for me, I can't seem to get past the idea that I'll never be able to have children."

"That's not selfishness," Dymple said. "That's a God-given desire."

"He's denied me the opportunity, and you and Aunt Mary." Kate stopped. "Did you want children when you were younger, Dymple?"

"I did. And God gave them to me."

"You've never mentioned kids."

"I was a schoolteacher for thirty years, so I nurtured dozens of children. I loved each of them, and they loved me back. My desire for a family was satisfied. Best of all, I got to go home to a peaceful quiet house each night."

Kate frowned.

"I know. It's not the same. For me, however, teaching was enough, more than enough. God will fulfill your dream. It might mean adoption, or maybe foster parenting."

Kate shook her head. "I couldn't do either, after all the awful foster parents I was stuck with. And, really, isn't adoption basically long-term foster care, a family the adoptee can't escape?"

Dymple searched Kate's face. "You realize, don't you, that you have a jaded view? For many thousands of individuals, both types of homes have been positive loving experiences."

Kate shrugged. "My payback for being a persistent runaway might be adopting a child who makes our lives as miserable as I made the lives of my foster parents." She ran her finger around the rim of her teacup. "The older I get, the more I realize my unhappiness wasn't always their fault."

Dymple patted Kate's arm. "You and Mike would be good parents, whether for adopted children or foster children. You'd provide a wonderful home, along with all the marvels of this beautiful ranch. Plus, you know the evil that orphans sometimes experience. Maybe God wants you to be an instrument for change." She pointed upward. "Don't forget, he adopted you into his family when you became a Christian."

Kate cocked her head. "Huh, I hadn't thought of it that way."

"I'm not telling you what to do, just throwing out suggestions." Dymple picked up her cup and took a sip." You could help with community or church youth organizations or act as a big sister to a troubled girl. Maybe open a daycare center. Lots of possibilities."

"Guess I need to start thinking outside the box, or the womb, in my case." She straightened. "So, Dr. Forbes, since you're solving all my problems today, what do you suggest for the bone-deep exhaustion I've felt since surgery."

"That reminds me." Dymple set her cup down and reached for her satchel beside the couch. "Almost forgot to give you this." She handed Kate a gift-wrapped box and card.

"How sweet of you. What's the occasion?"

"It's a get-well gift. Sorry it's a bit late."

"That's okay. This is exciting." She read the card. "Very cool that your sisters signed it too. Thank you." Inside the package, she found a cross-stitched sampler with bright pansies etched around the edges.

> *You chart the path ahead of me*
> *and tell me where to stop and rest.*
> Psalm 139:3

Tears in her eyes, Kate hugged the elderly woman. "This is beautiful. I'll hang it in our bedroom, where I'll see it every day and be reminded that God has already charted my path."

"My younger sister, Dahlia, stitched that for you. I picked the verse, knowing you'd find slowing down difficult. Time and rest heal our spirits as well as our bodies. Allow yourself this season of rest, Kate. Stay in the Word, take your vitamins, drink lots of water, soak up sunshine and fresh air, walk more and more each day, and you'll be fine. You will move on. Your path has already been chunked."

Kate grinned and hugged her friend. "I've said it before. What would I do without you?"

"I'm praying for you as well as for Mike and Laura and Mary. Now, tell me how I can pray for your friend in Texas. From our brief phone conversation, I gather she's in some kind of trouble."

"Amy weighs heavy on my heart every minute of the day. She needs lots of prayer. Before I tell you about her, I want to ask you something."

"Yes?"

"Do you have a recipe for raisin scones?"

Amy collapsed when Thomas finally stopped hitting her and sent the other men out of the room. He pulled her onto his lap. At first, she resisted his embrace, shattered by the pain and humiliation she'd just endured. But it felt good to have his arms around her and to breathe in the scent of his sweat mixed with aftershave. She fell against his chest, weeping.

"Baby, baby," he crooned. "You're gonna be fine." He smoothed her hair with gentle fingers. "I hated to do it, but I had to. You forced me, Natasha. If that john hadn't played it cool with the cops, told them he left his phone in a theater—and then wiped off fingerprints before they got their hands on it, Executive Pride would be on the hot seat, thanks to you."

All she could manage was a whisper. "I'm sorry, Thomas. I didn't mean to get you in trouble." What was she doing? Was she becoming one of those pathetic women she'd known in prison? Women who cursed their abusers one minute and said they couldn't live without them the next?

He pulled her close. "So, who's this person you texted?"

"A friend." The soles of her feet burned and throbbed like pulsing red-hot coals. She longed to elevate them yet didn't dare move until he released her.

"Where?"

"Wyoming." The pain rocketed up her legs.

"Man? Woman?" He kissed her forehead.

"Woman."

"Why her?"

"She knows how important my animals are—or were—to me." Feeling like a traitor, she shoved mental images of her pets aside.

He patted her head. "What was someone in Wyoming supposed do for animals in Pennsylvania?"

"I don't know. Maybe call the Humane Society."

"What's her name?"

"Kate."

"Last name?"

"Neilson." Almost as soon as she said it, she realized she'd given him Kate's maiden name, not her married name. She decided not to explain. He was asking way too many questions about her best friend.

"What does she look like?"

She leaned back to see his eyes. Why did he care? "White girl. Average height. Average build."

He squeezed her to his chest and whispered in her ear. "What color is her hair, baby?"

She hesitated. Why was he so interested in Kate? "Depends. She changes it every now and then."

"What color is it right now?"

"I have no idea. Haven't seen her lately."

"What does she do for a living?"

Amy shrugged. "She's married."

He raised an eyebrow.

"She doesn't have to work."

His other eyebrow shot up. "Does she—?" The phone on his belt rang.

She slid onto the bed. "I'll let you answer that." Maybe he would forget about Kate and stop asking questions.

Thomas put the phone to his ear. "Yeah?" As he stood, his leg rubbed against her calf.

A shockwave of pain shot all the way to her ribs. Amy sucked in her breath and curled into a fetal position. How was she going to survive the night with men who wouldn't have any idea how raw and tender her legs and feet were? And who wouldn't care even if they did know.

"Three new broads?" Thomas was saying. "Great. Hey, the border work is..." He gave Amy a sidelong glance. "Hang on." Hurrying to the door, he punched the code and slipped out of the room.

Kate fastened her snow boots and zipped her jacket. The sun was shining, and she finally felt like going outdoors again. She stepped off the porch but stopped to soak in the beauty of the snow-covered mountains in the distance. The snow that coated the ranch grounds and roofs sparkled, and the breeze that nipped at her cheeks felt wonderful. She filled her lungs with the crisp air. Maybe she wouldn't be so glum if she got out more.

She found Mike outside a stall watching Laura's horse, Honey. The mare paced the stall, stopping only to kick at her belly. Tramp sat next to him. Kate sneezed. The hay dust always did that to her, yet she loved the earthy barn smells.

Mike reached for her hand. "Bless you."

Tramp licked Kate's other hand. She scratched his ears. "Is Honey okay?"

Mike nodded. "She's in the first stage of labor and doing good, though she's foaling later in the year than we like."

The amber-colored mare snapped at her sweaty flank and pawed the straw, her tail switching about her legs.

Kate frowned. "She seems hot and uncomfortable."

"Yeah, that's normal for stage one." He caressed her cheek. "I'm glad to see you out of the house, sweetheart."

"It feels good to be out and to have your arms around me." She burrowed into his coat. "I'm sorry I haven't been much fun lately."

He pulled her close. "We have to give it time."

"Can you leave Honey for a couple minutes to help me with a project?"

"Sure. This could take a while. Mares usually birth at night. What do you need?"

"I thought I'd search for Aunt Mary's radio and telephone. Dymple suggested she might not sleep so much if she could work her prayer line again. And I'm hoping that having something to do will keep her from talking about *that man* all the time. Sometimes I think she's not just imagining him, but that she's talking about a real person."

He pushed back his hat to run his fingers through his hair. "The funny thing is, she glares at Mom every time she says it."

They crossed the barn to the stall where the boxes were stacked. Tramp curled in a corner and promptly went to sleep. The horse in the next stall nickered and shuffled its feet.

Mike shifted a parcel. "You did a good job labeling these. We shouldn't have much trouble finding the right box."

They began reading the contents listed on the sides of the cartons. "Let me know if you get tired," Mike said. "I'll pull a bale over for you to sit on."

"Thanks." Kate kissed his cheek. "You're so good to me."

He touched his lips to her forehead, like the very first time he kissed her.

Kate's pulse quickened. "Don't you dare try to distract me, Michael Duncan. I'm on a mission."

He nuzzled her neck. "Me, too..."

She pushed him away. "Later, my love."

"Is that a promise?" He reached for another box.

"That's a promise."

He grinned. "I'll be counting the minutes."

She slid a box around to read the label. "Can I ask you something, Mike?"

"Sure. What's on your mind?"

"Guess."

His forehead wrinkled. "Our hands are tied until we know where Amy is, Kate."

"I talked with Walt today. He said the last name of that Thomas guy is Mendiola. He's known around Dallas-Fort Worth nightclubs for being a smooth talker, and for always having a beautiful woman at his side."

Mike cocked an eyebrow. "Interesting."

She hesitated and then blurted, "Walt likes my idea."

He stared at her. "What idea?"

"My idea to infiltrate Executive Pride."

"You mean your idea to endanger your life?" He stiffened. "Walt is spinning his wheels right now, going nowhere with the investigation. No wonder he likes your idea."

Kate leaned against the railing. Convincing Mike was going to be a challenge. "If I let Executive know that you and others are aware of where I'm at, I'll be okay."

Mike blew out a long breath. "So, what exactly is it you're thinking of doing?"

"*Infiltrate* was probably the wrong word to use." She folded her hands and steepled her forefingers. "I don't plan to worm my way inside the organization. And I wouldn't do the escort bit. Instead, I could check to see if Executive needs hostesses for booths at upcoming conventions, that kind of thing."

"How does Walt fit into this plan of yours?"

"He could hang out at the convention, look for Amy, keep an eye on me. And contact the police if things turn ugly."

"So you admit things could get dicey."

"Nothing about life is safe. The plane could crash on the way there."

"That's not what I'm talking about, and you know it, Kate."

She stepped closer to take his hands. "If I've learned anything these past couple of years, it's to trust God, to listen to his voice and obey it." She wrapped her arms around his neck. "We're all Amy has, and I believe God wants me to help her. I have street smarts and a bit of an 'in' at Executive. I want to pursue it, even if it's a dead end." She kissed his cheek. "Walt doesn't think it's a dead end. He has a hunch, and I have a hunch there's a connection there."

He clasped her shoulders. "If you go, I'll go with you. But before we make any decisions, I'd like to pray about this to make sure we're doing the right thing." Mike rubbed his jaw. "Could be there's a civilian SWAT team for hire in Texas. You open to that?"

Kate laughed. "Even if there was such a thing, we'd have to find Amy first."

"Did you forget that her text suggested she doesn't want to be found?"

"That's not the real Amy. I know it's not. She's in some kind of danger." She grasped his forearms. "We have to act fast. The longer she's missing, the harder it'll be to find her. Is it okay if I ask Walt to see if Executive is involved in any upcoming conventions?"

"Aren't you getting the cart before the horse? I thought we were going to pray about this."

"Knowing what's available will help us determine whether or not my idea is even feasible."

"Okay." At the sound of a whinny, he kissed her cheek and hurried across the barn, Tramp right behind him.

Kate trailed the pair into Honey's stall, where the mare now lay on the straw bedding.

Mike sent Tramp out of the stall before pulling Honey's tail aside to reveal a large, dripping, white sac of fluid. "Her water just broke. Guess she's not waiting until dark to deliver this one." He shifted his position to rub the mare's neck. "You're doing good, girl. Won't be long."

They stepped out of the stall, and Mike latched the gate.

"Is there anything we can do to help her?" Sympathy pains washed through Kate, along with a wave of sorrow. She'd rejected her one chance to have a baby of her own.

"We'll leave her alone, unless she gets into trouble. This is her second pregnancy, so she should do fine. Her first birth was trouble-free." Mike folded an arm around Kate. "Will you be okay."

"I think I can handle it. Is it all right if I stay?"

"I'd appreciate your help." He tipped her chin up. "Foaling is messy."

"I don't mind." She eased into his embrace and let her husband's kisses drive her worries from her mind.

Chapter Fifteen

Amy handed her lunch tray to the boy who stood beside her bed. The slender child couldn't have been more than nine or ten. She smiled. "Thank you."

He took the tray without responding or making eye contact and left her bedroom. The boys and girls who brought her food and picked up her empty dishes, who took her dirty laundry and returned it clean, who vacuumed and dusted her suite and swabbed her bathroom, children who painted her nails without saying a word—they were her only contacts with the other employees, other than Thomas's thugs.

Yesterday, she'd realized the kids all had identical tattoos on their shoulders. The markings were simple and small—plain blue initials surrounded by a black circle. But what did "TM" stand for? Made more sense to use "EP" to indicate where they worked.

According to Thomas, a large segment of EP clients preferred fresh young bodies. Did these emotionless children work day and night? She brushed the dreadful thought aside and considered her own "advanced age," as Thomas phrased it. She was older than the kids, but she wasn't ancient. Ancient was the thirty-five-year-old hooker she met in prison who looked sixty-five. Of course, that woman was a streetwalker, not a cradled-in-luxury call girl, like herself. If she took care of her body, she'd wow the johns for years to come.

Amy settled into the pillows that lined the head of her bed. *Thomas must think I still look okay.* He was planning to use footage from her nightly sessions in the porn movies he sold online. He'd also promised she'd eventually get to do some real acting.

For the time being, she was supposed to act natural, whatever that meant in a brothel. It wasn't like she enjoyed servicing the johns. However, she'd been instructed to pretend each one was the best lover she'd ever encountered, so that's what she did. Amy shrugged. Maybe she was a real actor after all.

She checked the clock. Just a few more hours, and she'd have to go back to work, whether she felt like it or not. Five days after the beating, she could barely walk. Though the bamboo rod wasn't supposed to leave marks, the soles of her feet were swollen and pus-filled.

The equally distended welts on her legs and the cut on her knee from the bathroom mirror leaked fluid. She felt feverish, like she had the flu. And the thought of working another night was almost more than she could bear.

Twisting her legs, she examined her calves. The inflamed traces of her faded tattoos made her sick to her stomach. She was about to crawl to the bathroom for more ibuprofen, when the door opened and Damon strode in.

Her breath caught. What now?

He threw clothing on the bed. "Get dressed."

She hated the way anybody could walk in on her without knocking and do anything they wanted to her. And she despised Damon with his arrogant swagger.

"Move it, whore! We leave in five minutes." He left, slamming the door behind him.

She crawled to the end of the bed and picked up the clothing. A long-sleeved knit shirt, sweatpants and a sweat jacket, plus a coat. Amazing. The only clothing she'd been given so far came from Victoria's Secret and its ilk.

They must be taking her outside the building. Was that a good thing or a bad thing? Her heart began to pound. She tried to see the positive side. At least she'd get a change of scenery. And breathe real air again. Even if it was winter air. Surely Dallas winters, if that's where she was, weren't as cold as Pittsburgh winters.

Pulling the sweatpants over her raw calves one leg at a time was slow going. She kept at it until she'd maneuvered the pants above her hips. Donning the socks hurt her feet as much as the pants hurt her legs. Finally, with a whispered, "Hurry, Natasha," she slipped the shirt over her head.

As the top settled onto her shoulders, she realized what she'd just said. She narrowed her eyelids. She was not Natasha. She was Amy. Thomas might have stolen her life, but he couldn't have her name. She slid her arms into the jacket. The warm clothing felt heavenly after weeks of wearing nearly nothing.

She crawled to the bathroom. No matter where they took her, she wanted to at least brush her teeth and comb her hair. No time for makeup. Besides, she couldn't stand up to see herself in the mirror. If she looked as awful as she felt, she didn't want to see her reflection. Inching back to the bed, she put on the coat and tried to ignore the fear that fluttered like frantic moths against her ribs.

The door opened again. Damon was followed by a man who wore a headset and a coat and pushed a wheelchair. They lifted her into the chair, and Damon rolled her out the door and down the long hallway.

At the end of the corridor, an elevator door stood open. Damon bumped the wheelchair over the threshold. Amy winced and wished she'd taken a pain pill before they left.

The other man punched a button. Within moments, the doors parted, and a gust of wind swished inside the elevator. She slid the coat's zipper to her chin, surprised by how cold the outdoor air felt, air she hadn't breathed in weeks. Or was it months?

All she could see was sky and the tops of buildings. And a helicopter. She gripped the wheelchair arms, fearing the venture would lead to a hell worse than what she'd already endured.

Damon guided the wheelchair to the helicopter. He and the pilot lifted her out of the chair and into the aircraft. She strapped her seatbelt across her shoulder and lap as they climbed inside.

The helicopter momentarily hovered above the building before it whooshed across the Dallas business district. At least she thought she was in Dallas. Could be Calcutta, for all she knew. The buildings ranged from short to tall, from flat roofs to round or pointed pinnacles.

Just as the motion combined with her ever-present nausea was about to make her lose her scant lunch, the helicopter settled onto the roof of a flat-topped building. Again, Damon wordlessly dumped her into the wheelchair and whisked her toward an elevator. They descended several floors in solitude before the doors opened and two men and three women stepped in.

Damon clamped his hands on her shoulders, an obvious signal for her to keep quiet. She drank in the sight of *normal* people, people who chatted amongst themselves without fear. People dressed for success, not sex, whose clothing wasn't doused with perfume or aftershave.

Amy and her guards exited the elevator before the others. Three-quarters of the way down a hall lined with dentist and optometrist offices, Damon checked both ways before knocking on an unmarked door. The door slowly opened, and she was quickly wheeled to a room just inside the door.

She recognized the medicinal smell of a doctor's office and the familiar shape of gynecology stirrups. Did they think she was pregnant? She was nauseated, yet she couldn't be pregnant. Thomas had started her on the pill the moment he put her to work. Maybe they were planning to do an abortion. But shouldn't that be her choice? Then again, the last time she'd been able to choose for herself was the morning she boarded the plane bound for Dallas.

Damon and the pilot transferred her from the chair to the exam table.

Amy sucked in a breath to keep from screaming. Each time they moved her hurt worse than the time before.

The doctor, if that's what he was, handed her a paper gown. "Take off everything and put this on."

Amy hesitated. "What are you—?"

Damon snarled. "Do what he says."

The man motioned toward the doorway. "Have a chair in the hall."

"I'm keeping an eye on her." Damon folded his arms.

The doctor reached for the curtain. "Then give her some privacy."

"Whores don't get privacy." Damon sneered, but he stepped back when the doctor yanked the curtain between them.

Amy pulled her shirt over her head and gritted her teeth to keep from crying out when the sweatpants stuck to the backs of her legs. She folded the clothing at the head of the table and slipped her arms through the holes in the paper gown. She shivered. Warmth was such a short-lived pleasure. "I'm ready."

The doctor opened the curtain. "Slide your butt to the end and place your feet in the stirrups." He tugged two latex gloves from a dispenser.

She did as he said, letting only her heels touch the vinyl. When her feet came in contact with the cold metal supports, she flinched.

He carefully elevated one of her feet and then the other. With slow gentle movements, he examined the cut on her knee and her infected calves. He scowled at Damon. "Was this necessary?"

In her peripheral vision, Amy saw Damon shrug. "She asked for it."

The doctor didn't respond. Instead, he slid a plastic sleeve onto a thermometer and stuck it under her tongue. Then he proceeded with a vaginal exam.

She clutched the sides of the table. Did every EP employee have to go through this?

He finished, rolled the gloves off his hands and tossed them into a trash receptacle. "Everything's normal here, but I'll need to do some blood work to determine the severity of the infection in her legs." He talked to Damon, not her. "After I do a pap smear and a breast exam."

He took the thermometer from her mouth and glanced at the readout. "This is one sick woman. You'll have to take better care of her, if you want to make any money off her."

Amy felt like one of the horses at the stables where she worked. While the vets examined the animals from head to hoof, they discussed their condition with the owners. She was less than an animal. She was an object, a possession, a commodity, neither human nor animal. But at least she wasn't pregnant.

When the doctor was done with that part of the exam, he swabbed her legs and feet with a strong-smelling solution that stung and cooled at the same time. She was grateful when he replaced the curtain so she could put on her clothes.

She dressed slowly, relishing her momentary solitude on the tiny vinyl island behind the thin nylon barrier. Never again would she take privacy for granted, that is if she ever regained control of her life. This was worse than prison. Why had she so easily given in to Thomas? She remembered the snakes and grimaced. Even so, she couldn't let him control her forever.

Damon barked, "Hurry up!"

She wiggled the pants up and over her hips, biting her lip against the pain.

The doctor thrust the curtain aside, took two vials of blood, and then handed Damon several small squares of paper. "Get these prescriptions filled today and start the medications immediately. Once her legs and feet heal, use cocoa butter to reduce the scarring."

He paused. "I repeat. Don't delay. Get these filled today, or—"

Damon waved away the warning and pushed the wheelchair to the table. He took Amy's arm. The doctor grasped her other arm and leg, and they lowered her into the chair.

"Tell Thomas I don't want her to work for at least a week," the doctor said. "Maybe two weeks, depending on the blood results and how long it takes for her to heal. And keep her off her feet."

Damon frowned. "He won't like that."

The doctor dug through a file cabinet. He handed Damon a green sheet of paper. "Here are floor exercises she can do to maintain muscle tone."

Amy watched his face, but he avoided her gaze. Maybe if he didn't make eye contact he could continue to pretend she was a piece of equipment.

"Remind him he about the one he lost because he didn't listen to me." The doctor glanced at Amy and quickly averted his eyes.

She twisted toward Damon. "What's he talking about?" Thomas had warned her again and again that she wouldn't last long in the business if she didn't take care of herself.

He hissed, "Shut it, slut," and propelled the chair out of the room.

Kate gripped the stall door, wishing she could help the mare.

Honey grunted and pushed, and then pushed again. A dark spot appeared in the sac that bubbled from the horse's rump.

"Mike, I see something."

"That's a hoof. If the foal is positioned correctly, it'll be a front leg, not a back one."

The mare whinnied, stood, and plopped onto her other side. She rolled about before lowering her head on the straw.

"Is that good for her to do? Won't she hurt her baby?"

"She's just moving the foal to a better birthing position."

Honey pushed several times, her flanks quivering between the muscle spasms. The mare clenched again, three times. Fluids squirted from her body with each thrust. Finally, she dropped her head down, her breathing heavy and loud, her nostrils flaring.

Kate elbowed Mike. "That's a lot of water, yet there's still plenty in that sac."

"She's urinating. Might even poop before this is over and done with. I told you it'd get messy."

The pungent odor of horse urine mixed with straw wafted upward. Kate wrinkled her nose.

The mare got up again and staggered a few feet before rolling onto her knees. The amniotic sac dangled like a translucent melon from the tiny hoof. A second hoof appeared under her tail, barely visible in the vulva.

"Uh-oh." Mike yanked his two-way from his belt. "It's upside down. I'll radio Mom to call the vet. He's on his way over but said to call with problems."

"Your mom wasn't back from town when I left the house. I can run over and call him."

"His cell number's on the bulletin board by her computer. I just hope he's in range, not sandwiched between mountains."

Though she could hear the urgency in his voice, she took a moment to ask. "How can you tell it's the wrong direction?"

"The foal should look like it's diving out of the mare, feet pointed down. Those are pointed up." He grimaced. "Not good."

She squeezed his hand and was about to release it, but Mike held tight. "Don't slip and fall."

She smiled. "That's how we met. Remember?"

"How could I forget?" He waved her out the door. "Hurry, but don't..."

"I won't."

Tramp barked and took off for the door. She zipped her coat and trotted after him. "I'm coming, I'm coming."

Doc Hall was parking his pickup in front of the barn when Kate and the collie exited the side door. Tramp bounded toward the truck as the vet switched off the motor and opened the door.

Kate rushed over, each breath erupting into a cloud of frozen moisture. "I was just about to call you, Dr. Hall. Mike says the mare's in trouble. The foal is upside down." The diesel-laced air made her sneeze.

"Bless you." Dr. Hall climbed out of the truck cab and reached behind the seat for his medical bag. "I had a feeling things weren't copacetic." He placed his hat on top of his salt-and-pepper crewcut, closed the door and walked with her to the barn, snow crunching beneath their feet.

He held the door for her. "How long has Honey been in labor?"

"Not long, probably less than an hour. As soon as her water broke, the foal's foot came through."

He stopped at the sink just inside the door, removed his jacket, rolled up his sleeves and began scrubbing his arms. "That's how it usually is with horses. Quick."

Mike came around the corner. "Good to see you, Doc. She's struggling."

At the sound of a loud snort, they hastened to the stall, Tramp at their heels.

Dr. Hall stepped inside, drying his arms on a towel.

The mare tried to get to her feet and then fell back.

Kate grabbed Mike's shoulder. "Poor thing, she's exhausted."

The vet hung his hat on a peg and dropped to one knee before the horse. He patted her neck. "Remember me, Miss Honey? I'm here to help you. Just like last time." He pulled back her tail and saw the protruding feet covered by the bluish-white membrane. "Mike, come hold her head."

Mike opened the gate.

Tramp tried to follow. Kate grabbed his collar. "Stay."

The dog whined and sat beside her.

Dr. Hall dug a large jar of petroleum jelly from his bag. "I'll have to turn this one." With quick motions, he slathered the gel from his hands to his upper arms and then hunched over the horse's rump.

Kate leaned her forehead against a post and closed her eyes. *Please help Honey and her foal make it through this ordeal, God.* She took a breath. *And me, too.*

Amy lifted her head as two of the young girls who cleaned her room walked in. Both wore spaghetti-strap tops and short shorts, heavy eye makeup, rouge and lipstick. Their dark hair was unnaturally streaked with yellow highlights, and their expressionless faces looked older than their small childish bodies. Like the others, their shoulders were tattooed with a circled "TM."

One girl carried a white paper sack, the other a stack of clothing. They set the items on the end of her bed and then, like miniature soldiers, stood at attention, their eyes blank and distant.

Amy sat up. "Thank you."

Neither girl responded, nor did they move.

"Do you need something?" *Besides soap and water?* They smelled like they'd showered in perfume.

"Watch drink pill." The girl's heavily accented voice was barely audible.

"Oh." Amy flipped back the bedding and wormed her way to the foot of the bed. She picked up the bag and pulled out prescription bottles. While she read the instructions on the labels, one girl went into the bathroom and came back with a glass of water.

"Thank you. You're very kind."

A hint of a smile flashed across the youth's face. One appeared to be Asian, the other Hispanic. Maybe they didn't speak because they didn't know English, or maybe Thomas told them not to talk to her.

The moment she downed the pills, the girls took the vials from her, dropped them into the sack and carried it to the door. One girl stood on tiptoe to punch in the code. Amy tried to catch the pattern, but her finger motions were too fast. How did it happen that children, children who were probably illegal immigrants as well as EP prisoners, dispensed her medications and knew the code to get in and out of her room and she didn't? Her life was upside down and backward.

She examined the clothing. Three more sets of soft, warm, body-covering sweats. Apparently Thomas wasn't getting rid of her yet.

CHAPTER SIXTEEN

The door latch clicked, startling Amy, like it always did. What now? Did Thomas have second thoughts about the clothing?

Alfonzo stepped in and surveyed the room before waving in two women. As quickly as he'd come, he left. The women stayed.

"Hi." A willowy black woman with gorgeous hair held up a CD player and a tote bag. "In case you don't remember us, I'm Mikaylah Lovington, Mike for short. I brought snacks and music." She was dressed in a feather-trimmed scarlet teddy with see-through lace sides, fishnet stockings and stiletto heels.

The other woman, a curvaceous redhead similarly attired in blue strutted to the bed. "I'm Janessa Valentine. I brought catalogs. Thomas asked us to help you pick out a dress for when you're better and can go out on the town with him."

Amy squinted at the women. Was this some kind of trick?

Mikaylah eyed Amy's feet. "I see you got the special treatment."

Janessa dropped the catalogs on the coffee table and reached for the wheelchair. "I'll push you over to a loveseat."

The door opened again. One of the young girls held the door while the other carried in a tray with three glasses and a pitcher of what looked like cranberry juice. She set the tray beside the catalogs and walked away. Without comment, both girls marched into the hallway, the door closing after them.

Amy maneuvered into the wheelchair, reeling with the sudden influx of new people into her empty world. "What's with those girls? They never—"

"Have you started your exercises yet?" Mikaylah spoke rather loudly. "They'll help you get better faster."

Amy nodded.

Janessa parked the chair beside a loveseat and helped Amy transfer onto it. Then she pulled the other loveseat close and sat down, the coffee table between them.

"Thanks." Amy was breathless from the exertion. "Are you two...?"

"Mm-hmm." Mikaylah's nod was vigorous. "We're EP employees, just like you. Been with the company almost a year now." She plugged the player into a wall outlet and dropped in a CD before reaching for her snack bag. "Gum anyone?"

Smooth saxophone jazz filled the room, dancing through the heavy fragrances that trailed the women into her suite. Lightheaded and feverish, Amy felt as though she was spinning with the music.

Janessa took gum but Amy said, "No, thank you."

"Maybe later." Mikaylah sat beside Janessa. After she removed a piece of gum from the foil and popped it into her mouth, she spread the metallic wrapper on her knee, smoothing it with the backside of a long, red fingernail. "Where do you want to start, Janessa?"

The redhead held up a catalog. "I like this one. They usually have a good selection." She leafed through the pages and then pointed at one of the pictures. "I think this outfit would be good with Natasha's coloring. What do you think?"

Mikaylah, who'd been doodling a design on the foil with her long fingernail, slid the paper onto the page. "Nice. Gold is a perfect color for her."

Janessa moved to the other side of the coffee table. She put the catalog on Amy's lap and knelt beside her. "Do you like it?"

Amy started to push the wrapper out of the way, but Janessa whispered, "Read." Amy stared at the squiggles until she realized they formed a word. *Camera.* Without moving her head, she searched the room. Janessa aimed her chin at the far corner of the suite.

Amy took a long breath. She was an actress onstage twenty-four-seven, acting out her own pathetic life. It was one thing to be recorded in the brothel, but in her own bedroom? She released the breath. "I like the way the skirt flares." She tried to sound enthused. "Do I really get to go out with Thomas?"

"We take turns." Janessa pointed at another dress. "What do you think of this one with the bling-bling collar?"

"It's cute. How do we mark these?" Amy asked. "I don't have a pen."

Janessa folded the corner of the page down. "Like that."

"Can I see?" Mikaylah asked.

Janessa handed her the catalog.

Mikaylah spit her gum into the foil and scrunched it into a tiny ball. "I hate it when gum loses its flavor." She held up a box of Wrigley's Extra. "Anyone else want one?"

This time, Amy took a piece. Maybe she'd think of something to communicate to her coworkers. Could she trust them? The nastiest women in prison were kittens compared to Executive Pride men. What were these two females like underneath their teased hair, elaborate makeup and sweet smiles?

Mikaylah laid the catalog on the coffee table. "I brought a snack." She reached into her bag and produced a small vegetable tray. "Ta-da! Veggies. With low-fat dip, of course." She worked the plastic top off the tray before setting it on the coffee table. "And salt-free rice cakes."

"Rice cakes, yuck." Janessa pouted. "I was hoping for something with a little flavor."

Mikaylah wagged a finger at her. "Got to keep that girlish figure."

Janessa crossed her eyes and lifted the pitcher to pour each of them a glass of juice.

Mikaylah lowered her eyelids. "This was the best I could do." She dug through the tote, pulled out a deck of cards, and gave it to Janessa.

Amy looked from Janessa to Mikaylah. "Can I ask a question?"

Like cornered animals, her companions' expressions grew wary and their focus shifted from her face to the camera in the opposite corner. Mikaylah folded her arms. "Don't know if we'll have an answer."

"I was just wondering where we met before."

Janessa patted Amy's arm. "It's hard to remember everyone you meet and all that happens during 'welcome week.'"

Amy winced. If only she could forget that first week altogether.

Mikaylah placed three napkins on the coffee table. "Maybe you'll get to do the sports show with us."

"What happens at a sports show?" Amy asked. Was it some kind of competition between brothels?

"EP has another group of women who only do escort service and events." The dark-skinned beauty flipped her black curls behind her shoulder. "There aren't enough of them for the sports show, so Janessa and I and some of the others have been assigned to help them out. They need models for sports clothing, people to host booths for golf accessories, energy drinks, kayaks, camping gear, skis, all kinds of stuff. I think it'll be fun."

"I'd love to do that." The few minutes she'd spent away from EP that morning felt heavenly, even with Damon breathing his foul breath down her neck.

Janessa dealt the cards, sliding a silver square to Amy beneath one card. *Choker.*

Choke? Amy pretended to squeeze her own throat.

Janessa responded with a barely discernible head shake.

Mikaylah, whose back was to the camera, dropped her cards. "Whoops, you're going to have to deal them again, sista."

As Janessa gathered the playing cards and redistributed them, Mikaylah etched something on another foil and pushed it front of Amy.

Amy tried to decipher the word. *Necklace.* Oh. *Choker necklace.* She touched her throat.

Mikaylah nodded.

Amy looked at Mikaylah and then Janessa. Neither of them wore a choker.

Lips barely moving, Janessa whispered, "Mi-cro-phone," and jiggled her shoulders with the song's drum roll.

Microphone?

Mikaylah stuck another piece of gum in her mouth. "This sugar-free stuff is the worst for keeping its flavor." She scribbled something on the wrapper and slid it next to Amy's cards.

GPS.

Amy raised her eyebrows. This was like learning a new language. Did she mean GPS in cars?

Mikaylah picked up the hand she'd just been dealt, glanced at it, and glared at Janessa. "Hey, girlfriend, you can do better."

Janessa shrugged. "Sorry." She turned to Amy. "Shows are a nice way to see different people, different walls, diff—"

Mikaylah cranked up the stereo and sang along with the vocalist. "You'll never know, no, you'll never know...ooh, ooh, ooh...the tears..."

Janessa motioned to Amy. "You start."

Amy laid a card on the table and picked up a catalog. She turned pages, pretending to study each outfit before she inched her gum wrapper onto a page. With the corner of her nail, she wrote *ask T about show* and slid the foil off the table near Mikaylah's foot.

The sassy woman played her card before reading the foil.

Amy watched her face fluctuate from fear to affection to... She wasn't sure what she saw. Maybe resolve.

Finally, she spoke. "I know what cranks his case."

A soft smile flitted across Janessa's lips. "So do I."

Mikaylah raised her voice. "Thomas loves all of us—women, men, boys and girls. We're his family, and he's our big daddy. You just can't help loving that beautiful man."

"Even when you don't want to." Though Janessa whispered the words with her hand over her lips, Amy heard and understood her feelings. Her new friends were no different than she was.

They were all needy little flies trapped in Thomas's sticky web and somehow pleased to be his prey.

Was that how the young ones felt? How the men felt, too? How could he have such a hold on all of them? Did anyone ever break loose from his snare?

Kate paced and prayed from one end of the barn to the other, and then prayed and paced some more. Like Mike and Doc, she didn't relax until the foal was birthed, the placenta delivered, and the cord separated from the foal. Finally, the men stood and stepped back. Both animals were getting to their feet, an almost-humorous challenge for the newborn. Yet no one laughed. This was a crucial moment.

Kate couldn't stop the tears that rolled down her cheeks. The foal was wet, wobbly and adorable. And Honey was okay, thank God.

The horses stood motionless for a few minutes, resting. Then the baby began to search for her mother's udder. The three humans barely breathed while she rooted about. The moment she began to noisily nurse, slurping and smacking with abandon, Kate and the men shared a sigh of relief.

Kate wiped tears from her face. "Does that mean the foal is okay?"

"She'll be fine," Doc said. "But she has one more milestone to cross, and that's to expel meconium."

"What's that?"

"It's the first feces a foal—or a human, for that matter, passes." He leaned against the railing that divided the stalls, his dripping hands extended. "Meconium has several components—swallowed amniotic fluid, bile, intestinal secretions, and the like. If she doesn't expel it within three or four hours, Mike will need to give her an enema. Impaction can cause severe abdominal pain."

"I'll keep an eye on her." Mike ran his fingers through his hair. "That was a tough one, Doc."

The vet knelt to scrub his arms in the bucket of soapy water Kate delivered to the stall so he wouldn't have to walk to the sink to clean up. "I was afraid we might lose them both, but Honey hung on." He scratched at the end of his nose with the back of his hand, leaving bubbles on his grey-flecked mustache. "She's a tough little lady. However, I'm not sure she had one more push left in her."

Kate tossed Dr. Hall a clean towel. "I can't believe a grey horse came from Honey's reddish coloring." She looked at Mike. "Yes, I know. The proper term is *sorrel.*"

Doc studied the newborn. "Not a big surprise, really, with Lightning as her sire."

Mike stepped out of the stall. "We won't know the filly's coloring for sure until she sheds this coat. She does have a nice thick coat, doesn't she, Doc?"

"Good thing. The weatherman says it's going to be a long cold winter."

Kate wrapped an arm around Mike's waist. "I hope she keeps that white star on her forehead. And those cute stockings on her feet."

"Mom was hoping for distinctive markings. Too bad she missed the birth. She likes to watch."

Doc got to his feet and handed the towel and pail to Kate. "I saw Laura in Rawlins today. Don't think she saw me. Seemed fairly caught up with her escort."

Mike turned to Kate. "Do you know anything about an escort?"

She shrugged. "All she said was that she was going to town."

"It's none of my business," Doc said. "I was just surprised to see her with Hughes."

Mike's mouth dropped. "Todd Hughes?"

"Yep. They were huddled together cozy like. Or maybe he was helping her cross a slippery sidewalk. Hard to say. However, if I were a betting man..."

Mike opened his mouth and then closed it.

Kate patted his arm. "There's probably an explanation."

Doc's brow furrowed. "Uh, sorry. I didn't mean to meddle. Probably nothing." He grabbed his hat and settled it on his head. "Glad your mare got that over and done with. Maybe I can get a full night's sleep for a change."

He picked up his bag and stepped out of the stall. "I think your horses will both be fine. Give me a call if you have any concerns."

Tramp sidled up to the vet, nudging his hand with his nose.

Doc bent to scratch the dog behind his ears. "You're my bud, aren't you, boy? We spent a lot of time together after those wolves tore into you."

He straightened. "Your dog's doing good, considering his age and what he went through. Another patient I wasn't sure was going to make it."

Kate smiled. "Must have been all those people who were praying."

"Not the first time I've seen prayer do the trick."

They walked him to the door. He put on his coat and shook their hands. "Congratulations on your new filly. She's a beauty. Give me a call when you name her, and I'll add it to her record."

"Thanks, Doc, for everything," Mike said. "Have Connie send us a bill."

"Will do." The vet reached for the door, but then he stopped. "How's your bison herd doing? You haven't called about gunshot wounds lately."

Mike slipped his hands into his back pockets. "They seem to be healthy and safe, for the moment, anyway."

"Good. I'm glad to hear it." The vet saluted goodbye and exited the barn.

Kate squeezed Mike's arm. "I'd better check on Aunt Mary. She was napping when I left the house."

"I'll change out the straw in the stall." His brow furrowed. "What do you make of the stuff Doc said about Mom and Hughes?"

The worry lines on his forehead made her sad. "That was a surprise. Still, we don't know all the facts."

"Yeah, right."

"Maybe your mom is home by now. If she hasn't started dinner, I will."

"Sounds good."

She zipped her coat, hugged him and moved to go, but he held tight.

"What?"

"Thanks for helping today. I know it must have been hard for you."

She stood on her tiptoes to kiss him. "It was hard and scary—and wonderful. That new colt is amazing. So perfect and alert. Standing, nursing, looking around. And only a few minutes old."

"Uh, sweetheart. Remember?"

"Remember what?"

"A colt is a male. This is a female. She's a filly."

"Oh, right." She traced an "f" in the palm of her hand. "F for female filly."

The laugh lines beside Mike's eyes creased.

Kate punched his arm. "Are you laughing at me?"

"Wouldn't think of it. I was just thinking how cute you are."

"Uh-huh, sure." Kate smiled at the suckling noises the filly made. "What are you going to name her?"

"That's up to Mom. It's her foal."

"I can't wait to hear what she decides."

"I just hope it's a fitting name for Lightning's offspring."

"Oh, my." Kate threw back her head, laughing. "Aren't we the arrogant owner of the sire."

"You have to admit he's a handsome horse."

"And his daughter is lovely. I'm sure your mom will choose an appropriate name for her." Kate grinned. "With my help, of course. Remember, I was the one who named Trudy. Everyone thought it was a great name."

Mike laughed. "How could I forget a baby bison named Trudy?"

Kate kissed his cheek and hurried toward the house, crisp snow creaking beneath her feet like old gate hinges. Yard lights illuminated her breath and reflected diamonds in the blue-glazed snow. Her spirit soared. What a beautiful night and what a marvel she'd just experienced. God's creation never failed to astound her. The thrill of it all made her want a baby even more. She whispered, "I wish I could have a baby, too."

A clump of snow plopped from a nearby tree, and her mother's voice, one she'd thought she'd forgotten, came to her. *If wishes were horses, Katy Joy, we'd all take a ride.*

She grinned. How many times had her mom told her that? "Okay, God. I'll enjoy Laura's filly without feeling sorry for myself. Tell Mom 'thanks.'"

She rounded a corner. "Aunt Mary!"

Balanced on her walker and accompanied by Prissy, Mary blocked the snowy pathway.

"What are you doing out here without a coat? And in your slippers?"

"Just looking for my husband." Mary offered a feeble smile. "He's late for dinner."

Kate yanked off her coat and flung it across her aunt's shoulders. Prissy pranced and whined to be picked up, but Kate ignored the dog. She pulled the hood over her aunt's hair. Frost was already forming from her breath. "Stay here. I'll get Mike to carry you."

"I have to find Dean."

"We'll find him after we get you inside." She buttoned the top button. "Don't move. I'll be right back." She darted for the barn, slipping and sliding. "Mike, help!"

Mike clasped the elderly woman close to his chest, waiting for Kate to open the backdoor. Mary was so lightweight, how could she not be chilled through and through?

Kate opened the storm door and then the house door.

Two steps and they were inside. The lights were already on. He sniffed. Spaghetti?

Laura met them in the dining room. "I was just wondering where everyone…oh, my goodness. What happened to Mary?"

"I found her on the path just now." Kate touched Mary's leg. "Do you have any idea how long she's been outside?"

"I've only been home ten or fifteen minutes. I just assumed both of you were napping. No lights were on. The backdoor was ajar, but I figured one of the dogs had somehow nudged it open."

Mike gave his mom a long cold stare. She'd been cuddling with Hughes while they helped her mare through a difficult birth. On top of that, Kate's aunt could have frozen to death because no one was watching her. "We need to check for frostbite."

He carried Mary to the couch. Once they determined her core temperature was good and she showed no signs of frostbite, they wrapped her in a quilt and set her in a chair beside the fireplace.

Kate tucked the blanket around Mary's feet. "Laura, would you mind if we ate in the living room with TV trays? I want to feed Aunt Mary, so we don't have to unwrap her arms from the blanket."

"Great idea," Laura said. "It's a good night to cozy up to the fire."

They'd just started eating, when Kate turned to Mike. "Did you tell your mom the news?"

"Tell her what?" He didn't want to be in the same room as his mother, let alone speak to her.

"About Honey."

"What about? Oh." His focus flicked to Laura. "Honey foaled this afternoon. You missed it."

Laura frowned. "Why didn't you tell me?"

He glared at her. "You weren't here, Mom."

"I know that, Mike." She looked puzzled. "You could have called me."

Kate glanced from mother to son. "It's a filly. Right, Mike?"

Mike took a bite of spaghetti. Kate could tell his mom about the birth. He didn't feel like talking.

CHAPTER SEVENTEEN

Although she'd seen the new foal the night before, Laura was anxious to see her in daylight and headed to the barn right after breakfast the next morning. When she approached the stall, Honey nickered, stepped to the railing and hung her head over the gate. The filly slipped behind her mother. Laura stroked the mare's neck. "You did good, Honey. I heard you had a rough time, but you persevered and gave us a beautiful little filly."

As if she understood, Honey swung her head toward her offspring.

Laura laughed. "You have every right to be proud. She's perfect. I'm sorry I missed her birth."

She chewed at dry skin on her lip. Not only did she miss the foaling, Aunt Mary wandered into the snow because no one was home to keep an eye on her. Laura ran her fingers through Honey's flaxen mane. Why couldn't she enjoy a couple hours away? And why did she always have to feel guilty when she treated herself to time with Todd? It was her life.

She stepped into the stall to hook a lead rope to Honey's halter. Again, the foal hid behind her mother. Laura patted Honey's neck. "Time for some exercise, girl. Your baby will follow." She led the two of them out of the warm barn and into the snowy corral, frosted breaths haloing their heads.

The foal snuffled the cool air and then stuck her nose in the snow. With a snort, she hopped backward, eyes wide.

Laura laughed. "Welcome to winter, little one."

They circled the enclosure, Laura leading Honey. The filly trotted at the mare's side, clinging like a shadow. Laura walked backward, watching the filly. "Such a beauty you are. I bet you turn as black as your father. He started out grey like you, you know."

Horses in the other corral whinnied and nickered. Honey responded. The foal's ears perked.

Laura pulled her coat hood over her head and continued talking to the filly. "What shall we call you? Inkspot? Midnight?" She pursed her lips. No. Too common. Besides, the filly might not turn out as dark as Lightning. Maybe she should think of a name that wasn't color related. Missy? No. That was too much like *Prissy*.

Honey pricked her ears, and Laura turned to see Cyrus tromping along the path, his greasy cowboy hat crammed low on his head.

The weatherworn cowboy stomped through a snowdrift to reach the corral, his breath crystalizing before him. "So you got yourself a filly, Mrs. D. She's a purty little thing."

Laura grinned. "I'm hoping she'll be black when she loses the first coat and that she keeps her markings."

Cyrus leaned against the top railing. "I was rooting for a colt you could name Harley or Piston. You know, something powerful and full of vim and vigor, 'cause it's Lightning's foal."

"Oh, my goodness, Cyrus." Laura laughed. "Those are crazy names. Good thing she's a filly."

"So, what are you plannin' to name her?"

"I haven't the slightest idea."

He rubbed his stubbled chin. "Guess I'd better help."

"I get final say because I don't think I could ever name a horse after an engine part."

He grunted. "Well, here's one for you. Star Crossed."

"Isn't that kind of negative?"

"I like the sound of it. And she has that white star on her forehead. Or you could name her Knee-High 'cause of those sock marks on her legs."

Laura reversed the horses to circle the corral in the opposite direction.

The filly skittered to the other side of the mare.

"I like your star idea," Laura said. "Let's think of a name with 'star' in it."

A flash of white slammed against Cyrus's hat and knocked it off.

"What in tarnation?" He twisted and slipped, joining his hat in a snowbank.

Manuel came hopping through the snow. He reached down to help Cyrus get up.

Cyrus slapped his hand away and scrambled to his feet. He picked up his hat, shook off the snow and plopped it onto his head. "What in blazes are you doing here, Ortega? Aren't you s'posed to be in school?"

"I'm on my way home for the weekend." He tried to brush snow off Cyrus's shoulder, but Cyrus twisted out of reach. "You keep your bloomin' snowball-throwin' hands to yerself."

Manuel laughed. "I couldn't resist, Cyrus. You were a perfect target." He waved to Laura. "Hi, Mrs. D."

"Hi, Manuel. Good to see you."

He stuffed his bare hands in his coat pockets. "That's a muy bonita filly you got there. When was she born?"

Laura smiled. "Yesterday."

"Got it!" Cyrus said. "Starling."

Manuel gawked at him.

"Just thinkin' of a name for the filly."

"Aren't starlings those nasty black birds that kick sparrows out of birdhouses?" Manuel asked.

Laura stopped the horses near the men. "Starlings don't have the best reputations."

Honey nuzzled the filly and it immediately began to suckle.

Cyrus kicked at the snow. "Okay, so how about you spell star backwards and call her *Rats*?"

Laura put her hands on her waist. "Cyrus Moore, you are impossible today."

Manuel laughed. "How about *Estrella Blanca*?"

Cyrus glared at him. "Speak English."

"It's Spanish for white star."

Laura smiled. "I love it, a beautiful name for a pretty little horse."

"Sounds mighty high falutin' to me," Cyrus said. "Maybe I'll just call her *Rats*."

Half irritated, Laura said, "I think I smell a stubborn rat."

His eyes narrowed. "If you're so good at smelling rats, why're you hanging around Hughes?"

She glanced at Manuel. He was waving at Mike, who'd just parked Old Blue in front of the barn. "Don't call my filly stupid names." She pivoted and led the horses inside the barn without waiting for a retort. How did he know about Todd? Did Mary tell him? Or did rumors about her clandestine dates reach the ranch? She exhaled a cloud of frost. It had to happen eventually.

Maybe she should call it quits with Todd. He drank more than she liked, yet he treated her like a queen. And it was nice to have someone in her life to help her across a slippery sidewalk, to hold her hand when she was worried.

She tethered Honey to a post and began cleaning the stall. The filly didn't stray from her mother's side. In fact, she was already nursing again.

Estrella Blanca. Laura smiled. Such a beautiful name. She couldn't wait to tell the others at dinner. Too bad Dan wasn't around to enjoy the new foal.

She thought of Todd. Did he like horses as much as her husband did? They were such different men. Dan loved God and his family with every fiber of his being. She wasn't sure what Todd loved, other than himself and his ranch.

His plan to enlarge his huge spread and turn it into an exotic game ranch sounded a bit crazy to her. Yet she knew a man had to have his dreams. She was grateful Dan's dreams for a family and a guest ranch were fulfilled before he died.

They'd designed the ranch headquarters on the back of a paper placemat down at Grandma's Café one afternoon. The final layout turned out almost exactly as they'd hoped, with an adjustment or two. Dan was happy at the Whispering Pines, and so was she. Until he died.

Without him, the place felt empty. If Mike hadn't needed her to help keep things going, she might have moved away. She didn't know where, but some place where Dan's absence didn't smack her every time she turned a corner or stepped into a stall, like now.

She could see her husband walking on the path. Hear his voice greet a guest. Smell his clothes when she opened the closet. She saw him in the growing crinkles around her son's eyes, in the way Mike walked and how he wore his hat. She even saw her husband in Mike's sweet smile when he teased his wife. Though she thrilled at Mike's love for Kate, her own loss hurt so much she had to turn away.

Laura forked clean straw into the stall. More than once, she'd considered leaving the ranch to escape the pain, yet she knew she never could. Maybe that's why Todd appealed to her. She could escape the memories for a few hours yet go home to the bed she shared with her true love for so many years.

Her conflicting emotions were hard to explain, even to herself. She longed for Dan and often relived sweet memories of their time together. Yet, she wanted to distance herself from thinking about him.

Todd tried to understand the tug-of-war that tore at her heartstrings, but he'd lost his wife so long ago, he didn't seem to miss her as much as he missed having a woman around the house. Maybe he wouldn't spend so much time at the bar if there was someone to go home to. She set the pitchfork aside. What if he couldn't break his habit of hanging out at Bogie's? Would she feel just as lonely as she did now if she married him?

She pushed a loose strand of hair back under her hood. Marriage to Todd Hughes was not something she cared to think about right now, even though she liked him, could maybe learn to love him. On the other hand, Mike would never understand.

Or Cyrus, for that matter. Not that Todd would have anything to do with either of them, or Aunt Mary. For some reason, neither person could tolerate the other.

Kate held the door while her great-aunt maneuvered her walker out of the neurologist's office and onto the sidewalk. They worked their way around an icy patch in the parking lot and then Kate helped Mary get into the car. After depositing the walker in the back of the SUV, she slid in the driver's side and closed the door.

Mary laid her mittened hand on Kate's arm.

"What is it, Aunt Mary?"

"Will it hurt?"

Kate patted her aunt's hand and started the car. "Will what hurt?" She tested the heater. Thank God the motor still held a hint of warmth. They'd been in the doctor's office over an hour.

Mary fumbled with her seatbelt.

Kate reached over to fasten the strap for her.

"This, this..." Mary's gaze dropped to her lap. "This disease, or whatever you call it."

"The doctor called it Alzheimer's." Kate smiled. "You're cute in that hat, Aunt Mary." She put the car in gear. "She didn't mention pain. Just said your memory might get worse as time goes on."

She drove out of the parking lot onto the street. "You're doing great. You remember how to dress and feed yourself. You remember me and Laura and Mike, and the dogs."

Mary released a long sigh. "I don't remember where I am half the time. Or where I'm going. Sometimes I stand in my bedroom turning in circles."

"That must be really frustrating for you." Kate squeezed her hand. "But you have the three of us. We'll help you all we can. And we'll love you, no matter what." She stopped for a red light.

"You've always been such a sweetheart."

"Not always."

"You went through some rough years, yet you came through them and grew into a wonderful young woman. I'm very proud of you."

Kate peered into her aunt's eyes, delighted she sounded like her old self, at least for a moment. "I couldn't have survived without you praying for me and writing to me all those years I was in foster homes and jail and prison."

The traffic light changed and Kate maneuvered the car onto Grand Avenue. "Now it's my turn to take care of you."

"Just keep that man away from me."

Kate frowned. "What man?"

"You know."

Kate peeked at her aunt again. The light was gone from her eyes. Was *the man* imagined or real? "No, I don't know."

"She knows."

"Who?" They'd had this conversation before. Kate wanted to see if she got the same answer.

"That lady. The one I live with."

"You mean Laura?"

"She knows." Her voice was barely a murmur.

"Speaking of Laura, I told her I'd pick up some groceries while we're in Laramie."

Kate's phone rang. She pulled to the curb and picked up the phone. Maybe Laura needed something else from the store. "Hello."

"This is Walter Harnish, private investigator, calling from Dallas."

His formal introduction made her smile. "Hi, Walt. Good to hear from you. Any news?" Maybe, just maybe he'd found Amy.

"That Executive Pride bunch is contracted to supply hostesses for a big ol' convention coming up in a couple weeks."

"What kind of convention?"

"Sports show. Everything from golf shoes to backpacks, bicycles to tents, they say."

Surely Mike wouldn't object to a sports convention. "Are they hiring hostesses?"

"Got an ad in the newspaper."

"I'll call Executive's office and ask them about it. Any other news?"

"That's all I have for now. I'll keep working on it." He burped. "S'cuse me, ma'am. What does your hubby think about all this?"

"He's not exactly excited about me going to Dallas again."

"I hear ya. If I was in his shoes, I'd feel the same way. You don't have to come all the way down here, Miz Duncan."

Kate smiled. She had to remind him almost every conversation to use her first name. "Please call me *Kate*."

"I can keep an eye on your friend, Miz Kate, and let you know when things get fired up."

"Amy might not trust you, Walt. She knows me."

Mary reached for the door handle.

Kate touched her arm. "Just a minute, Aunt Mary. We're not at the store yet."

"Make sure Mike comes to Dallas with you," Walt said, "so the Executive people understand you're not runnin' solo. Tell 'em your husband plans to hang out at the convention center, but don't tell them about me. I'll be there all day, every day, wearing a disguise or two."

That afternoon, Kate and Mike returned to the horse stall where they'd stored Mary's boxes. Kate examined the box they'd left balanced across two sawhorses. "This might be the one we're looking for."

Mike shifted a parcel on the stack. "This box has your name on it, Kate."

"That must be the one Amy and I found in Aunt Mary's attic with mementos from my parents. I meant to separate it from the other boxes before we packed the truck in Pittsburgh."

The new filly nickered on the other side of the barn.

Kate smiled, tempted to go watch the little foal.

Honey answered with a soft whinny.

Mike arched an eyebrow. "You never said anything about it."

"I planned to open it that night, but we were all so tired, I decided to wait. And then... Well, you know all that's happened since."

"You found a box of stuff from your parents and you're not excited? You've said more than once you missed having family keepsakes."

"I know." Kate stepped close to finger her name on the box. "When Amy found this it was like finding treasure."

He removed his hat and scratched his head. "So why aren't you ripping it open right now?"

"Part of me wants to share the moment with you..." She hesitated. "And part of me wants to also share it with Aunt Mary and your mom, and Amy. I promised her we'd open it together, so I hate to do it without her." She paused again. "And I have to admit, another part of me wants it to be private, just me and my family." She looked down. "I'm sorry."

He took her hands. "You don't need to be sorry. This is all you have from your family."

"I'm not sure what my problem is." Kate laid her head on his shoulder. "Maybe I'm afraid I'll be disappointed or that the contents will trigger painful memories and I'll become more depressed than I already am."

Mike rested his cheek against her head and stroked her hair. "It's possible you might be disappointed, but I doubt it."

"You're probably right."

He lifted her chin. "Why are you making this so difficult?"

After a moment, she said, "You're right. I'm dragging my heels." She took a breath. "Okay. I'll open it in private, get my crying over with, and then show you what's inside. After that, I'll show the others." She tapped the parcel balanced across the sawhorses. "Guess what I found."

"Zane Grey books?"

"Silly man." Kate shook her head. "Aunt Mary's phone and radio are both in here. Plus her call log. This will be a fun surprise for her."

"See?" Mike winked. "Good things are coming from these boxes."

"Do you know where the antenna is?"

"Yep. In the corner behind the boxes. I can attach it to the side of the house later."

"Great. While you're doing that, I'll put the phone and radio on her desk and help her organize things." She hugged him. "I'm so excited for Aunt Mary. I'll feel better going to Dallas knowing she has something to occupy her time and her mind."

"Hey, I thought we were going to talk more about Dallas before we made a decision."

"Right." She nodded. "Guess I got carried away 'cause of the phone call."

"What phone call?"

"Just before I came out here, Executive Pride offered me a job at a sports convention in two weeks."

His eyebrows rose. "What did you tell them?"

"I told them..." She put her hands on her waist. "I told them I would talk with my husband and call them back." Kate jutted her chin. "Satisfied?" After a lifetime of confrontations, arguing with Mike was something she usually tried to avoid. However, she didn't like his tone of voice.

"I didn't mean..."

"Don't you trust me?"

"You've been so anxious about finding a way to help Amy, I got the feeling my opinion doesn't count."

"Of course it counts, Mike. We're in this marriage together, and we've prayed about Amy together." She tilted her head. "I have to ask you what you asked me. Why are you dragging your feet? This may be our only chance."

"Because I don't like putting you in the line of fire."

"God will take care of us."

"God expects us to use our brains, not intentionally walk into risky situations."

"Of course it's risky, yet God is bigger and stronger than anything we might encounter in Dallas." She took a long breath. "We can walk by faith, or we can walk in fear. I'm not only in a unique position to help a friend, I'm convinced God wants me to help her. I'll regret my failure to act every day of my life if we never see her again."

"Okay, we'll go to Dallas." He folded his arms. "Clint's been hammering me about looking for Amy, so I know he'll want to tag along. But we can't barge in there like some kind of maverick militia. We've got to work with Walt, let him take the lead. He's the expert."

She kissed his cheek. "I'll call Clint before I make our flight reservations."

CHAPTER EIGHTEEN

From his vantage point facing the Highway Haven House of God congregation, Mike saw Todd Hughes step into the mountainside chapel and look around. Mike's fingers froze on his guitar. He couldn't strum, couldn't sing. What was the jerk up to now?

He watched Todd slide into the empty space beside Kate, who sat next to Laura. Laura turned her head and then quickly looked away, her cheeks flushed. Kate shifted closer to her mother-in-law.

Mike focused on his fingers and tried to remember the words for the final verse of the song. Todd's presence ruined his concentration the same way Tara had distracted him from the music before she went to prison. Although her attendance at Highway Haven was sporadic, when she was there, sparks flew. Until now, her father only entered the chapel for weddings and funerals, and to eat at the receptions and dinners afterwards.

What did the man want from them? The answer hit him like a sledge hammer. Their ranch. Mike choked, missed a word, missed a chord. Todd Hughes wanted their ranch. Had that been Tara's intent all along? Why she'd talked as if the Whispering Pines belonged to her? He'd blown her off, thinking it was crazy talk from a crazy woman.

He clenched his jaw and strummed harder. What if his mom married Hughes? He could only imagine how awful it would be to live with the arrogant man. But that would never happen. He and Kate would have to leave Whispering Pines.

He saw his wife bow her head and knew she was praying, probably because she knew how he felt about Hughes. Mike swallowed. He had to get ahold of himself before he made a mountain out of a molehill. Just because Todd Hughes walked in the church door and sat down didn't mean he was up to no good—or did it?

After church, Mike took his family and Dymple to Grandma's Café. Cindy, the young girl he'd met earlier, set up a table for five. Mike was glad Todd slipped out of the sanctuary during the final prayer. He didn't care to buy lunch for him—or eat with him.

"This place is much nicer than it used to be," Laura said. "More welcoming."

Kate glanced around. "Smells good, too. Makes me hungry."

The girl led them to their table, and Mike helped seat the women. "Ladies, this is Cindy. She and her family just moved here from Pittsburgh."

Mary eyed the girl. "Are you the Raeburn's daughter?"

Kate touched her aunt's shoulder. "Aunt Mary, just because she's from Pittsburgh doesn't mean—"

"Yes, I'm their daughter, and you're…" Cindy's mouth dropped open. "Mrs. Anderson! I didn't know you live here."

Kate glanced from Mary to the girl. "You really do know each other?"

"We went to the same church." Cindy grinned. "My mom was Mr. Anderson's caretaker when he was sick. Sometimes we all went with her to visit them."

"That's right," Mary said. "Dean and I loved it when your family came over."

"I've got to get Mom and Dad." Cindy pivoted, her ponytail flipping from side to side. "They'll be so excited to see you."

Moments later, a balding dark-haired man and a blond woman rushed toward them from the kitchen, aprons flapping. "Mary!" The woman hugged her. "I'm so happy to see you again—in Wyoming, of all places."

"Oh, are we in Wyoming?" Mary squinted out the window. "I s'pose we are. My niece, Katy, and I are traveling. Seeing the world together."

Cindy turned to Mike. "I thought you said you have a ranch near here."

"We do. Mary is Kate's great-aunt. We relocated her here a couple months ago."

The woman took Mary's hands. "The last time I called your prayer line, you didn't answer. And your home number was disconnected, so I called the church. The secretary said you were living with relatives. Never thought we'd see you again."

She stepped back. "We'll have to get together for coffee. I'll make some of those blueberry muffins you like so much."

Mary's eyes shone. "That would be wonderful, dear."

The woman touched Kate's shoulder. "We saw your beautiful wedding pictures. Congratulations. This must be your husband."

"Thank you. Yes, this is my husband, Mike."

The man hugged Mary. "It's fantastic to see you again. You'll always be the belle of Pittsburgh to me."

"Oh, my." Mary beamed like a star-struck teenager.

He motioned to the others. "I'm Martin Raeburn, and this is my wife, Joyce. I take it you already met Cindy. We also have an eleven-year-old son named Casey."

Mike introduced the others at the table. Laura said, "Come up to the ranch, anytime." The couple thanked her for the invitation, said their goodbyes, and scuttled back to the kitchen.

The Duncan crew had just given Cindy their orders, when Marshall Thompson walked into the café with his wife and mom and dad. Mike watched the Thompsons settle into a booth and take menus from Cindy. He hadn't heard from Marshall in a while. Maybe he and his dad were over their red-deer scare. He took a sip of water. It would be great if he didn't have to worry about brucellosis.

The jukebox switched from a Diana Ross song to Dolly Parton. Mike chuckled. The Raeburn family must have struck a musical compromise. And the son must have lost. No rap music for Grandma's Café.

Marshall closed his menu, said something to his wife and walked to Mike's table. He tipped his head. "Good afternoon, ladies and gentleman."

Mike stood. "Marshall, I believe you know everyone here except Kate's Aunt Mary. We moved her here from Pennsylvania not long ago."

Marshall squeezed Mary's hand. "Pleasure to meet you, ma'am. How do you like the West so far?"

"To be honest, I expected to see buffalo dotting the prairies thick as flies on honey. To date, I haven't seen nary a one."

Mike raised his eyebrows and looked at Kate, who appeared to be as surprised as he was by the comment. He didn't know Mary could be so eloquent or that she wanted to see his bison.

Marshall elbowed him. "I believe Mr. Duncan here is just the man for you. If he's too busy to set you up with a bison tour, I'll be glad to do it."

"I'd like to go, too." Dymple's eyes were bright. "I've heard all about your bladder, Mike, but I've never been nose to nose with one."

Marshall's wide-eyed gaze flicked from Mike to Dymple and back again.

Mike fought to keep a straight face. "Come spring, I'll drive you two to the bison pasture for a front-row visit." He turned to Marshall. "How's your herd doing?"

"That's what I came over to talk about. Dad's research is turning up—"

Mike cleared his throat. "These ladies give me a hard time for talking about bison all the time. Why don't we step outside for a few minutes, so we don't bore them."

After stopping to say hello to Marshall's wife and parents, Mike followed him and Robert out of the warm restaurant into the cold parking lot. Had the Thompsons told their wives about the possible brucellosis outbreak? Maybe he should tell his mom and Kate. But, really, there was nothing to say at this point. He buttoned his coat. "What's up?"

Marshall zipped his jacket. "Leonard Gruber sold out on us."

"How's that?"

Robert folded his arms and widened his stance. "He sold his place to Hughes last week and is already loading his stuff in that five-ton truck of his."

"His family has owned their ranch for generations," Mike said.

"We went over there to ask what was going on." Marshall crammed his hands into his jacket pockets. "Leonard didn't have much to say, didn't even want to talk about it. Right, Dad?"

Robert nodded. "His wife acted strange when she answered the door, said Leonard couldn't talk, and then she shut the door in our faces. Didn't invite us in or say goodbye. Just left us standing there in a subzero gale. We stepped off the porch and were about to leave, when Gruber came out in a t-shirt, obviously not planning to talk long. He was real short with us, like he couldn't wait for us to leave."

"Doesn't sound like Leonard. He's a decent sort of guy." Mike pulled his coat collar up around his neck. "Any idea what's going on?"

"He rain-danced all around our questions," Robert said. "We finally gave up and started for the truck. That's when he whispered, 'Check the locks on your closets.'"

"Who locks their closets? Did he explain?"

Marshall shook his head. "He did an about-face and bolted for the house."

Mike shrugged. "Maybe it has something to do with a skeleton in his closet. You think Hughes blackmailed him?"

Robert pushed back his hat and scratched his forehead. "That's the only thing we can figure."

"You think Leonard would talk to me?"

"Worth a try," Robert said.

Mike edged toward the restaurant. "I'll run by his place this afternoon."

Marshall grabbed his coat sleeve. "One more thing, Mike."

Mike steeled himself for more bad news.

"My boys were out riding horses in the hills, and they swear they saw three red deer."

"Were they near your bison?"

"No…"

"Or your cattle?"

"No, but deer get around."

Kate set the carton on the bed and closed the bedroom door. Mike was visiting a neighbor, so this was a good time to delve into her mystery box. She climbed on the comforter, crossed her legs and readied herself for an afternoon of memories. One by one, she pulled back the flaps. The musty aromas of yesteryear saturated her senses. She sneezed and rubbed her nose.

Inside the carton were the remnants of her childhood. Was that how it was in heaven? People standing in line to meet their Maker holding their life boxes? She slid her wedding ring up and down her finger. What would her box hold when her days on earth were done? Would she fulfill her purpose, whatever that was?

She toyed with a flap, not yet ready to look inside. Like Mike said, it was crazy to be so hesitant to check out the box's contents. This was a dream-come-true moment after all her years of longing for her family.

So what kept her from opening the box? She thought about her ambiguous feelings for a moment. Maybe she was afraid the contents would be the end of it all, that she'd never have another connection with her family. "That's not true," she whispered to herself. Her aunt was alive and well and napping in the next room. They'd packed dozens of her diaries and stored them in Pittsburgh. Surely the journals contained references to her mom and dad and brother.

She smiled, remembering the fun she and Kenny shared while climbing the big trees in Aunt Mary and Uncle Dean's backyard and exploring their basement and attic. She would never run out of memories, especially with a boxful of mementos to help her recall long-forgotten events.

She picked up the baby book and opened it to where she'd left off. The next entry appeared to be a letter to God.

Thank you, God, for blessing us with a perfect baby girl. Rosy cheeks, bright brown eyes, and a headful of dark hair. Her father declared her to be the prettiest baby in the nursery. He was right, of course.

Paul wanted a boy. However, the instant I delivered our sweet Katherine Joy into his hands (the doctor let him "catch" her), he fell head-over-heels in love with her. I saw it in his eyes and in the tears that rolled down his cheeks. He's already calling her Joy Belle.

I'm so glad to be home, where we can have her to ourselves, instead of sharing her with all those people who poked and prodded her and made her cry. But I was happy to share her with our pastor and his wife, who stopped by today to meet Katy Joy. They brought her an adorable angel mobile that plays "Jesus Loves the Little Children."

Before they left, the two of them laid their hands on her tiny body nestled in my arms, and Pastor prayed God would grow her into a woman who always returns to him, no matter how far she strays. It was a strange prayer. I was offended until he said we all are prone to wander away from the fold and need to be reminded often to follow the Shepherd.

Stray? Kate sat back, her shoulders against the headboard. That was an understatement. She'd been the ultimate lost sheep stumbling through life furious with God. For too many years, she believed he stole her family and replaced them with jerks, those foster families who treated her like an outsider, at best, and like trash to be used and abused, at worst. Some robbed her of her virginity and her youth. Others took her dignity, her reputation and her possessions.

Yet, she admitted, things might have gone better with some of the nicer families if she hadn't built a wall around her soul. One couple tried especially hard to help her, but she couldn't allow herself to trust them.

Smoothing the pages of the baby book, she finished reading her mother's letter.

May our precious little girl always yearn for you, Lord, and return to you each time she strays.

Kate hugged the book to her chest. *I'm back, Mom, back in the fold.* She put the baby book in the box and picked up a manila envelope. Lifting it high, she jiggled the envelope until construction paper art fell onto the bed.

One sheet with her name on the back labeled "My Family's Cow and Horse Farm in Wyoming, US of A" was a chalk drawing of jagged mountains behind equally pointed pine trees next to a building with a severely peaked roof, probably a barn. Several stick animals were drawn in what appeared to be a corral. Plus, four stick people stood or lay, depending on how one viewed the drawing, outside the corral. Each figure sported tall boots, a wide hat and a crooked smile.

Kate grinned. She'd drawn the picture the day she and her brother received a surprise parcel from their father, a traveling salesman. He'd sent a big package from Wyoming with boots for her, a cowboy hat for Kenny, and clothes and jewelry for her mom.

"Yes, Katy Joy," she murmured to her little girl self, "living on a cow farm makes me smile, every day." She wiped away a tear. Her family would have loved the Whispering Pines. She could honor their memory by making the ranch a happy place for Aunt Mary.

Digging through the box, she found school papers, class pictures, favorite children's books, and a sweater and a hat with her name on them, along with a story she'd written about riding on her pretend horse, her dad's leg. She even found a packet of savings bonds marked "for our children's college education."

Kate set the bonds aside. She would put them in the safe later to preserve for their children. The thought made her stop what she was doing and sit back. Was she beginning to open up to the idea of adoption? Maybe so. Now she possessed keepsakes to share with their children, if God chose to bless her and Mike with a family.

The phone on the nightstand rang. She picked it up. "Hello."

"Darling..." The voice was male. "When can you escape that nasty old lady's talons again? I've been missing you and your sweet smile. This morning wasn't enough."

Kate frowned. Did she hear right? "This is Kate Duncan. I'm not sure who you're—"

Click.

A moment later, the phone chimed the double ring for the office. Still holding the handset, she read the number on the screen. Local number. The phone only rang once. Laura must have answered it.

CHAPTER NINETEEN

Mike parked in front of the Grubers' house. Curtains covered the windows and a tractor sat beside the small barn, yet the place felt deserted. Had the family already moved? He buttoned his jacket and stepped out of Old Blue. No sign of life, not even Tuffy and Tess, Leonard's energetic border collies.

He walked to the porch, eyeing wide tracks in the trampled snow. Leonard's big truck?

Tramp sniffed the tracks before marking his visit on the tree beside the porch.

Mike knocked at the front door and waited. No response. No sound of footsteps or the drone of a radio or television. Just the flapping of a "holiday greetings" flag on a short pole attached to the porch railing.

He peered through the slit between the drapes that covered the picture window. The living room was empty, stripped clean. Mike frowned. Must have been quite the skeleton in Leonard Gruber's closet. Holding his hat to keep it from blowing away, he stepped off the porch. Next stop would be the Williams place.

He climbed into the pickup behind Tramp, glad the cab was still warm. But he didn't start the engine. Instead, he scanned the empty barnyard. Why did he feel like someone was watching him?

His two-way crackled to life. Mike jolted to attention.

"Hey, Bossman, can you hear me?"

Tramp's ears perked.

Mike chuckled and lifted the radio from the seat. Tramp and Clint were buddies. He pressed the talk button. "I'm here, Clint."

For several seconds, all he heard was static. Then Clint came on. "I hate to be the bearer of bad news, but the bison sniper struck again."

Tramp settled on the seat, his chin between his front paws.

Mike groaned. "Another cow?"

Clint grunted. "This time they got a bull, the one I bought at the Denver stock show."

Mike slammed the dashboard with his fist, causing his dog to jump to his feet and look at him as if he'd lost his mind. It'd been over a year since the last buffalo was shot. "Someone's playing hardball now."

"Yeah. Want me to call the sheriff?"

"The department wasn't much help last time."

"Remember," Clint said, "Caldwell was fired after he messed up the theft investigation. Maybe whoever they assign this time will do a better job."

"Okay, go ahead and call. Do you have any idea when the bull was killed?"

"The carcass is cold, and the blood is frozen around the wound. All I can say is it wasn't today."

"See any snowmobile tracks?"

"Nope. The bull is near the road. My guess is that the jerk didn't even have to get out of his—or her—truck. Just leaned out the window and pulled the trigger."

Mike squinted at the barn. The main door was partially open. He thought he saw movement inside. "Tell the deputies everything you know and remind them of past incidents, just in case they've forgotten. You can fill me in on details when I return. Over and out."

He opened the truck door and slid his shotgun from behind the seat. Holding the gun at his side aimed downward, he circled the house to approach the barn from an angle. An icy wind whistled through the doorway, swirling a cloud of hay particles.

Mike motioned to Tramp to stay put and slipped into the barn, his back against the wall and the shotgun grasped between his cold fingers. As his eyes adjusted, he made out a short stack of hay bales. Other than that, the barn was empty.

A shadow flickered beside the bales.

He swung the gun around.

Squawk.

Mike froze and Tramp bounded in, charging for the scrawny rooster hunched against the wall.

"Stop!" Mike pointed to the opposite corner. "Sit."

Tail between his legs, Tramp slunk to the corner and lay down.

Shaking his head, Mike lowered his firearm. A rooster. Leonard had left a chicken behind. By now, the poor critter was probably as hungry as it was frozen. He set the shotgun by the wall, pulled gloves from his coat pocket and slipped them on. Roosters could be mean.

He pointed a second time at his dog and held up his palm. "Stay."

Tramp laid his chin between his front paws.

Mike tiptoed toward the bird.

The rooster flapped a wing and croaked a pathetic protest.

Tramp whined.

Mike bent down and reached for the rooster.

"Keep your hands off my bird."

Still crouched, Mike whipped around.

Todd Hughes stood in the doorway, feet planted wide.

Tramp leaped to his feet, ears pinned and teeth bared. Snarls rumbled in his throat.

Mike's heart hammered his throat as he got to his feet. His dad wasn't joking when he said Hughes could materialize out of nothing. "This bird belongs to the Grubers."

Tramp bounded to his master's side, growling. This time Mike didn't send him away.

"I own this property now." Todd jutted his chin. "Anything left behind belongs to me."

"I doubt leaving the rooster was intentional."

"Intentional or otherwise, it's my bird. And this is my property. Better git before I call the sheriff."

Mike clamped his jaw. *God, don't let my mother marry this idiot.* He swiveled, grabbed the rooster and thrust it inside his jacket. The bird didn't fight him.

"Drop it, Duncan! Or I'll file charges."

"You do that. In the meantime, I'll check out your illegal acquisition of the Gruber homestead. I'm sure my mom will find my research fascinating."

Hughes scowled. "Leave her out of this."

Mike pressed the motionless fowl against his chest and grabbed his gun.

Todd stepped back, eyeing the shotgun.

Mike pointed the barrel at the ground. "I don't know what you're trying to pull with my mother, but she's not stupid."

Todd smirked. "Could of fooled me. Now git outa here."

The wind blew open a door on the other side of the barn, and Mike caught a glimpse of Todd's truck through the doorway. Why did he park behind the barn, in a snowdrift, when he supposedly owned the place? He motioned to his dog. "Let's go."

Todd reached beneath the flap of his jacket and pulled out a pistol. "Hand me the rooster."

"You'd shoot me over a chicken?" Mike shook his head. "You're crazier than I thought."

A smug expression crossed Todd's face. "I'll kill your mangy mutt." He pointed the gun at Tramp. The dog growled and bared his teeth.

Todd sneered. "I can say I shot him in self-defense."

"That'll impress my mom." Mike stepped to the doorway and shouldered the heavy door all the way open. "C'mon, Tramp."

Todd brandished his gun. "I said, leave her out of this."

Tramp snapped at him, and Todd jerked away. "Keep the stupid chicken. It's only a matter of time before I get it, along with your two-bit ranch."

Mike ignored him and tromped toward his pickup. His dog would follow, unless Hughes was stupid enough to tangle with an irate ranch dog.

"Next time you pull a gun on me," Todd yelled, "I'll shoot first."

Mike shoved the rooster behind the pickup seat, ignoring its feeble squawk. Tramp sniffed the bird and jumped inside. Mike followed him, closed the door and started the engine.

The collie snarled once more at Todd, who stood in the barn doorway, his gun aimed their direction. And then, with a whine, the dog sat. Mike slid the heater level to high. Tramp was as anxious to leave as he was. That was good, because they were both ready to tear into the crook.

The ride to the Williams ranch was quiet. Tramp stretched across the bench seat and laid his head on Mike's lap. Mike stroked the collie's soft fur, hoping to calm both of them. Soon, Tramp's feet began to twitch. Mike envied his dog's ability to shed the anxiety that still gnawed at his own stomach.

He hadn't heard a peep from the rooster behind the seat. Did it die of fright? Or, like Tramp, was it happily soaking up the heat that now coursed through the cab?

So Hughes had his eyes on the WP as well as the other adjoining ranches. What did he do to Leonard and his family to make them take off so fast? And why was he parked behind their barn? Was he watching to make sure they didn't come back? *Or waiting for me...*

Mike scowled. Hughes didn't know he planned to stop by Leonard's place, or did he? He'd told his mom where he was headed. Maybe she talked with Hughes. But why would she tell him his whereabouts? Were they in cahoots?

He rubbed his temple. Even if his mom loved Hughes... He cringed at the thought. Even if she loved him, the man had no respect for her, not to mention being deranged enough to threaten him and Tramp over a half-frozen rooster.

Mike slowed for an icy patch on the road. If it wasn't so cold, he'd open the door to release the bile roiling in his belly. What would he find at the next ranch? At least he wouldn't run into Hughes there. The only way Todd could beat him to Arnie's ranch was to pass him on the highway.

Mike didn't have to knock on the Williams' front door to know Arnie's family was gone. No vehicles or equipment were parked in the yard. No smoke drifted from the chimney. No drapes covered the picture window and no furniture graced the living room. Tire tracks in snow churned dark with dirt indicated a hectic few hours loading their possessions. What kind of power did Hughes wield against them?

He and Tramp climbed back inside the truck. Discouragement sucked at his soul. The Gruber and Williams families vanishing without an explanation or a goodbye didn't make sense. They were good people who were well-liked in the area as well as longtime friends of his family.

Then there was the brucellosis scare and red deer appearing and disappearing. Plus another dead buffalo, which wasn't just any buffalo. It was his latest acquisition, a bull that cost a fortune and would have enhanced the quality of his herd. If Hughes was the one behind the bison deaths, it didn't make sense for him to kill off valuable livestock.

He thought of his mom's secrecy and how Kate's exuberance evaporated after the hysterectomy. He thought of Aunt Mary's fading mind and the night she wandered outside in the snow, of Amy's disappearance in Texas, and Kate's willingness to go to dangerous extremes to find her.

Mike released a long sigh. Like blowing snow, everyone and everything he loved was drifting away. Would he lose his family entirely?

Tramp whimpered.

Mike patted his dog's back and recalled a scripture verse he'd learned as a young child. *Trust in the Lord with all your heart and lean not on your own understanding.* His own understanding was definitely finite. He didn't have a clue what to do next. Should he talk with his mom about Hughes? Tell her and Kate about the red deer and the threat of brucellosis? About the dead bull? Should he track down the missing families or leave them be? Maybe they didn't want to be found.

He drove to the top of the next rise, parked beside the road and pulled out his cell phone. Good. He had service.

Marshall answered on the third ring. "Howdy, Mike. What's up?" Mike could hear cattle in the background. "They're gone."

Marshall waited a moment before responding. "The Williams family or the Grubers?"

"Both."

Again, silence. "Animals and equipment?"

"Everything."

As if offended to be overlooked, the rooster behind the seat croaked a garbled cluck. Either the bird was thawing, or that was its deathbed farewell. "Except for Arnie's rooster," Mike added. "I found it in his barn. Ran into Hughes there, too."

"Uh-oh."

"Yeah. He threatened to kill my dog if I took his rooster. But then he said he'd get the bird when he gets our ranch."

"So he's after your place, too. I figured as much."

Mike watched a porcupine waddle across the highway. "Appears he's going after it by romancing my mother."

Marshall swore. "That's hitting below the belt."

The prickly animal reached the base of a tree on the other side and began to climb.

"Don't tell anyone about my mom, Marshall. I've got to talk with her and find out what's going on between her and Hughes, if anything."

"I'll keep it under my hat." Marshall groaned. "What are we going to do about this mess? We can't keep sitting on our hands doing nothin'."

"I'm thinking there has to be something illegal about these sales. The Williams and the Grubers have been here for decades, yet neither family said goodbye to anyone, that I know of."

"My wife and Betsy Williams were good friends," Marshall said. "They went shopping together in Cheyenne just a couple weeks ago. Maggie would have told me if Betsy said they were planning to move. This happened mighty fast."

"Can a person renege on a sale if they change their mind?"

Snow plopped from the disturbed branches, heaping in piles beneath the tree as the porcupine worked its way upward.

Marshall was quiet. "Might be possible. Moving out lock, stock and barrel the way they did, it's like they were burning bridges. I'll ask Dad to do some research. You have any idea how to reach Leonard or Arnie?"

"I don't have cell phone numbers for either of them."

"I doubt they left forwarding information with the post office or the phone company, but we can check." Marshall paused. "The county must have some information, because they'd need to send copies of sales documents."

"Think they'll give that info to you?"

"Should be public."

"I'll talk with my mom and get back to you to compare notes. Time to nip this craziness in the bud." Mike took a breath and blew it out through his nose. "I'd better go. Oh, one more thing. My foreman just called to say he found my new bull shot dead."

"You're kidding."

"Wish I was."

"Any idea who?"

"My gut instinct tells me it's Hughes, but I'm having trouble connecting the dots between him trying to take over my ranch and whoever's killing off my herd." Mike closed his eyes but opened them again. "You're in the same boat, Marshall. You've got a ranch he wants, plus you've got bison. Better keep an eye on your herd."

Kate stood in the doorway of Mary's bedroom, watching her arrange her desk. "Are you glad to be back at your desk?"

"Oh, my, yes." Mary placed the phone to her left and her notebook on the right, just the way they were in Pittsburgh. "I've missed helping people give their problems to God." She filled a wooden pencil holder with pens and pencils and positioned it above the notebook.

"You look beautiful this morning, Aunt Mary."

"Thank you, dear." Mary had insisted on wearing one of her nicer dresses. "I'm working for the Lord," she said. "I need to dress appropriately." She'd even asked Kate to arrange her hair, after she finished her bowl of raisin-less Raisin Bran. "Regularity. I don't want irregularity to distract me from my work."

Mike set her scanner to a local channel, although he'd told Kate it might never receive a message. Not only was the ranch far from town, the mountains would interfere with signals. However, occasional chatter from a passing patrol vehicle and messages bouncing from mountain to mountain might be enough action for her faltering attention span.

Kate prayed the telephone would jump to life soon. She'd called the phone company last week and made arrangements to have the Pittsburgh line ring in Mary's room. "Would you like something warm to drink while you work?"

"Tea, please. You know how I like it."

Kate grinned. That was one thing neither she nor her aunt forgot. Steep green tea for three-and-a-half minutes, add a teaspoon of honey and a "splash" of cream, stir three times. "Coming right up."

In the kitchen, she switched on the burner under the teapot and opened a cupboard door to find a toothbrush propped in one cup and a tube of toothpaste in another. She sighed. "So that's where she put them."

"Katy," Mary called from the bedroom, "I have a message."

"Thank you, Jesus," Kate whispered.

By the time the tea was ready, Mary had the phone clasped against her ear. "How you love this precious woman who's grieving the tragic loss of her grandson, Lord. Her heart is broken. Please send your..."

Kate set the mug on a coaster and tiptoed out of the room. Her aunt was serving others again. Tears welled in her eyes. No one knew better than she did that God heard and answered Aunt Mary's prayers.

CHAPTER TWENTY

Amy fastened the second diamond-studded dangle earring, sprayed her hair and stepped back to survey the results. Not bad. She hoped Thomas would be pleased. He said they'd have dinner her first time out with him and wouldn't spend too much time on their feet. No dancing. That was good. She wasn't sure how long she could tolerate high heels.

Satisfied with her appearance, she sat on the edge of the bed and crossed her legs. Her short black dress with its diagonal silver stripe crept up her thighs. Leaning back, she rested her weight on her wrists and practiced her smile.

Thomas entered, took one glance at the plunging neckline, and whistled. "You blow my mind, gorgeous. I can't wait to show my favorite woman around town."

She tilted her head and studied him through lowered lashes. "You're looking real fine, yourself, handsome." His tailored black suit accented his dark eyes, wide shoulders and narrow hips. The silver vest over a purple silk shirt provided just the right blend of elegance and showmanship. And his aftershave was as tantalizing as ever.

"I brought something beautiful for a beautiful lady." He lifted a silver choker from a velvet case.

She stood, wobbled, and then stepped toward him. "Thank you, Thomas. It's… dazzling." She hoped the word was strong enough. She reached for the necklace.

He stepped back, swinging it between his hands. "See anything unusual?"

She stared at the rows of flowers studded with sparkling diamonds. "It's really unique." Two tiny disks swung on short chains from the wide clasp. One was engraved with the letter "T" and the other with an "M." Touching one, she asked, "Is that the designer?"

"Guess again."

She fingered the delicate chains. "Are those your initials? I don't know your last name."

"Bingo. Now, turn around and hold up your hair."

So that was what the "TM" tattoos on the kids meant. They'd been branded, like Mike's cattle. Amy swallowed her disgust and did as he instructed.

He clasped the choker behind her neck. "This means you belong to me, baby." He kissed her earlobe. "It's like a wedding ring, only much bigger and far better. The diamonds alone are worth a fortune."

Belong? He might possess her body at the moment, but she didn't belong to him. Amy could see the diamonds' twinkle reflected in the night-darkened window. And, no, the necklace wasn't the same as a wedding ring. Getting involved with Thomas because she was desperate for a job was stupid, but she wasn't a total idiot.

Thomas fidgeted with the necklace a moment longer.

"Is something wrong?"

"Got to make sure it's locked tight."

She tilted her head. "Locked?"

He waved a small key in the air. "The only way this is coming off, sugar, is if I take it off."

She dropped her hair and watched him pocket the key. "I don't understand."

"You don't need to understand. You just need to be pretty and remember who owns you."

Seated beside Thomas in the limo, Amy soaked in the sights and sounds of the city. Instead of watching silent distant traffic from high above, she was immersed in civilization again. At least for tonight, she was a bona fide member of the human race.

She was fairly certain they wouldn't eat at the same restaurant where they'd eaten before. And she was right. Even so, the ambience was just as elegant as the first restaurant.

Heads turned when they entered the intimate dining room. Someone whispered, "Exotic couple."

Thomas winked at Amy.

She smiled. He was treating her like a queen tonight. Even though she knew this was not the real Thomas, she enjoyed his attention. The real Thomas was evil and sadistic, unlike the benevolent charmer who smiled and held her chair for her and murmured she was the most stunning woman in the room and that he couldn't wait until dessert, the dessert the two of them would share later in her suite.

Amy waited until the waiter placed the napkin in her lap and left to get their drinks. "You're by far the best-looking man in this restaurant, Thomas. You look great in that suit." She dipped her head. "Thank you for bringing me here. This is a really nice place."

She fiddled with the napkin, not knowing what else to say and wishing she could scream her real thoughts. *You may think you own my body, Thomas M, but you'll never own my soul!* Not if she fought his magnetic power, something that was easier said than done on a night like tonight.

"I think you'll like the food here, Natasha."

Amy bit her lip. Wasn't that the line he used when he drugged her? She ran her tongue across her front teeth to eliminate any lipstick residue.

His voice was low and seductive. "You'll also enjoy the music." He indicated the string quartet across the room.

"This restaurant is lovely and relaxing." Her stomach gurgled. She was so hungry and anxious to eat something besides salad.

"We'll come here again when you're ready to dance."

"That would be wonderful. I can't wait."

Thomas ordered for both of them, prime rib for himself and tilapia for her.

Amy's mouth watered at the mention of prime rib. She shoved her disappointment aside. Surely the almond-crusted fish would be delicious.

When the waiter left, Thomas leaned across the table and placed his hand over hers. "I'm glad you're better and back to work. I was very pleased with your performance this past week."

She slipped her hand from under his to pick up her water goblet. "You watch us?"

"I check in on our guests now and then. Gives me pleasure to see my employees making other people happy. However, I mostly watch the numbers. You're cranking 'em out, Natasha, like the pro you are. I'm pleased to have you on staff."

She took a sip of water. "Thank you." She was a mindless fool answering to the wrong name, a moron who'd probably thank him the next time he beat her, too. Staring out the window at the glittering lights below them, she was caught off-guard by his next comment.

"I think you're ready for work on the outside."

Her grip on the goblet tightened. "Outside?" Was he going to send her to the streets? Kate had told her what it was like to walk the streets, so she was well aware of the hazards. Still, the freedom and the possibility of escape would compensate for the danger.

"Executive Pride occasionally provides hostesses for events in the Dallas-Fort Worth metroplex. Next week, several of our people will be hosting booths at a sports tradeshow, including Mikaylah and Janessa, the coworkers who visited you recently."

Amy hoped her disappointment wasn't obvious. Working with her new friends would be fun, but being stuck in a booth would limit her escape options.

"We have a fitness center that wants a woman whose anatomy does justice to a tank top and short shorts," Thomas was saying. He eyed her cleavage as he spoke. "She'll pass out literature and supplement samples. Doc says you can do it if you wear tennis shoes and sit down between customers. We'll double your tanning time this week to cover those ugly tattoos."

He didn't ask for a response, so Amy said nothing. The change of pace would be nice, but convention halls were notoriously cold. How sexy would goosebumps look on her unseasonably tanned body? She adjusted the choker. It was heavier than she expected and felt like hands squeezing her neck.

"Don't do that."

Amy blinked. "What?"

"Don't mess with that necklace. It cost more money than you ever stole in your life."

She dropped her hands into her lap. Was the choker really that expensive? Then she remembered Janessa and Mikaylah and their warning about a microphone. If the necklace had such a device, why did Thomas make her wear it tonight? He could hear her every word, see her every movement, except when she was in the ladies room.

She offered Thomas a coy smile, hoping to cover her resentment. He actually believed he owned the right to monitor her every move.

He winked. "So, what do you think about the outside job?"

What did it matter what she thought? She didn't have a choice. "Sounds fun. How long does it run? All day, or just an evening?"

"Three days. Friday through Sunday. We'll provide a chaperone to escort you to your meals and breaks."

In other words, to keep her from sneaking away. But maybe he'd let her sleep at night instead of tending to the demands of his endless clientele. If nothing else, she might get to chat with Mikaylah and Janessa.

He cocked an eyebrow. "Thanks to that expensive necklace, we'll always know your whereabouts."

"Oh." So that's what Mikaylah meant by GPS.

"Remember, the authorities haven't stopped searching for Amy Iverson, the chubby woman who came to town to murder a total stranger."

She was about to object when he held up a palm. "I realize you're no longer that homely person, Natasha, and I am fully aware the best place to hide from cops is right under their noses, but we can't let our guard down."

The moment Kate and Mary left the house to go see the new filly, Mike headed for the office. Finally, he and his mom could talk in private.

Laura concluded a phone call and turned to Mike. "A man from British Columbia wants to bring his entire family here in July, including his parents. Sounds real excited to visit Wyoming."

Mike sat at Kate's desk. "How many people in his party?"

"Seven."

"That'll fill a couple cabins."

"At the rate people are calling, we'll be completely booked before Easter."

"Great." He leaned toward her, his elbows on his knees, hands clasped. It was now or never. "Mom, something's come up that you and I should, uh, discuss."

Her forehead wrinkled. "Right now?"

"Yes."

"I'm awfully busy."

"This can't wait."

"If it's about yesterday…"

Oh, so she already knew. "What about yesterday?"

Her cheeks colored, and she looked away. "Well, I mean, whatever happened with the chicken, I'm sure it'll all work out."

"This isn't about chickens, Mom." His voice got louder. "This is about Hughes threatening to shoot me. He even threatened to kill Tramp."

She shook her head. "That's not how I heard the story. I think both of you are being childish. If that rooster belongs to Todd, you need to give it back."

"Don't you get it? He's trying to take over our ranch, like he took over the Gruber and Williams ranches."

She checked her watch. "I have just enough time to get to my hair appointment in town." She jumped to her feet and rushed out of the room.

Mike gaped at her retreating figure. He'd pushed his mom's buttons more than once as a kid, but she'd never left in the middle of a conversation. He stepped to her desk to check the calendar she kept on the wall. No hair appointment was listed for today.

He frowned. Not only had she never walked out on him before, she'd never lied to him. What had Hughes done with his mother?

Kate found Mike in the kitchen staring out the window above the sink. She filled the teapot and placed it on the stove, then wrapped an arm about his waist. Resting her cheek on his shoulder, she asked, "What do you see out there, sweetheart?" All she could see was snow and trees.

"Nothing much. Just thinking, I guess." He aimed his cup at the coffee maker. "I finished off the pot, but I can brew more."

"Thanks for the offer. I'm heating water for tea." She rubbed his back. "You seem preoccupied. Anything wrong?"

He pressed the space between his eyebrows with his fingers. "Yeah. Everything."

"Everything?" She studied his somber blue eyes. "It's not like you to be so pessimistic."

His shoulders dropped, and he blew out a long breath. "We need to talk."

She stepped back. "About us?"

He pulled her close. "No, sweetheart, it's not about us. It's about that new rooster."

Kate nearly laughed out loud, but his expression told her he wasn't joking. She leaned away from him. "That rooster sounds sick. Where did you get him?"

"I took him from the Grubers' barn."

She raised her eyebrows.

He nodded. "Yep. I stole a rooster."

Kate stretched around him to open a cupboard door. "I stole all kinds of stuff back in the day, but I have to say I never swiped a rooster." She took two cups from the shelf. "I'll fix myself and Aunt Mary some tea, and then you and I can sit in front of the fire with a couple of the raisin scones I baked earlier, while you tell me all about the rooster."

Chapter Twenty-One

Kate set her cup on the coffee table. "Todd Hughes pursuing your mom to get the ranch is bad enough. To think he ran off our neighbors and threatened you and Tramp is beyond understanding."

"We don't have all the facts about the Williams and the Grubers."

"Whatever happened, both families taking off so suddenly without saying goodbye is super strange." She folded her hands around her knee. "On top of all that, someone shot another bison, and you didn't tell me."

Mike bit into a scone and spoke from the side of his mouth. "That just happened."

"You've known about the possibility of brucellosis for weeks, and I heard nothing about it."

"That's the thing." He chewed and then swallowed. "It's only a possibility, nothing more at this stage. You almost bled to death and then had emergency surgery—and your best friend disappeared. I didn't think you needed any more trauma."

"Did you tell your mom this stuff?"

"I tried to talk with her about Hughes and didn't get far."

"So you've been carrying this huge load of worries all by yourself."

"I've prayed about it. God knows what's going on."

"Sharing burdens is what marriage is all about, Mike." She took his hands. "I appreciate you wanting to protect me, especially while I was healing. But you forgot that I'm here to help you through your struggles, too." She tilted her head. "I just remembered something I should have told you."

He sat back. "So I'm not the only one with secrets."

"I wasn't sure what to think, so I didn't say anything about a weird phone call we got." She combed her fingers through her hair. "Now it makes sense." She told him what she'd heard and how the office phone rang immediately after. "Makes sense the caller was Todd, but I can't believe he called my aunt a nasty old lady." Kate twisted a lock of hair around her finger. "I wonder if your mom would rather Aunt Mary didn't live with her. Maybe I should put her in a nursing home while we're gone."

"Mom has said several times she likes having Mary here." Mike scratched his chin. "But she's not the mom I remember."

Kate wrinkled her nose. "I can't believe she's hanging out with Tara's dad."

Laura Duncan sat alone in a corner booth at Grandma's Café, sipping coffee and wondering what else she could do now that she was in Copperville. She'd already grocery shopped, mailed the bills in her purse and topped off the gas in her SUV. Maybe she'd drop by the beauty shop to get a quick haircut and redeem the fib she told her son. But even if she did, a lie was a lie.

What was wrong with her? It wasn't like she was in love with Todd, at least not in the way she'd loved Dan. She enjoyed his company, yet he didn't come close to being anything like her sweet husband. She watched a couple walk across the snow-covered parking lot to their car holding hands.

Maybe it was because Todd made her feel like a woman again, rather than a widow. She swirled the dark liquid in her cup. But what about his drinking and his trips to Vegas? He told her he gambled a little and enjoyed a few night shows.

What did he do the rest of the time? He never called her from Vegas. If they married, would he continue the gambling trips?

She lowered the cup to the table. Todd had been single for over twenty years. He was accustomed to doing what he wanted when he wanted. Yet, he also tried hard to please her.

Laura sighed. How did she get into such a whirlwind of emotions?

Joyce Raeburn, who'd been circling the room refilling coffee cups, walked over to her table. "Care for a refill?"

"No, thanks. I've had my quota of caffeine for the day."

"I'd like to sit and visit a moment, if that's okay with you."

"Please do." Laura motioned to the seat across from her. "I'd love to get to know you better. Mary speaks so highly of you and your family."

Joyce pulled a potholder from her apron and placed the carafe on it. "Please give my sweet friend a hug for me when you get home." She slid into the booth. "She's a very special lady."

"I'll be glad to do that."

After turning over an unused cup, Joyce poured coffee for herself. "You seem to have a lot on your mind today, Laura. Anything I can help with? I'm a good listener."

Laura smiled. "I'm not surprised to hear that. When Mary talks about Pittsburgh, she always mentions your name." She leaned forward. "We haven't had you and your family up to the ranch. What days work best with your café schedule?"

"At this moment? None. We're open seven days a week from six a.m. to ten p.m."

"That's a killer schedule."

"It's catching up with both of us." Joyce massaged her neck. "Martin and I are thinking of closing on Sundays. We do good business that day. However, we'd like to attend church and have some family time as well as a few hours to relax."

Laura could see the exhaustion in Joyce's eyes. "Are you still needing more help?"

"Yes. Cindy started at the university this semester, so we hired two young women part time. Then one of them developed pregnancy complications and her doctor put her on bed rest. A couple weeks later, the other girl decided to move to Denver with her boyfriend."

She picked up her coffee. "Enough about my problems. What's happening in your life? Anything you'd like to talk about?"

Laura hesitated. She barely knew Joyce. But that could be good. Her new friend might be the perfect person to help her think through her relationship with Todd. As a newcomer to the community, Joyce could act as an impartial third party. Laura folded her hands and rested them on the table. She wouldn't have to give Joyce all the details. Just the basics. "Maybe you can help me sort through my thoughts."

The sound of Kate's knife clinking against the butter dish echoed in the silent dining room. She glanced at Mike and Laura, who'd barely spoken throughout the meal. Normally, Mike would have commented on how good the bison steaks smelled and tasted. And his mom would have teased him about his buffalo obsession.

Mary giggled. "Molly is the cutest little thing." She held out her hand. "Her lips on my fingers are so soft and gentle."

Kate grinned at Laura and Mike's perplexed expressions. "Aunt Mary nicknamed Estrella today. I think Molly was the name of her donkey."

Mary sat tall. "Of course that's my donkey's name."

Mike rested a forearm on the table. "Tell us about your donkey."

"She likes me." Mary beamed like a child with a new puppy.

"It's true." Kate touched Mike's arm. "That shy little colt, I mean *filly*, sidled right up to her and started playing with her scarf."

"When can we see my Molly again?" Kate's aunt practically bounced in her seat.

"How about tomorrow?"

Mary grinned and wiped her mouth with her napkin. "I'd better go to bed, so I can get up early." She grabbed her walker. Once she was on her feet, she pointed a bony finger at Laura. "You can come with us to see Molly. But not that man. Dean doesn't like him. Goodnight."

"Goodnight." Kate sighed. Would she ever stop talking about *that man?*

The moment the bedroom door clicked shut behind Mary, Laura cleared her throat. "Speaking of *that man...*" She pushed her plate aside. "I owe you an apology, Mike."

He folded his arms. "So he's a real person."

Laura ran her fingers along the edge of the table. "Like you, Mary doesn't think much of Todd Hughes."

"Thanks for telling us, Laura." Kate laid her fork on her plate. "Makes me less concerned about how fast her dementia is progressing."

"I'm sorry I didn't explain earlier." Laura looked at Mike. "I shouldn't have left the office in the middle of our conversation today. Or lied to you." She paused. "I didn't have a hair appointment. I just wanted to avoid talking about..." She took a breath. "I didn't want to talk about Todd, so I ran away." She scooped breadcrumbs into a pile beside her plate. "I spoke with a friend in town, who's going to pray with me and help me sort things out."

Mike arched an eyebrow. "What's to sort? I can tell you—"

Kate squeezed his arm. "Let her finish."

Laura swept the crumbs into her hand and dropped them on her plate. "I know you miss your dad, Mike, and you understand I miss him, too. Yet I don't think you comprehend the depth of my loneliness. Despite you and Kate and Mary living here with me, I've felt alone ever since your dad died. More alone than I can express. Todd helps me forget the loneliness. I enjoy his company." She held her hands over the plate and brushed off residue.

Mike placed his palms on the tabletop. "Of all the people..."

"I've seen a side of Todd Hughes you haven't. He's lonely, too."

"That's no excuse." His voice grew louder. "Mom, he's trying to get his hands on our ranch. He's using you."

She held up her palm. "All I can tell you is that I plan to seek God's direction for our relationship."

Kate reached for Laura's hand. "Dozens of people have told me Dan was a kind, generous, loving man. You can't help but miss him."

Tears welled in her mother-in-law's eyes.

Kate grasped Mike's hand with her free hand. Maybe she could be the link that reconnected mother and son. "You and Dan raised a wonderful son, Laura. I'm privileged to be married to him and to be a part of your family. We want what's best for you, God's best. Don't we, Mike?"

He didn't respond.

Kate elbowed him. She wanted things to be right between her husband and his mom before they left for Dallas.

"Yeah." His voice was hard, like his eyes. He pulled his hand from her grasp, picked up his plate and left the dining room.

The limousine ferrying Amy, Janessa and Mikaylah, five children and four EP bodyguards wound through the traffic to the beat of country-western music blaring from the stereo system. The kids stared out the windows with blank eyes and impassive faces. Amy wondered if they realized other boys and girls would envy their limo ride. Not that she was thrilled about it.

She twisted to see the backs of her bare legs. The painful dermabrasion and laser sessions plus daily tanning time hadn't quite eradicated the tattoos. At Thomas's insistence, she'd applied tattoo concealer. She hoped the makeup didn't rub off on the leather seat and make the guards angry.

The sight of her unadorned calves made Amy sad. Her animals were her family. She missed them.

The car slowed and pulled into an alleyway. What happened to her pets? Did nice families adopt them? She closed her eyes and dug her long nails into her wrist, derailing her nostalgic thoughts with pain. She was supposed to be perky and cheerful for her job today, not depressed and gloomy.

The car stopped. Damon stepped out first to stand on the pavement, arms crossed against his chest. "Move it, people!" The others clambered out of the vehicle.

Amy followed Janessa. One of the men pulled Janessa from the limo and then grabbed Amy's arm and jerked her to a standing position. Dressed in a tank top, shorts and a waist-length jacket, she had little defense against the chilly air.

They were parked in what was probably the back side of the convention center. Ahead of her, men unloaded tables and chairs from a truck trailer and carried them through an open doorway.

"Here's the rest of the whores," Damon said.

A second limo stopped behind the car she'd ridden in and the doors opened. Several more children, women and men stepped out. She surveyed the group. EP was out in force today. Watch out, Dallas.

At least they'd get a break from their usual work. Or would they? Did Thomas have enough people left at headquarters to keep the brothel going while they slept tonight? She exhaled. What did she care? This was her weekend to escape.

She watched the men unload the truck. Something about ordinary guys working at an ordinary job was refreshing, like the outdoor air she breathed. Maybe she could slip unnoticed into the back of their truck and be driven somewhere far away.

Steel fingers bored into her neck, and she felt hot breath on her ear. "Eyes ahead." Damon snarled. "You're not here to gawk or solicit business."

A dozen retorts raced through her mind, but she gritted her teeth and did as he said. Damon was wrong. She was here to gawk at everyone and everything and find a way to escape. She would watch for openings but remember the GPS and microphone. The reminder that she wore a necklace embedded with electronic surveillance devices made her scratch at her neck. She'd had the choker on less than an hour, and she already detested it.

"Hands off the jewelry." Damon pinched her arm. "You break the necklace, and you'll find out snakes are just the beginning of the fun and games we like to play."

A shudder shook her body.

He laughed.

She strode ahead of him, hating her weakness and despising him and everything he represented.

They checked in at a registration desk by the back door. One-by-one, the women were dropped off, each one instructed to remain at her booth until an EP guard picked her up for breaks and meals. When they reached Amy's booth, *Vertical Leap Health and Fitness*, the men separated from her, herding the children to an unknown destination.

Amy felt sorry for the kids, who were as wide-eyed and wary as cornered animals. What was their role at the sports convention? Would they demonstrate bicycles or skateboards or what? Would they pretend to be happy children who lived with loving families, not with a monster who imprisoned their souls and pimped their innocent little bodies?

She watched the last child straggle around a corner. Too bad the kids' t-shirts concealed their tattoos. That oddity alone would tell people things weren't right. Branding children was insane. Amy clenched her fists and turned to her booth. Her heart hurt more for the EP youth than for herself. At least she'd experienced a childhood. She had to find a way to help the young ones.

CHAPTER TWENTY-TWO

Mike wrapped his arm around Kate's shoulders and kept it there while they walked the two blocks from their hotel to the convention center. Early morning traffic sped past, occasional honks erupting above the rumble of engines. A bus pulled up next to them and the doors wheezed open. Kate and Mike slowed for the handful of passengers who spilled onto the sidewalk in front of them.

"I'll leave my cell phone on all day." Mike brandished his phone. "Call me anytime for any reason. Don't worry about interrupting my meetings. If someone is suspicious or hangs around your booth too long..." He steered her out of the path of a street vendor pushing a breakfast burrito cart along the sidewalk.

"I'll be careful," Kate said. "Don't forget that Walt and God will also watch over me. He didn't bring us here to abandon us—or Amy."

Someone called, "On your left." Mike pulled Kate to the side. After the bicyclist sped by, they resumed walking. He held up the phone again. "Text me."

"I will, when I have a chance." She kissed his cheek. "Just remember, they said I'll stay busy most of the time."

Security guards stopped them at the front entrance. The one with the clipboard asked her name, while the other studied her western attire.

"Katherine Reynolds." Kate displayed her nametag before slipping the lanyard over her head and onto her neck. "I'm hosting a gun booth for Bart's Guns, and this is my husband. He's dropping me off."

The guard checked his clipboard and nodded to an attendant. The woman motioned for them to follow her. "This way, please."

Mike clutched Kate's hand as they hurried to keep up. "That guard noticed how good you look in those new jeans."

"He was checking to see if I dressed for the part."

"I doubt it."

"So, slap him for me on your way out."

They jogged across the huge hall, weaving in and out of aisles, until their guide came to an abrupt halt, nearly causing them to run her over. "Here we are. Bart's Guns." She motioned to the man behind the table. "And this, I believe, is Bart."

The thirty-something man shook Kate's hand, and the attendant left.

In Mike's estimation, the guy was way too good-looking, but at least he wore a wedding ring.

"Nice to meet you," Kate said. "I'm Katherine Reynolds, and this is my husband, James. We're from Colorado."

Mike was impressed by Bart's firm handshake.

"What do you do in Colorado?" Bart asked.

"We run a working guest ranch," Mike said. "In addition to the usual trail rides, campfires and fishing, our guests can help brand cattle and round up horses."

"James also has a bison herd," Kate added. "Our guests love to take pictures of them. Next best thing to Yellowstone."

"Bison, huh." Bart's eyebrows lifted. "They're fascinating animals and becoming more and more popular with ranchers, I hear."

"That's right." Mike nodded. "Come visit us sometime. I'll give you our royal bison tour."

"I just might do that. Do you have a card?"

Mike pulled a business card from his shirt pocket. "I need to get back to the hotel to help our foreman set up a room for a meeting, so I'll get out of your way." He handed the card to Bart, glad Kate reminded him to stock his pocket with the Colorado business cards rather than his usual Wyoming ones. "What time can I pick Katherine up for lunch?"

"Whatever fits your schedule." Bart took cards from a stack on the table and gave one to Kate. "I plan to roam the floor and network with folks, but I'll keep an eye on the booth and help when things get busy. You can call me to cover meals and breaks and any other time you need to stretch your legs." He slipped Mike's card into his pocket and offered him one of his own. "Here's my card. Feel free to call if you need anything."

Mike kissed Kate and was about to leave, when he decided to check out the guns Bart was unpacking. "I've been thinking about getting a new elk rifle. You'll have to show me what you've got before the show is over, Bart."

Kate placed her hands on her hips. "I knew it was dangerous to let you visit this booth."

"I just want to see what he has."

Bart winked. "Yeah, a little harmless window shopping, that's all. We have a new Winchester I think you'll like. It's a beauty." He leaned close and stage-whispered, "Maybe your wife will let you take advantage of our generous employee discount."

"Hey, I like that idea."

Kate waved Mike away, blowing him a kiss.

He winked at Kate and saluted Bart, who seemed like a nice guy. A booth full of guns would discourage people from bothering his wife. In addition, Walt had promised to roam the convention floor all day, looking for Amy and keeping an eye on Kate.

Amy pressed the DVD on-button and dropped the Vertical Leap Health and Fitness video into the tray.

The young man in the next booth walked over carrying a shoebox. "You ever do this before?"

"No, this is my first time. I think it'll be fun."

"It will, but you'll get tired." He opened the shoebox and put the lid on the table next to him. "Sit down whenever you get a chance."

"Thanks. I appreciate the advice."

He held out his hand. "I'm Colin."

She took his hand. "I'm, A...uh, Natasha." She clutched the choker. Would they catch it that she'd almost said her real name? "Who are you representing?"

"I'm with a start-up company." He held up the box. "My boss designed a new kind of running shoe that will revolutionize—" His eyes widened and he stepped back.

Amy turned to see Damon stomping around the corner.

He grabbed her elbow. "Quick blabbing and get the booth ready."

She felt heat flood her cheeks. The first normal conversation she'd experienced in months, and Damon decided to run interference. She pulled from his grasp. "Nice to meet you, Colin. Good luck with your shoes."

Colin's gaze skipped from her to Damon and back again. "Yeah, sure. You, too."

Damon glared at her. "No more talking."

"What was I s'posed to do? Ignore him?"

His jaw muscles twitched. "Forget the chitchat, or Thomas will be here before you can say, 'Please, Thomas, don't hurt me.'"

Damon's mimicry of her pathetic pleas sliced at her self-esteem more than his demands did. She punched the DVD button. "I've got work to do." The Vertical Leap logo appeared on the blue screen.

He sniggered and strutted away.

Amy moved to the first of two stacks of boxes. Talk about hell on earth. Here she was with ordinary people again, yet she was unable to talk to them. But, she reminded herself, she wasn't an ordinary person. She was a bad girl dressed like a good girl—or maybe not. She tugged at her short shorts. At least she was wearing more than she did in the brothel.

She read the instructions taped on the top box. Basically, she was supposed to talk up the fitness center and hand out brochures and energy wafer samples. She broke the box seal, and her mouth began to water. Chocolate! Pushing back the flaps, she leaned close to indulge herself in the heady scent. Crazy as it was, the sweet aroma filled her with a sensation she'd hadn't experienced in a long time. For a moment, she couldn't identify the forgotten feeling. Was it hope?

Mike wandered from aisle to aisle on his way out of the convention center. Walt was supposed to be searching for Amy, but it wouldn't hurt for him to hunt for her, too. Booth after booth was filled with every sport accessory imaginable. Sunglasses, golf gloves, bicycle helmets, fishing poles, baseball bats, sports drinks and much, much more.

At a trampoline display, he saw a burly man with hard eyes and muscular arms standing between two trampolines, his stance wide. Somber dark-haired children climbed inside the nets and began to hop about like drunken rabbits.

Mike frowned. The kids seemed so serious, like bouncing on a trampoline was work, not play. They glanced at the man every few seconds, as if fearing his reaction. Another equally subdued child stepped onto a mini-tramp situated in front of the larger ones.

A blond lady next to the mini-tramp flashed a bright smile and lifted her arms. "Smile, boys and girls. You're having fun, right?"

No one answered her.

The man balled his fists. "Smile." His voice was harsh. "Laugh. Now."

Brief smiles flitted across their young faces, and the noises they made sounded more like strangled squeals than happy giggles. It was as if the children didn't know how to laugh.

Mike put his hands in his pockets. He didn't have a whole lot of experience with kids, yet something about these slender children struck him as odd. Maybe they were from an orphanage, one staffed by indifferent caretakers. He decided to check on them again later in the day. Maybe it was too early and they weren't quite awake.

The next booth featured one-hundred flavors of popcorn. The popcorn machine was already hard at work and the smell was tantalizing, but he kept walking. All he could think about was the kids. They were so thin. Were they malnourished?

Several aisles later, he ran smack into an unobstructed view of the backside of a woman wearing even shorter shorts than what some of their summer guests wore at the ranch. Bent over boxes, she revealed far more goose-bumped flesh than he cared to see.

Mike focused on the booth banner. *Vertical Leap Health and Fitness Center.* That's what city folk did to keep fit. Joined a club. All he had to do was walk out of the house and some chore would require most of the muscles in his body as well as his brain. No sweaty gym for him. He'd also get a good dose of clean air and sunshine to boot. Thank God for the WP.

Amy straightened and pulled down her shorts. A man passed her booth shaking his head, apparently deep in thought. "Mike?" She clutched the choker. Though she'd whispered his name, she shouldn't have spoken out loud. What was Mike Duncan doing in Dallas? And why was he at a sports show? He was a rancher, not a retailer.

Stepping into the aisle several feet behind Mike, Amy waved at Mikaylah. "Mikaylah, you look great in that outfit."

Mikaylah, who was attired in a form-fitting black-and-gold cyclist outfit, waved from across the aisle and down several booths. "How's it going, sista?"

"Okay. I bet you're a lot warmer than I am."

Mike stopped, eyed Mikaylah and then Amy, yet showed no sign of recognition. After a moment, he moved to the display on the other side of the aisle.

Amy's heart pounded so hard she feared Thomas's men would hear and rush over to find out what was going on. If only she had a way to get Mike's attention without speaking.

Mikaylah raised her elaborate eyebrows, fanned her face and mouthed *hot.*

Amy knew Mike truly was a hot guy, not because he was handsome, but because he was a genuine gentleman, something neither she nor Mikaylah encountered these days.

Cold fingers clamped onto her bare shoulder. She jerked away, and came face to face with Damon.

His nicotine breath nauseated her. She bit her lip to keep from gagging.

"Who were you talking to?"

She pointed to her coworker at the other end of the aisle. "I was talking to Mikaylah. She looks terrific in that outfit. Maybe she should take up cycling."

"You said, 'Mike.'"

"That's her nickname."

"Get to work. It's almost nine." He shoved her toward the booth and left.

Amy drew in a long breath and didn't bother to mention how stupid the diamond-studded choker looked with the cycling outfit. She fingered the chains that circled her own neck, knowing her necklace was just as strange.

Colin was eyeing her. He seemed to be a decent guy. Too bad she couldn't talk with him. She rubbed her arms. The place was like a refrigerator. If only she could borrow one of the furs the "Trading Post" across from her displayed. But she knew that out of love and respect for her pets, she could never wear an animal skin. Unless, of course, Thomas forced her to.

She opened an energy wafer packet and stuck the wafer in her mouth. Video running? Check. Brochures splayed in an attractive manner? Check. Samples nicely arranged? Check.

Energy wafers tasted? Check. They were delicious. She ate a second one and planned to eat many more, not just because she was hungry. She needed strength and energy to escape.

A shiver shook her from head to toe. Goosebumps out of control? Check.

Crossing her arms, Amy clasped her cold shoulders with her even colder hands and jogged in place. Thank God her feet had healed. The question was, would they tolerate three days of standing? No matter how much they hurt, this was better, so much better, than working at the brothel.

Still jogging, she rotated to watch the video. Might be good to know a little about the product she was pushing. But her thoughts kept returning to her best friend's husband. If she saw Mike again, how could she connect with him? How could she explain her predicament while wearing a microphone on her neck?

She trotted to Mikaylah's booth. "Got any gum with you? My mouth is dry, and I haven't even talked with anyone yet."

"Here, take this." Mikaylah handed her a package with only a few pieces in it. "I have another pack."

"Thanks."

"Happy chewing. May all your gum-wrapper balls hit their targets."

Amy laughed. "You're a funny lady, Mike."

A muscular EP employee appeared at her elbow. "Last warning. Stay in your booth."

Amy returned to the Vertical Leap table, grabbed her jacket and slid it over the tank top. She didn't care how unsexy it was, she'd wear the jacket until they made her take it off.

She pulled out a stick of gum and slid the remaining pieces into the jacket pocket. What was Mike Duncan doing at a sports convention? Promoting his guest ranch? Could be he was in town for a bison convention.

No matter the reason, she hoped he would return. She tried not to get her hopes up. After all, he didn't recognize her, probably because she'd lost weight and her hair was longer than when he'd last seen her. Plus, it was highlighted. She touched her face. Before Executive Pride, she'd never worn much makeup. Now she wore so much she hardly recognized herself in the mirror.

First trip to the restroom, she'd wipe off some of the makeup. And flatten her hair. If only she could dump the stupid choker. She sat on the cold metal chair and felt another crop of chill-bumps erupt. If she got Mike's attention, what would she do? Wave a gum wrapper in his face? That would be weird.

And what would she write on it? *Help* would catch his attention, although, if he didn't recognize her, he'd think she was a crazy woman. Maybe *prisoner* or *kidnapped*. But those were long words. The shorter the better. Maybe she could use her name. It was short, but if one of the guards saw it...

Three men in business suits walked toward her booth. She smoothed the gum wrapper on her leg. With the sharp corner of her fingernail, she carved one word into the foil before she unwrapped the gum and slipped the paper inside her bra. She stuck the gum in her mouth and chewed several times before tonguing it between her teeth and cheek.

Amy stood, took off her jacket and hung it on the back of the chair. "Good morning. Would you gentlemen like to sample an energy wafer? They're a great way to start the morning."

CHAPTER TWENTY-THREE

Amy faltered in her sales pitch to the middle-aged couple on the other side of the table. In her peripheral vision, she could see two burly EP employees, Marco and Alfonzo, working their way through the people who wandered the aisle. What did she do wrong this time? She'd been very careful with her words.

She handed the man and woman each a sample. "Try this and tell me what you think."

The men were one stall away. But surely they wouldn't hurt her in front of all these people.

They stopped beside the couple.

The woman asked her husband, "Do you like the taste?"

"Doesn't matter if I like it or not. I know how much you like chocolate." He reached into his back pocket. "I'll buy a box."

"Maybe we should get several."

He handed Amy cash. "Three boxes, please."

Amy put their wafers in a sack with a Vertical Leap logo printed across it and wrote a receipt for them. She held out the bag. "Enjoy!"

"Thanks, we will." They moved to the next booth, where Colin was in the middle of an enthusiastic promotion of his special shoes.

Marco walked behind the table to stand next to her while she put the money in the cash box. When she finished, he said, "Go."

Alfonzo jerked his chin, indicating she should follow him.

Her throat constricted. Was this a bathroom break or punishment for her earlier misdeeds? Amy swallowed, lifted her jacket from the chair and followed Alfonzo. If only she could lose herself in the crowd. But they'd track her every step, with or without the GPS.

She was working her arms into the sleeves of her jacket when they passed Mikaylah's table.

Mikaylah winked.

Amy lifted her fingers in greeting, but her smile was weak. For all she knew, she was headed for another bastinado session. Even if it was just a bathroom break, this wasn't how she'd pictured the convention. She'd hoped to spend time with Mikaylah and Janessa to get to know them better. Instead, they were all monitored and controlled, just like at the brothel.

Outside the women's restroom, Alfonzo gripped her arm. "No talking. No loitering. I'll be waiting."

She pulled away from him. Of course, he'd be waiting.

The line to the toilets was long, which was okay with her. She enjoyed being among normal women again. For a brief second, she was tempted to fall to her knees and beg them to save her. What would she say? *Help, I'm a prisoner!* They'd look at her like she was crazy. After all, she wasn't chained or behind bars. And then, Thomas's thugs would crash in and drag her away.

The line moved forward. Amy checked her reflection in the mirror and saw that other women gave her side glances that quickly slipped away. She stared at the floor. If she ever escaped, she'd wear ankle-length muumuus like her grandma and never use eyeshadow or rouge again. Or a choker necklace.

Once she was inside the privacy of the toilet stall, Amy checked the foil. It was warm and flat, yet her word was visible. Small as it was, the little paper gave her courage. When she washed her hands, she used a damp paper towel to dab at her cheeks and eyelids, all the while ignoring the gawking teenager beside her. She ran her fingers through her hair and shoved it behind her ears, hoping her appearance was a little less vampish.

Outside the restroom, Alfonzo seized her arm and pushed her toward the cafeteria, where he deposited her at a corner table far from other diners. He told her there'd be hell to pay if she moved and then walked over to the food line.

Amy put her feet up on a chair and leaned her head against the wall, more exhausted than she'd expected. For just a moment, she would rest, and then she'd look for a way to escape. Maybe she'd see Mike. She was almost asleep when she felt a hand slide from her knee up her leg.

"Hey, sexy lady..."

Amy slapped the hand away. "Get your hands off."

The man leered at her chest, a lustful smile contorting his features. "Natasha, isn't it?"

She recoiled. How did he know her EP name? She didn't recognize him as a customer, but then, she rarely looked at johns. Mostly, she closed her eyes and hoped they'd finish their business and leave.

"You high-priced babes like to see the cash, don't ya?" He pulled a wad of bills from a jacket pocket. "Tell you what. There's a hotel across the street. How much for two, maybe three hours?"

Alfonzo came up behind the man and grasped his arm. "What's going on here?"

Her accoster whipped around. "Cool it, dude."

"You harassing my woman?"

The man sneered. "You call that a woman?" He curled his lip and strode toward the entrance.

Amy lowered her eyes. The guy was a pervert, yet his words hurt.

Alfonzo tossed a tiny tray of apple slices onto the table. "Eat."

She pulled back the plastic cover. The crisp smell of apples filled her senses. She removed the top from the small caramel container that accompanied the apples and was about to dip a slice into the sauce, when Alfonzo shoved his finger into the brown goo.

"Thomas's women don't eat sugar." He circled his finger in the caramel, a sardonic smirk twisting his lips.

Amy dropped the container on the table.

Alfonzo licked his finger. "Thomas isn't going to like it when he finds out you were soliciting business."

"I was not soliciting."

"Shut up and eat."

Kate, who'd stayed busy all morning in the gun booth, finished talking with a customer before she turned to Mike. "Sorry about the wait."

He handed the gun he'd been examining to Bart. "No problem. Gave me a chance to take a gander at this rifle."

"More window shopping, right?"

"Right."

She gave him a knowing glance before smiling at Bart. "Is this a good time for me to go to lunch?"

"Perfect. Take all the time you need."

"Thanks." If they ran into Amy, they might need extra time.

Holding hands, she and Mike walked to the end of the aisle. "I passed a couple restaurants on the way over," he said. "Want to check them out?"

"We're more likely to run into Amy if we stay in the building."

"You're right." They started for the cafeteria, but then he stopped. "Before we go over there, I want to show you something."

"If Amy is eating lunch in the cafeteria, I don't want to miss her."

"This won't take long." He led her to an open area with a sign that read *Jumping Beans Trampolines.* Cheered on by a small crowd, several children were flipping and twisting on two large trampolines, while others took turns bouncing on a smaller one.

Kate looked at Mike. "Is this what you wanted to show me?"

He gave a slight nod. "Notice anything unusual?"

She surveyed the scene again. An energetic cheerful woman seemed to be in charge. Or was the beefy man who stood between the trampolines the real boss? She leaned toward Mike. "That guy reminds me of a correctional officer."

"Yeah. Anything else?"

"Okay, boys and girls…" the woman called. "Time to switch."

Kate watched the children change positions and, with barely a moment's rest, begin to jump again. They were obviously tired, yet something more than that was going on. What was it? She tilted her head. That was it. They weren't having fun. Most kids would be giggling and shouting. They'd be relaxed and loose-jointed, but the tension in these kids' bodies was obvious. Every time they slipped or fell, they leaped to their feet and peeked at the man, their eyes big.

"The children." She winced. "They're afraid."

"Yeah."

She pulled Mike close. "That guy is giving us the evil eye."

He wrapped his arm around her. "Let's go."

"Where do you think those little kids came from?" Kate asked as they walked away. "They're a mix of nationalities."

"A heartless orphanage is my guess."

"We could ask the trampoline company."

"Good idea. I'll call the Jumping Beans office this afternoon.

Kate returned from lunch disappointed she hadn't seen anyone who even slightly resembled Amy. Mike and Clint were planning to look for her as soon as they finished their meetings, and Walt was supposed to be watching for her. Maybe on her next break, she'd jog around the arena to see what she could see.

Marco, Kate's EP contact for the weekend, and another man approached her booth. As soon as she spotted them, the Matthew verse surged through her mind. *Be on your guard against men.* "Hello. Are you interested in the guns or just checking up on me?"

Marco cracked his knuckles. "A little of both. You can take a break now. We'll cover for you."

"I just got back from lunch. Besides, Bart never said—"

The other man jumped in. "We talked to him."

Kate eyed him for a moment. He was way too anxious. "I'll take a break with my husband later."

Marco frowned. "You a newlywed or somethin'?"

"No. I just happen to love my husband and enjoy his company."

The other man pointed to a pistol in the display behind her. "Let me see that handgun."

A mental picture of him holding the gun to Amy's head made her shudder.

He jutted his chin. "Got a problem with that?"

She handed him the gun. "Do you hunt wild hogs? I hear that's a huge sport in Texas."

He fingered the pistol from end to end, admiration gleaming in his eyes. "Nah. My dad used to hunt 'em. The taste is too gamey for me."

Marco nudged him. "You like target practice, don't you, Alfonzo?"

"Yeah. Target practice." Alfonzo aimed the pistol at the back of a man who stood at the next booth and pretended to pull the trigger. "Pow, pow."

Kate fought the temptation to rip the revolver from his hands and hit him over the head with it. She'd done that once, to protect another hooker when she worked the Hill District in Pittsburgh.

Alfonzo stroked the gun barrel. "This baby is my kind of toy."

By the time Alfonzo took her to the cafeteria for her afternoon break, Amy had the drill memorized. Make a quick toilet stop, avoid eye contact with the other women in the restroom, wipe off more makeup, hustle to a secluded table, listen to a lecture demanding she not leave her chair, act disinterested while scanning the room for Mike or a cop or... She exhaled, not sure who or what she was searching for but hoping she'd recognize the way out of EP when she bumped into it.

Not seeing any potential saviors or brothel clients nearby, Amy rested her head against the wall while Alfonzo went for food. She closed her eyes. It had been a long cold day already, and many more frigid hours loomed ahead of her. The convention wouldn't shut down until ten.

What about the kids? How were they handling the endless day? She hadn't seen any of them since they arrived. She hoped they were being treated well. They'd probably fall asleep in the limo on the way back to headquarters, poor things. She knew she'd sleep like a baby tonight, if Thomas didn't beat her for messing up this morning.

Her stomach tightened and her toes curled at the memory of the bastinado. Surely he wouldn't hit her while she was working the convention. She groaned. Of course not. He'd wait until the show was over and she was out of the public eye.

Mike took Kate's hand, and they walked away from the booth. "Ready to go put your feet up?" He could tell she was tired.

"Sounds good."

They neared the entrance to the cafeteria in time to see a string of young boys exit the men's restroom. The brawny man they'd noticed at the trampoline display was at the rear of the lineup. Holding the door, he flicked the head of a small boy walking out of the bathroom. "Move it."

The child grabbed the top of his head and ran after the others, eyes wide, mouth open.

The man looked Kate up and down and then made eye contact with Mike.

Mike saw recognition click in the other man's glance, followed by loathing. Kate's fingers tightened around his. Why was the guy so rough with the kids? They appeared to be too intimidated to misbehave.

Kate stopped at the entrance. "I'm surprised this place is so crowded in the middle of the afternoon."

"Might have something to do with the fact Dallas has two or three more people than Copperville."

She grinned. "Could be."

Mike ordered a cup of coffee and an apple, and Kate asked for ice tea along with a packet of peanuts. They found a seat near windows. Kate sank into a chair. "I can't tell you how good it feels to sit."

"You don't have to do this," Mike said. "In fact, I doubt your doctor would approve of you standing so much." He patted his leg. "Put your feet on my lap, and I'll give you a foot rub."

"Wow, thanks, sweetheart." She pulled her boots off. "I sit down between customers."

"We don't need the money."

"You know I'm doing it for Amy. This convention is our only connection to her." She rested her legs on his.

Mike bit into the apple. "Reminds me." He wiped his mouth with the back of his hand before he began massaging her feet. "I called the trampoline place just before I came over here."

She ripped open the nut bag. "What did they say?"

"They didn't hire the kids directly. They hired them through an agency." At the sound of loud swearing, he turned to see a muscular man in a tight t-shirt scowl at a little boy. "Stupid brat. Pay attention to where you're going." He huffed. "The coffee burned my leg. Too bad it didn't spill on you."

"Watch your mouth, mister." A tall man two tables away jumped to his feet. "He's just a kid. It was an accident." He motioned to the child. "Come here, Jakey. It's okay."

The boy scrambled to his side. The moment he wrapped his arms around his father's leg, he began to cry.

The angry man swore again and brushed his hand across his pant leg. "No, it's not okay. I'm covered in coffee. Hot coffee. And it's your fault for not controlling your brat."

Mike tensed, ready to jump in and break up a fight.

Kate touched his arm. "Wait." Her voice was low. "He's with Executive."

Mike raised an eyebrow.

The boy's father glared at the irate man. "I'll buy you another cup. And pay your laundry bill."

The man sneered. "Forget the charity. Just take your brat home where he belongs and lock him up." He stomped to a table in the far corner, where a stone-faced woman sat, her hands gripping the table edge.

The father's face contorted. He started to follow, but the woman next to him, who was now holding the crying child, grabbed his arm. "He's a hothead, Spencer. Ignore him."

Spencer hesitated.

A man at a nearby table said, "He's a jerk. Don't waste your time on him."

Spencer's wife clutched his arm. "Please don't give him the satisfaction of a confrontation."

Spencer finally sat down, still staring at the other man's back.

Jakey snuggled into his mother, who kissed the top of his head and patted his back.

Mike felt Kate's fingers dig into his arm.

She was staring at the rude man with unusual intensity.

He placed his hand over hers. "You all right?"

She blinked. "That woman he's with..." Her lips barely moved. "Does she look familiar?"

The woman was scrunched low in her chair, her eyes as big and frightened as those of the little boy. Probably wasn't the first time the guy lost his temper. "I don't recognize her. Wait, maybe I do. I think I saw her this morning. She's wearing a crazy necklace like that escort we took to the banquet."

"Not only is the choker necklace similar, I think she may be..." Kate paused. "Amy."

Amy? He gave Kate a quizzical glance.

She nodded.

He peered at the frightened woman over the lip of his coffee cup. It might be her. On the other hand, she could be any made-up female wearing a weird necklace. Was this wishful thinking on Kate's part? It didn't seem likely that Amy would hang out in a public place when the police were after her. Or that she'd be with that kind of guy. She certainly wasn't enjoying his company. In fact, she was as cowed under as the Jumping Beans kids.

The kids! He plopped the cup down, spilling coffee on the table. He hadn't finished telling Kate about the phone call. Swiping at the liquid with a napkin, Mike watched his wife study the other woman. Maybe now wasn't the time to tell her. "You really think that could be her?"

"Mm-hmm," Kate murmured. "With weight loss, a different hairdo and highlights, plus a whole lot more makeup than she used to wear." She gripped his arm. "What do we do? She's obviously terrified."

Maybe that's why he didn't recognize her. The Amy he knew was vivacious and happy-go-lucky. Always smiling. "Probably not a good time to talk to her."

"What if we never see her again?"

He leaned closer and murmured, "I know how to tell whether or not that's Amy."

"How?"

"Tattoos."

"Oh, of course." She squeezed his fingers. "They're getting ready to leave. Let's follow them." She slipped her feet into her boots.

The couple stood and started toward the entrance.

Kate jumped up.

Mike grabbed his coffee, and they wound between tables, following as quickly as they could. The other pair moved at a brisk clip. They exited the cafeteria and turned toward the exhibits. By the time he and Kate entered the hall, the couple was nowhere in sight.

"Oh, Mike, where could they have gone?" Kate looked ready to cry.

He pulled her from the milling crowd to stand against a wall. "They couldn't have gone far. I didn't see tattoos on her legs, did you?"

"They could be covered with makeup or maybe they were removed."

"As much as those things cost?" Mike snorted. "I doubt it."

"I still think it could be her." She lowered her voice. "If it is Amy, then she's somehow connected with Executive Pride, like we suspected."

He pulled his phone from his pocket. "Clint is walking the floor. I'll text him to say we think we saw her."

Kate nodded. "I'll text Walt."

Laura picked up the telephone in the living room. This was a good time to call Todd. Mary was talking to someone on her prayer line. She took a breath. "Okay, God. Here I go."

Inviting Todd to join her and Mary and the Raeburns for Sunday lunch was definitely stepping out of her comfort zone. Despite her misgivings, they needed to bring their friendship into the open. Maybe by the time Mike and Kate returned from Texas, she'd have a better idea of where her relationship with him was headed.

She dialed Todd's home number. It rang until the answering machine clicked on. Rather than dial his cell phone, she left a message and then stared out the living room window. What was her problem? She'd never felt wishy-washy about Dan. In fact, almost the moment she met him at a Jubilee Days rodeo in Laramie, she'd known he was the one for her, for forever.

She closed her eyes. But forever was cut short. Fighting tears, she reminded herself that her years with Dan were good years, and now it was time to move on.

Was she hesitant about Todd because her feelings for him didn't measure up to her feelings for Dan? She ran her thumb across the phone screen. That really wasn't fair. Dan was young love, her first love. In fact, he was her only love, until Todd came along. The question was, did she love Todd or just enjoy his attention and companionship? Her feelings for him were so different than her feelings for Dan.

She replaced the phone in the receiver. If she wasn't so lonely, maybe she could think more clearly. Could be a platonic friendship was the answer. Would Todd want that? Probably not. According to him, he'd been single long enough.

Talk with Dymple. The thought badgered at the back of her brain. But she couldn't do that. Dymple wouldn't approve of her dating a man who displayed little interest in God, though she'd been excited to see him in church and said kind things about him at lunch.

Laura opened the patio door for a quick breath of fresh air. Hot flashes and frustration were not a good mix. For a moment, she stood in the cold, debating whether or not to invite Dymple to the Sunday afternoon get-together. Was she brave enough to receive Dymple's input along with Joyce's? She already knew Aunt Mary's opinion of her suitor.

Todd's rooster crowed its sick squawk. Laura shut the door and hurried to her office. She had work to do, after she called Dymple.

CHAPTER TWENTY-FOUR

Before returning to her booth, Kate stopped in the nearly empty restroom. She was washing and drying her hands, when she heard a flush and the squeak of a stall door. An auburn-haired woman wearing a tennis outfit appeared in the mirror.

"Janessa!"

Janessa's eyes widened. "I, I don't..." She grabbed her necklace.

Kate gaped at the choker. It was the same one she'd worn the last time they met and just like the one the woman with Alfonzo wore. Why identical necklaces? Was it an Executive Pride thing? She hadn't been issued a choker for the convention. "I'm Katherine Reynolds, from Colorado. You accompanied me and my husband and our foreman to a stock grower's banquet several weeks ago."

"Oh..." Janessa lowered her hand. "I remember now. We went out for coffee afterward." She smiled. "Sorry I didn't recognize you."

"That's understandable. We only met once." Kate sneezed. Janessa's perfume was more potent than she remembered.

"Bless you." Janessa pulled a lipstick case from her waistband. "Are you in town for the sports show?"

"Yes." Kate smiled. "In fact, I was hired by your agency to work in a booth."

Janessa studied Kate for a moment. "Executive Pride?"

"Yes, just for this show. My husband scheduled some meetings in Dallas for his bison business, so I decided to tag along and have a little adventure while he works."

"No offense, but..." Janessa wrinkled her nose. "A sports show doesn't seem like much of an adventure to me."

"We spent part of the winter snowed in. I was starting to get cabin fever."

"I bet your ranch is beautiful with everything covered in snow." Janessa slipped the cover from the tube.

The only other woman in the facility washed and dried her hands and left the room.

Kate inspected her hair in the mirror. "I love winter there, yet Dallas is a nice change of pace." Arms folded, she leaned against the wall and watched Janessa apply lipstick. "Mind if I ask you a question?"

Janessa twisted the lipstick down and replaced the cover. "I need to get back to work."

Kate checked her watch. "Me, too. I was just wondering if you've ever met anyone at Executive Pride named Amy Iverson."

Janessa shook her head. "That name isn't familiar."

"Amy's coloring is similar to yours. Have you seen anyone else there with your hair color?"

Janessa yanked at a faucet handle, turning the water on full blast. "Don't know why my fingers are so sticky." She scrubbed as though her hands were covered in glue.

Kate frowned. Did she say something wrong? "I was just thinking—"

Someone hammered on the door. Both women jumped.

"Hurry up in there!" The masculine voice was harsh.

Janessa shoved the lipstick into her waistband and ran for the exit, wiping her hands on the short skirt. When she opened the door, the man started swearing. The door swished shut behind her, but Kate could still hear the abusive language.

She stopped the water flow and pressed her palms against her pounding heart. What was that all about?

I'm sending you out like sheep among wolves. Be as shrewd as snakes and as innocent as doves. Be on your guard against men.

Kate gripped the counter edge. *God, show us how to be shrewd.* She straightened, adjusted her vest, and ran to the door. Mike had to be wondering what happened to her.

Laura leaned back in her desk chair and stretched. She'd worked on the computer project for over two hours.

Mary wandered in, pushing her walker, a lost expression in her eyes.

Laura smiled. "Taking a break from phone calls?"

"Where's Katy?"

"She and Mike are in Texas. They'll be home soon."

"Oh." Mary's gaze flitted around the office like a butterfly seeking somewhere to settle.

Laura stood, rubbing her lower back. "Would you like to go to the barn to visit Estrella Blanca—or Molly, as you call her?" It would do both Mary and herself good to get out of the house.

Mary brightened. "I'll go put on my snow boots."

Laura grinned, amazed Mary remembered the boots Kate and Mike gave her for Christmas. "Good idea. The snow is melting, so it's messy out there."

When Laura and Mary approached the stall, the filly nickered and stuck her nose through the gate. Laura wondered if the little horse remembered the sound of Mary's walker.

"Hey, little girl." Mary pulled a carrot from her coat pocket. "I brought you a treat."

Estrella sniffed the carrot before pulling it into her mouth.

Laura laughed. "No wonder she likes you best. You spoil her."

Honey pawed at the straw, stirring up hay and urine odors.

Mary produced another carrot. "No need to be jealous, momma horse. I brought you one, too."

Honey took the carrot, and Estrella nibbled Mary's coat sleeve. She stroked the foal's neck. "Such a curious baby."

At the sound of whining, Laura said, "Tramp wants in. I'll be right back."

"Don't worry about me. Molly and I will entertain each other."

The dog bounded in, more energetic than he'd been since Mike and Kate left. Laura scratched his ears. "So Mary and I are suddenly good company, huh?"

Tramp stiffened and growled.

"What's the matter, boy?"

Hackles raised, he barked and took off for the back of the barn.

Laura grabbed a hayfork. A wild animal must have gotten in. She rushed to open the back door so Tramp could herd the raccoon or whatever it was outside. But then she heard a door slam, followed by a loud yip.

Rounding the corner, she saw Tramp clawing at the tack room door. Threats rumbled from his throat. Strange. They usually left that door open. She unlatched the barn's back door and swung it wide.

In two strides, she was at the tack room. She yanked at the door but stopped before she opened it all the way. What if it was a skunk? Before she could shut the door, Tramp charged inside, barking furiously.

Laura dropped the hayfork and flattened herself against the barn wall. Covering her mouth and nose with her hands, she squeezed her eyes shut. If she got sprayed, at least those crucial body parts would be protected.

Tramp yelped, and someone shouted, "Git outa here, you stupid dog!"

Snatching up the long fork, she stepped inside, nearly stumbling over Tramp, and switched on the light. The dog was crouched, hips back, front feet extended, snarling like she'd never heard him snarl before.

The man kicked at Tramp. "Call off your stupid mutt!"

"Todd. What are you doing in our tack room?"

"Call him off."

"Come here, Tramp."

Either the dog didn't hear her or he was ignoring her, because he continued to bark.

She set the hayfork down and grabbed his collar.

The dog gave her a "have you lost your mind?" glance and continued to growl.

She dragged him out of the room and shoved him outside. As soon as she shut the door, she spun around to glare at Todd, who'd followed her from the tack room. "What on earth were you doing in there?"

"Trying to get away from that mongrel."

She could hear Tramp scratching at the door. At least he'd stopped barking. "Let me rephrase. What are you doing in our barn?"

He sidled toward her. "I was hoping to get a chance to see you, beautiful."

She backed away. "You could knock at the front door of my home, like every other visitor to this ranch does." She remembered Dan telling her how spooky it was when Todd appeared out of nowhere on their property. One minute there'd be no one else in the barn, and the next, Todd Hughes would be standing there watching him work.

"But, baby..."

"Do not call me that."

He smiled a sly smile. "Whatever you say, darling. Your wish is my command."

Laura rolled her eyes. "Get on with it. I need an explanation."

"I wanted to see you, but I didn't want the old lady running interference, like she does every time I try to spend time with you."

"Mary does not do that."

"Well, she makes it clear she doesn't like me, same as your dog."

"Laura, where are you?" Mary's feathery voice floated through the tension and the hay particles drifting in a nearby shaft of light.

"I'm putting Tramp out, Mary. Be there in a second."

"Is someone with you?"

"Just one of the guys. He's leaving right now."

She pushed Todd toward the door. "Next time, call. And use the lobby door. That's where you'll find me, at the house."

"Nice barn you have here."

"Dan and I built it ourselves, with help from neighbors." She eyed him. "I don't recall you being on any of the work crews."

"Oh, I was here, every day. You just don't remember."

She was fairly sure he hadn't helped. However, that was years ago.

"Laura?" Mary's voice sounded closer.

"Coming." Laura spoke louder. "Stay there. You can help me feed Honey."

She shoved Todd outside and grabbed the door handle.

He tried to kiss her.

She backed out of reach, half tempted to slap him. The man could be so aggravating. For now, she'd ignore his audacity and go ahead with her plan. "Did you get my invitation?"

Todd's eyes lit. "Invitation?"

"To lunch on Sunday."

"Just you and me? No old lady?"

Laura let out an exasperated huff. "Mary will be there, along with several others."

He lowered his eyelids. "You gonna tell 'em we're a couple?"

Laura heard the rattle of the walker coming around the corner.

Mary cleared her throat. "Dean is going to be worried if I don't get home soon."

Laura whispered, "This is not an announcement party. I'm having some people over for lunch after church and thought you might like to join us. It'll be simple. Soup and sandwiches, something like that."

"Nobody will notice the food when they see how good we look together."

"Oh, brother." She shut the door.

Kate dashed from the convention hall restroom and almost slammed into Mike.

He grasped her shoulders. "What's going on in there?"

"Did you see Janessa?"

"The guy who pounded on the door grabbed her."

"I tried to talk to her." Kate couldn't see the pair anywhere in the wide hallway. "She was real jittery. And she's wearing one of those choker necklaces again."

Two women passed them on their way into the restroom.

Mike led Kate to a quiet corner. "Let's pray before you return to work."

Leaning against her strong solid husband, Kate whispered, "Give us wisdom, God, and show us how to help these women."

"And the children," Mike added.

Kate blinked. "You mean...?"

He opened his eyes. "The trampoline company got those kids through Executive Pride."

"Oh, Mike. That man treats them awful."

"I told the woman the kids were mistreated. She said their representative at the sports show voiced concerns, but they have to honor their contract."

"That's callous."

"Exactly what I said. She finally agreed to send someone to observe the trampoline activities." He pressed his lips together. "I hope those kids aren't punished because of my interference."

"Or you. They could come after you."

After he walked Kate to her booth, Mike jogged to the Vertical Leap stall. The woman they'd seen in the cafeteria was surrounded by a cluster of people. He moved closer. She was offering something called "energy wafers" to the onlookers. He'd have to try one. That would be a good conversation starter.

He strolled across the aisle to the Trading Post display and was greeted by the smell of leather. Fur coats and capes lined the stall and unfinished pelts hung from a rack at the front. He couldn't resist stroking one. The smooth silky feel made him realize how much he missed his dog.

The attendant got up from his chair. "That's a beautiful fur, isn't it?"

"Sure is. I should have asked before I touched it."

"That's why I hang the pelts there. So people can experience how luxurious a real fur feels."

Mike rubbed a coffee-colored fur with the back of his hand. "Which animal did this come from?"

"Sable. This lighter one over here is also sable. Their coats vary in color. Are you shopping for your wife or for yourself?"

Mike saw the group across the aisle move on. It was now or never. "I need to go. I'll try to bring my wife by later."

The booth hostess was straightening her display when Mike approached her table. They made eye contact, and her fingers froze.

He hesitated. Was she afraid? He started to speak.

She placed her finger on her lips. "Hello, sir. Would you like to try one of our energy wafers?"

"Uh, sure, if they don't taste too bad."

Her eyes were wide, and he thought he saw her lip tremble. "Like you," she said, "I was cautious at first, yet I found them surprisingly good, and they really do provide an energy boost."

"Okay." He scratched his chin. "You convinced me."

"Give me a second to get that for you." Though a box of wafers sat on the table, she twisted away from him.

Mike raised an eyebrow. What was she doing?

As quickly as she'd turned away, she faced him again. She picked up a wafer and handed to him, along with a piece of paper.

He stared at the paper. It looked like a gum wrapper. He turned it over. It *was* a gum wrapper. He gave her a quizzical glance.

She mouthed what he thought was *read*.

He studied the silver foil. The lines on it could be letters. *T-R...* tramp? He looked her up and down. She was dressed rather suggestively. If she was soliciting his business, her method was odd. The woman's face reddened. She tugged at her shorts and then grabbed the foil from him. Plopping it on the table, she etched something with her long red fingernail before handing it back to him on top of a brochure. "Here's some information about Vertical Leap. We have eleven locations in Dallas, nine in Fort Worth, and twelve in Houston."

"That's a bunch."

She'd added two letters at the edge of the foil. *W* and *P*. *Whispering Pines?* Now it was his turn to blush. His dog's name was a clue, one he'd almost missed. He studied her face. Yes, this was Amy, just like Kate thought. A very thin version of Kate's best friend, but it was her.

She circled one hand around the other, as if encouraging him to keep talking.

"Uh, I didn't realize you have so many locations. There's probably one near us." He cleared his throat. "Okay if I take another wafer for my wife?"

Amy's eyes brightened. "Your wife... is she...?" She coughed and fidgeted with the choker. "I mean, do you live in the area? Couples' memberships are discounted."

"I'll show her the information. She might want to join. Me? I'll stick with the wafers, if they're any good."

"Why don't you taste one and tell me what you think."

He unwrapped the wafer and bit into it. Chocolate. Kate would love it. He gave her the okay sign. "Good stuff."

Her eyes wild and desperate, she mouthed *help.*

He wanted to assure her, but her attention had shifted. Following her focus, he spied the bully he and Kate saw her with earlier. The brute was headed their direction. Mike stuffed the gum and wafer wrappers into his shirt pocket and moved away.

At the next booth, he picked up a running shoe. The young man behind the table handed him a pamphlet and began telling him all the wonders of the unique shoe. Mike listened with one ear, his thoughts with Amy.

Did he cause trouble for her? They didn't talk much, didn't have physical contact. Their communication couldn't have been observed, unless someone was sitting above the exhibits with a pair of binoculars.

An elbow in his side almost knocked him over.

He swiveled. Alfonzo. The beefy man's stance reminded him of a bull pawing the ground, readying for the charge.

Alfonzo's eyes flashed. "Give me what you took from that booth over there."

"I didn't take anything, except samples and a brochure."

Alfonzo gripped his arm. "I'm with security. We'll search you in the office."

Mike jerked from his grasp. "No you won't."

The brute cursed and reached for him again.

Mike sidestepped and crouched, ready to tackle him.

The shoe salesman cheered. "Take him down!"

A crowd gathered.

Alfonzo scowled at the bystanders and waved them away. No one moved. He swore at them.

Mike grabbed Alfonzo's shoulder and swung him around.

Alfonzo threw a punch. Mike blocked it and slammed his fist against the angry man's jaw.

Alfonzo swore, but before he could take another jab at Mike, an equally brutish man appeared at his side. "Boss says get outta here." In an instant, the two of them disappeared around the end of the corridor.

Mike did an about face and saw Amy huddled in the far corner of her booth. She looked ready to pass out. They had to steal her away soon.

CHAPTER TWENTY-FIVE

Kate didn't join the discussion at supper that night or eat much. Her stomach had twisted into a tight knot the moment she learned the frightened woman they'd seen in the cafeteria was indeed Amy. The fact that her best friend couldn't talk freely with Mike but communicated via a gum wrapper, of all things, said volumes. Add in Alfonzo's attack on Mike this afternoon, and things were beginning to get serious.

"How could her tattoos just disappear?" Clint was asking. "If I remember right, those birds on the back of her legs were fairly obvious." He stabbed his fork into a piece of meat. "And probably expensive."

"You bet. And even more pricey to remove." Walt rolled up a sleeve and held out his arm. "When me and my ex divorced, I wanted her name removed from my arm along with all the doo-dads around it. Can you see anything?"

They all leaned close, squinting in the dim lighting.

Kate examined his forearm. "Maybe a little bit of darkness, like here." She moved her finger to another spot. "And there. Someone did a good job."

"How'd they do it?" Mike asked.

"Dermabrasion. Cheaper than laser." He grimaced. "Not fun. Took a bunch of sessions and too many paychecks, but it was worth it. If the woman wanted out of my life, I dang well wanted her erased from mine."

Clint raised his eyebrows. "That bad, huh?"

Walt grunted and turned to Mike. "Tatts or no tatts, you're convinced she's Amy Iverson. Is that correct?"

"That's correct."

"Then we need to tell Barker she's at the show."

Kate started to protest.

He held up his hand. "For her protection and yours. If she's innocent, like you believe she is, it'll come out in the courts." He folded his arms and sat back. "Wearing my different disguises today—"

Kate interrupted. "What disguises? I didn't see you."

"You saw a skate skier and a clown on a unicycle. Don't know if you saw the mountain man disguise."

"You were all those people today?"

"I've got dozens of alter-egos in my closet. Just remember, even when you suspect it's me, don't say anything. You never know who's watching. I'm fairly certain your Executive friends have people stationed upstairs at one of those windows."

Mike rapped the table with his knuckles. "I was afraid of that."

"I checked out every Executive Pride person working this show," Walt said. "A handful of people appear to be ordinary citizens, but—"

Kate couldn't wait. "Is Amy Iverson's name on the list?"

"Yours is, but I didn't see hers." He shrugged. "Your friend is probably working under an assumed name. Some of those women have exotic monikers. As far as I can tell, a few women act normal and have normal names. The other employees, including those kids you saw, are as skittish as dogs during Fourth of July fireworks. And the older females are all wearing those bizarre necklaces."

Kate smirked. "They're called chokers."

"Name makes sense." He paused. "Couple odd things about the jewelry. They're identical and, somehow, they don't seem right."

"They look like necklaces a woman would wear for a night on the town or maybe to a bar, but not with tennis dresses and cycling outfits," Kate said. "Is that what you're trying to say?"

"Yeah. Did they ask you to wear one?"

"No." She shook her head. "The receptionist didn't mention anything like that. Just wanted identification."

"Did you show them that driver's license I made for you?"

"Yes."

"Good, good."

Clint slapped the table. "That's it!"

Kate jumped. "What?"

"Those choker things. They're bugged."

Mike, who was cutting his steak, stopped. "What makes you think that?"

"Remember how Janessa grabbed her throat when she was talking with us at that Italian restaurant? And how she and Amy act like they're afraid to talk? I bet those necklaces have microphones in them."

"Bingo." Walt aimed a trigger finger at Clint. "You hit the nail on the head, bud."

Kate gasped. "That's horrible. Surely not..." The more she thought about it, however, the more Clint's logic made sense.

"Fits with what I've been ponderin'." Walt fiddled with his steak knife. "One more thing I should mention."

She could tell by his tone she wasn't going to like what he said. If he told them they needed to step out of the investigation, she'd resist with every ounce of her being. She would not, could not abandon Amy. They were too close to walk away now.

"From what I've seen so far, I'm thinking the women with the necklaces are..." Walt rubbed his nose. "Not sure how to say this without dissing your friend..." He scratched his head. "I'm convinced those women are...well... Dang it, I'll just say it. They're, uh..." He planted the knife on the table, blade up. "Ladies of the night."

"No! That can't be." Kate leaned toward him. "I worked the streets in Pittsburgh, but Amy never did."

Walt arched an eyebrow.

She sat back. "We met in prison."

Without even a blink, he said, "So this ain't your first rodeo." He burped. "S'cuse me. Seems you'd have noticed your friend isn't exactly dressed for a revival."

She'd wondered about the changes in Amy. Surely she wouldn't...

Mike put his arm around Kate but spoke to Walt. "What makes you think they're call girls, other than appearance?"

"The thought that keeps coming home to roost is that they're not just hookers, they're human-trafficking victims." He paused. "Sex slaves. I think Executive Pride is running an illegal brothel with slave labor. Every last one of the women with the necklaces is as nervous as a cat in a dog pound, and they have all those sorry-lookin' bodyguard types hanging around 'em. It's the same with kids."

Tears filled Kate's eyes. "That would explain why Amy disappeared so suddenly."

Clint placed his hands on the table. "So let's go grab her."

Walt swallowed some coffee and then set his cup down. "You've seen the bozos who guard these people. Any one of them would be more than happy to take out you and you..." He pointed to each one of them. "And you, if you make trouble for them. Those women and children don't act the way they do without good reason."

Kate knew he was right. She'd seen the sick grin on Alfonzo's face when he aimed the gun at a man's back. "This isn't about us, Walt. It's about Amy. Our sole purpose in coming here this weekend was to find her."

"And rescue her," Clint interjected.

Walt nodded. "I'll give Barker a buzz."

"Good." Mike ran his fingers through his hair. "The cops can do the dirty work. In the meantime, Clint and I'll patrol the convention center to keep an eye on Kate and Amy."

"How can we let her know we're trying to help her?" Kate asked. "Without putting her in more danger?"

"I have an idea." Walt pursed his lips. "She likes dogs, right?"

"Yeah, she does," Clint said. "I'm working on an idea, too."

Later that evening, Amy saw a man wearing a fishing hat pulled low over his eyes approach her booth. He was leading a large leashed dog with one hand and pushing a pet stroller with the other.

"Can I pet your dog?" The instant she asked, Amy clamped her mouth shut, wishing she could retract the words. Thomas would make her pay for touching an animal.

The man rolled the stroller partially into the booth. The dog followed.

She held her hand out to the retriever.

"This big guy is Leo," the man said. "He's a golden retriever. The backpack he's sporting was designed for comfort as well as efficiency."

Leo sniffed her hand before licking it.

"He's beautiful." Amy stroked the dog's head, reveling in the feel of his soft fur.

"And this pet stroller is handy for small dogs with short legs."

Amy dropped to one knee to peek inside. "What an adorable puppy. What kind is it?"

"She's a Shih Tzu. Her name is Miz Sadie."

Sadie whined.

Amy placed her finger on the mesh screen. "Poor baby. You're feeling left out."

The little dog stuck its wet nose against her fingers.

Amy laughed. "You're a cutie."

"You want to feed her a treat?"

"Sure, that would be fun."

He reached into his shirt pocket, pulled out a bone-shaped dog biscuit and handed it to her, along with a scrap of paper the size of a fortune-cookie strip.

She took the biscuit and started to hand the paper back to him, yet he ogled the paper like it was a hundred-dollar bill. That's when she saw the hand-printed words. *Help coming. Be ready.*

She curled her fingers around message. Who was this man?
A loud noise made them both jump.

Marco pounded the table again. "What's going on here?"

Amy gave the dog biscuit back to the man. How could she
have forgotten she was never allowed a moment of pleasure?
Blinking away tears, she crumpled the paper, dropped it on the
floor and stood.

The dogs growled.

The man in the fishing hat slowly got to his feet. "I was just
letting her pet my dogs."

"Move out, buster. Can't you see she's working?"

Leo bared his teeth. The man tugged his leash. "Let's go, Leo."

Head lowered, Amy placed one foot on the piece of paper and
began to rearrange the brochures Marco knocked askew.

He charged around the end of the table, jerked her close and
hissed, "Thomas is not going to like this."

The sensation of spittle striking her ear made her shiver.

"Keep slacking and you'll find yourself staring at the Trinity
River from the bottom up." He shoved her aside and stomped away.

Amy bent down to retrieve the wadded note. Feeling Colin's
gaze, she avoided eye contact and stepped to the stack of boxes
at the back of the booth. Once her hand was hidden inside a half-
full case of brochures, she opened her fingers and smoothed the
paper to read it one more time.

Though she longed to roll the words across her tongue, to
taste their deliciousness and savor their meaning, she crushed
the strip into a tiny spitball. Should she toss it into another booth?
No. Too risky. Better save it until the next bathroom break.

Reaching into her pocket to deposit the paper, she felt the
gum packet. She slid a piece out, unwrapped it and popped it in
her mouth, along with the tiny strip of paper. Once the paper was
mashed into the gum and stuck to the underside of the table, no
one would be able to decipher the words.

Chewing slowly, she thought about the man with the dogs.
She'd never seen him before. Was he with Mike? Did he know

what he was up against? And what about Colin? He glanced her way often, always with a concerned expression on his face.

Lots of people seemed to want to help her, yet what could they do? Did they realize how dangerous it was for them to tangle with Thomas and his henchmen? And what could she do on her own to escape? If a real cop walked by, would she have the courage to turn herself in?

After the convention ended that night, Kate and Mike helped Bart lock up his guns and close down the booth. On the walk to the hotel with Mike and Clint, no one spoke. She assumed the guys were thinking what she was thinking. Even though they'd found Amy, they weren't able to help her.

They reached the hotel and rode the elevator in silence. When the doors opened on their floor, Clint said goodnight and trudged toward his room three doors down from theirs. Kate watched him go. With his bowed head and drooping shoulders, he looked as dejected as she felt.

Mike unlocked the door to their hotel room and motioned her inside.

She threw her purse on the bed. "We sure spun our wheels today."

He hugged her. "I'm sorry, sweetheart. I know you're disappointed, but if you think about it, we made progress. We know a lot more about Amy now than when we flew into town yesterday."

She clutched his shirt. "How can we sleep knowing Amy is imprisoned somewhere in this city? We could be out searching for her. Instead, we're wasting precious hours sitting in a hotel room."

"We have no idea where to begin."

"That's not true. We know she works for Executive, and we know where their office is."

"Doesn't mean she lives there."

"We could start there."

He sat on the edge of the bed and tugged off a boot. "Yeah, and get in the way of the cops, who can put two and two together just like we did."

The room phone rang and Mike picked it up. "Hello... Oh, hi, Clint." There was a pause. "Yeah, Kate was just saying the same thing." Silence. "You're right. I'll meet you downstairs."

Amy switched on a bedside lamp and fell across her bed, so exhausted she considered sleeping in her clothing. She heard footsteps outside the door and sat up. What did they want now?

Thomas opened the door and leaned in. "You're still up. Good. I was hoping I could talk with you."

Like he wouldn't have awakened her? What was with the politeness? It wasn't like him to not get right to the point.

"Hi, Thomas." She tried to sound upbeat, but she was so tired.

"Hey, baby." He sat next to her and caressed her arm. "Long day?"

"Uh-huh."

"How'd it go?"

"People seemed to really like the energy wafers I gave them."

He drew her to him.

Too tired to resist and knowing better than to try, she let him hold her.

For a moment, he rocked her. "Remember that friend you told me about?"

"Huh-uh."

"Someone named Kate."

Amy peered at him. "I had a friend in prison named Kate."

"Is her real name *Katherine*?"

Uh-oh. Something about Kate had captured his attention again. "Could be. I don't remember."

"You said she was married to a rancher. Remember his name?"

"Something short." She fought to keep her voice relaxed. "Maybe Bob or Bill."

"Does *James* ring any bells?"

She yawned. "There was an officer in prison with the last name of James. That's the only one I can think of."

He released her. "Change your clothes. You've got a client waiting and several more on the schedule for tonight."

"I thought…"

"You think too much, Natasha. I'll do the thinking and you do the—"

She blanked out the last word. She'd do her job. That's what kept her sane, calling what she did a job.

He walked to the door and punched the buttons. "Five minutes. Fix your face and comb your hair."

CHAPTER TWENTY-SIX

Kate blocked the hotel room exit, hands on her hips and legs planted wide. "No way, Mike. You two are not going without me."

"We'll just wander around. See what we can see. I'll text you if we run across something noteworthy."

"*Noteworthy*? Are you kidding me? We're talking about Amy's future, maybe even her life."

He held out his hands. "It could get dicey."

His cell phone rang. He glanced at the screen before lifting the phone to his ear. "Yeah, Clint. I'm on my way."

Kate folded her arms.

Mike cleared his throat. "We'll be there in a minute."

He dropped the phone back into his pocket. "Taxi's here."

"Wait!" Kate held up a hand. "We need disguises. I need a moment to think about how to change our appearance."

Following a brief stop at a discount store, the taxi driver dropped them off two blocks from Executive Pride's office building. Kate took in the loiterers outside a club called Rolly's Rockout Place. They, in turn, gave her and Clint the once-over, while Mike paid the cab driver.

She chuckled to herself. The kids must be wondering what three lost-looking gringos were doing at a hip-hop inner-city nightclub. She wondered the same thing, but at least they'd left the hotel and were actually doing something.

She crouched on her heels to check her makeup on the taxi door mirror. After they'd made their purchases at the store, she'd hurried to the restroom to revive her streetwalker persona. First, she'd rimmed her eyes with heavy black eyeliner and applied multiple layers of smoky mascara. Then she striped her eyelids with glittering green, yellow and orange eyeshadow, followed by accents to her eyebrows. Final layers included a green swath beneath her lower eyelashes, rose-hued blush, thick purple lipstick and a fake mole beside her left nostril.

Kate studied her reflection, sad she recognized her former self, yet pleased she was no longer that person. Tucking a wayward strand of dark hair under the knit cap snugged against her head, she was pretty sure no one would connect her with the western-clad gun salesman at the sports show. Both her husband and Clint had done double-takes when she walked out of the bathroom.

She straightened, and Mike closed the door. The taxi sped off. Ignoring curious stares, the trio walked toward their target. All three were dressed in sweats and tennis shoes. The men also wore ball caps with the bills pulled low over bifocal glasses they'd found at the store.

Kate tipped her head, trying to see the top of Executive's building. Did they own the entire building or just rent the fiftieth floor? Where did they keep people like Amy and Janessa and the kids?

The whap-whap-whap of a helicopter caught her attention. Lights blinking, the aircraft momentarily hovered above them. Clint and Mike slid their hats back to watch the helicopter land on the roof of the Executive building.

Cliff removed his glasses. "Sure is hard to see with these things."

"Is that a Life Flight helicopter?" Kate asked.

Mike lowered his glasses to the tip of his nose. "I don't think so."

"Seems like an odd time of night to be landing on a building other than a hospital."

"A lot of wealthy people live in Dallas." Mike slid the glasses back in place. "I s'pose they can come and go whenever, however they please."

"Or maybe..." Clint straightened his hat. "Maybe it's part of that helicopter-brothel deal Walt talked about."

Kate squinted at the top of the building. Was Amy up there right now?

They made their way to the corner across the street from the Executive building. Clint stuck his hands in his pockets. "Shall we start at the front or the back?"

Mike waited until a motorcycle raced past. "Let's check out the front." He took Kate's hand as the three of them trotted across the street and stepped onto the sidewalk that ran alongside the tall structure. Mike took a long breath and squared his shoulders. "We should have grabbed a couple of Bart's guns."

Clint raised his eyebrows. "Now you're talking."

The threesome looked both ways before stepping into the trees that skirted the nearly deserted parking lot. Only two cars and one pickup truck occupied slots. Through the lobby's glass front, they could see that the lobby was also empty.

Clint pushed branches aside to peer over the top of his glasses at their surroundings. "What next?"

When Mike didn't respond, Kate said, "You guys got a plan?" She looked at her husband, who looked at his foreman.

Clint murmured, "I've got a plan." He pulled his sweat jacket hood over the ball cap and strode across the parking lot. When he reached the glass doors, he tugged at one of them. It opened, and he stepped inside.

"Amazing," Kate kept her voice low. "A lobby door unlocked at midnight." She'd tried a multitude of locked doors on dark Pittsburgh nights. Once in a while she got lucky, like tonight.

Mike took a step. "Stay here."

She grabbed his sleeve.

Two burly men in jeans and t-shirts materialized from around the corner of the building. They stopped outside the lobby, and then one headed for the doors. The other crouched in the shadows.

Clint was already at the elevators when the entry door opened. He turned around.

The man motioned Clint outside.

As the two men exited the building, Clint said, "Doesn't make a whole lot of sense to lock the elevators without locking the lobby doors." He pushed the glasses up the bridge of his nose and pulled the ball cap bill lower on his face.

"Easier for tenants who need to work at night. They have the code for the elevators." The man's voice took on an edge. "You obviously don't know the code, so why are you here? And, how'd you get here? I don't see a car."

"Took a cab. Like I said, I hired an escort from that Executive Pride place upstairs a few weeks back and thought if she was around, we could go dancing or something." He snapped his finger. "I've got it! We could take a helicopter ride. I just saw a 'copter land on the roof of this building. Do you know if I can rent it?"

"It'll cost you."

Kate nudged Mike, who muttered, "Interesting."

"That's okay." Clint chuckled. "Just got my annual bonus at work. I'm rollin' in the dough."

Kate frowned. What was Clint up to?

"You have that in cash?" The man, whose hands were at his side, wiggled his fingers.

The other man crept forward.

Clint cocked his head, as if he'd heard something. "Steer me to an ATM machine and I'll have it in a jiffy."

"What's her name?"

Clint hesitated. "Who?"

"The escort."

"Janessa. Don't know a last name."

"What if she's not available?"

"I guess someone else would be okay, but I'd rather it was her, you know." He shrugged. "What kind of helicopter rides are available? Must be a price breakdown."

"We can talk about that on the way up." The man walked over to a door and opened it.

Clint followed him to the entry.

The man in the bushes rose to full height.

Kate gripped Mike's arm. "We can't let him get in that elevator."

"I'll tackle the closest guy while you distract the other one," he whispered, "so Clint can take him down."

"Okay." She could handle him herself, but this was no time to argue with her husband. Then she heard Clint say, "Uh, sorry for the trouble. I changed my mind."

"What?" The man scowled.

Clint edged toward the parking lot. "It's late, and I just remembered I have an early meeting tomorrow morning."

The man wiggled his fingers again.

"Which one do you want?" Kate whispered.

"I'll take the one by the door. Clint will—"

"Clint will help."

"Okay. Let's go."

Kate darted across the parking lot, leaped at the second man and knocked him to the ground.

He jumped up, grasping for a hold on her body.

She kicked him in the stomach.

He grabbed her leg, twisting her to the ground.

Kate rolled with the twist and yanked her leg free.

He was on top of her in an instant, his arm around her throat.

Now on her knees, Kate didn't have the leverage she needed to fling him off. Instead, she bit his bicep as hard as she could.

He let out a piercing curse and ripped his arm away.

Kate sprang to her feet, spitting his flesh back at him.

With a roar, he bounded upright, blood streaming down his arm, and charged her.

She sidestepped.

The furious man tripped past her.

She whacked him across the neck, and he collapsed at her feet, air whishing from his lungs in a loud growl.

Kate stepped away, ready to counter his rebound. He didn't move. That's when she noticed how quiet it was. She glanced up and saw Mike and Clint staring at her above the inert body of the other man. "Can I borrow your handkerchief, Mike? I think I have blood on my mouth."

He tossed her his bandana and picked up his hat and glasses. "We'd better clear out of here before these thugs wake up."

Secluded in the far corner of an all-night diner, the three of them replayed the evening over waffles and hot chocolate. "I'd heard you'd been in street fights, Kate," Clint said. "I only half believed the stories, until tonight. You don't hold anything back."

Mike chuckled. "Now you know why I never argue with my wife."

"It's just instinct, Clint." She waved his admiration aside. "I have a question for you."

"Fire away."

"Why did you change your mind about riding the elevator?"

"I had a feeling the first guy wasn't alone and I'd never make it to their headquarters or be able to help Amy."

Mike gave him a thumbs-up. "Good call, man."

"As fast as those two showed up," Kate said, "they must have seen you on camera."

"The hood and the hat probably hid my face." Clint yawned and rubbed his eyes. "Or at least shadowed it. Plus, I had those glasses on."

"Yeah." Mike nodded. "But if we come back, you need a different disguise." He looked at Kate. "That goes for you and me, too. We may have also been caught on video."

Clint leaned his chair back. "I doubt Walt will be pleased when he learns what we just did."

"He won't." Kate dabbed her mouth with a napkin. "Even so, we have to tell him we stirred the pot tonight."

When she returned to the booth after her Saturday lunch break, Kate found Bart between customers. "Your turn," she said. "This is your chance to put your feet up."

He studied his watch. "I'll run over to the cafeteria and grab a soda."

"Like you tell me, take your time, relax."

"Well, maybe for a few minutes. Call me if things get crazy."

Seated in a chair, watching people pass by, Kate could feel fatigue and discouragement sap her enthusiasm. She hadn't seen Amy or Janessa during lunch nor heard if the guys made contact with either of them. The convention was half over, yet her friends and the kids remained prisoners.

She checked the aisle, hoping to see her husband and wondering if she'd recognize him in the disguise Walt gave him. He and Clint were roaming the arena incognito to keep an eye on her and Amy. Mike had changed clothes for lunch and refused to tell her what he wore on the floor. "For your protection," he'd said.

According to Walt, plain-clothed cops were also watching over them. She chuckled at the irony of the situation. She and Amy, of all people, were being protected by policemen rather than chased by them. But she was surprised they didn't arrest her friend. After all, she was wanted for murder.

Walt, who'd been none too happy to learn of their late-night escapade, told them the authorities were planning some kind of sting operation and didn't want to jeopardize it by grabbing Amy. "I just hope," he said when they met for breakfast, "you didn't put that Executive bunch on alert."

She sighed. If nothing else, at least they'd proved to themselves that Executive's offices were open for business late at night and that they didn't like surprise visitors. She wished they knew where Amy went at night. Did she live in that building or stay somewhere else? Kate sighed and tapped her fingers on her leg. Too many questions and not enough answers, or action.

A middle-age man stopped to examine the pistols in the case. She stood. "Hi! Any particular gun you'd like to check out?"

He asked about several guns, and by the time she finished with him, Bart was back.

Kate shook her finger at him. "That was a really short lunch break."

"Katherine Reynolds." The voice was loud and demanding. "We need to talk."

She swiveled. Damon. What did he want? Kate lifted her chin. "Okay."

"Privately." He reached for her arm.

She stepped away. The last person she wanted a private meeting with was Damon. "We can talk here."

He gave Bart a hard stare, glanced at the people walking by, and lowered his voice. "The social security number you gave us is invalid."

Kate frowned. "Invalid? I don't understand."

"Our bookkeeper says it's not a legit number. We need to go to a quiet place where you can tell me the right one."

"I'm sure I wrote the correct number. I'll stop by the office later and talk with your bookkeeper."

"We need it now for your paycheck."

"I can wait for the check."

His eyes narrowed. "We have to have that information today, or we can't pay you."

Bart moved closer.

Kate placed her hands on her hips. "I'm more than happy to work without compensation."

"You'll be paid." Bart folded his arms. "I'll skip this middleman clown and pay you direct."

Damon's face reddened. He glared at Bart. "You stay out of this, unless you want us to sue you for breaking your contract."

Bart waved him away. "Get lost."

Kate turned her back on Damon.

He grabbed her from behind, one arm around her waist and his free hand gripping her upper arm. She yanked her arm free and jabbed her elbow deep into his stomach.

Damon grunted and doubled over.

Kate swung around and smacked his backside with her knee.

He landed with a thud on the cement floor but jumped to his feet, cursing.

Bart moved to stand beside Kate. His hand was inside his open vest. "Leave her alone."

Damon's eyes narrowed. "She's coming with me."

Bart murmured, "This one is loaded, bud."

Kate retreated, more than happy to let her boss handle Damon.

By now, a crowd was forming. Damon pivoted and tore through the onlookers, knocking spectators aside. Kate saw Marco and Alfonzo meet him at the end of the aisle.

Bart pulled a cell phone from his pocket and called security.

Kate fell into a chair. Knocking Damon on the floor was not the way to help Amy. Her response to his attack was pure instinct, but maybe he'd gotten the message to leave her alone. She rubbed her shoulder. Why was he so anxious about her social security number?

Two convention officers made their way through the crowd and cordoned off the aisle. Kate watched while one officer spoke with Bart and the other took statements from individuals who'd witnessed the assault. She'd been told to remain seated, which was okay with her. The adrenaline was wearing off, and her hands were beginning to shake.

Finally, an officer approached her.

Kate sat up. Would he believe her when she told him her actions were solely self-defense?

"I'd like you to come with me, ma'am, so we can hear your story in private."

Private. Wasn't that the word that started all this? "Can't we talk here?"

"Our office is on the second floor. We won't keep you long."

Kate hesitated. Walt said Executive's men observed them from the second floor. But even if they did, she didn't have a choice as to whether or not to go with the officer. With her three-strikes-you're-out legal status, she couldn't afford to thumb her nose at authorities.

She nodded and followed the officer to an elevator. They rode up one flight and then he led her down a long empty hallway, opened a door and motioned her inside. Kate hesitated but finally stepped into a brightly lit room that smelled like coffee and...corn chips? Two dark-haired men with crew-cuts, stern eyes and rigid jawlines sat behind a long table. One officer was dressed in street clothes and the other wore a police uniform. Both men stood. She remained near the door.

"This is Detective Barker." The security guard indicated the man in street clothing.

Barker nodded.

"And Officer Vogel." The uniformed man nodded his head.

Kate eyed the detective. So that's what Barker looked like. She'd pegged him, although she'd pictured him a bit shorter and stockier.

He indicated the chair across from them. "Please have a seat." Then he motioned to her escort. "Thanks, officer. Go ahead and open up that aisle again. That'll make those vendors happy."

"Yes, sir." With a salute, he was gone, closing the door behind him.

Kate remained by the door. "Why am I here?"

"We'd like to discuss the attack you just experienced and how it might relate to your friend, Ms. Iverson."

Kate frowned. "She didn't—"

He lifted a hand. "I realize she most likely didn't instigate the attack." He pointed to the chair. "Please sit down."

Kate sat, noting the bag of Fritos in the middle of the table.

He aimed a thumb toward the other man. "Officer Vogel is aware of the details of Miss Iverson's disappearance and the warrant for her arrest."

Vogel nodded.

Barker focused on her again. "What's this about a social security number?"

CHAPTER TWENTY-SEVEN

Kate focused on the coffee stain on the detective's notebook. Not even Mike knew what she'd done. Could he ever forgive her if she landed in prison again? She swallowed. Telling the truth was important. If she'd learned anything in recent years, she'd learned the value of transparency.

Looking the detective in the eye, she prayed he'd understand. "I was concerned that Executive Pride would use my social security number to check my background and discover Amy and I were incarcerated together in Pennsylvania. So I wrote a fake number on the W-4."

She placed her hands on the table. "My plan was to give them the correct number once this weekend was over. What I keep wondering is why was Damon so determined to get my info?"

"So you know your assailant's name? Security said he disappeared right after the confrontation."

"He's the man I dealt with the first day I walked into Executive's office. I have his card in my purse and can get it, if you'd like."

"Thank you. We'll pick it up after the interview."

Officer Vogel wrote something on the notepad in front of him.

"I can give you other names of people associated with Executive Pride."

"Shoot."

"I only know first names. Marco. Alfonzo. Thomas. Janessa."

Vogel continued writing.

Kate clasped her hands in her lap. "Can I ask you something?"

"You can ask," Barker said, "although I can't promise an answer."

"Why haven't you arrested Amy Iverson? You told me she's wanted for murder."

Officer Vogel rested his pen against his chin, his eyes on Barker, who sat back, hands folded. "I'll put it this way. Your friend is just one pony in a pasture full of wild horses we'd like to corral. If we pull her in, it's likely Executive Pride will lock up tight, and we'll never see any of these women again."

"Executive has children, too," Kate said. "I'm terribly concerned about the ones here at the show."

"We're keeping an eye on them."

"I can't tell you what to do." She leaned forward. "But wouldn't Amy and the others be safer behind bars than with those bullies?"

"That may be the case. As I said, we're trying to topple an empire, not just rescue a few serfs, or cowboys and cowgirls, to stick with the analogy."

Kate clenched her fists. They were talking about flesh-and-blood people, not storybook characters. She stood. "I'm here to rescue my best friend and whoever else I can snatch from the evil empire's clutches. I'll do my best to stay out of your way while you're toppling that empire. However, I make no promises."

Barker got to his feet. "I catch you interfering with our investigation, and you'll find yourself behind bars—again."

Almost as soon as Kate returned to the gun booth, Bart left to find a quiet corner where he could make phone calls. She'd barely sat down, when two boys in baggy pants, t-shirts and camo jackets came riding on a bicycle painted in camouflage green and black. The smaller one was balanced on the handlebars. Both boys laughed and waved at the booth attendants as they weaved between visitors, honking the bike horn and blowing whistles.

Kate chuckled. First time she'd seen that duo at the sports show. Were they Executive Pride kids? She shook her head. No, they couldn't be. They were too happy and loud.

With an extra-long horn honk, the bicycle crashed in front of the gun booth.

Kate jumped to her feet. "Are you okay?"

The older boy righted the bicycle and pumped a fist into the air. "We're tough dudes. Right, Lenny?"

The other boy sprang to his feet, holding his elbow. "I'm fine, man."

His friend helped him onto the handlebars, and they took off again.

Kate called after them, "Nice bike."

The older boy waved but kept peddling. "Thanks."

Boys. They reminded her of her daredevil little brother. Sometimes males were too macho for their own good. For a moment, she allowed herself to wallow in the anguish of knowing she and Mike would never have sons of their own. But only for a moment. Amy's plight was their concern right now.

Amy was opening another box of wafers when she heard someone clear his throat. She turned and saw a man in shorts and a t-shirt. Beneath the brim of his baseball cap, he wore sunglasses.

She readjusted her shorts. "Hello, sir. Would you like to try one of our energy wafers? They're really good." She ought to know. So far today, she'd eaten at least a dozen. That was the only way she was able stay awake.

The man blinked at her over the top of the sunglasses, eyebrows lifted.

Something about the guy was familiar.

He removed the glasses and winked.

She stepped back, surprised by his brash behavior.

He grinned.

And then she knew. No way could she forget Clint Barrett's infectious grin. She returned the smile and handed him two samples.

He pulled the bill of his ball cap low on his forehead before he tore the packet open. Holding up the wrapping, he asked, "Can you throw this away for me?"

"Sure." She'd put the scrap in her pocket and toss it the next time she visited the restroom.

With the wrapper wedged between two fingers, he held out his hand, palm up.

That was odd. She frowned.

He focused on his hand, twitching it ever so slightly.

She looked again and saw writing. *Here to help you* was written in three lines across his palm. *You* was underlined. Tears sprang into her eyes. His presence at the sports show wasn't a coincidence. She took the wrapper from him and put it in her pocket. "Do you like the flavor?"

"Yeah. It's good. I'd like another one, if that's okay. And maybe some for my three friends who are at the show with me."

"Of course. I'll also give you some brochures to give to them."

Three friends? Why did he specify three? She knew Mike was at the conference and maybe Kate. Who was the third person? Susan? Amy checked Clint's ring finger. It was bare, but that didn't mean a whole lot. Kate once told her that farm and ranch workers didn't normally wear rings because the metal could catch in machinery and cause them to lose their fingers or hands.

She tilted her head. "How are you feeling? Most people say they feel more energetic within a couple minutes."

He stuffed the extra wafers in a jacket pocket and slipped the brochures into the back of his Levis. "I'm feeling great, thanks." He replaced the sunglasses, put his hands on the table and leaned toward her. "Say, I hope this doesn't sound too forward. Do you live around here?"

She'd told other men who'd asked personal questions that she didn't give out contact information. Yet she wanted Clint to have at least a general idea of where she lived. "Twin cities."

"Doing anything after the show tonight?"

What could she say to give him a clue about her life? "It's nice of you to ask, but I have another job, my regular job, so I'll be going straight there." She pulled a stick of gum from her pocket and tried to think of a message she could give Clint. Out of the corner of her eye, she saw Marco making his way through the crowd.

"After working here all day, you go to another job?" Clint lowered his brow. "Sounds like a lot of hours to me."

Amy dropped the gum into her pocket. "The sports show is a one-time thing. I don't do this kind of work every weekend."

"What days are you off work?"

Marco shoved through the crowd to stand next to Clint. "Quit pestering the woman and get lost."

"Nothing wrong with trying to talk to a pretty lady."

"Move on."

Clint scratched his temple, hiding the wink he aimed at Amy over the top of his sunglasses before he merged into the crowd.

When Mike came to pick her up for dinner, Kate reached under the table to get her purse and couldn't feel it. She squatted on her heels to check the box where she usually stored the handbag, but it wasn't there. "That's strange."

Bart stepped closer. "What's the matter?"

"I don't see my purse."

The two men hunkered down beside Kate. Bart pulled out another box. "Maybe it's in a different one." But that one was empty.

Mike slid out other boxes, some empty, some partially filled with brochures, business cards, gun holsters and other accessories. "Not here."

Kate walked to the front of the table and pulled up the table skirt. Nothing. "How could something as big as a purse disappear?"

Mike pushed boxes back in place and got to his feet. "Maybe it was stolen."

"One of us was here all day." She massaged her neck. "This booth never went unmanned."

Bart checked the boxes stacked at the back of the stall. "That's right. I don't see how it could have been taken by anyone."

"Oh." Kate groaned.

Mike stared at her. "What?"

"If anyone should have recognized a couple little thieves, it should have been me." She let out a frustrated huff. "Can't believe I fell for their act."

Bart's eyebrows pinched together.

"Two boys came riding through on a bicycle and pretended to crash in front of this table." She pointed to the spot where they'd tipped the bike. "One of them fell off and fumbled around the curtain. I bet that's when he took it."

"Wouldn't you have seen it?" Mike lifted his eyebrows. "You were too close to miss something like that."

"My attention was on the bicycle and the boys, not under the table, and they both wore those big, baggy, camouflage jackets. The kid could easily have hidden my purse under his arm inside the coat. Who knows how many other people they conned today."

Bart wiped his hand over his cheek and heaved a heavy sigh. "I'm sorry about this, Katherine. You'd better report the theft to security."

"They're going to think I'm a troublemaker."

Mike hugged her. "You're not a troublemaker, sweetheart. Trouble just seems to be finding you at this show. We'll talk to security on the way out."

They said goodbye to Bart and left the booth holding hands. "I guess we know how I'll be spending my supper break," Kate said. "Canceling credit cards and the Colorado phone. I'll have to wait until tomorrow to cancel my Wyoming driver's license, but at least I don't have to worry about the bogus Colorado license. Plus, I still have my regular phone in my pocket, so you and I can—"

She stopped and clutched his arm. "Do you think it was a setup because I wouldn't give Executive my social security number?"

He shrugged. "I s'pose it could have been a setup, but the question is—why?"

"If they get their hands on that purse with my dual IDs and business cards, the game is up. They'll know who we really are."

He grunted. "We'd better tell Walt. He's planning to stop by the restaurant to talk with us for a few minutes."

Phone to her ear, Kate listened to canned music while she waited to connect with credit card representatives. She ate her dinner with her free hand and tried to follow the conversation around the table. Mike, Clint and Walt had all seen Amy throughout the day. Kate felt a tinge of jealousy, although she'd agreed with the guys when they suggested she keep her presence a secret, so the Executive crew wouldn't get suspicious.

She wished they'd eaten at the cafeteria, where she might have at least glimpsed Amy. However, Walt wanted to meet somewhere private, so he could bombard her with question after question about the theft. She answered as best she could between bites.

Before he left them, Walt said, "By the way, Barker was fit to be tied when he found out you Wyoming mavericks were hanging around that Executive place last night. He said to tell you to tend to your own knittin' and stop meddlin' in police affairs."

"He might think it's a police affair," Clint said. "But Amy is our friend, and the cops haven't done a thing to help her."

"I believe God brought us here to rescue her," Kate added. "And that's what we'll do."

Walt shrugged. "Just passin' the word. Keep in mind, Barker is so mad right now, a pressure cooker is tame in comparison. If he decides you're interfering with the case, he'll have you on a plane outa here faster than you can say *Dallas/Fort Worth International Airport.*"

On the walk back to the convention hall, Kate saw a green sweater in a store window that made her think of Amy. They were running out of time to save her friend. Surely there was something more they could do to help her.

They stopped at an intersection, and Clint pushed the button to cross the street. "We're going to ignore what Walt said about Barker being mad, right?"

"I was just thinking about that," Kate said. "I want to do whatever we can to help Amy and the others, yet I don't want to do anything stupid. You have to admit we didn't accomplish much last night."

"But we learned quite a bit," Mike said.

"I agree." Clint nodded. "Maybe we can learn more tonight."

"Maybe." She took both their arms and walked between them. "Let's see how it goes during the final hours of the convention and decide what to do after that."

Kate hoped the boys on the bicycle would come through again that night, so she could ask what they'd done with her purse. She'd promise not to press charges, if they told her. However, no boys on bicycles came her way. And no Executive thugs harassed her. Her only excitement was the cell phone picture Mike sent of Amy talking with a customer.

The picture made her sad. She'd never seen her friend so thin and forlorn, not even in prison.

A familiar-looking man approached the table, his gaze flicking from her to the guns and back to her. Kate slipped the phone into her back pocket, trying to remember where she'd seen him before.

He pointed to the display behind her. "Hand me the revolver in the second row, two from the left." His shirtsleeve slid away from his wrist, exposing a snake tattoo that began on the back of his hand and wound up his arm.

The hair on her own arms rose. It was him. The man she'd ridden the elevator with weeks ago. She smiled. "I'll get it for you."

Kate lifted the revolver out of the case, feeling his gaze and knowing he was mentally undressing her. Any other man, and she might have put him in his place. But something told her this one was associated with Executive Pride, even though he appeared more refined than the other Executive employees she'd seen. Maybe she could learn more about the organization from him.

She laid the gun in his hands, her sweetest smile in place. "Do you shoot targets, or are you just wanting some extra protection?"

He smirked. "Katherine, baby, I've got all the protection a man could ever want."

He'd obviously read her nametag. Big deal. "So you shoot at targets?"

"You could say that." His gaze slid from her face to her chest before returning to the revolver.

The steel in his tone and in his eyes reminded her of Alfonzo. She shuddered and buttoned her vest. "I can get the specs on that handgun for you, if you'd like." She opened the laptop that lay on the table. "What's the model number?"

He read the numbers to her.

Bart finished with a customer and walked over. "I can help with questions, if you have any."

"Yeah, what's the range of this thing?"

"I just found the specs." Kate showed Bart the computer screen. "I'll let you take it from here. You're the expert."

The man scowled, as if irritated she was handing him over to Bart.

Be on your guard against men. The words floated across her vision, stippling the man's face. So he was one of them. Now she knew what to do when the conference closed for the evening.

Amy stumbled into the limo that would deliver her and the others back to the brothel. She made her way to the farthest seat from the door. Even if she'd been allowed to talk with anyone, she was too tired to think, let alone converse. She watched the kids totter in, obviously exhausted. Almost as soon as they dropped onto the leather benches, they curled into little clumps and fell asleep.

If only she could tuck each boy and girl into bed, kiss their cheeks, and promise they'd wake up in their momma's arms. *God,* she prayed, *even if you don't care about me, surely you care about these sweet babies. Get them out of this hellhole.*

The engine started and the car pulled through the alley and into traffic. She rested her head against the window. The music was subdued tonight, which was nice. The kids would get a little bit of sleep before they were dragged out of the car and onto an elevator.

She closed her eyes, longing for sleep yet knowing she should use these few minutes of peace to plan her escape. The dog guy said to be ready. But how could she be ready when she didn't know him or his plan. Or what Clint and Mike had in mind. She couldn't hang all her hopes on men she might never see again. Besides, they'd all be useless against Thomas and his sadistic sidekicks.

She watched Alfonzo through the slits of her eyelids. He and the others were ruthless evil men who would relish the opportunity to gang up on her friends. For their sake, it would be better if they didn't get involved with her sordid life.

Amy rubbed her tired eyes. She needed her own escape strategy. Truth was, she'd thought of a dozen options, from throwing herself at a security guard and begging him to take her to the police, to slipping into the crowd and out the door, to asking Colin to call the cops for her. None of her ideas seemed feasible, knowing how EP monitored her every move—and how they would hurt, maybe kill, anyone who tried to help her.

She chewed at her lip. Whatever she did, tomorrow was her last chance at freedom. She had to come up with a plan.

Seated in the deserted hotel lobby, Kate, Mike and Clint discussed their plans for the rest of the evening. "How about dressing in grunge," Kate suggested. "Mike has a couple flannel shirts with him. You could wear those—untucked, of course, over t-shirts, with faded jeans."

Mike stretched his legs out. "What do we wear on our heads?"

"Same as last night. In fact, your ball caps will be even better 'cause they got messed up." But then she shook her head. "That won't work. Someone might recognize the hats. Better pick up some new ball caps on the way. Be sure to rub dirt on them and scrunch them up, so they appear well used."

"What about the glasses?" Clint asked. "They're hard to hang onto in a fight."

Mike nodded. "Yeah."

Kate cocked her head. "I thought this was an exploratory venture, but it sounds like you two are itching for another fight." Knowing she was more experienced at fighting dirty than they were made her regret she wasn't going with them. On the other hand, they were both able to take care of themselves, and anyone who got in their way.

Mike took her hand. "We'll be careful."

"I know." She pursed her lips. "Those glasses don't fit the grunge look. We'll have to think of something else." She studied Mike's face. "Assuming you'll stay out of direct light, I could use makeup to draw in sideburns and maybe give hints of mustaches and beards."

Clint's brow wrinkled. "Makeup?"

"It won't be much. Like I said, just hints. In fact, I have an idea." She stepped to the breakfast counter, found what she needed and hurried back. "This is perfect."

Mike and Clint eyed each other, their doubt obvious.

Kate tore the corner off a packet labeled "dark hot chocolate" and shook the powder into her palm. "A tiny bit of this instant cocoa mixed with your day-old stubble will give the impression you have a good start on some serious beards."

For a moment, neither man spoke. Finally, Clint said, "If nothing else, we'll smell good. Might even attract a babe who's tired of men who use regular aftershave."

Mike chuckled. "Or a dog who likes chocolate."

When both men appeared as unlike themselves as possible, Kate sent them out of the hotel room with a prayer for their safety. They were headed back into enemy territory.

She secured the chain lock and reached for her cell phone. Though she longed to go with them, she was staying behind to fight the enemy on her own terms. Seeing the guy with the snake tattoo today had convinced her they'd never win the battle without heaven's armies behind them. She punched speed dial and began pacing from the window to the door and back.

Laura answered on the fourth ring. "Hi, Kate. I was hoping to hear from you two today. How are things in Dallas?"

"Not so good." Kate stopped in the middle of the room. "I'm calling for prayer. Is Aunt Mary still up?"

"She went to bed a couple hours ago, but I can check to see if she's awake. She hasn't slept good since you left."

"Don't disturb her. But first thing in the morning, please ask her and Marita to pray for us."

"What's going on?"

Kate heard worry in her mother-in-law's voice and quickly added, "We found Amy."

"Oh, that's wonderful. Is she at the convention?'

"Yes, but she's heavily guarded."

"Guarded. Why?"

"We're not sure why. Every time one of us gets close, a bouncer-type guy shows up. She looks terrified and has lost a lot of weight."

"Poor thing."

"We've also run across little kids who are guarded like Amy. It's possible they're human trafficking victims."

"Oh, Kate, that's terrible. I'll pray for them, too."

Kate could picture her mother-in-law's concerned expression. "Please ask God to show us how to help them."

"If they need a safe place, they can come to the ranch."

Kate hadn't focused any further down the road than rescuing Amy and Janessa and the children. "That's really sweet of you to offer the ranch." She thought of the Matthew passage and of her husband and his best friend headed back into the lion's den. "We'll talk about that later. Right now, we need to be shrewd yet innocent, like the Bible says. And we only have one more day to do whatever it is we're going to do."

Next, Kate called Dymple Forbes, who sounded groggy when she answered the phone. "Dymple, I'm so sorry to wake you."

"That's okay, sweetie." She cleared her throat. "You should know by now you can call anytime you'd like."

"It's an emergency, or I would have waited until morning."

"This is about Amy, isn't it? You found her and she's in some kind of trouble."

"Oh, Dymple, it's awful. We found her, but we can't get to her." Kate began to cry. "She may be a sex trafficking victim."

"Oh, my."

"We've seen little kids who may also be trafficking victims."

Dymple groaned. "God help them."

Kate fell to her knees beside the bed. "Would you pray with me right now?"

CHAPTER TWENTY-EIGHT

Mike asked the cab driver to drop him and Clint off several blocks from Rolly's Rockout Place. They walked the rest of the way. As they passed two women in platform heels and short tight skirts standing under a streetlight, one of them gave Clint the once-over and winked at him. He ignored her and continued walking.

Mike laughed. "She likes that sexy chocolate beard of yours."

"You'd better hope nobody gets close enough to smell our Hershey faces."

"Yeah, if someone happens to touch us and they get cocoa powder on their hands, our gig is up and our shorts are fried."

"Shorts are fried?" Clint scrunched his eyebrows. "Sounds like something Walt would say."

"Well, yeah, that's where I heard it. Kinda like the sound of it." Mike stepped out of the way of a skateboarder.

"If you say so, boss."

They walked through a cluster of smokers standing outside the bar and into Rolly's, where they found a table in a murky corner. The music was loud and the crowd young and enthused. The smell of alcohol hung heavy in the air. They ordered beers.

No one other than the barmaid seemed to notice them. Mike was okay with that. He wanted a chance to get their bearings and listen, if that was possible in such a noisy place, for clues about

Executive Pride. They'd decided the nightclub was as close as they'd get to the Executive building, and even then, they needed to be careful. He was thankful Kate remained behind to pray. She was convinced they'd learn something helpful tonight. He hoped so.

They nursed their beers as long as they could and pretended to enjoy the wild antics on stage. They'd just ordered a second round when three men swaggered in. Mike recognized one of them from last night's encounter. He signaled Clint and slouched deeper into the shadows.

The threesome took seats at a nearby table just as the band announced they were taking a break.

Clint murmured, "We better talk about something."

Mike cleared his throat. "Remember the red deer rumors I told you about?"

"Uh-huh."

"Got a call from Marshall Thompson today." Mike took a sip from his bottle. "His son talked an assistant game warden he knows into tracking the red deer with him. They were able to get close enough to tranquilize one and take a blood sample. Don't know yet if it carries brucellosis. He said the animal appeared healthy, and now that there's proof red deer are in the area, the Game and Fish people are going to round 'em all up."

"Great..." Clint stretched. "Hey, I caught a few minutes of the UW game against Air Force."

"Been wondering about that game. What was the score?"

"Seventy-one to—"

With an almost imperceptible shake of his head, Mike cut Clint off.

"I'm tellin' you," one of the men was saying, "I was attacked by a banshee."

The broad-shouldered man next to him snorted. "You hittin' the bottle again, Harry?"

"No, it's true, man." Harry held up his hands. "Some broad shot out of the bushes, bit my arm and knocked me out." He touched his upper arm and sucked in a breath. "Hurts worse than a dog bite. And there were others. I don't know how many. They knocked out Butch, who was on duty with me. When we came to, they were gone."

"Did they take your wallets?"

"Nothing missing. Still haven't figured it out."

"Sure it wasn't dogs?"

A waitress approached the threesome's table with a tray of drinks.

"What was that score again?" Mike asked.

"Wyoming seventy-one, Air Force sixty-nine."

Mike nodded. "Close one."

"Yeah, wish I'd seen the whole game."

At the next table, the third man asked, "Did you tell the boss?"

"Are you loco? He'd think we were sleeping on the job and give us hell."

"Yeah, or worse." The man paused. "If anything suspicious happens again, report it. Might mean something funny's going down."

"One guy tried to go upstairs," Harry added. "Said he wanted to see Janessa."

The bigger man snickered. "Wouldn't we all? How'd he know her name?"

"Said she was his escort once."

"What d'ya mean, he tried to go upstairs?" asked the other.

Clint pulled his cap lower.

Harry rubbed his forehead. "He tried to get on the elevators. When Butch told him he'd have to take him up, all of a sudden he changed his mind." He paused. "And then this, this cyclone hit, and we both were knocked flat on our faces. Don't know how long we were out. I'm glad the boss didn't catch us."

"What did the guy look like?"

"Couldn't make out his face. Wore a hood over a hat."

Mike allowed himself a quick breath.

Harry brightened. "He wore glasses."

"Like half the other dolts in this town."

"Well, it's something."

"Don't think you're off the hook," said the first man. "If the guys in the video room were paying attention..."

Harry waved the comment aside. "They're too busy watching the whores." He lowered his voice and whispered something more. They all laughed.

"What about the woman?" The big man continued his interrogation.

Again, Mike held his breath.

"All I remember is wild makeup and blazing eyes."

"Blazing eyes?"

"Could of been a man in drag, but those eyes..." His voice trailed off and he whistled. "She, or he, was mad, *real* mad."

Mike smirked and saw Clint's mouth twitch.

One of the men glanced over at them.

Clint slid a napkin to the center of the table. "You ever play hangman?"

"Long time ago. You pick the first word."

"Okay." Clint drew seven dashes and then a gallows above them. "What's your first letter?"

"All that makeup." said one of the men. "Could be any of the tramps upstairs."

"That's it." Harry smacked his forehead. "Why didn't I think of it before? She's one of those two we caught trying to escape last month, and she's back for revenge."

"Quiet." The big guy shook his head and looked around.

Mike squinted at the lines on the napkin. "Think I'll try an 'e.'"

Clint wrote "e" on the last dash.

"Huh." Mike studied the drawing. "Doesn't help me much."

One of the men whispered something about a river.

Clint gave Mike a side glance.

Harry moaned. "Aunt Edith was right."

Mike snuck a glance at Harry, whose face twisted as he spoke. "She said the ghosts of the dead who die unjustly always come back to haunt us." He grimaced. "A dead whore, an *angry* dead whore, is going to chase us to our graves."

"Stop talking nonsense." The big man shook his head. "Or Thomas will think you've lost your marbles and dump you in the river, too."

The other man nodded. "He's right. Forget all that craziness, man, if you know what's good for you." He leaned in. "I heard Thomas is bringing in a new hussy tomorrow night. If we want to help break her in, we can volunteer for an extra shift. Unpaid, of course." He hoisted his glass and downed the rest of his drink. "You guys going to do it? He says this one's really good. She's experienced."

"I don't know." The big guy tapped the table. "I like 'em young and fresh—and scared, if you know what I mean."

Mike swallowed the bile rising in his throat. "Uh, how about an 'm'?"

Clint drew a noose on the gallows.

Like the night before, Amy entertained clients for what felt like an eternity before Damon finally escorted her back to her room. Barely able to keep her eyes open or to stand upright, she fought the urge to lean against the wall while he punched in the code to open her door. If she relaxed her muscles for even a second, she'd crumple to the floor. Knowing Damon, he'd kick her inside and leave her where she landed.

Amy counted beeps. By now, she knew the code consisted of six numbers. But she didn't know what those numbers were. Maybe someday she'd figure them out. Tonight she was too tired to try.

She'd slipped out of her work teddy before she crawled into bed last night, every joint and muscle in her body throbbing. Tonight, she wouldn't bother. Each second of sleep counted if she was to be alert enough tomorrow to find a way to escape, with or without help.

Damon twisted the knob and shoved the door open.

She stumbled into the dimly lit room. Even before the door closed behind her, she was kicking off her heels. Next, she released her fishnet nylons from the garter fasteners. Too tired to stand any longer, she sat on the edge of the bed and rolled the first nylon down her leg.

"Tell me about your friend."

Amy swiveled. "Thomas."

Her boss lounged on a loveseat, his eyes and hair glittering in the moonlight that shone through the big window. Uh-oh. She'd forgotten to pull the drapes so his snakes could sleep. He'd propped a leg on the cushions and positioned his arm across the back of the sofa, the perfect picture of relaxed elegance.

Yet she knew better. The way he squeezed and released, squeezed and released the leather upholstery told her everything she needed to know about his state of mind.

"What friend?" She bent low to remove the other stocking, her heart pounding against her leg. *God help me. I have no idea what to say to him.*

"Katherine." He spat the words one-by-one. "Joy. Duncan. Recognize the name?"

"I don't know—"

"Oh, yeah. That's right." He squeezed and gripped without releasing. "You said her name was Kate Neilson."

Amy straightened. "I have a friend with that name. I told you about her. She lives on a ranch in Wyoming." Why was he so interested in Kate?

He shifted both legs to the floor and leaned forward, hands on his knees. "Where is she now?"

"At the ranch, I guess." She shrugged. "How should I know? I haven't had contact with anyone outside EP since I've been here."

Thomas jumped to his feet to tower above her.

Amy flinched. Even if he hit her, she wouldn't betray her friend.

He grabbed her by the hair and yanked her upright. "Don't lie to me! She's here. In Dallas. She came to see you."

Amy stifled a scream and couldn't stop the tears that sprang to her eyes. "If she's in town, I missed it, Thomas. You know I don't have visitors."

He glowered at her, veins popping from his temples and forehead, and latched onto her throat with both hands. "You stupid slut!" He whipped her from side to side and flung her to the floor. "If I find out you're lying to me, you'll pay."

Striding across the room, he pounded in the code, wrenched the door open and stepped through the doorway.

Amy slumped on the floor, gasping for breath. When she could breathe again, the smell of the aftershave he'd left on her neck made her gag. She watched the door, waiting for it to close, but it remained open. Light streamed in from the hall light. Was this her opportunity, her moment to run?

She was about to push herself upright, when Thomas stepped back into the room. "And I suppose you know nothing about her friends hanging around your booth." His voice was low and menacing.

She squinted at him. How did he know that?

He swore. "I'll deal with your lies when the convention is over." For a long moment, he glared at her.

Amy dug her fingers into the carpet. Maybe he was thinking of how to punish her now, not later.

And then he smirked. "Since I first saw your friend's sexy body, I've been thinking about how to put her to work for us. What better time than now?"

Amy sat up, her head swimming. "But—"

His lip curled. "But what?"

"She's married."

"You think I didn't know that?"

Amy's legs felt like noodles when she climbed out of the limo the next morning. She'd had such high hopes of escaping today. Now she wasn't sure she could even walk from the car to the building. Shoving one foot in front of the other felt like slogging through mud.

The other women who'd ridden with her appeared equally beat. And the kids. The poor babies had dark circles under their eyes. Could they hold out one more day?

She hoped they'd gotten more sleep than she did. After learning Thomas was after Kate, she'd tossed and turned the entire three hours she'd been allotted for sleep. It was her fault Kate was in Dallas. And now she was in danger of being kidnapped, too.

Damon grabbed her arm. "Hurry up." He shoved her toward the door. She tripped yet managed to remain on her feet and stagger into the building. A gray-haired man with a dust mop eyed her, his eyebrows tight.

Damon waved him away. "Mind your own business."

Amy dug her nails into her palms and marched ahead, wishing she could thank the man for caring and beg him to help her. They reached her stall, and once again, Damon reminded her to stay in the booth. The moment he left, she dug into a box and grabbed a handful of energy wafers. She'd already eaten so many she could barely tolerate the smell or the taste, yet they were her only hope for surviving the day. That and coffee, if Alfonzo would buy it for her.

After the church service ended, Laura hurried Mary to the car. She needed to finish preparing the food before their lunch guests arrived at the ranch. They drove in silence, Mary nodding in and out of sleep in the passenger seat and Laura trying to settle the butterflies that flitted about her abdomen.

Mixed feelings sparred in her brain. Todd could be a brat. That was true. On the other hand, he'd been single so long he needed a wife to civilize him, which would take time. Another major factor was her son. Would he ever accept Todd as part of the family? She wouldn't expect him to consider Todd a father figure. However, it would be nice if they could at least get along.

She slowed for three does and a buck that stepped out of the trees and bounded to the other side of the road. She'd been so lonely and so determined she had a right to companionship that she'd left God out of the equation. Today's sermon confirmed her narrow focus.

She stepped on the gas again. Todd hadn't attended the service. If he'd been there, would he have heard God's voice the way she did?

A pair of hawks circled above a meadow. She watched them for a moment. Like the raptors, she and Joyce were partners, circling above the Todd situation, seeking God's direction together. Maybe it was silly to compare her collaboration with Joyce to two birds hunting lunch, yet it was good to know her new friend was praying with her.

As she drove, Laura asked God for specific signs of his will and for her will to align with his. By the time she pulled up to the lobby, the butterflies were at rest and she was prepared for whatever the day would bring.

Mary awakened. Laura helped her out of the car and up the ramp. What if at the end of the day she concluded that she and Todd weren't meant for each other? How hard would it be to end her relationship with him? He was a determined man.

CHAPTER TWENTY-NINE

Laura opened the lobby door. "Come in, come in. It's cold out there."

Dymple and the four Raeburns greeted her and filed inside. Todd bounded up the steps behind them. He gave her a quick peck on the cheek. "I'm excited about this coming-out party."

She stood on tiptoe to whisper in his ear. "This is just a simple lunch with friends and neighbors."

He gave her a knowing look. "Yeah, sure."

Laura closed the door. "Please lead the way to the living room, Dymple. Mary is anxious to see all of you." Maybe Todd sensed something was up regarding their relationship. That was okay. Today would be a defining day.

In the living room, Dymple gathered coats to hang on the antler rack by the back door. "Anyone hear the forecast? I saw some nasty clouds headed our way."

"I know I'm from Pennsylvania and not yet accustomed to Wyoming weather," Martin said, "but those clouds seem extra ominous to me."

Todd smirked. "That's the way you city folks are. You get all worked up over a few gray puffs in the sky. I heard the weather report out of Laramie this morning, and there was no mention of a storm."

"Pennsylvania?" Mary leaned forward in her chair beside the fireplace. "Who's from Pennsylvania?" Prissy jumped off her lap to check out the visitors.

Joyce knelt beside her and took her hand. "Mary, we're the Raeburns, your old friends from Pittsburgh. Remember us?"

Cindy picked up Prissy and joined the two women.

Mary studied Joyce's face and then Cindy's. She hesitated. "Maybe, but who are those people?" She pointed at the other family members.

"That's my husband, Martin, and our son, Casey. He's grown quite a bit since you last saw him, so he may not seem all that familiar to you."

Mary winked. "Buster Boy."

Casey's cheeks reddened.

Martin grinned. "Yeah, good ol' Buster Boy, the sock monkey." He rubbed his son's head. "Casey carried it with him everywhere he went until it fell apart and Joyce threw it in the trashcan. Poor little guy was heartbroken. Cried for weeks."

"Da-ad."

Todd snorted. "Only momma's boys have dolls."

Laura elbowed him. "Stop it."

Mary waggled a finger at Todd. "You are not a nice man. You should leave right now."

He flexed his jaw muscles and appeared ready to fire back a retort.

Laura squeezed his arm. "Don't go there."

Todd gave her a dirty look, and she could see Dymple eyeing the two of them. Maybe she should have been more open with Dymple about her relationship with Todd. This wasn't the best way to break the news.

Joyce jumped to her feet. "What can I do to help with lunch? It was so nice of you to invite us, Laura."

"Yes, thank you very much," Martin said. "This is a real treat for us to have someone else do the cooking." He sniffed. "Something smells wonderful."

Laura smiled. "I've got beef stew simmering in the slow cooker."

Casey raised his hand. "Can I see your foal?"

"How about we eat first?" Laura said. "Then we can all go out to the barn to meet Miss Estrella Blanca."

Laura laughed at Casey, who jabbered and fidgeted and hopped about the room while the others donned their winter gear. "You remind me of my boys when they were your age, Casey." She zipped her jacket. "So much energy."

"Hurry, Cindy." Casey bounced on the balls of his feet. "We don't have much time to be with the filly." He tried to help his sister put on her coat, but she slapped his hand away.

"Settle down." Martin grabbed his son's shoulder. "And stop pestering your sister."

Laura laughed. "Good thing Mary decided to nap, or you'd have a really long wait, Casey. Takes a good half hour to get her ready for a trip to the barn, yet it's worth it. She loves Estrella Blanca, or Molly, as she calls the foal."

Joyce buttoned her jacket. "I don't get the relationship between those names."

"Mary used to have a donkey named Molly. Some kind of synapse connection there, I guess." Laura wrapped a scarf around her neck and peeked out the patio door. "Anyone need boots? The snow is coming down hard." A light snowfall had begun almost as soon as they sat down to eat but now big flakes were falling fast and furious.

Todd frowned. "Wasn't in the weather report."

Joyce touched her husband's arm. "Maybe we should leave now, while the roads are open. We can see the horse another time."

Casey groaned. "Please, just for a few minutes, please..."

Todd grunted. "Whiny kid."

After a moment, Martin said, "Okay. But we can't stay long."

"Whoo-hoo!" Casey held the patio door while the others filed onto the deck.

Snowflakes danced in the crisp air. Casey and Cindy caught them on their tongues and threw handfuls of snow at each other. Laura was sorry Mike's dog couldn't join the fun.

Tramp normally would have met them at the back door, his tail wagging furiously. Today, however, she'd encouraged Cyrus to take the dog with him when he drove down to the pasture to check the cattle. She didn't want to chance a confrontation between Todd and Tramp.

Todd came up beside her and took her arm.

She pulled away. "Not now."

"It's slick."

"I've walked this path hundreds of times over the years, in rain, snow, wind, sleet and hail. Even when it was crawling with slippery Mormon crickets." She cringed at the memory. "I am quite capable of walking it today without your help, thank you."

"My, my, aren't we becoming the women's libber?"

"Call it what you want. This is the real me."

"You've been spending too much time with the old lady."

"What?" Laura would have stopped if they'd been alone and if the Raeburns weren't so anxious to see the horses and head home. "What does this have to do with Mary?"

"She was practically breathing fire at me all through lunch."

"You deserved it. You didn't even try to be nice to her."

"Why should I?"

"Why should you?" Laura took in his tight jaw and thin lips pressed in a hard line. He was still angry—angry at a helpless confused woman who hadn't said a word, good or bad, to him during lunch, though her visual daggers were obvious. *If Todd really loved me, he'd make an effort to accept the people I love, no matter their idiosyncrasies.* She stared up into the snow cloud. *I think I'm getting the message, God.* Snowflakes gently tapped her face.

With a shake of her head, she squared her shoulders and marched ahead of Todd to open the barn door and hold it while the others trailed inside, one after the other. He lingered at the door, obviously wanting to speak to her. She pushed him inside and latched the door behind them, closing out the brisk breeze and shutting in the sweet smell of hay and the warm earthy aroma of horses.

Kate searched the cafeteria for Amy and didn't see her. She scanned the room again, and again. Finally, she picked up her turkey sandwich. But then she put it back down. She couldn't eat knowing today was their final day at the convention.

Mike offered a sympathetic smile. "Sorry she's not here." He tore open a packet of mustard and squeezed it on his hamburger.

"Did you see her this morning?"

"Yeah. Looked like she didn't sleep much."

Remembering that Amy told Clint she worked another job after leaving the sports show, Kate wondered if she'd gotten any sleep at all. "Did she see you?"

"She didn't act like she recognized me."

"What did you do all morning?"

"Something to do with my disguise. Clint and I alternate spying on you two."

Kate broke off a piece of sandwich. "So, what are we going to do about Amy? Today is our last chance to help her."

Mike caressed her cheek with the backs of his fingers. "I know, sweetheart, I know. Walt says to hold tight and wait for the cops to act. I'm thinking we should walk out the door with her between me and Clint, and that would be the end of Amy and this Executive bunch."

"I have a feeling it wouldn't be that simple."

"You're right." He bit into the hamburger and spoke out of the side of his mouth. "Maybe we can get Walt to put pressure on Barker, remind him they might not see her in public again."

Kate leaned close. "Janessa and her bouncer buddy just sat down three tables away. She looks as miserable as the last time we saw her. Maybe worse, like she hasn't slept or seen the sun in weeks. We have to put an end to this, for her sake and for Amy and the kids."

He eyed her. "We?"

"Well, with help from Walt and the cops."

"Remember the scripture we read this morning, the one that says, 'Rescue me from my persecutors, because they're too strong for me?' Amy and the others need to be rescued. However, we're no match for their persecutors."

"You're right. God is the only one who can rescue them, but I hope he lets us participate."

Mike arched an eyebrow. "To think you accused me of itching for a fight."

She glanced at Janessa again. "I used to pray another verse from that psalm when I was incarcerated. 'Set me free from my prison, so I can praise your name.' That's my prayer for all the Executive Pride prisoners."

Back at her booth, Kate checked the time whenever she had a chance, counting the hours until the sports show ended at six. The convention was almost over, and they hadn't rescued Amy. On top of that, they were flying home tomorrow night. Was this all for nothing?

You gave me that scripture, God, and you led us to Amy. We can't leave without her. She paused. *Well, I guess we could, but how would we ever connect with her again?*

Her phone buzzed, and she pulled it from her hip pocket. Though she didn't recognize the number, she read the text. *If you care about your friend and your husband, walk to Exit D. Alone.*

Kate looked around. The only people in the convention hall who had her Wyoming cell phone number were Mike, Clint and Walt. Like she suspected, the Executive creeps must have gotten hold of her purse. Should she respond to the message or ignore it? It could be a trick. After all, Mike was disguised and Amy was already under their control.

Kate read the message again and was tempted to ask Bart's opinion, but he was busy with customers. Plus, the message said to go alone. She squinted at the domed ceiling above her. Approaching the exit by herself was dangerous. Yet, she couldn't ignore the possibility that Mike and Amy's welfare might depend on her.

She reached under the table for her purse. She'd take her pepper spray and conceal it in her palm. But as her wrist landed on the box edge, she remembered. No purse. She straightened. Now what? Of course. Text Mike. Fingers flying, she typed, *Everything OK?* and hit *send.*

Her phone beeped. Good. He'd answered. However, only one word appeared on the screen. *NOW.*

Kate surveyed the row of windows that ran along a wall above the arena floor. Was someone watching her, like Walt suggested? Stalling for time, she replied, *not finished with work.*

The response was immediate. *NOT A JOKE.*

Okay. She'd play the game their way yet take her time walking to the exit. Maybe she'd hear from Mike before she arrived at Door D.

Laura put her arm around the boy's drooping shoulders. "I'm sorry you have to go so soon, Casey. But your parents are right. You need to leave before this snowstorm turns into a blizzard. It doesn't take much wind for the roads to become impassible up here."

As if to prove her point, a big gust shook the rafters and rattled the doors.

Todd harrumphed. "This is just one of our spring storms. A little extra moisture, that's all."

Laura ignored him and continued talking to Casey. "You're welcome to come back whenever you want to see Estrella Blanca. You can even help me train her, if you'd like."

"Really?" The boy's eyes brightened.

When Martin opened the barn door, wind caught it and sucked him outside with it. The others followed. A flurry of snow-laden air took their breath away as they stepped into deeper snow than was on the ground when they entered the barn.

Martin gave Todd a dirty look. "Just a little extra moisture, huh?"

Todd anchored his hat to his head and hurried ahead of the others. Cindy and Casey took Dymple's arms. Martin helped Joyce and Laura, and they all leaned into the wind. Covering their faces the best they could, they pushed their way back to the house through ever-deepening drifts.

Once they were all safely inside the lobby, Laura said, "We should check the road report before you go." She opened the screen to put another log on the fire.

Martin peered out the window and then at his wife. "We don't have anyone to open the restaurant for us tomorrow. And we can't afford to miss another day of business now that we're closed on Sundays. I think we should at least try to make it down the hill."

"I need to get back to school tonight," Cindy said. "I have class tomorrow."

Laura wondered if they understood the severity of Wyoming blizzards and how dangerous mountain roads could be when slick. "Please don't hesitate to turn around and come back, if you need. We have plenty of empty cabins this time of year."

"I'd like to spend the nightingale," Dymple said. "If you don't mind."

Laura smiled. "I was hoping you'd stay."

A log in the fireplace crackled, and the smell of pine wafted into the room.

"Is it okay if I peek in on Mary before we leave?" Joyce asked. "I'd like to say goodbye."

Cindy bobbed her head up and down. "Me, too."

"I'll go start the car and clear the windows." Martin reached for the door. "We'll leave as soon as it's ready."

Dymple followed Joyce, Cindy and Casey into the hallway.

When they were alone, Todd laid his hat on the fireplace mantle and sidled close to Laura. "They're making an awful big stink over a demented old lady."

Laura stepped away from him. "You're such a grouch today. Do you always have a hard time being friendly? Or has it been too long since you had a drink?"

He narrowed his eyes. "You're such a nag today. Do you always have a hard time—?"

Martin burst into the room. "The snow is coming down harder than ever." He shut the door and wiped his boots on the rug just inside the doorway. "We've got to get going immediately, or you might have to put us up for a week, Laura. If you don't mind, would you tell my family we need to leave now?"

Laura nodded, even though she wished they'd spend the night. At the same time, she hoped Todd didn't think the invitation to stay included him. He'd been so rude today. God seemed to be showing her the man's true colors.

Martin turned toward the door again. "I'll go finish scraping the windows."

Joyce ran into the room, followed by the other three. "We can't find Mary."

"The back door was open." Casey's eyes were wide. "I checked outside and didn't see her, so I closed it."

Laura started to speak but couldn't. The horrible thought of Mary wandering in the storm, most likely without a coat, closed her throat and brought tears to her eyes. How long had the frail woman been outside? Was there any hope of finding her alive? If only they hadn't stayed so long at the barn.

Martin opened the door again. "I'll turn off the engine, and we'll help you look for her."

Laura bit her lip. She needed to think, not panic, and remember how Dan handled emergencies. "Dymple, I'd like for you to man the phones and the CB radio. I'll show you how. Todd, you can—"

He waved away her words. "Leave me out of this. That old biddy isn't my problem."

She gaped at him. "She's not a problem. She's a human being who could freeze to death if we don't find her soon."

"That's how the Indian squaws used to do it when they got past their prime. They'd go sit on a mountaintop and let the weather and the wolves deliver them to that great teepee in the sky." He pointed a finger at the ceiling.

Her jaw dropped.

Casey glared at him. "You're crazy, mister."

Todd started to backhand the boy.

Laura shoved the red-faced man away. "Get out of my house."

Todd spun around, eyes flashing. "Don't you—"

Martin stepped back inside.

"Leave the door open," Joyce said. "Mr. Hughes is on his way out."

Todd swung toward her just as Martin moved between them. "Don't even think about it, Hughes."

CHAPTER THIRTY

Laura couldn't take another moment of drama. They had to find Mary before it was too late. She pointed to the door. "I said *get out!*"

Todd grabbed his hat from the mantle. "You'll be sorry."

She didn't respond.

He crammed his hat on his head. "I hope the witch freezes." He swung the door wide and tromped onto the porch.

Shaking his head, Martin shut the door.

Joyce put her arm around Laura. "I think you have your answer."

Laura took a long breath. How could she have been so blind? Mary was right all along. She released the breath. "Dymple, if you'll take charge of the phones and the radio, I'll get two-ways for the rest of us, so we can keep in touch. How should we divide up?"

Dymple raised her hands, palms up. "Dear God in heaven, creator of both sweet Mary and the beautiful snow."

The others joined hands and bowed their heads.

"You alone know where she is. Keep her warm, keep her safe. Lead us to her and don't let any of us get lost in the storm. You're our shepherd. Bring each of us safely back into the fold. Amen."

The sound of amens rang around the room, and the search party began pulling on their hats and gloves again. Laura tugged Casey's hat over his ears. "Zip your coat all the way to the top."

Cyrus stomped into the room, Tramp beside him. "I just met that yahoo Hughes charging down the road to the pastures. Has he gone loco or what? I barely made it back up the hill. Nearly slid off the road."

Dressed in a baseball uniform, sunglasses and a ball cap, and posing as a batting cage demonstrator, Mike found himself giving batting lessons. He reached around the nine-year-old girl whose hair smelled like green apples to reposition her hands on the bat. He glanced at her mother, who nodded her approval.

She'd asked him to show her daughter how to hold a bat. Said the dad was overseas with the military and wanted to enroll the little girl, whose name was Josie, in softball when he returned home. Mike knew playing little league coach was going above and beyond his duties. Even so, he could take a few minutes to teach her a couple things.

He pulled Josie's bat into position and turned the pitching machine on the lowest speed. He'd watch her bat ten pitches, give her some suggestions, and then let her try again, unless he got a line of people anxious for a turn.

His cell phone buzzed, and he slipped it out of his shirt pocket. Text from Kate. *Everything OK?* He'd respond as soon as he finished with the girl.

After Josie and her mother left, two teenage boys walked up to the batting cage. He quickly punched buttons. *Things are good here. How about you? See you soon.* He pressed "send" and greeted the teens, who wanted to practice their batting skills.

Finally, he found a moment to jog to the restroom. After that stop, he'd check on Kate and Amy to see how they were doing. Just inside the bathroom, his cell phone rang. Probably Kate.

He leaned against the wall. "Hey, sweetheart. How's it going over there?"

"Mike, this is Dymple."

"Oh, sorry. I thought you were Kate. What's up?"

"Your mom asked me to ask you and Kate to pray for Mary."

He adjusted the ball cap he was wearing. "What's wrong? Is she sick?"

"This bad bullfrog came through." Her voice quavered. "We were all out at the barn and she must have awakened from her nap. Then—"

"Whoa, Dymple. You lost me at bullfrog."

"Bullfrog?"

Mike moved away from the noise of the hand dryers. "Maybe you should start over."

She cleared her throat. "After lunch, the kids wanted to meet Laura's new filly, so we all went out to the barn, except Mary, who decided to take a nap."

"What kids?"

"You remember the people who bought Grandma's Café? I think their name is Raeburn. Your mom invited their family and Todd Hughes and me to your place for lunch after church today."

He heard what sounded like static and a woman's voice in the background.

"Mike, I think that's the Sheriff's Department. They want to establish radio contact with us, in case the phones go out. I'd better talk with them. Your mom showed me how to operate your CD. Hope I push the right buttons. I'll call you right back." With that, she hung up.

He raised an eyebrow. Dymple must be talking about their CB radio, not the CD player. Lowering the phone, he stared at the screen. What was going on? A man brushed past him. Mike moved to the side and dropped the phone back into his shirt pocket. Why was the sheriff radioing the ranch? And where was his mom?

He leaned his head against the wall. The scent of the hand soap that dripped in a nearby sink competed with the urinal stench and lost the battle for dominance. He rubbed his temples. What was Todd Hughes doing in their home? Checking it out so he could move in? He wanted to believe his mom hadn't invited him to lunch. Maybe he showed up when the others did and she politely asked him to join them.

Mike grunted. He wanted to kick something, hit something, or someone. However, that someone was too far away—hanging out at his house, no less.

He reached for his phone to call Kate but then stopped. She'd want answers to all the questions floating through his head and more. And he didn't want to chance missing Dymple's call. He'd wait until he talked with her again before he called his wife.

Men and boys came and went. Toilets flushed. Hand dryers blasted. Water whooshed. Someone blew his nose. Mike took the phone from his pocket and held it in his palm. He'd give Dymple one more minute, and then he was calling home. Maybe she'd forgotten her promise to call back.

The phone vibrated and then rang. He pushed a button. "Hello."

"This is Dymple."

"What's going on there?"

"I'm sorry to tell you this, Mike. Mary wandered away."

He frowned. Kate would be horrified. "How long has she been gone?"

"We're not sure, probably less than an hour. We were all down in the barn seeing Laura's new horse and weren't watching the time."

Knowing Mary, she was wearing slippers and a sweater, maybe her bathrobe over her clothes. "What's the temperature there?"

"I don't know. It's cold. A surprise buzzard blew in just after we got here. It's nasty out there."

Mike scratched his head. She probably meant *blizzard*. "How can we help? Even if we flew home right now, we couldn't get to the ranch 'cause of bad roads."

"Pray. Your mom and the Raeburns and Cyrus are outside searching for Mary. Pray for them and for the ambulance and deputies trying to get here through the storm."

"I'll call Kate right now. Please keep us informed." Kate's aunt was so thin, she wouldn't last long in a blizzard, especially if she wasn't dressed properly.

"I'll do that, Mike. Don't forget the psalm that says God is our refuge and strength, an ever-present help in trouble."

He smiled. Leave it to Dymple to refocus his thoughts. "Thanks. I appreciate the reminder. We'll talk later." He hoped he hadn't cut her off, but he was anxious to tell Kate about Mary.

Kate's voicemail came on after the fourth ring. He left a message. "Just got a call from home to tell you about. Give me a buzz when you're free. I love you."

He left the bathroom and made his way through the crowds to Amy's booth. She seemed to be doing okay. He hurried from there to the aisle where Kate worked. She wasn't at the gun table. He perused the guns on display until Bart finished with a customer. Pulling down his sunglasses, he leaned close. "Do you know where Katherine is?"

"Oh, Mike, hi." Bart looked him up and down but didn't comment on the baseball outfit. "I've been wondering the same thing. She's been gone quite a while."

"How long?"

"Hard to say." His brow furrowed. "Half-hour, forty-five minutes."

"That long?" Mike dug for his phone. "I just remembered an odd text she sent." He clicked on the message.

"What did she say?"

"She only wrote two words—everything okay. With a question mark."

"Hmm." Bart edged toward a couple who'd stopped to examine the guns in the case. "I noticed her messing with her phone a couple times before she told me she needed to leave."

Mike checked the time of Kate's text and then looked at his watch. Forty-nine minutes difference. If the text timing was any indication of when she left, his wife had disappeared almost an hour ago. How was it possible both Mary and Kate went missing the same afternoon? Worse, Kate vanished in Dallas, just like Amy.

Seated in the stark conference room with Clint, Detective Barker and a handful of other officers, Mike answered yet another question. "No. We made no plans for after the show ended other than to go to dinner with Kate's boss." He motioned toward Clint. "And Clint Barrett and Walt Harnish."

"And what is your relationship with them?" Detective Barker leaned forward.

"I'm fairly certain you already know Clint is the foreman for our ranch and Walt is the private investigator my wife hired to find Amy Iverson." He drummed the table with his fingertips. "Kate's been missing for almost two hours now. Sitting here talking about it isn't helping her."

The detective folded his hands and rested them on the table beside a bag of corn chips. "I understand your concern, Mr. Duncan. For your information, we have a couple men checking the exits, asking people if they saw Mrs. Duncan leave."

Mike grasped his knees to slow the jiggle. "Did you search Executive's headquarters? They harassed Kate all weekend. And one of them attacked her. "

"We don't know that Executive Pride took her or, for that matter, that anyone took her."

Mike cocked his head. "Meaning what?"

The detective held out his palm. "Knowing your wife is a past felon, have you considered the possibility she tired of being a good girl and decided to rejoin the dark side? Could be the lure of the big city was too much for her to resist."

"No!" Mike jumped up, knocking his chair over.

The other officers were instantly on their feet.

Mike placed his hands on the table and bent eye-to-eye with the detective. "The only reason Kate came to this convention was to find her friend."

Clint stood next to Mike. "I can vouch for that, sir."

Barker studied the two men. "We'll pursue the Executive Pride possibility, along with others, and keep you informed. Meeting dismissed."

Mike and Clint took the stairs and stopped at the landing just inside the door to the main floor. Mike fisted his hands. "Possibility? We know as well as they do that Executive is the prime suspect."

"Maybe he was bluffing, to see how you'd react." Clint shoved his hands into his pockets. "What now?"

Mike waved his phone in the air. "First we call Walt. And then we find my wife."

The phone rang.

Mike's heart jolted. He pushed the button and crammed the phone to his ear. "Kate?"

"It's Dymple again."

"Oh." He stifled a groan. "Hi, Dymple. Any word on Aunt Mary?"

"Yes, thank God. Your mother found her curled against a bush. She must have slipped down the hill below your dining hall. The bush stopped her from sliding all the way into the pond. That ice would have frozen her for sure."

"So she's alive?"

"Yes, but not very coherent."

"Frostbite?"

"We're not sure. An ambulance is following a snowplow up here right now. The EMTs should be able to give us an idea of her condition before they transport her to the houseboat."

Mike rubbed his neck with his free hand. Surely she meant *hospital*.

"You can be proud of your puppy dog."

"How's that?"

"He and Prissy saved Mary's life. They were snuggled up with her, which was good, because she wasn't wearing a coat or boots. Just slippers. It was Tramp's barking that caught Laura's attention, although she could barely hear him above the howl of the wind. She said the snowfall was so thick she couldn't see that far down the hill. Martin and Cyrus helped carry Mary to the house."

"We can't stop praying yet, Dymple."

"No, we can't. The ambulance ride to the hospital is going to be long and treacherous. And besides frostbite, there's the chance she might catch pneumonia. I don't know how it will affect her multiple sclerosis. Like me, she's no spring chicken."

"Please have everyone pray for Kate, too."

"Oh, dear." Dymple stopped. "Is she having constipation from the surgery?"

"Uh, you mean *complications*?"

"Yes. That's what I meant."

"Worse. She's been kidnapped."

There was a long pause. "No."

"I don't know for certain, but I'm pretty sure she was taken by the same people who kidnapped Amy." He shoved his hand through his hair. "I'll explain later. Ask Mom to pray for Kate, please."

"I'll do that. I'm so sorry this happened, Mike. Just remember, God is with her, just like he was with Mary."

"Thanks. I'll keep you updated." He opened the exit door. "Gotta run."

Amy gazed out the limo window. All she saw was a blur of color and lights that seemed to pulse with the country music blasting from the speaker above her head. She couldn't remember ever feeling so disappointed or drained. Not only did she not see any of her Wyoming friends all day, she didn't see the other guy either, the one whose note said to get ready to be rescued.

And even though Colin in the next booth waved a sad-faced goodbye, he'd made no effort to help her. What a wimp. But then, she was no braver than he was. She sighed. She hadn't even tried to escape. As a result, here she was, headed back to Thomas's skyscraper hell, never to see her Wyoming friends again. She'd dared to hope that tonight she would return to a normal life. She'd also hoped to warn Kate about Thomas. Now it was too late.

Across from her, the children were draped over each other like rag dolls, obviously done-in. Poor babies. She'd failed them.

Amy tried to hold back the tears, yet one trickled down her cheek. She wiped it away. Death would be better than growing up at EP, if the kids lasted that long. Surely God was concerned about them, even if he ignored her.

A familiar strip mall flashed by the window. After three days of riding to and from the convention center, she now recognized landmarks. The limo was getting close to headquarters—and to Thomas and his latest punishment. What was he planning this time? She swallowed. How much more could she take?

The limo passed the drive that led to the back entrance they usually used.

Amy sucked in a breath. What was going on?

Marco's bored but alert glance slid her direction.

She yawned and covered her mouth, shifting her position to see out a different window. The driver made a left turn, drove a few blocks, and then turned right. The limo that followed did the same. Several blocks later, they took another right. And another left.

Right, left. Left, right. Straight three blocks, and another turn. Though seemingly random, she got the feeling the idea was to confuse the passengers. The vehicle slowed and pulled into a dark alley lined with dense hedges and an occasional dumpster. The headlights went dark, the interior floor lights dimmed, and the music stopped. The guards put their feet on the floor and their hands on their knees, as if preparing to leap out of the car.

Amy chewed at her lip. Something was up.

The limo stopped. Marco shook the kids awake. Even in the murky lighting, she could see the terror on their normally expressionless faces. Were they waking from happy dreams about home and family to the nightmare of reality? How sad they endured horror day in and day out. If only she could hold them and tell them she'd help them return to their homes.

Marco hissed, "Shh. No talking."

As if any of them would dare speak a word.

A slender man with a revolver opened the limousine door from the outside.

Marco motioned for the guards in the car to get out, and then he signaled the other passengers. "Move it, whores." He pointed to a doorway in a brick building ten feet away. "In that door and down the stairs." He lowered his voice. "No noise, no funny stuff." He reached inside his jacket and pulled out a pistol.

The children staggered out after the men. One girl fell from the car onto the ground.

Marco snarled and yanked her to her feet. "I said, no funny stuff." He gave her a shove, and she stumbled toward the doorway.

Amy hurried to catch up with the girl and take her hand before she tripped down the stairs.

The girl's hand tensed.

Amy whispered, "It's okay."

Though the stairway was not lighted, a sconce at the base offered enough illumination for the group to safely maneuver the stairs, despite prodding by the guards and the stiletto heels many of the women wore. The captives huddled together at the landing, reminding Amy of chicks about to slip under a mother hen's wing.

However, there was no mother hen to shield them from the sadistic foxes that dictated, tormented and dehumanized their fragile lives. Maybe there wasn't a Father God, either. If there was, he didn't appear concerned about their plight.

CHAPTER THIRTY-ONE

Amy gripped the girl's hand and scanned the wide shadowed hallway. The place smelled familiar, a stronger smell than the usual dank basement odor. Somehow, the sewer-like stench embodied violence and fear. She shivered. Maybe it was related to some long-forgotten childhood trauma.

Loud cursing pierced the silence.

Amy jerked.

The girl clutched Amy's hand with both of hers.

"Move it, you idiots," Marco shouted. "Get out of the way."

The guards shunted the group farther into the hallway. Two men carrying an ornate chair worked their way down the stairs. Amy recognized the chair. She'd sat in it several times in the brothel while waiting for the next customer. The man behind them lugged a stack of bedding. Following him, two men struggled to balance a mattress and navigate the stairwell.

Someone switched on a light in room across from Amy. The men deposited their loads inside and hastened back up the stairs. She surveyed the contents of the room. Bed parts, foundations and mattresses were stacked high, along with piles of bedding, lamps, end tables, more chairs, and computer monitors.

Maybe Thomas was relocating the EP headquarters. She grimaced. Would this dark basement be where they lived and worked from now on? How much worse could things get?

The girl patted her hand.

Amy smiled. She had a friend, a beautiful little Hispanic friend. She took a breath and tried to act calm, for the girl's sake.

"Take them to the back," Marco ordered.

Another guard, one she hadn't seen before, flicked a whip. The sound crackled like a gunshot and made her jump. She frowned. Why did they think they needed a whip? The prisoners were already as docile as a flock of butterflies.

There might have been twenty captives who were being herded like cattle through the long passageway. She couldn't tell exactly how many. Almost half of them were children. They passed several empty rooms. One chamber, however, contained barbells and weighted disks. So that's why the guards were built like gorillas.

As they moved beyond the weight room, something about it nagged at the back of her mind. Amy slowed. Though the girl propelled her forward, her thoughts began to gel. If the guards used the equipment regularly, the room would likely be located near EP's headquarters. In that case, the circuitous route the limos took from the convention hall may have ended right back where they started. If that was true, and if she ever escaped, she could find her way downtown. For the first time since they left the convention center, she felt a glimmer of hope.

Dark rectangular objects sat in the middle of the next room. Stereo speakers. Amy winced, remembering the horrible moment she'd awakened to Thomas's voice booming around her. That's why the place smelled familiar. She stumbled. Again, the girl pulled her along, keeping her one step ahead of the whip.

Mike and Clint met Walt outside the Executive building in the lighted parking lot. "Got any news for us?" Mike asked.

Walt aimed his chin toward the glass-enclosed lobby, where a cluster of policemen stood by the elevators. "Just talked with

Barker. They're meeting with Executive's head honcho, Thomas Mendiola, on the fiftieth floor in a few minutes. Barker says Mendiola seems anxious to cooperate with an investigation and is opening the office."

A large bird flew into a nearby tree and began to whistle and screech.

"What kind of bird is that?" Clint asked. "It's even noisier than a crow."

"It's a type of blackbird called a grackle," Walt said. "They're real aggravating when they get to squawking first thing in the morning." The grackle's shrieks and clicks nearly drowned out his next words. "Barker thinks the guy was a mite too friendly on the phone, too willing to assist."

Mike folded his arms. "You going up with the cops?"

"Maybe." Walt glanced toward the windows. "Better get back in there, just in case they decide to include me." He touched his forehead in a quick salute and strode toward the double doors.

"Should we follow them?" Mike asked. "Kate could be up there."

Clint shook his head. "If the guy's so willing to show them around, the cops won't find anything."

"Makes sense." Stepping back, Mike tried to see the fiftieth floor. From that angle, it was impossible. "So, what can we do down here?"

The grackle flew to a lamppost and upped its decibel level.

Mike gritted his teeth. The bird's raucous noises sawed at his tattered nerves.

A black limousine entered the parking lot from the access lane at the side of the building and stopped in front of the lobby. Several men got out of the car and joined the officers inside.

Clint moved so he could see around the car. "There they go, and Walt's with them."

"Good."

Clint turned to Mike. "I just saw someone step into that hedge over there and disappear."

"You sure? I mean, we're both pretty jumpy right now."

"Maybe I'm seeing things, but we should check it out. Might have something to do with that Executive bunch."

"Let's go."

Several yards ahead of the group, Amy could see that the hallway widened to an opening a dump truck could drive through. Strange. Thomas liked doors. Doors that locked.

Like sheep headed for slaughter, they shuffled through the entryway, shoulders rigid, eyes wide. The first thing she noticed, other than the girl's death-grip on her numb fingers, was an eerie glow at the far end of the long, narrow, concrete room. The air was warm and musty. And the fetid smell was stronger.

She looked around. The dimly lit space appeared empty, except for... Were those people illuminated by the odd lighting?

Lined up against the back wall, the figures didn't move, didn't speak. Just stared straight ahead. Could they be manikins? She was used to EP silence. In fact, the convention noise was overwhelming at times. Here, the lack of sound and motion was as unnerving as the shifting shadows on the ceiling.

Now that she was closer, Amy saw that the light radiated from the floor and white-washed the faces of the two guards who bent to pick up a long wide grid. Half carrying, half sliding the grate, they skidded it toward the light. The screech of steel against cement jarred the silent bystanders to action. People on both sides of the light clasped their ears, including Amy and the girl.

With a loud metallic clang, the grid fell into place. The light flickered, as if disturbed by the commotion. The men straightened and motioned them forward.

Amy reached for the girl's hand again. What were they getting into now? She clamped her jaw and tried to steel herself for whatever lay beneath the grid. It couldn't be good.

They inched forward. Now she could see those on the far side of the light. They were coworkers. She could tell by the way they were dressed.

Someone at the front of the group screamed and fell back. Another voice cried, "Please, no."

The whip cracked, and the pleading ceased. Guards pushed people onto the grate. Someone groaned, yet no one spoke, no one cried out. And they all ran across the metal bridge as if chased by a specter, even those in high heels. One tripped and fell, slipped out of her heels and charged across. A guard swore and threw the shoes at her.

Amy's chest constricted and her heart pounded against her ribs. She tried to smile for the girl, who watched her with terrified eyes. And then it was their turn.

"Drop the hand," a guard ordered.

She released her grip on the child's tiny fingers.

The guard thrust Amy onto the grid.

She stumbled to her knees on the hard metal and found herself staring into the light. Snakes. Hundreds of slithering, coiling, tongue-flicking snakes. Amy froze, unable to move.

Someone jabbed a pole into the mound. The reptiles hissed and rattled. One of them struck at the stick.

She screamed, jumped to her feet and leaped to the other side.

Harsh male guffaws followed her.

Marco shouted, "I see you haven't forgotten our mascots. They're hungry. Haven't fed 'em in months."

Mike and Clint crossed the Executive Pride parking lot and stopped at the lane that ran alongside the skyscraper. The hedge on the other side was tall and dense. Mike looked from one end of the greenery to the other. "I don't see an opening anywhere."

Clint trotted over to the bushes and began tugging branches.

Mike scanned the area, noting the solitary side door in the Executive building. What would they do if someone walked out right now? They needed a plan. He looked back at Clint, who now yanked the bushes with both hands. A wide chunk of hedge loosened, and he nearly lost his balance.

Mike rushed to his side.

"It's fake," Clint whispered. "Feels like rubber." He motioned toward the opening. "You first."

Mike stepped into the gap in the greenery. The cavity was high enough for him to remain upright, and then some. Two more steps, and he was through the foliage and standing on a driveway that appeared to access a narrow alley. A bare bulb over a garage door on the other side of the alley provided the only light.

He heard rustling behind him. Clint was wiggling the artificial branches into place. "Clint," he whispered. "Let's go." The less noise they made, the better.

Clint emerged from the bushes.

Mike pointed to the black limousine parked between the metal building on their right and the brick building on their left. They slipped between the car and the wall and were working their way forward, when Mike heard something in the hedge. He tapped Clint's shoulder, and they both crouched behind the long dark vehicle.

Peeking around the windshield, Mike saw two husky men carrying what appeared to be furniture, maybe a dresser. They lurched their load around the car and turned toward the brick building.

He swiveled on his heels to shadow Clint, who was creeping between the building and the car, tracking the men.

Clint stopped and cocked his head.

Mike did the same.

A man was speaking, his voice low. "This is the last of it."

"Take it on down. The sports-show whores should be out of the way of the stairs by now."

Clint looked back at Mike, eyebrows raised.

Mike clenched his fists. What were the women doing down there? Was his wife one of them? Before his imagination could run wild, he shut it down and refocused. God would take care of Kate. His job was to find her.

More shuffling, and then the footsteps faded into silence. The grackle, which must have flown from the other side of the parking lot to the hedge, started in again, screeching and squawking, clicking and warbling. How one bird could make so many obnoxious sounds, he didn't know. Yet, he was grateful for the noise cover.

He was trying to figure out what their next move should be, when he heard footsteps and heavy breathing.

"Glad that's over." The voice was masculine. "My back is starting to ache."

"What do you mean, over? Once the heat is off and the cops butt out, the boss'll have us drag everything up those stairs again and put it right back where it came from."

"This is a weird job," the first man said. "First, we hang out at the convention center for days, barely moving a finger, and then in hardly no time at all, we move out beds, rake and vacuum carpets like Mr. Clean on steroids, throw rugs over the furniture marks, and haul in tables and chairs."

"We'd better get back up top before someone comes for us."

"We've been on the job over ten hours. Why—?"

Another voice broke in. "Around here, we don't ask why. We just do whatever it takes to please the man upstairs, and I'm not talking g-o-d."

"Yeah," the other man said. "Because if you don't." There was a long pause. "Let's just say your family'll never know what happened to you."

Amy pushed her way to the back wall, as far from the snake pit as she could get. She sat down and pulled her knees to her chest. *Breathe,* she told herself. *Breathe, Natasha.*

She groaned. No. Her name was *Amy*. She took a long shaky breath. Thomas had them right where he wanted them. Paralyzed by fear. Yet, they couldn't live indefinitely behind a snake pit, or make money for him here. So this must be temporary jailing. But why?

She lifted her head. How many women and children did EP keep? Three dozen? Four? Like perfectly sculpted statues, they all faced the pit, its undulating shimmer reflected on their beautiful though pale faces.

Marco called, "Time to shut down the party."

Again, two men grasped the grate. This time, they pulled it away from the pit, screeching the heavy grid onto the cement.

The onlookers winced and shrank back.

Amy covered her ears against the unbearable sound and stared at the trench. It ran from wall to wall and was five, maybe six-feet wide. Who knew how deep it was. Or how many snakes it held.

Someone sobbed. "Please don't leave us here."

The men laughed and sauntered out of the room.

Something nudged Amy's foot.

She jerked away and then looked down. A boot had touched her shoe, not a snake.

"Amy…"

The whispered word in the silent room might as well have been a shout. All heads swiveled toward the sound.

Amy followed the boot to a leg and the leg to a body and then Kate's face. Her friend lay next to her, rubbing her eyes as if just awakening. Amy moaned. Thomas had kidnapped her best friend, and it was her fault. "Kate, I'm so sorry."

Almost as soon as she spoke, she clasped her hands around the necklace. The women around her did the same.

Kate tried to sit up but fell back down. "Where are we?"

Amy pointed toward the pit.

Kate squinted, obviously confused.

Amy helped her sit and lean against the wall.

Kate's gaze moved from woman to child to woman. And then, as if everything was coming into focus, she grasped her throat, a question in her eyes.

Amy "zipped" her fingers across her lips.

Kate pointed to the light and gave Amy a questioning look.

Amy pursed her lips. How could she say *snake* without speaking? She traced a zigzag line on the floor with her finger.

Kate frowned.

Amy tried again with the zigzag. Then she spread her fingers beside her face and opened her eyes and mouth wide to indicate terror.

Kate, who still appeared confused, balanced on her hands and knees and then slowly crawled toward the pit.

The others gawked at her as if she'd lost her mind, horrified expressions plastered across their painted faces.

Amy checked the doorway. Were there really no guards standing by? Or did they assume the snakes were sufficient insurance against escapees?

Mike watched the men round the car and walk toward the bushes. The bird exploded with a loud whistle followed by a harsh scraping sound. One of the men waved his arms and growled, "Outa here, stupid bird."

Leaves rattled and wings flapped. Above the hedge, Mike saw the profile of the retreating grackle in the lamppost light. So much for the noise cover. He twisted just in time to see Clint poke his head around the corner of the building and extend a finger.

Mike nodded. Just one guard.

Clint motioned to him.

Mike moved closer, wincing when his boot scraped the cement.

Clint pointed to himself and then to the front of the brick building.

Mike indicated he'd go around the car. He picked up a pebble and pretended to toss it at the driveway.

Clint gave him a thumbs-up.

Mike edged around the limousine, checked the bushes and stood. He'd throw rocks to get the guard's attention, and Clint could ambush the guy as he walked past. But then he heard more voices and ducked behind the car again. Would they ever get inside the place?

"We're the last ones out," a masculine voice said. "I'll lock the door and give you the key, even though it isn't necessary. Those morons are scared spitless of the sidewinders."

Another male laughed. "Yeah. They're down there cowering like rabbits cornered by a pack of—"

The first man broke in. "Quiet. The boss is calling."

Silence.

"Marco here." Pause. "Natasha? Got it. We'll bring her right up." A moment later, he said, "We need to go back down to get one of the broads. He wants her upstairs. Some kind of deal with the cops."

Mike heard retreating footsteps and then nothing. He couldn't tell how many men were in the group or whether any of them stayed with the guard. Probably not. It was too quiet. He tapped Clint's back and pointed to the driveway. Then he sent up a quick prayer and moved to the other side of the car.

CHAPTER THIRTY-TWO

Kate reached the edge of the pit. Still feeling lightheaded from whatever drug was stabbed into her leg when she stepped out the back door of the convention center, it took her a moment to comprehend what she was seeing. Was that wriggling mass really snakes?

She sat on her heels, hands on her thighs. The sight of hundreds of slithering reptiles crawling over and under each other in the bright light made her dizzy. Or maybe it was the warmth and the nauseating smell. She looked at Amy, whose eyes were almost as big as her open mouth.

The women and children gaped at her. It was one thing to be afraid of snakes, Kate thought, and another thing to be petrified.

She could tell the odor was irritating her sinuses. Placing the back of her hand against her nostrils, she tried to stop the sneeze, but it came anyway. Again, the women clasped their necklaces, as if even a sneeze was a dangerous sound.

"Kate." Amy's whisper was loud and insistent. "They're coming!"

Mike threw a handful of pebbles toward the middle of the driveway.

The response was instant. "Who's there?"

He waited and then flung more rocks.

Footsteps headed his way.

Mike darted behind the car.

A slight man with a revolver stepped into view.

Clint sprang from the shadows, knocking him to the ground.

The man landed with a loud groan. His gun skittered across the concrete.

Mike ran toward the pair, ready to grab the gun and whack the guard's head with it, but the downed man didn't move.

Clint rolled him onto his back.

Mike snorted. "You really slammed him, dude."

"All my years of steer wrestling finally paid off."

Mike released the clasp on the guard's belt, yanked it from his pants, and then shoved him back onto his face. "Hold his arms, so I can wrap this around them. Then we'll dump him in the limo. It's unlocked."

They were about to pick up the inert man, when Clint whispered, "Wait."

Mike frowned. "We gotta move it."

Kate twisted her head to see Amy motioning for her to return to the group. She scurried back to the wall and had barely positioned herself next to her friend, when several men marched through the archway.

"Natasha, get over here."

Amy sucked in a breath.

"Now!" One of the men stomped toward the far edge of the pit.

Amy stood, her hands shaking.

Kate glanced from Amy to the men. What was going on? Despite her confusion, she jumped to her feet to stand beside her friend. The two of them had been a formidable team in prison. They'd give the Executive monsters a run for their money.

The man swore. "Not you, dimwit. Sit down."

Marco! Kate ignored him. She hadn't gotten this close to Amy to abandon her now.

He pulled a gun. "Time you learned the rules around here. When we speak, you jump."

Kate sat down. No use making things worse for Amy and the others.

Marco waved his pistol at Kate. "You'll pay for your insubordination." He aimed the gun at Amy. "Get over here."

She hesitated.

Kate patted Amy's leg. "Jesus goes with you."

Amy took a breath, squared her shoulders and stepped to the pit.

Marco gestured with the pistol. "Jump."

"What?"

"Jump. Now."

The silent onlookers came alive, gasping and whimpering as if they were the ones being ordered to hurdle the snakes.

Amy rubbed her palms against her shorts. "I can't jump that far."

Marco motioned to the other men. Two of them stepped to the edge and held out their hands.

Amy looked at the pit and then at the men.

Kate could tell she didn't trust them, yet it was obvious she didn't have a choice.

Amy stepped back as far as she could, sprinted across the open space and leaped over the gap, landing on one foot.

The men caught her by the arms and then dipped her down into the pit.

Amy screamed.

Kate sprang to her feet.

Shrieking and thrashing about, Amy nearly dragged the men into the pit with her.

Finally, they jerked her out.

The other men laughed hysterically, as if they were watching a comedy. One of them whispered something to Marco, who trained his gun at Kate's chest. "That's twice."

Mike looked both ways. "Hurry."

Clint pulled a bandana from his back pocket. "I'll gag him in case he wakes up." He spread the handkerchief open. "Only a couple boogers." Pulling two corners taut, he twisted the fabric into a long roll, slipped it between the guard's teeth and double-knotted it behind his head.

Together, they half carried, half dragged the limp body to the vehicle and dumped him in the back. The dome light remained on. Mike opened the front door and turned the light off while Clint retrieved the gun. Then they stepped to either side of the building entry.

Clint whispered "I hear something," and ducked behind a dumpster.

Mike slipped between the car and the building. The sound of his pulse thumping in his ears competed with the laughter and footsteps coming their way.

"Ha-ha, Natasha," one of the men was saying. "We got to see you make a fool of yourself one more time before we hand you over to the cops."

Mike heard more harsh male laughter. And then Amy appeared between two of the mafia types they'd seen around the convention center. Tears streamed down her face, but she didn't utter a sound.

"Hey," one of the men said. "She can't go to jail wearing our special jewelry. The cops'll be on to us in no time."

"Oh, yeah." The man snickered. "Anyone got a sharp knife on them?"

Even in the dim lighting, Mike could see Amy's eyes widen.

"You don't need no knife," someone said. "Thomas gave you a key. You were s'posed to collect all the jewelry tonight."

"Uh, right." The man, apparently the leader, caressed Amy's tearstained face and then reached into his shirt pocket. "I was hoping to run a blade up that lovely neck of yours."

She pressed her lips together.

He pinched her rear, and she jumped.

Mike clamped his jaw. *God help her.*

A cell phone rang. The ringleader reached into his shirt pocket. "Marco here." There was a pause. "We got her. Taking the necklace off now. I'll tell her. Be right up." He stuck the phone in his pocket and jerked Amy around so that her back was to him. "Don't move."

Mike gripped his thighs. If Amy hadn't been headed to police custody, he would have taken on the jerks.

The man pulled the choker off her neck, and Amy touched her throat. He dangled the sparkling chains in front of her. "If you tell the law about what goes on around here and they come snooping again, Thomas says your rancher friend will die a slow painful death." He jutted his chin. "Do you understand?"

Amy turned away.

He grasped her jaw and pulled her face close to his. "Understand?"

She lowered her eyes. "Yes." Her voice was barely audible.

He pocketed the choker. "Let's go. The boss is waiting."

One of the men asked, "Where's Jose'?"

The others looked around.

"Probably taking a leak. Wouldn't want to be him when the boss finds out he left his post." Marco started forward. "Those whores ain't going nowhere, and we'll be right back. Once the cops are gone, we'll take the furniture upstairs, so we can do some business tonight."

When the last man disappeared into the hedge, Mike scooted around the corner of the building. "Clint?"

Clint inched from behind the dumpster into the doorway. "If I ever get my hands on those goons…"

"Sounds like Amy's headed to jail." Mike kept his voice low. "She'll be safe there."

Clint brandished the revolver. "I was tempted to mow 'em all down." He stared at the bushes. "Maybe I should follow them."

"We're not done here."

Clint exhaled. "We may never see her again."

"We know where she's headed, but we don't know where Kate is. We need to find her."

Kate stepped closer to the pit. What was she seeing on the other side? After a moment, she realized she saw metal grates, three of them. Most likely, the grids covered the entire trench when all were in use. She picked out Janessa in the crowd and moved to sit by her. The woman didn't seem to notice her presence. "Janessa, it's me, Kate."

Janessa stiffened and covered her necklace.

Kate mouthed, *Sorry*. Just because Amy and her choker were gone didn't mean the others could talk. She pointed at the pit and tried to act out her plan to pull one of the grates around to serve as a bridge for the captives to cross to freedom.

Janessa's eyebrows crumpled. She drew a zigzag line on the floor with her finger.

Snakes. Kate nodded. Of course they were a factor. However, they weren't nearly as bad as the reptilian men who controlled these people's lives. She pointed to two young girls with matching tattoos on their shoulders, gorgeous girls whose beauty was marred by the terror in their eyes, and tried to plead their case with hand gestures. If she wouldn't fight for herself, maybe Janessa would fight for the girls.

Kate stood and reached out her hand. Janessa hesitated but finally joined her. The others watched, eyes wide and unblinking.

Janessa motioned to a beautiful black lady Kate remembered seeing at the convention. The woman looked at them and then at the pit. After a long moment, she got to her feet.

Kate took their hands and led them like children to the pit. The closer they got, the more the other two hung back.

A car horn beeped erratically in the distance.

Kate peered down the long hallway beyond the archway. She'd pictured their location as rural, far from Dallas. After all, that's where snakes usually lived. But maybe they were in a city. God would have to show Mike where to find her. Dallas was huge.

They stopped at the lip of the pit. Kate steeled herself. Time to do what God brought her here to do. At least she had some protection. Unlike the others, she wore boots and jeans.

She jumped into the pit and slipped on the squirming reptiles. Struggling for a foothold, she lost her balance, screamed and grabbed for the edge.

The limo horn honked and kept on honking. Mike spun around.

Clint jumped behind the car, gun ready.

Mike snuck alongside the vehicle, peeking through the dark windows, but he couldn't see anything. Bursting out onto the driveway, he charged for the driver's side door and wrenched it open.

Draped across the front seat, the bound-and-gagged guard butted his head against the steering wheel horn again and again. Though his hands were secured behind his back, he'd managed to wiggle through the open window between the passenger and driver compartments.

Mike slammed the man's temple against the steering wheel, knocking him out again. Then he shoved his limp body back through the opening, slid the window closed, shut the door and ran for the building. Hot on Clint's heels, he skidded inside the doorway and waited, holding his breath, but he didn't hear anyone coming their way.

They looked around the small area. The floor they stood on wasn't much more than a landing for a flight of steps that led downward. In addition to the door they'd just entered, there was another door opposite it. Clint turned the knob. It was locked. The only other option was the stairway. He whispered, "Didn't those guys say something about stairs?"

Before Mike could answer, his phone buzzed. He snatched it out of his pocket, frustrated he hadn't silenced it earlier. But maybe Kate was calling. He looked at the screen. *Finished upstairs. No sign of women or children. Where are you?*

He whispered, "Walt," and showed Clint the message before he punched in a reply. *Next door, thru bushes, brick bldg, bring cops.* He pressed *send*, changed vibrate mode to silent mode and signaled for Clint to descend the stairs.

Kate crouched beside the rattlesnake pit, breathing hard. She didn't dare make eye contact with the others after confirming their worst nightmare. She shuddered. Slipping on the snakes was a hideous experience, but she wished she hadn't screamed and possibly alerted Executive.

She walked the length of the pit, still trying to catch her breath. The writhing mass and the stench nearly overwhelmed her senses, but she noticed that fewer snakes congregated at one end. Motioning for Janessa and the other woman to join her, she placed her palms together, aimed her fingers upward and whispered, "Pray."

They folded their hands.

She mouthed her prayer. *Give us courage, wisdom and strength. Amen.* With that, she lowered herself into the pit again and placed one foot in a bare spot. Using her free leg, she gently nudged a knotted reptilian mass with the side of her boot. No reaction other than a squirm or two. *Thank you, Jesus.* She remembered what Mike had said about rattlesnake fangs being able to penetrate boot leather and added a prayer for protection.

With a few more shoves, she was able to clear enough space to stand with both feet on the cement floor, which was coated with a dark substance. So that's what she smelled. Snake feces. Inch by inch, she pushed snakes aside. When she'd cleared enough room for two people to stand, she tugged at the grate, but it didn't budge.

She tried again, with no discernible progress. She looked at the women who hovered above her. Pointing at the grid, she motioned for them to help her pull it.

Janessa shook her head. The other woman squared her shoulders and stepped to the edge.

Kate held out her hand. But then she thought of another approach. Instead of making a lot of noise dragging metal across cement, she'd stand inside the pit and lower people next to her. Janessa's friend could lift them to the other side.

Kate pantomimed her new plan, but the woman didn't move. Kate tapped her watch, hoping she'd understand that time was crucial.

Finally, she grasped Kate's hand and stepped down, her face contorted with fear. Kate helped her climb to the other side and then motioned to Janessa, who stared at Kate and then at her friend, who was beckoning to her.

Again, Kate pointed to her wrist.

Janessa was breathing so fast and shaking so hard, Kate thought she might pass out. But she took Kate's hand and dropped into the pit, her squeal barely audible. The woman on the other side helped her scramble from the snake hole.

Kate checked the snakes. The mass was separating. She waved to the others huddled against the wall. One little boy jumped up and then another and another. Others followed. Their expressions were fearful and their bodies tense, but at least they'd come to life. Kate wondered how long it had been since they'd felt even a hint of hope.

One by one, they dropped into the trench and were lifted to safety. Only three people left. Kate felt a weight on the top of her foot and looked down. A big ugly diamondback was working its way onto her boot, one scale at a time. *Please, God, don't let that slimy thing crawl up my leg.*

Mike crept down the steps to the basement. Clint followed close behind. At the bottom was a long dark hallway with doors on each side. They'd have to check each room, even though the place was so quiet it felt deserted.

Clint wrinkled his nose and gave Mike a questioning glance.

Mike shrugged. Maybe there was a septic tank somewhere nearby.

Clint stepped to the nearest open doorway and peeked inside.

Mike followed, listening and watching for movement. He squinted into the darkness.

Clint checked the hallway and then switched on the light. The room was full of furniture. Mattresses, beds, nightstands, chairs.

They waited for a moment but heard nothing. Mike shut off the light and they entered the room across the hall. Same thing. Room after room held furniture, much of it identical.

Mike frowned. Where was Kate? He blew out a breath and swallowed his frustration. If he let his emotions get out of hand, he might do something stupid.

By now, they'd stopped turning on lights. At one open doorway, he could tell the room held workout equipment. Another was bare, except for stereo speakers and rolls of duct tape. They were about to search the room across the hall, when they heard voices. Clint slid to one side of the doorway, and Mike slipped behind the door.

Three men stopped not far from them.

His breath shallow and silent, Mike prayed they couldn't hear his pounding heart. Through the crack between the door and the wall he saw that one of them had a phone at his ear. "He's gone, boss. We don't see Jose' anywhere. It's like he disappeared into thin air."

Silence, and then he spoke again. "That's where we're headed right now, to check on the whores. The audio guys said they heard strange sounds." Pause. "Yeah, I'll call you right back."

Kate offered her hand to the wild-eyed Hispanic woman who teetered at the edge of the trench.

The lady moaned. "I no can do."

The blonde waiting behind her clasped a hand over the ter-rified woman's mouth.

Kate pointed to a bare spot inches from the snake now coil-ing on her boot. If only she'd thought to put her pant legs inside the boots.

The woman's eyes bulged.

The other woman whispered something in her ear, and the dark-haired woman stepped down, her foot inches from a lethar-gic rattler. Kate transferred her to the waiting hands of those on the other side and reached for the two remaining individuals, the blond woman and a young Asian girl. Maybe she could move two at once across the gap, dump the snake and jump out before it reacted.

"Well, well, well." An acrid male voice sliced the silence like a butcher knife. "What do we have here?"

The escapees gasped.

Kate whirled. *Damon.*

"Miss Smarty Pants at it again. That's three times."

Kate could tell her movement disturbed the snake. She prayed it wouldn't strike.

Damon sauntered over to stand above her on the metal grid.

She looked him in the eye. The guy was as cocky as a cor-rectional officer. No way would she show any sign of weakness.

He shook his head. "Thomas is not going to like this, not one little bit." He bent down, hands on his thighs, his eyes glistening in the pit light. "We're going to have to teach you and all these other whores a lesson none of you will ever forget."

Kate's breath caught in her chest. Something was crawling up her leg. Was it inside or outside her pants? Which was worse, the snake or Damon?

CHAPTER THIRTY-THREE

Mike and Clint waited until the footsteps became distant before they snuck out of the room and followed the men. Step by silent step, Mike prayed he could get to Kate before they did, wherever she was.

Near the end of the dark hallway, a wavering glow outlined the forms of three men, and the sewer smell grew stronger. Careful not to scuff his boots against the floor, Mike inched around the archway. It was warmer in here.

Clint nudged Mike and jerked his chin toward the side of the room.

The flickering light made it hard to see. Mike squinted and realized he was seeing people. Thirty, maybe forty women were bunched together in a silent shoulder-to-shoulder semi-circle, like bison protecting their young from wolves. Were they shielding children? He thought he saw a child peek around a bare leg and then realized most of the legs were bare. The women didn't have all that much clothing on their upper bodies, either.

The man nearest the odd light laughed and waved a hand at his companions. "Isn't that right, boys? This is going to be the best lesson of all. They'll never do something this stupid again."

The other two joined his laughter, their strident cackles reverberating in the hollow chamber.

Mike and Clint glanced at each other.

"You, Katherine Duncan..."

Mike whipped around.

The man crouched on his haunches and talked to someone whose face Mike could now see. Wrapped in the odd, vacillating glow, Kate's expression was unreadable. She didn't speak, didn't move, and didn't blink. What was going on? Mike started toward her.

Kate refused to give Damon the satisfaction of a reaction or allow herself to kick away the rattler that now clung to her kneecap.

Damon straightened then tilted toward her again. "Slut!" Veins popped from his neck and forehead. "You'll learn not to mess with Thomas."

Kate twisted to the side, grasped the snake behind its head, and flung it at Damon.

The snake wrapped around his neck.

Damon yelped. Arms spinning like a windmill, he fought for balance and then stumbled across the grid toward his cohorts. "Help me!"

Both men back-stepped, hands extended as if protecting themselves.

Damon whirled and charged at the women and children, who screamed and cowered against the wall.

Damon clawed at the reptile. "Get this thing off me!"

The snake hissed and sunk its fangs into his cheek.

Damon staggered, tripped on the grate and fell to his knees.

Mike looked at Kate and then at the panicked man, who clambered to his feet and lurched toward the cluster of people. "Take it off," he yelled. "Now!"

A tall black woman stepped from the group. "I'll help you. Turn around."

Damon pivoted, his back to her, just as Kate scrambled up the other side of the trench.

The woman raised her high-heeled foot and kicked Damon over the grid and into the light, the very spot where Kate was standing moments earlier.

He shrieked and then shrieked again.

"Yes!" The woman pumped a fist into the air, and the others began to clap and cheer. But Kate was eyeing Damon's buddies.

One of them shouted, "That's enough!" and snapped a whip. The sound shattered the short-lived celebration like a crack of thunder. Women and children cringed against the wall, their terror a silent movie playing to the garbled wails that emanated from the pit.

Mike signaled to Clint.

Clint nodded and hurtled across the floor to tackle the guy with the whip, while Mike bolted for the second man.

Kate squinted, trying to see beyond the light. What was going on? A gun bounced across the cement floor and landed in the pit on top a mound of snakes. Kate leaned over to retrieve the weapon before it disappeared beneath the slimy mass. Almost as soon as she grabbed it, a man fell into the trench.

She jumped back.

He crawled toward her and she realized it was Alfonzo, the one who'd bullied Amy, the one who pretended to shoot a man at the sports show. She trained the gun at his head. "Don't move."

Snakes hissed and struck his body.

"Let me out," he begged. "I won't hurt you."

"Don't believe him, Kate."

She looked up and saw Clint on the other side. Mike couldn't be too far away.

The woman on Kate's side shouted, "Damon's climbing out."

Kate spun around, and in three strides bridged the gap to tromp his knuckles with her boot heel.

He cursed and fell back into the pit.

Clint called, "Behind you, Kate."

She wheeled around in time to see Alfonzo charge at her. She jumped to the side.

He landed on the concrete with a thud and a grunt but was on his knees in an instant.

She kicked him back into the trench, where he flailed and swore amidst the squirming mass.

"Sorry, Kate." Clint waved a gun. "I was afraid I'd hit you or one of the others if I tried to shoot him."

"Where's Mike?"

"Over there."

In the gloom beyond the pit, she saw her husband astride yet another kicking cursing man. "Mike," she shouted. "Throw him in the pit. We've got to get these people out of here, fast."

He yelled, "Clint, grab his legs."

Clint shoved the gun into the back of his jeans and grabbed the man's legs. Together they dragged him to the edge of the trough and flung him over the side. Like the others, he thrashed among the reptiles, howling and pleading for help.

Mike gawked at the trench. "What in the world?"

Clint shook his head. "A real sick mind thought this one up."

Mike motioned Kate. "I'll jump over and help you get out."

A loud male voice bounced between the walls. "No you won't!"

Mike pivoted.

Clint yanked the gun from his Levis.

Kate saw a tall man in an expensive suit stride through the archway, followed by three armed men. Her heart plunged to her stomach. It had to be him. Thomas Mendiola, the Executive kingpin. The man on the elevator who'd visited the gun booth.

They'd come so close to freedom. Amy may have been taken from the snake den, but now she and Mike and Clint and the others were the alpha snake's prey. *Help us, God.*

"Drop the guns!"

Neither Kate nor Clint responded.

Thomas motioned to his men. "If they don't cooperate by the time I count to two, pick off the whores one at a time. First a broad, then a brat. Then another broad, and another brat."

Kate released the gun. It clanked against the cement.

Clint did the same.

Thomas guffawed. "Thought that would get your attention." He pointed at Kate. "You are a smart ass. I'll cure you of that while my men dump your friends' bodies in the river."

Kate's breath caught. *Oh, dear God. Not Mike and Clint.* She'd gotten them into this mess.

The thud of booted feet whooshed into the room. "Police. Drop your weapons!"

Thomas's men swiveled, guns aimed. A deafening explosion roared through the chamber, and all three fell to the floor.

Thomas leaped across the pit, grabbed Kate and shoved a knife under her chin. "Me and my whores walk out of here now, or this one gets her throat slit."

No one spoke. The only sounds were the screams and curses rising from the pit.

Kate clenched her fists, hating the man's touch and his hot breath against her ear. Most of all, she despised his evil aura. She would not go without a fight.

Mike stepped onto a grate. "Release my wife."

Detective Barker appeared at his side. "We'll handle this, Duncan."

Kate's captor brandished his knife. "Push the grid over. Me and my broads are walking outa here."

"Mr. Mendiola," Barker said, "It's over. These people are going home."

"No." Thomas stabbed the air with the knife. "They're mine. This one is mine. Those two over there are mine. They all belong to me. "

His spittle landed in Kate's ear and she flinched.

"You'll never take them from me." His voice grew louder. "I'm their big daddy. I give them everything they need for the good life."

Mike eyed the knife, met Kate's gaze and then focused on the knife again.

She signed "okay" with her fingers.

"I make ugly people beautiful and desirable," Thomas ranted. "I clothe them in the latest fashions, give them expensive jewelry, introduce them to wheelers and dealers. They get to glitter and dance. Without me, they're nothing but stupid little goats grubbing through the garbage pit for another rancid bite of food."

Mike slapped his leg. "That's hilarious, Mendiola. You don't own anybody. In fact, you won't even own the shirt on your back in prison."

Officers rushed to Mike's side. He ignored them.

Thomas jabbed the knife at him. "You're as stupid as your bimbo wife."

Kate grasped his flailing arm and twisted. Following the momentum with her own weight, she wrenched him around her body and into the pit.

He landed on his back on top of Alfonzo, the knife still in his hand. Calling Kate a name she hadn't been called in years, he rolled over and grasped the ledge, his knees churning amidst the snakes.

Mike jumped into the pit.

Kate was about to stomp Thomas's fingers, when Mike grabbed his shoulder, spun him around and slugged his jaw.

Thomas's head snapped back. He swore, stabbed Mike in the shoulder and raised his arm to strike again, but Kate kicked the knife away.

Mike slammed his fist into Thomas's face again and again. The evil man collapsed like an empty sack.

Kate took a long breath and leaned down to rest her hands on her knees. She stared at the boot where the rattlesnake had coiled before it climbed her leg. Thank God the nightmare was over.

Mike yelled, "Kate, watch out!"

She looked up in time to see Thomas fling off a snake and crawl toward her. She reached for the gun she'd dropped.

Shots rang out, and the evil man slumped face down in the writhing, hissing, rattling, stinking mass.

Kate looked from Mendiola to Mike. Her husband's shoulder was bleeding. Detective Barker and Clint stood above him on the other side of the trench, guns fixed on the brothel kingpin. A huge rattler, the biggest she'd ever seen, separated from the mound and slithered onto his back.

Kate followed Detective Barker from his office to the interrogation room.

He opened the door and motioned for her to enter. "I'll ask the guards to bring Miss Iverson down. Have a seat. It'll take a few minutes." He left, closing the door behind him.

Kate couldn't sit. Instead, she paced the small room with the one-way window, tiny table and three metal folding chairs. How many such rooms had she entered handcuffed and dressed in orange? Funny how interrogation rooms all looked the same—and how this room unnerved her as much as the others did.

She clasped her hands, trying to stifle the queasiness that threatened to unsettle her breakfast. How could she help Amy? What could she say to encourage her best friend to talk? Detective Barker said she hadn't spoken a word to anyone since she'd been arrested.

Kate gripped the back of a chair. She didn't know if her presence would help Amy or what she could do to show her support. But she did know how to pray. God would guide her. With a trusted friend and God's presence in the room, maybe Amy would relax and tell her story.

The door opened and Amy entered, followed by the detective. Small and thin, she looked pale without all the makeup she'd worn at the sports show.

Kate smiled. At least they didn't shackle her.

Amy stopped just inside the doorway. "Kate." Her hands went to her throat.

"It's okay, Amy." Kate moved toward her. "The microphone is gone."

"You're alive?" The words were more breathed than spoken.

Kate opened her arms. "Hug me, and you'll know."

After a moment's hesitation, Amy stepped into her embrace.

"Oh, Amy," Kate whispered, pulling her friend close, inhaling the scent of soap and shampoo. "I've waited so long for this moment."

"Me, too." Amy began to shake. "Me, too."

Though she wanted to be brave for her friend, Kate started to cry. "You're going to be okay. I know you are. God brought you out of Executive Pride, and he'll clear the charges against you."

Amy began to weep.

Kate rubbed her back. "I can't help you, Amy, and Detective Barker can't help you, unless you talk. Unless you tell us what went on at Executive Pride."

Amy wiped her eyes and glanced at the detective, who was now seated at the table. "You trust him?" Her voice was barely audible.

"Yes." Kate dabbed at her own eyes. "He helped rescue both of us."

Amy stared at the floor.

"What's wrong?" Kate took her hands.

Amy whispered in her ear. "Thomas said he'll kill you if I tell the cops about EP."

"I should have known you were protecting someone other than yourself." Kate hugged her again. "Thank you. The good news is that Executive Pride is no more. The doors are locked, Thomas is dead, and his henchmen are either dead, jailed or chained to hospital beds."

"Really?" Amy's eyes widened. "How?"

"Snakebites and bullets. You missed all the excitement."

Amy blinked several times, as if she was trying to digest the news that she'd finally escaped her kidnapper's clutches. "Where are the others? Am I the only one who—?"

"The women are all safe and in protective custody," Detective Barker interjected. "The children have been placed in an orphanage until social services can figure out where they came from, how they got here, who their parents and guardians are."

He indicated the two chairs across from him. "Please sit."

Amy hesitated.

Kate took her hand. "I'll be right beside you."

As they were sitting, another officer walked into the room with a folding chair. He shut the door and sat next to Barker.

Kate asked, "Can I show Amy that picture now?"

Barker nodded and winked.

She grinned, glad she'd included him in the fun secret she was about to reveal. She pulled a folded piece of paper from her jacket pocket and handed it to Amy, who opened it.

A sad smile crossed her friend's face. "My sweet puppies. Thank you, Kate. At least I'll have something to remember them by."

"That picture was emailed to me by your neighbor, Kevin."

"He must have taken it last winter. There's snow on the ground."

Kate and the detective exchanged a glance. "Kevin sent the picture yesterday. He's been keeping an eye on your animals since you left."

Amy's mouth dropped open. "Where are they?"

"At your duplex. Mike and I made sure the lease didn't expire."

"Oh, Kate, I can't begin to thank you."

Detective Barker cleared his throat. "Let's get started. I'm Detective Barker. This is Officer Gorman." He placed his forearms on the table and smiled. "Our records show you're from Pittsburgh, Miss Iverson. What brought you to Dallas?"

Amy heaved a long sigh. "Doing exactly what my friend told me not to do."

Kate stood with Mike, Clint and Walt on the roof of Executive Pride's headquarters. A cool breeze tossed her hair and fluttered the flag on the building across from them. She snuggled under Mike's good arm. "It's colder up here than down on the street, but the air smells better."

He hugged her close. "We're fifty-two stories high. A bit of an elevation change."

Clint placed a foot on the ledge. "This is quite the view."

"Yeah." Walt swept his arm across the panorama. "You can see clear across the city." He pointed. "Way over yonder in those hills is where I grew up on the outskirts of town. Saw my share of coyotes when I was a kid, and diamondbacks."

Mike said, "We've all seen our share of diamondbacks lately."

Walt turned to Mike. "How's the shoulder?"

"It's sore but not serious." He shifted his arm in the sling. "The doc who stitched it up said the damage could of been a lot worse."

"Thank God he didn't get bit," Kate said.

"Yeah." Clint snorted. "Those Executive guys are chock full of rattler poison. Poisoned brains and poisoned bodies."

Walt shook his head. "Bizarre bunch of devils."

"Has anyone heard an update on those guys?" Clint asked.

"Detective Barker filled me in when I saw Amy this morning," Kate said. "Damon and Thomas are both dead. A couple others are hanging on by a thread. They arrested several men who were hiding up here on this roof and some who tried to hide in the stairwell. The good news is that they're fairly certain they got them all."

Clint's expression turned serious. "I never wanted to go to war, never desired to kill anyone. But if I had to take someone's life, I couldn't have asked for a more deserving target than that Mendiola guy."

"Uh…" Walt cleared his throat. "Barker says the medics only found one bullet in him."

"Then the cop missed."

Walt shrugged. "They say the bullet was theirs."

"But—"

Mike interrupted. "Maybe they're trying to cover for you, dude. I doubt that gun was registered, and last I knew, you'd let your handgun permit expire."

"Oh, yeah…"

Kate shivered, remembering that as an ex-felon, she wasn't supposed to handle guns. In the heat of the moment last night, that was the last thing on her mind. She could only hope and pray her fingerprints wouldn't be used against her.

Walt motioned to her. "How's that aunt of yours doing?"

"Good." Kate was happy to think about something other than the possibility of returning to prison. "Mike's mom says Aunt Mary will probably go home in a day or two. In the meantime, she tells every person who walks into her hospital room the story of Queen Esther in the Bible."

"Speaking of stories..." Mike looked at Kate. "We heard a doozy this morning."

"Does it have anything to do with bison?" Clint asked.

"How'd you know?"

Clint gave Walt a knowing look. "Mike's bison herd has experienced a rough couple of years."

"We'll get the full rundown later," Mike said. "The short version is that Todd Hughes was at our house yesterday afternoon when Kate's aunt wandered away. He wouldn't help search for her, so my mom kicked him out, which made him mad."

Clint guffawed. "Wish I could have seen that."

"Even though the ranch was socked in by a blizzard, Hughes drove down the mountain to the bison pasture, climbed through the fence, and shot a cow."

Clint groaned. "Not another one."

Kate sighed. "Yes, another one."

"Before she died," Mike said, "she evidently charged Hughes, because they found him underneath her carcass."

Walt grimaced. "Nasty way to go."

"Must have crushed every bone in his body," Clint said.

Mike shook his head. "He didn't die."

"What?" Clint's eyes widened.

Kate helped Mike zip his coat over the sling, and he continued the story. "The cow landed on Hughes's legs. Her body heat kept him warm enough he didn't freeze to death."

"Cyrus saw Todd drive onto the road that leads down to the pasture," Kate added. "Otherwise, no one would have known he was there, and he would have frozen for sure. Later, after all the hubbub about my aunt died down, Cyrus remembered Todd and told the deputies who'd helped with Aunt Mary that he might be missing."

A strand of hair blew across her face and she tucked it behind her ear. "They snowmobiled into his yard, but he wasn't home. So a search-and-rescue helicopter was sent out early this morning. They spotted Todd's pickup parked on the road and eventually found him under the cow, half frozen yet still alive. I guess it was quite a process to winch the bison off his legs. Somehow they managed to get him out from under the cow and airlift him to a Denver hospital."

Walt adjusted his ball cap. "That's the most bizarre thing I ever heard."

Clint pounded a fist into his palm. "Proves your theory, Mike. Hughes is the one who's been killing your bison."

Mike shrugged. "Maybe. If nothing else, I have a feeling the Sheriff's Department will rethink past events, including our bull being gunned down a few days ago. Plus, the Thompsons may have enough evidence gathered by now to interest authorities in Hughes's quick acquisition of the Gruber and Williams ranches. Someone told my mom they heard that Arnie Williams's and Leonard Gruber's grandfathers made land deals with Rodney Hughes that weren't on the up-and-up. That knowledge may have given Todd Hughes some leverage with them. Who knows."

The elevator door opened, and Janessa and her friend stepped out, followed by one of the policemen assigned to guard the Executive Pride quarters. The women, who wore jeans, jackets and high-heeled boots, glanced warily around the rooftop, dazed expressions on their faces.

Kate met them in the middle of the helicopter landing pad. She understood their confusion. They'd need time to sort through their ordeal. She prayed God would give them each a mentor like she had in Dymple Forbes to walk with them on their journey to wholeness.

She smiled. "I'm so glad you two could come. I wanted to say goodbye and give you an opportunity to stand on the Executive Pride roof as free women."

Janessa hugged Kate. "Thank you for risking your life for us."

"My privilege. God and those guys..." She indicated Mike, Clint and Walt. "They all had my back."

The other woman took Kate's hand. "We didn't get to officially meet. I'm Mikaylah. Thank you for what you did. That was really brave of you."

Kate hugged her. "You were the brave one. You knew how dangerous it was for you to help me."

The women turned to Mike and Clint. "Thank you for all you did," Janessa said. "I'll never forget either of you."

Clint introduced the two to Walt and told them how he'd helped with the rescue.

Walt, who with Mike and Clint had been warned by Kate that the women might not want to have physical contact with them, dipped his head. "Pleased to meet you, Miz Janessa, Miz Mikaylah."

Janessa asked Kate, "Do you know what happened to Natasha? Is she okay?"

"I am fabulous!" Dressed in an orange jailhouse jumpsuit labeled *Dallas County*, Amy posed in front of the elevator, arms raised and a big smile splashed across her face. A second policeman stood behind her.

"Natasha!" The women ran to her.

Mike nudged Kate. "Natasha?"

"That was her name in the brothel."

"Oh, yeah. I remember the EP guys calling her that when they were taking her to the cops. So the other names are fake, too?"

"Probably."

Clint whispered, "How'd you pull off this get-together?"

Kate grinned. "Take a bow, Mr. Private Investigator."

Walt tipped his ball cap.

"Walt and I convinced Detective Barker that standing on this rooftop would convince these women they're free from Executive's power and help them share details about the brothel, something that's often hard for trafficked victims to do." She nudged Clint, who was watching the three women. "Now you can see Amy before we go."

His ears turned red but he kept his eyes on Amy, who shouted, "We're free, we're free!" She grabbed Mikaylah's and Janessa's hands. "Come on, everyone, let's dance."

The men refused the offer, but Kate joined the celebration. Round and round the women danced, their hair flying. Tears ran down their faces as they chanted, "Freedom, freedom, freedom!"

Despite the tears, Kate couldn't stop smiling. She hadn't been this happy since her wedding day. As Dymple would say, God outdid himself again.

Janessa stopped and leaned against a pipe. "Sorry. I'm getting dizzy."

Amy twirled again. "So many times I wished I could sneak up here, climb in the helicopter and fly away. And now, here I am. I'm so happy I feel like I could sprout my own wings and sail over these skyscrapers."

Kate, who'd returned to Mike's side, whispered in his ear. "It's so good to see Amy happy again, even if for just a moment of celebration. She was so sad and scared this morning."

He pulled her to him. "And I'm happy to have you in my arms again."

She laughed. "One arm, anyway." Then she kissed his cheek. "This is my happy place, beside you."

Janessa sat on the roof ledge and put her head in her hands.

Mikaylah hurried over to her friend. "I don't want you to fall off the edge." She guided Janessa to a wide vent. "This is a safer place to sit."

Kate knelt beside the pale woman. "You okay?"

"Pregnancy is for the birds." Janessa held her stomach. "I can't keep anything down."

Kate studied her face. So that's why she'd looked so pale all weekend. Thank God she was out of the brothel. "I was wondering what your plans are, now that you're free. Sounds like motherhood is next on your list."

The young woman scowled. "Motherhood was never a part of my plan, or Thomas's plan. When I told him I thought I might be pregnant, he scheduled an abortion for next week. Now, I don't know what to do."

"I can't tell you what to do." Kate took her hands. "However, I can tell you I've been there done that. Every day of my life, I regret aborting my baby. Please wait before you do anything drastic. You've been through a lot. Give yourself time to adjust."

Janessa shrugged. "My mom and stepdad are picking me up tomorrow. I'll wait 'til I get home to decide."

Mike came over to stand next to Kate.

She stood. "If you decide to give your baby up for adoption, Janessa, please keep us in mind."

Mike took Kate's hand. "Do what's best for you and your baby, Janessa. We'll never pressure you in any way."

Janessa hesitated. Finally, she nodded. "Okay, I'll think about it."

"Where are you from?" Amy asked. "I don't know anything about either one of you, except that Mikaylah likes gum." She winked at her dark-haired friend.

"I'm from Kansas," Janessa said. "A Kansas farm, to be exact. When my mom remarried, she leased the land to a farmer and the house to a retired couple and moved in with my stepdad." She brightened. "She said she'll ask the renters to vacate the farmhouse, so I can start a bed-and-breakfast there, like I've always wanted to do."

Amy grinned. "That's a great idea. You'll be good at it."

"Yeah, I cook a mean breakfast, nothing like what we ate down there." She pointed at the roof.

"Real food." Amy clapped her hands. "Let me know when you're open for business."

Clint motioned to Amy. "What are your plans? I mean, after..."

"After I get out of prison?"

"Yeah."

Mikaylah's eyes widened. "Prison?"

"Possibly for murder."

Mikaylah and Janessa gasped in unison.

"If all goes well, that won't happen." Amy pushed windblown hair from her face. "Thomas set me up for murder charges, but now that the police know about EP, my lawyer says those charges should be dropped soon. However, I violated parole by coming here, so I'll do time for that. Stupidest thing I ever did." Her shoulders drooped and she looked down.

"What's done is done," Clint said. "You'll move on from here."

"You're right." She smiled at him. "I need to think about the future, not get stuck in the past." She looked at Kate. "When I called Elaina to tell her where I've been, she said she's now planning to go to college in Colorado instead of Pennsylvania. She got a scholarship. Maybe I'll move out west to be near her."

"That's perfect, Amy." Kate grabbed her hands. "You can live at the ranch and be close to Elaina and to us."

Clint grinned. "I'd like that."

Amy returned his smile. "So would I."

Mike motioned to the others. "You're all welcome to visit our guest ranch, free of charge. That offer includes you, Walt. We couldn't have pulled this off without you."

"Thank you," Janessa said. "I'd love to see your place." She touched Mikaylah's arm. "What are your plans?"

One of the officers called, "Five minutes."

"Okay." Mike waved at him. "Thanks."

Mikaylah stuffed her hands in her jacket pockets. "I don't know what I'll do. My husband in Chicago doesn't want me back, that's for sure."

Amy raised her eyebrows. "I didn't know you were married."

"I was 'til I walked out on him. He's probably filed for divorce by now."

"Do you have children?"

She scuffed the toe of her high-heeled boot against the roof. "Two. One of them is a brat and the other is severely handicapped. I was worn out from taking care of him without any help from my husband and trying to deal with the other one. And then I met Thomas online..."

"You met him online?" Amy's eyes were wide. "You mean you knew him before you came here?"

"Yeah. He's very charming when he wants to be."

Janessa rolled her eyes. "We know all about that."

"When he promised me a job where I'd never have to cook or clean or take care of kids, I jumped at it. A wistful expression crossed her face. "Thomas said he loved me and wanted me to be with him in Dallas."

Amy snorted. "We know all about his idea of love, too."

Kate reached for Mikaylah's hand. "What now?"

"Maybe I'll take to the streets. At least now I know what I'm good at."

"What?" Amy squinted at her.

Kate tilted her head. "You want to be a streetwalker?"

Mikaylah shrugged.

"You heard me tell Janessa I've been there done that with an abortion," Kate said. "I can say the same about streetwalking. It's dangerous, it's demeaning, it's soul-deadening, it's—"

Mikaylah dismissed the subject with a wave of her hand. "I hear you."

Kate paused. "I'll pray for you to find a new career." So much she wanted to say, but Mikaylah wasn't ready.

"You could go to beauty school," Amy said. "You do amazing things with your hair."

Mikaylah's well-defined eyebrows arched. "I kind of like that idea."

Kate reached into her jacket pocket and pulled out her Wyoming business cards. "I'll be praying for all of you. Transitioning back to real life won't be easy." She gave both Mikaylah and Janessa a card. "Call anytime. I'm not a counselor, but I've experienced a fair amount of trauma. And, like Mike said, we'd love to have you visit us."

The policeman's hands were on his hips. "One minute."

Amy grabbed Kate's arm and pulled her to the ledge. "See that flag?"

"I noticed it when we first came up here."

"I used to stare out my window at rooftops for hours. I can't tell you how many times I watched that flag flap and wondered if I'd ever feel the wind on my face again. It's hard to comprehend that here I am, a free woman." She raised her arms. "I might be wearing orange, yet I'm free, thanks to an amazing God and courageous friends."

"The star-spangled banner still waves for you, my friend." Kate hugged Amy. "I'm so glad you're back in the land of the free and the home of the brave."

The day of the hayride dawned cold and crisp, but that didn't keep the Duncans' guests away. With Laura's help, Kate wrapped Mary and Dymple in buffalo robes, while Mike and Clint assisted the others as they climbed onto the flatbed truck. The men had stacked hay bales three high around the perimeter of the truck bed to provide protection from the wind yet allow the passengers to see the scenery. Within that barrier, they'd placed bales for seating.

Casey Raeburn clambered to the top of the highest bales. "I can't wait to see the bison. Maybe they'll snort and paw the ground and charge at us."

"I certainly hope not." Joyce Raeburn took a quilt from the stack Laura provided and sat next to her husband. "Get down from there, Casey, and sit with your sister."

He huffed. "Do I have to?"

Martin lowered his eyebrows. "Now."

The boy hopped down but refused the corner of the blanket Cindy offered. "Maybe Indians will stampede the buffalo. That would be so cool."

Cindy rolled her eyes. "You watch too many old westerns."

"I do not."

"Everyone ready to go?" Mike tossed one last bale onto the truck and climbed aboard.

Clint followed and sat beside Amy, who'd snuggled into a corner.

After a chorus of yeses, Mike motioned to the driver, one of the WP ranch hands, and the truck began its slow descent down the two-track road, tires crunching on the crisp snow.

"Go? Are we going somewhere?" Mary asked. "I love road trips."

Kate smiled at her sweet aunt, who was so thoroughly bundled only her eyes were visible. They'd tried to convince her and Dymple to ride in the warm cab as they rolled down the mountain to the bison pasture. However, both women insisted on riding with the others. "We're traveling through a winter wonderland, Aunt Mary."

Early morning frost had crusted every fencepost, wire, twig and leaf with brilliant white crystals. As the truck bumped out of a fog cloud and into sunshine, the world around them glistened as far as she could see. Beyond the white hills, snow-capped mountain peaks gleamed against a dazzling blue sky.

"Ah, sunshine," Laura said.

They drove between frosted trees and whipped-cream meadows. Mary peered over the bales. "Oh, my. What a wonderful sight."

Amy turned around to lean with her forearms on an upper bale. "This is incredible. I didn't know snow could be so beautiful."

Kate squeezed Mike's gloved hand under the quilt, and he squeezed back. Amy had always been full of vim and vigor, as Cyrus would say. Today, her joy seemed to bubble over. Kate thought her own heart might burst with happiness.

"Every day is a gift from God," Dymple said, "but it appears he decided to add snarls to our celebration today."

The others squinted at Dymple, confused expressions on their faces. Kate was about to change the subject, when Casey said, "I don't get what snarls have to do with anything."

Dymple made an exasperated sound. "Is that what I said?"

"Uh, yeah."

"I meant to say something else." She paused, her lips pressed in a determined line. "Sparkle. That's what I wanted to say. God gave us sparkle today."

Amy clapped, the sound muffled by her gloves. "Sparkle. I like that, Dymple. I'm going to remember this sparkling day the rest of my life." She settled next to Clint again.

Kate smiled. How could she even begin to express her gratitude to God and to her friends for all they'd done? "Every day I thank God that both Aunt Mary and Amy are safe and sound. Thanks to him and each of you, they're with us on this hayride."

Amy's eyes brimmed with tears. "I've said it before, and I want to say it again." She held out her hands. "Thank you for praying for me and risking your lives for me and Aunt Mary. I claim her as my aunt, too, and would have been heartbroken if..." Her voice trailed off.

Clint put his arm around her.

Everyone but Mary grew somber. She was looking upward, apparently enjoying the ice crystals that floated and glittered around them.

Cyrus cleared his throat. "Some people call that diamond dust."

"I like that name," Cindy said.

Casey bounced on the bale. "Me, too."

Martin leaned toward Amy. "The Duncans told us about your situation, Amy. Do you mind if I ask a couple questions?"

"Go ahead. My life is an open book, unless you're a member of the media."

Everyone laughed, puffing out clouds of moisture that frosted their hats and hair and eyelashes.

"I don't understand how you can be wanted for crimes in Texas and Pennsylvania, yet be with us in Wyoming. Either you have a top-notch lawyer, or..."

"Or I'm a fugitive from the law?"

He shrugged. "Something like that."

"You're right. I have a terrific lawyer. Actually, two lawyers, thanks to Kate and Mike. One in Dallas and one in Pittsburgh. Even better, I have an amazing God who answers prayer."

She paused. "It took me a while to learn to trust God, yet the way things worked out is truly a miracle, starting with these guys getting me out of EP. And then my Texas lawyer got the DA to drop the murder charges."

Her eyes flashed. "Evidently, I wasn't the first person Thomas set up as a murderess. Who knows how many women are wanted for crimes they didn't commit."

But then she brightened. "As far as Texas is concerned, I'm no longer a criminal. Although my activities in Dallas were illegal, what I did there was against my will. So they let me out of jail—after I told them everything I could about EP and promised to testify in court, if needed."

Joyce cocked her head. "I'm surprised the Pennsylvania authorities didn't try to have you extradited."

"Oh, they know all about me," Amy said, "and they'll probably put me back in prison for violating parole. But they haven't yet asked for my return. My lawyer says I can wait until I have a court date. She figures it'll take a couple weeks."

Amy lifted her hands to the sky. "In the meantime, I get to enjoy this beautiful day with you-all."

Clint frowned. "I'm sorry you have to go back to prison."

Kate held up a hand. "I don't mean to contradict you, Clint, but I hope the state returns you to Patterson, Amy."

Mike seemed as surprised as the others by her statement.

"Prison helped me with my warped thinking." She looked directly at Amy. "Take advantage of the recovery classes and counselors Patterson offers as well as Bible studies and church services. Meet with the chaplain. Take correspondence courses or online courses. That's how I earned my degree. Get all the help you can get. I needed guidance to sort through my confusion in prison, and I have a feeling you do too."

Amy nodded, obviously sobered.

"Hey, there's a fox!" Cindy pointed at a hillside, where a bushy-tailed fox hopped through the snow chasing a jackrabbit. She balled her gloved fists. "I hope it doesn't catch the rabbit."

The fox has to eat," Martin said. "That's how it works out here in the wild. The big critters eat the little ones."

Cindy folded her arms. "Doesn't seem fair."

Laura, who hadn't said much, spoke up. "You're right, honey. Life isn't fair. However, life can be good, if we do things God's way instead of making up our own rules."

Beneath the quilt, Mike squeezed Kate's hand. She squeezed back. They were all learning, together.

When the truck crunched to a stop at the bison pasture, Casey jumped off, rolled in the snow and hopped to his feet. Kate laughed, but his parents sighed and shook their heads.

"He's all boy," Laura said. "Sometimes I miss those days of my two boys jumping, climbing, throwing rocks, and falling out of trees and off horses and roofs."

The men pulled bales from the truck bed and deposited them on the ground for seating before helping the others down. The guests joined Casey, who was already at the fence ogling the hump-shouldered bovines. "Be careful," Mike called. "That top wire is electric."

Kate and Laura rewrapped Mary in the buffalo robe and sat her on a bale facing the bison herd. Several of the huge animals were grazing near the fence, their shaggy brown coats dusted white with snow and their huge nostrils billowing clouds of moisture. "Oh, my," Mary said. "Such grand ghosts."

Laura chuckled. "You're right, Mary. They are a bit ghostly."

Her comment reminded Kate of the Indian legend about a maiden who turned into a white buffalo calf. The glint in the air and the silvery wonderland that surrounded them felt almost as mystical as that myth. But these were real animals, Mike's pride and joy, and she couldn't ask for a more real day.

Casey pointed to a bull that stuck his nose in a snowbank and was sweeping his massive head back and forth and then pawing the ground. "What's that buffalo doing?"

"He's using his head like a snowplow to clear away snow," Mike said. "That's how he gets at the grass below."

"Wow, that's cool."

"Bison are tough. Unlike cattle, they face into storms instead of away from the wind."

"That must be why their faces are all crusted with snow," Cindy said. "They look like they're wearing masks." The only dark spots in the behemoths' white heads were their brown horns, black eyes and black nostrils. Icicles dangled from their scraggly beards.

Laura called, "Who wants hot chocolate?"

Casey whipped around, shouting, "I do!" and fell on his face in the snow.

Laughing, his father helped the sputtering boy get back on his feet.

"We also have coffee and tea," Kate said. "And raisin scones."

Amy sidled up to Kate. Her cheeks were pink and her eyelashes frosted, like everyone else's. "I take it Aunt Mary hasn't stopped eating Raisin Bran."

"Dymple gave me a great recipe. Try one."

"The pie was good, so I guess I'll take my chances on the scones. Want one, Clint?"

Clint, who hovered at Amy's elbow, grinned. "Sure. I'll get us drinks. Want coffee or hot chocolate?"

Kate smiled. Clint and Amy were already taking care of each other.

"Everyone have a seat, please," Laura said, "and I'll bring your drinks to you."

The visitors sat on the bales facing the bison. A bull elk and two cows stepped out of the trees on the hill beyond the pasture.

"I feel like I have a front row seat to the wilderness," Joyce said with a shiver. "However, I must say this theater is a bit chilly." She raised her cup. "Thanks for the hot chocolate, Laura."

Casey asked, "You gonna shoot 'em with your new gun, Mike?"

Shortly after they returned from Dallas, Kate had surprised Mike with an elk rifle from Bart's Guns, and he'd brought it along on the hayride. "No," Mike said. "Hunting season is closed, and our freezer is full. Today, we just enjoy the elk. They're beautiful creatures, aren't they?"

Casey gave Mike a funny look. "I think they're kinda ugly, but not as ugly as your buffalo."

The others laughed.

Mike squeezed Casey's shoulder. "I like an honest man."

Kate helped her aunt drink some tea and then gave her a bite of scone. "Sorry we wrapped your arms inside the robe, Aunt Mary."

"That's okay. I'm nice and toasty."

Dymple, who shared a bale with Amy and Clint, asked, "Amy, have you thought about what you'll do when you're free again?"

"I'm not sure. Depends on where I end up after I get out of prison."

Clint put his arm around her. "I'm going to get you a bumper sticker that says *Wyoming or bust.*"

Cyrus chuckled. "That oughta do the trick."

Kate glanced from Mike to Laura. The three of them had talked at length about opening a home for the handful of Executive Pride children who couldn't be returned to their families, for one reason or another. In time, they hoped to take in other young trafficking victims.

After they conquered government paperwork, licensing and training, hired counselors and secured start-up funding, they planned to invite Amy to join the staff as a mentor and as a fund-raiser, provided she was willing to undergo extensive counseling and training. Kate turned back to Mary. As excited as she was about the project, now wasn't the time to mention their dream or offer Amy a job.

Mike walked over to the truck and returned with a cardboard box in his arms.

Casey jumped up. "What's in the box?"

Mike pulled out a paperback book. "Each of our guests today receives a copy of *The Thundering Herd* by Zane Grey."

Kate grinned. Only her husband would think his friends wanted to read about bison.

Casey stared at the cover. "Wow, millions of buffalo."

"I gotta warn you, dude, there's some kissing in there."

Casey screwed up his face. "Yuck."

"Mostly, it's about bison." Mike rubbed Casey's head. "You'll like it."

He handed Cindy a book. "There's a place in here that says the bison's big shaggy heads are what enable them to face danger, whether it's blizzards, sandstorms or wolves. No matter the enemy, they meet it head-on." He winked at Kate.

She smiled. They'd faced the enemy side-by-side, and that's how they would continue through life. She hoped they never stopped having adventures together and that her heart would never stop flip-flopping when he winked at her.

Martin took a copy. "Sounds like we can all learn a few things from those prehistoric-looking beasts."

When Mike came to Mary, he said, "You're wrapped up tighter than a burrito, Aunt Mary. I'll give your book to Kate."

Mary's green eyes twinkled. "Does it have a happy ending?"

He thought for a moment. "We know from history that the bison story didn't end well. But the main character? That's a different deal."

"Queen Esther's story ended happily."

Kate hugged her aunt. "Yes, after all kinds of twists and turns."

"Just like you." Mary reached from inside the buffalo robe to touch Kate's cheek. "You've experienced a rollercoaster of ups and downs, Katy Joy, yet your story has a happy ending."

Kate took her aunt's mitten-wrapped hand. "This chapter of my life—all our lives—had a wonderful finale, Aunt Mary. I can't wait to see what God has planned for us in the next chapter."

"Really?" Amy leaned past Clint to look at Kate. "You think God knows what's going to happen in the future? I mean, the Bible predicts the end of the world and all that. But to say God can fig-ure out what will happen to individual people seems unrealistic. There's gazillions of us."

"Dymple," Kate said, "tell her about the scripture your sister cross-stitched for me."

The older woman nodded. "There's a verse in Psalms that says God charts the path ahead of us."

Amy's eyebrows crumpled. "Surely God didn't plan for me to go to Dallas and meet Thomas...and..." Her voice faltered.

Dymple set her cup on the bale and wrapped her arms around Amy. "Sometimes we wander off the trail, sweetie."

Kate thought of her own years of drifting off-trail and how her parents' pastor had prayed she would return to God each time she strayed.

"But Jesus doesn't give up on us or leave us to flounder by ourselves." Dymple tilted her head back. Her breath formed a frost cloud above her.

Following her lead, the others gazed into the diamond-dusted sky.

She lifted her arm high. "He's always reaching out, waiting to rescue us from our messes. All we have to do is grab hold of his hand."

ACKNOWLEDGEMENTS

So many people graciously helped me find my way to "The End" of *Winds of Freedom*. From critique partners Lisa Hess, Valerie Gray and Peter Leavell, to beta readers Steve Lyles, Patricia Watkins and Alissa Lyles, to proofreaders Lisa Phillips, Jim Ketterling, Heather Humrichouse, Brady Lyles and Hilarey Johnson, to the members of Idahope Writers headquartered in Idaho's Treasure Valley, to Chris White, editor extraordinaire, writing instructor and author Dr. Laurie Bower, and Maryanna Young, Aloha Publishing CEO and tireless cheerleader for Idaho writers—all have provided incredible support and guidance.

I also received input from experts "in the field"—in this case, the great outdoors. Dr. Charles R. Peterson, zoology professor at Idaho State University in the Department of Biological Sciences, graciously shared his expertise, as did Jerry Cates, a Texas writer and editor for *Bugs in the News,* an extensive website featuring informative articles about insects, spiders, reptiles, and mammals in North America (bugsinthenews.com).

Even more fun than research (smile) was hearing from fans of *Winds of Wyoming* who not only enjoyed the first book in the Kate Neilson series but who also said they were anxious to read the sequel. Many thanks to each of you. Your encouragement and enthusiasm gave me the "umph" to stick with the project through endless edits and rewrites. You're the best!

Organizations that highlight the horror of human trafficking and efforts to rescue its victims include but are not limited to: Idaho Coalition for Justice, (http://www.icjustice.org); Destiny Rescue (http://www.destinyrescue.org/us); Wipe Every Tear (http://www.wipeeverytear.org); The Justice Conference (http://thejusticeconference.com); A Heart for Justice (http://aheartfor-justice.com); Shared Hope (http://sharedhope.org); International Justice Mission (http://www.ijm.org); Abolition International (http://abolitioninternational.org); and The Salvation Army's Initiative Against Sexual Trafficking (http://www.iast.net).

Thank God for the tenderhearted individuals who fight for those trapped in modern-day slavery. May He richly bless their efforts and grant freedom and wholeness to imprisoned souls in this country and around the world.

ABOUT THE AUTHOR

Rebecca Carey Lyles grew up in Wyoming, the setting for her Kate Neilson novels. She and her husband, Steve, currently live in Idaho (not to be confused with Iowa!), the beautiful state that borders Wyoming on the west. In addition to writing fiction and nonfiction, she serves as an editor and a mentor to aspiring authors and as a transition coach for women transitioning from prison to "the outside." *Winds of Freedom* is the sequel to the award-winning first book in the Kate Neilson series, *Winds of Wyoming.*

Contact: beckylyles@beckylyles.com
Facebook author page: Rebecca Carey Lyles
Twitter: @BeckyLyles
LinkedIn: Becky Lyles
Blog: widgetwords.wordpress.com

Visit the author's website to read a free eStory:
http://www.beckylyles.com

OTHER BOOKS BY THE AUTHOR

FICTION
Winds of Wyoming
A Kate Neilson Novel

Fresh out of a Pennsylvania penitentiary armed with a marketing degree, Kate Neilson heads to Wyoming anticipating an anonymous new beginning as a guest-ranch employee. A typical twenty-five-year-old woman might be looking to lasso a cowboy, but her only desire is to get on with life on the outside—despite her growing interest in the ranch owner. When she discovers a violent ex-lover followed her west, she fears the past she hoped to hide will trail as close as a shadow and imprison her once again.

NONFICTION
It's a God Thing!
Inspiring Stories of Life-Changing Friendships

When it seemed the best years of his life were over, Larry Baker gained a new passion for living through unexpected, life-changing friendships and adventures. He invites you to join him in the daily exhilaration of discovering the surprises and relationships God has waiting for each of us, just around the corner.

On a Wing and a Prayer
Stories from Freedom Fellowship, a Prison Ministry

The night God told Donna Roth he was sending her to jail to share his love with incarcerated individuals, she said, "Lord, you have the wrong house!" She had no experience or interest in prison ministry; yet, she was obedient, and Freedom Fellowship was formed. "On a Wing and a Prayer" features stories of inmates who found freedom inside prison walls through the ministry of Freedom Fellowship.

EXCERPT FROM

WINDS OF WYOMING

THE FIRST BOOK IN THE

KATE NEILSON SERIES

Chapter One

Kate Neilson peered into the slot on the collection box lid. Was that money she saw on the bottom or crumpled paper? Sometimes people put weird stuff in offering boxes.

The early morning sunshine hadn't reached her side of the dark log chapel, but she didn't dare turn on the interior lights and attract attention. Maybe she should grab the flashlight from her car. Though she'd opened the side door at the front of the sanctuary, she still couldn't see inside the box.

She toyed with the padlock. All she needed was enough cash to get by until payday at her new job. If she left a note saying she'd pay it back right away, with interest, surely they'd understand. After all, she was down to her last ten—

The floor creaked.

Her heart stopped.

"That box is empty, sweetie."

Stifling a gasp, Kate dropped the lock and spun around. A white-haired woman stood in the open doorway at the far end of the chapel.

"We haven't used it ..." The woman's voice cracked. "Since two-thousand and three."

Kate darted for the foyer, her pulse pounding at her temple. No way were they going to catch her this time. She slammed against the front door. One twist of the handle and—

"Please don't leave."

Drawn by the plaintive plea, she glanced back.

"Didn't mean to scare you." The lady lifted the canvas bag she was carrying. "I came to arrange the flowers for this morning's service."

Kate hesitated, her heart drumming her ribs, her breath locked in her lungs.

The woman extended her palms. "Stay and visit. Please."

"I thought—" Kate released the breath and sucked in a gulp of dry mountain air. "I thought, because it's a church, it was okay to come inside. The door was unlocked. I ..."

The lady's red-tinted lips parted in a wide, denture smile. "That's why we call this the Highway Haven House of God. We want travelers who've been enjoying the drive through the mountains to feel free to spend time with the creator of those hills." She hobbled toward the altar table at the front of the room. The wood floor squeaked with each step.

Kate clutched her chest to slow the hammering inside. What happened to the nerves of steel she'd honed on the streets of Pittsburgh? She took a breath. "I've never heard of a church called Highway Haven before."

The woman slid a vase from the center of the altar to the side. "Our little cathedral is a one-of-a-kind place, at least in Wyoming. Old-timers say this used to be the site of the rowdiest saloon this side of the Missouri, until ..." She chuckled. "Until, as the story goes, a couple inebriated, arm-wrestling patrons knocked over a kerosene lamp, and the bar burped to the ground."

Burped? Kate squinted at her. How could someone with so many wrinkles, someone who said *burped* instead of *burned* call other people old-timers? Oh, well. At least she was harmless. Moving from the foyer into the sanctuary, Kate dropped into a pew at the back of the room.

The lady reached in her bag.

She's got a gun. Kate grabbed the bench in front of her, ready to dive beneath it.

But the smiling woman produced a tulip instead of a pistol. "My name is Miss Forbes. What's yours?" She pulled more tulips from her satchel.

Kate gripped the pew back. Wouldn't the cops love that? Her fingerprints *and* her name, even though she hadn't done anything wrong, this time.

After the tulips came lilac blossoms and a glass jar of water. Miss Forbes unscrewed the metal lid, poured the liquid into the vase, and added the flowers. She glanced at Kate, eyebrows raised.

Kate folded her arms and sat back.

"That's okay. I shouldn't be so nosy." Miss Forbes plucked a tulip from the arrangement. "For a long time, this was just an ugly pile of blackened rubble. But in the early fifties, a small congregation purchased the land and built this chapel in two days." She indicated the walls, the flower in her fingers bobbing back and forth. "Raised the log walls the first day, added the roof the second."

She slipped the tulip into the center of the blossoms. "They called it Church on the Mountain."

Kate rubbed her stiff shoulder muscles and stared through the large window that dominated the front of the chapel. The opening framed a postcard-perfect scene of evergreens and newly leafed aspen in the foreground with snow-crowned peaks in the background—a far cry from the cement prison yard she'd circled twice a day for five long years.

If only she could immerse herself in her beautiful surroundings. But her mind wouldn't let go of the fact she hadn't heard the woman approach the building. She should have heard her footsteps outside the door, despite her slight stature.

She chewed at her bottom lip. A senile senior citizen had not only caught her off-guard but scared her half to death. Had she been seduced by the serenity of the place or too focused on the collection box?

Kate checked the windows again. No one else around. Standing, she stepped into the aisle and started for the front, determined to persuade the old lady to tell her where the church kept its stash. If she resisted, she'd explain her plan to repay the money. If that didn't work, she'd have to do a little arm twisting.

Her approach was no secret. The floor groaned with each footstep, but Miss Forbes continued to talk, her back to Kate. "Years later, after the state constructed a highway right next to the parking lot, the congregation decided it was time for a name change."

Six feet from the altar, Kate halted, knees flexed, feet planted wide.

The woman turned from the flowers, her hands on her waist. "Haven has a *peaceful* sound to it, don't you think?" Her blue eyes flashed. "Similar to *heaven*."

Kate flinched. *She knows. She knows what I was about to do.* She clenched her fists. *What's wrong with me? Why would I even consider harming an elderly person? Or helping myself to church money?* She wanted to run, but it was as though the woman's stare pinned her sandals to the floor.

Her shoulders sagged. Would she ever get it right? She could have stayed on her knees asking God to bless her new endeavor. That was the plan—to pray. She could have ignored the offering box. That would have been smart. She could have walked out the church door with God's favor and no regrets. That would have—

"Are you okay?"

At the sight of the woman's creased brow, Kate blinked and shifted her gaze. "I meant to stop at the overlook, but this little church seemed so inviting I stopped here first." The pungent perfume of the lilacs invaded her sinuses, making it hard to breathe.

Miss Forbes returned the vase to the center of the table, made some adjustments and smoothed the altar cloth. "The overlook is a half-mile down the road, well worth the stop. We also have a nice view from the rear of the church property. I can take you there, if you'd like. We have time before the church service begins."

Kate sneezed and rubbed her nose. "I would love to see it." She had to get out of the building before her sinuses swelled shut—and before she did something she'd regret the rest of her life, something that would put her back behind bars.

She followed Miss Forbes, who was shorter than she was by several inches, out the side door of the log structure and onto a dirt path that led into a shaded cemetery. Though the pink blossoms swinging at the end of her guide's long, white braid made her smile, all Kate could think about was how close she'd come to doing something really stupid again. Might as well bang on Patterson State Penitentiary's gate and beg the guards to let her back inside.

She'd left her past in Pittsburgh, but thieving was apparently as natural as breathing for her—no matter where she was or how fervently she promised God she would change her ways. No wonder cell doors were revolving doors for her. She shuddered. With the three-strikes-you're-out law, another mess-up would mean life without parole.

Shaking away the unbearable thought, she focused on the hillside cemetery speckled with headstones of every shape, tilt and shade of gray—and an occasional clump of snow. For the first time since they'd left the chapel, she heard the birds warble in the treetops and smelled the earthy, fresh fragrances of the forest— cleansing scents that soothed her spirit and cleared her head.

Miss Forbes paused to pluck a withered knot from a cluster of jonquils. Her braid slid forward to dangle above the flowers. "We had quite the storm a few days ago, full of moisture, which is fairly typical of spring snows around here. I didn't need to water the grass this morning, but I washed the grave markers." She straightened, her joints snapping. "Some think I'm silly, but my grandpa always said a society that honors the dead will honor the living."

She kicked a pinecone off the grass that topped a grave. "He was a deacon in this church for more than fifty yogurts." She pointed to tombstones several feet away. "His and Granny's stones are those two matching ones. My parents are buried next to them."

"*How long* was your grandpa a deacon?"

"For fifty …" Eyebrows scrunched, the woman turned to Kate. "Did I say something wrong?"

"I just didn't understand."

"It's not you, sweetie. It's me." The woman sighed. "My friends tell me I've been saying the craziest things ever since I tripped and hit my noggin on a headstone a couple years ago. They find it highly amusing. I'll be talking along fine then something silly pops out. The doctor says it's a form of ambrosia."

"You mean amnesia?"

The older lady pursed her wrinkled lips. "I don't know what I said, but my problem is called *aphasia*. I was told I might get over it—or I might not. The good news is that it's a language problem, not an intelligence issue, thank God." She snorted. "Although some might question that."

Kate knelt beside the markers. "You must have meant to say your grandpa was a deacon for fifty years."

"What did I say?"

"Uhm … Yogurts."

"Oh, my. No wonder my friends laugh."

"They shouldn't." Kate shook her head. "They must know what you're really thinking." She'd endured her share of ridicule in school and foster homes, not to mention prison.

Miss Forbes patted her shoulder. "Thank you, but they're just teasing. Sometimes I tease them, too."

Kate studied the gravestones. Damp granite glistened around the hand-etched engravings. *Otis Elmer Haggerty 1883-1966. Dymple Elizabeth Haggerty 1885-1973.* "Your grandparents were named Otis and Dymple?"

The lines at the woman's temples crinkled. "Yes, Granddad Otis and Granny Dymple."

"I never heard of anyone named Dymple before."

"Me neither, except for me."

"No kidding?"

"No kidding. I was born with a dimple in the middle of my chin, just like Granny. See?" She touched her chin.

Kate nodded, though she wasn't sure it was a dimple she saw or a crease. A single white hair jutted from a mole, brilliant in the morning sunlight.

"My parents used to say they argued about what to name me until the moment I was born. That's when they saw the dimple. I was named after both grandmothers. Dymple–with a *y*–Louise Forbes. You can call me Dymple."

Kate stood and offered her hand. "I'm Kate. Kate Neilson."

Dymple grasped her hand with both of hers, a look of recognition, maybe revelation flooding her face.

A chill shot up Kate's spine. She shouldn't have revealed her full name.

"Kate Neilson ..." Dymple smiled. "I have a feeling you and I will become very good friends."

The trail wound through the cemetery and ended on a rock outcrop that overlooked a river. Bounded by a metal railing and topped with wrought-iron tables and chairs, the ledge looked as urbane as a backyard patio. Whiskey barrels scattered between the tables brimmed with pansies and petunias. Puffs of lobelia and tufts of sweet alyssum cascaded down the wooden sides.

Kate stepped to the railing. "This is a beautiful setting."

"Residents of our little community gather here often. We have parties, weddings, marshmallow roasts—all sorts of get-togethers on this rock patio."

"The flowers smell wonderful. I'm amazed the church has such beautiful flowers this high in the mountains—and this early in the summer."

"I trick them into early growth."

"Really?" Though the effervescent lady intrigued Kate, she wasn't ready to believe everything she said.

Dymple chuckled. "Really, but it's no trick. I have a little greenhouse in my garden, where I start my own plants early in the spring as well as seedlings for the church."

Kate leaned against the top railing. Below her, hummocks of snow clung to the rugged mountainside. Water seeped from the crusted mounds and trickled downhill to feed a river that ambled like a lazy snake through the verdant valley. She pointed to barely visible buildings at the far end of the basin. "Is that Copperville?"

"Sure is."

Rows of concrete cellblocks marched across Kate's memory. "Patterson is bigger than—"

"Bigger?"

Kate felt her cheeks warming and ducked her head. "The town is smaller than I expected."

"Copperville was a fair-sized mining town in the late eighteen hundreds and early nineteen hundreds." Dymple swept her hand across the panorama. "A hundred or so years later, as you can see, it isn't much more than a few businesses and a smattering of houses. I feel for those who couldn't make a living here, but I prefer a small community. Wouldn't live anywhere else."

"Too bad I left my camera in the car. My Great-Aunt Mary and my friend Amy in Pennsylvania would love to see this."

"Don't you worry, sweetie. You can get good pictures at the overlook up the road." Dymple patted her arm. "Are you vacationing in worm?"

Kate hesitated. She'd prepared herself to answer questions about her schooling and past employment without mentioning prison but hadn't expected this one. "It feels like a vacation, because I'm finally out of college. But I came to *Wy-o-ming* to do a marketing internship at the Whispering Pines Guest Ranch. They're going to train me this week for their tourist season, which starts next weekend, Memorial Day weekend."

If Dymple caught the *Wyoming* emphasis, she gave no indication. "Good for you. The Duncans are wonderful people and their ranch has an excellent reputation. A bright young lady like you will fit right in."

Kate wrinkled her nose. Maybe, except for the reputation part—and the bright part. She'd done so many stupid things, like trying to steal from yet another church. "So you know the owners?"

Dymple slid her hands in the pockets of her denim jumper. "Laura is a dear friend, and her son ..." Her eyes sparkled. "Michael is a remarkable young man, my adopted grandson. You'll like him."

"Wow, small world. You even know my new employer."

Dymple shrugged. "This is a typical small community, Kate. Everyone knows everybody in our little corner of the world—and everything they do."

Kate stifled a groan. She should have stayed in Pittsburgh, where she was just another face in the crowd.

Dymple tilted her head. "You're a long way from home. Why Wyoming?"

Kate stared into the woman's transparent eyes. She'd come west to distance herself from her past. But that was a secret nobody, not even a kindly little old lady named Dymple, could ever pry out of her. "Oh, I just wanted a change of scenery when I finished school."

"You made a good choice, Kate. Welcome to Wyoming." She motioned toward the chapel. "Feel free to stop any time. The Sunday service begins in about an hour. I think you'd like Pastor Chuck."

A bug crawled toward Kate's fingers on the railing. She brushed it away. Not that the pastor would like her. She wasn't *ecclesiastical*, the first word she'd learned in English 101 after Professor Eldridge challenged her online prison class to learn a new word every day. Over time, she'd become comfortable with multi-syllable words and with attending church services on the inside. But she wasn't good enough to attend church with regular people, people who hadn't done all the bad things she'd done. "Thanks, but I'd better not stay. I need to get to the ranch. The internship starts tomorrow morning."

"Vaya con Dios, Miss Kate."

Kate cocked her head.

"That's how my Mexican neighbors in California said *goodbye*. In English, it means *go with God*. Isn't that beautiful?"

"Yes, but I'm not sure God wants to go with *me*." Embarrassed by her confession, Kate turned to leave.

Dymple grasped her arm. "What did you mean by that comment?"

"Nothing, really." Kate chafed against Dymple's grasp, but the older woman held tight. She looked down. "I've done a lot of dumb things. I know God supposedly loves me and all that, but ..."

Dymple released Kate's arm to gently lift her chin. "God not only loves you, sweetie, he delights in you."

Kate pulled back. "Delights?"

"Yes, Zephaniah—he wrote a book in the Bible—said God delights in you and sings about you."

"That'll be the day."

"He's singing right now. Your ears just aren't tuned to his frequency."

"I'll have to think about that." Kate looked at her watch. "I'd better get going. Thanks for the tour."

"You're welcome. I'll keep you in my prunes."

"Prunes?"

"Oh, dear." Dymple's crinkled cheeks turned pink. "I'm jumbling *all* my words today. Prayers. I'll keep you in my *prayers*." She waved her hand toward the cemetery. "Come see me again. I live on the other side, just beyond those trees."

"I'll do that." Kate started for the parking lot.

"One more thing," called her new friend. "Live your dream, Kate Neilson. Every day."

Indefatigable. Kate smiled, pleased to remember another word from English 101. She didn't know much about Dymple Forbes, but the petite lady appeared to be a woman of boundless energy.

She swiveled to tread the path back to the chapel. If only half the people she met in Wyoming were as interesting as … She slowed, nearly stopping. What was that strange look on Dymple Forbes's face when they were talking in the cemetery? *Like she recognized me.* But that was impossible. Her arrests had caught the local media's attention more than once, but surely Dymple didn't get Pittsburgh news out here in the middle of nowhere.

Made in the USA
Thornton, CO
02/21/23 20:03:58